"I AM YOUR DEATH."

• • •

The goblins stared into his dark eyes. Foam flecked their lips. One swung a mighty blow with his long sword at the warrior's head. Smoothly, Margawt caught the blade on his shield and caught the goblin with his sword deep in the thigh.

Margawt the Morigu withdrew his sword. Another attacker had reached him and swung an ax toward the elf's head. Margawt took a step forward with his left foot and went into a crouch. The weapon missed his back by mere centimeters, as he knew it would. The goblin's ax was driven into the earth. The sword which he now held two-handed cut through the goblin's elbow and completely through his body. Blood sprayed into the air as the bisected body fell to the ground.

The last of the goblins had had enough and turned and ran. Briefly, Margawt entertained the thought of chasing the creature and cutting him apart piece by piece as he tried to escape. But the earth cried for its vengeance....

With five strides the elf caught the panic-stricken goblin and with one swift stroke removed its head in midflight.

MORIGU:
THE DESECRATION
BY MARK C. PERRY

POPULAR LIBRARY

An Imprint of Warner Books, Inc.

A Warner Communications Company

POPULAR LIBRARY EDITION

Copyright © 1986 by Mark C. Perry

Popular Library® and Questar® are registered trademarks of Warner Books, Inc.

Cover art by Gary Ruddell

Popular Library books are published by
Warner Books, Inc.
666 Fifth Avenue
New York, N.Y. 10103

W A Warner Communications Company

Printed in the United States of America

First Printing: November, 1986

10 9 8 7 6 5 4 3 2 1

This work is dedicated to Sharon Claire Lorenz—
because it is the right thing to do...

Acknowledgments

There are several people who contributed to the success of *Morigu* and it is hard to thank them all. Brian Berkley has been a great help since the beginning. I shudder to think how many times the poor guy typed up the manuscript, not to mention all the late nights (and early mornings) he spent discussing the book with me.

Denise Workman also contributed a great deal. My wife Christine has been a constant source of inspiration and support. And it was Ben Greer more than anyone who taught me my craft.

I'd also like to thank Brian Thomsen, my editor, who knows and understands the Morigu as well as anyone and is the only human being alive who could've got me to make certain unnamed changes in the book. He did it by the unlikely manner of convincing me he was right.

And last, but probably most importantly, Lynn Abbey and Bob Asprin who have believed in my work and who I owe more than I can ever repay.

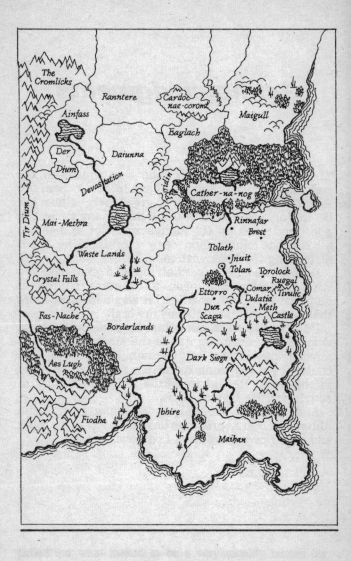

The Legend

It is in the tenth year of the newly formed empire of Tolath that our tale begins, 160 years ago. For that is the year that the dark powers of the inner and outer world rose up and sought the domination of the land and nearly was the world riven in that time. The Dark Siegn Wars had begun.

Three hosts did the enemy gather and the land shuddered beneath their weight. In the south from the country of Dark Siegn the cruel Dragon Lords unleashed their might on the empire and the free states of Maihan. In the north fell creatures marched from Maigull, invading the elven kingdom of Cather-na-nog and laying siege to the dwarf hold of Cardoc-nae-corond. But it was from the west that came the greatest threat.

There over the mountains of Tir Dium marched the third of the evil host, an army of endless numbers, led by none other than the black Princes of Hell. In that dark time elf, man, and dwarf joined forces and created the Alliance of Light with which to face their deadly foe.

The war raged on for a full twenty-seven years. The whole of the north-west fell to the invaders.

In that time the dwarf kingdom of Der Dium fell, Mai-Mathra was destroyed and her magic forest burnt to dust. And one by one the city states of Daiunna were overthrown. Such was the destruction of those three lands, that now that part of the world is known as the Devastation.

But there were other lands, and other peoples, and from them great heroes rose to lead the Alliance, determined to fight the enemy to the bitter end.

King Fergus Strong-Arm led his people from Cardoc-nae-corond and broke the enemy's siege that had lasted twelve years. Few of Maigull host made it back to the haunted lands. But the dwarven folk paid a heavy toll in that battle. They went back to their caverns, barred tight the gates, and marched no more to war.

The elves of Cather-na-nog left their forest led by their Ard Riegh Lonnlarcan, and he was as a demigod. Bright and deadly was the army of the elves, riding upon their magic steeds. They strode the battlefields of the world, bringing hard death to their enemies. How many of the immortals died in that most desperate of wars? Who can say? But the world is poorer for their loss. And of the great elven princes only Ceallac, King's cousin, Breeda the battlemaid, noble Cucullin and the Ard Riegh himself survived.

From the dwarven caves of the Crystal Falls came the greatest of the ally host. They came to the west to fight with the elves and the tread of their army's feet brought fear to the dark ones. It took the two allies nine years, but in the end they crushed the enemy and revenged the lost kingdoms of the Devastation. And together the two victorious armies marched to the aid of the beleaguered empire of Tolath and the dwarves at last came to grips with their most hated of enemies, the Dragon Lords of the Dark Siegn.

And one more army did join that battle there in the gentle plains of Tolath. From the magical land of Aes Lugh did they come, and it was Arianrood who was their queen. The Ead, the eldest of all the world's children. Beauty and power are her birth right. But it was a hard lot her armies faced and all of her great lords were slain.

So it was that the last battles of the great war were fought in the empire, and the world shook with the wrath of the Alliance of Light.

In those last years of the war the emperor fell in battle and his son was proclaimed emperor, Fealoth the Bright, the savior of the land. It was he who led the allied armies with the Arch Mage Dammuth ever at his side.

The enemy fell before them, and one by one were their strongholds overrun. All that remained were those in the fell marshes and scarred mountains of the Dark Siegn and the evil ones' fate lay before them.

In desperation did the enemy commit their final desecration, for they called to their master in Hell and made a pathway for him into the world. And, He came.

Now the whole land still sings of those days. Of how bright Fealoth was gifted power by the world's greatest wizards and how he did battle the Master of Corruption for three nights and days before casting the Dark One beyond the world's path. For that great deed Fealoth was raised to godhood and now his temples cover the land.

With the Bright One's victory the Alliance did

win the war and the Golden Age began. The time when evil would no longer plague the peoples of the world and all the hurts of the war would be remade.

And now the tale is told and most of the heroes of that time are long dead. The nations of the land have prospered and few of the dark ones walk the earth in any form.

But still, even now evil stirs in the land. Who would travel through the Devastation? And the haunted lands of Maigull is as black a realm as ever. It is known that those along the Dark Siegn border do still sometimes hear the cries of war when goblin raiders come ahunting. And have you not heard the rumors of trolls and darker things? And even has it been said that not all the dragons had been destroyed in the great war...

Prologue

On the outskirts of the ancient forest of Cather-na-nog, a young elf slumped against the bole of a large oak, his slim hands picking idly at the tree's bark. His black hair hung well past his shoulders, surrounding the thin face in a dark halo, and his eyes were so dark no pupils could be seen. Like all his people, he was exotically handsome.

Margawt slid further down the tree until only his head rested on a fat root. He took a deep breath, sighing in exasperation.

It just wasn't fair, he told himself. Not two weeks ago, the Ard Riegh Lonnlarcan had announced to the royal council that Margawt was one of the Shee. 'One of the Shee!' he mouthed to the sky. The Shee were the greatest of the elven kind and rarely did they appear among any but the noblest of the elves. Though his father was a respected scholar, no aristocratic blood flowed in Margawt's veins.

The Shee have many powers. They can learn and control more diverse and powerful magics than any other elves, and they are much hardier and stronger. But perhaps their greatest power, and weakness, is that they haven't the power of Aislinneena, the dream knowing.

It is the Aislinneena that sets the elves apart from all others. Time is not an absolute to them, it is controllable. The power of Aislinneena is the power to relive any moment in time and change the outcome of that event. The elf, while in the dreamstate, not only changes the decisions he made at any point in time, but all his actions from that time to the present. So an elf may emerge from Aislinneena a completely different creature from what he had been before the process.

The elven people cannot know true love since they never know pain. Their growth as individuals is controlled by themselves, not by fate. Rarely do they feel powerful emotions since anything causing such emotions can simply be relived and eradicated from their life. Thus an elf is the product of ultimate free will.

It was the Aislinneena that was frustrating Margawt at the moment. Neither of his two sisters were Shee, and, being young for elves (barely twenty) they used the dreamstate often and randomly. Margawt's younger sister, Downet, jealous of her brother's newfound importance, had used the power to relive the events of the last weeks.

Now in her mind Margawt was dead, having died in an accident on the way to see the king. Thus, she was in mourning for her elder brother. He did not exist for her and nothing he could do would change that. Such is the power of the Aislinneena that even when Margawt pushed her, his hands passed right through her. He wanted to return the favor and make her dead, but being Shee, he did not have the power.

Now his mother was guiding Downet in the dreamstate to reverse what had happened, and Margawt was looking forward to his sister returning to normal. 'Then,' he planned, 'I will make a squirrel bite her, and personally punch her harder than she's ever been punched before.'

Margawt left off his fantasies of revenge and leapt to his feet. His skin burned as if a hot fire blazed nearby. He was too new to his power to understand the meaning of his doomsense, but he was able to understand that what was happening to him was a warning of danger. Before the thought of action formed in his mind, Margawt was off and racing with the speed only the elves can attain.

Something cried inside him as pictures of his mother and sister floated to his consciousness. *Danger, death, rich red blood*. "Goddess!" he cried to the wind as he sped through the forest.

Margawt's shout of anguish filled the clearing as he saw goblin arrows pierce his mother and sister. They had been deep in the dreamstate, sitting near the hill that was their home. Even as Margawt turned toward the band of goblins racing at him, the grass turned bright red as mother and daughter died arm in arm, completely unaware of their own lives passing.

He clasped his hands together and started the chant his mother had taught him, tears blurring the tableau before him. A large goblin, clad in dirty furs, whirled a staff above his head and Margawt felt a jagged pain along his throat. His spell was broken and the magic dissipated into the air.

Suddenly a door appeared in the hillside and Margawt's other sister flew at the invaders. A colorless light shot from her brow into her cupped hands, and this she flung at the goblins. Three of them burst from the inside out into a purple, smokeless blaze.

Before the elf maid could attempt another spell, the goblin shaman spoke a word of power, and she was blown off her feet to smash unconscious into the hill.

The shaman's earlier spell still bound Margawt so he could do no magic. With a hoarse croak of rage he tore into the nearest goblin. He grabbed it by the neck, crushing its windpipe and bone in one convulsive motion. The goblins, some forty in all, rushed to meet the attack of the berserk elf.

Margawt picked up the dead goblin's spear and plunged it deep in another's stomach. The shaft passed through the mail corset and caught in the spine of the raider. The young elf lifted the dead goblins by the shaft and, with the terrible strength of the Shee, threw the body into the faces of two more. The shaft broke in half, and, using it as a club, Margawt waded into the goblins.

The end came suddenly, a mace to the head, a sword into the thigh, and a spear straight through his unprotected torso, but eight more goblins had died before they brought Margawt down, and all who came within range were wounded.

Margawt fought to stay conscious under the kicks and punches of the goblins, as they pushed and dragged him across the clearing and chained him to a tree, his wounds leaving thick trails of blood across the grass.

His eyes turned up to the sky as the earth turned and tried to tip him toward the great void above them. The pain was beyond his understanding and slowly it dragged him to unconsciousness.

He woke to the panic of drowning, but he realized some liquid had been thrown in his face to wake him. Only one swollen eye could still open. At first all he saw was a dancing red/orange haze and then what he thought to be chunks of half-cooked meat. Slowly, his mind recognized the still steaming bodies of his mother and Downet thrown at his feet.

The bodies had been hacked and mutilated beyond anything sanity could bear. One bright-green eye stared at Margawt from the pulped mass. Something inside him screamed, trying to escape, but in midflight it fell shattered, broken for all time.

Something landed on the bodies. It was his older sister, naked and beaten, her eyes rolled white. Her mouth opened in a scream, but Margawt could hear nothing. It made what was to follow even more terrible, as one by one the goblins raped his sister, the bodies of her family beneath her.

Somehow Margawt broke the spell that silenced him and cried a howl of denial. The sound of it lingered in the forest, making even the goblins shudder and pull away from him. But they took heart when he made no more sounds and passed out once again.

He awoke to see his sister on her knees facing him, two

grinning goblins holding her in front of him. Her eyes fastened on his, but he had nothing left to give her. Another goblin stepped into his limited view and slowly unsheathed a wicked-looking knife. The weapon came up. A flash of blood colored the air. Pain, bright pain, shot through him, making him vomit in agony. It took him a moment to realize the goblin had castrated him.

Nightmare, blood, horror, what were these but words to the young elf? His life slipped from him as the goblins continued their mad game. Margawt could never remember what happened, just flashes of scenes his mind refused to digest. Eventually his sister died. At one point the bitter pang of flesh burning assaulted his senses. The goblins, all teeth and red-veined eyes, laughed as they threw the insides of his sister at him, the organs smacking wetly against his numb body, her blood mingling with his.

A pulse, a steady beat, building, pounded inside him. Agony, fire searing his bones. Slow, thick warmth running from his wounds. A brief struggle to open his eyes, muscles dead. His body a weight of stone, immovable, dying.

Fighting the cloak that covers his thoughts, he concentrated not on the pain, but on the drum of a heartbeat. His? No, no, he should be dead, dying long ago from the wounds, the gaping wounds that tore his flesh, jagged, white cracked bone, reaching through the skin.

The pain drained away as the body died. *Soon, soon,* his mind whispered, *soon* . . . but there was another call that turned his soul from Lord Death. The beat, the beat. It stirred something in him, woke it, shook it. It was red, dark red, and hot. It grew in his mind, piles of formless meat, quivering, groping together. It was more than hate or rage. It folded about him, surrounding him in its caress of soft despair.

"It is vengeance, vengeance that keeps you alive."

The voice was warm and stifling. There was no escape from it. Nowhere to hide, nowhere to flee. And with a fierce

thrill—the sharp power of defiance. He knew he did not
want to run.

*"You want blood, blood streaming through your tearing
fingers."*

The voice came through the ground, vibrating up through
his dead loins. Now he knew, the heartbeat wasn't his, for
his heart was cold, long dead. No, it was the earth, the earth
Herself, and he could feel the life of it surging beneath him.

And now there was more than death, more than despair.

There was a choice.

It was there, around him, in him. The choice. Release the
rage and feel death's cool hand, or, or . . . *REVENGE!* A lifetime of revenge; a thousand lifetimes of revenge . . . his soul
to the earth things for the hard edge of a weapon to fight.

"You will be that weapon."

He felt the voice stronger now. The choice made, he followed the flow of his blood sinking into the earth. His body
shook for a moment, death striving with him one last time,
. . . but the choice was made. A sigh from far away as Lord
Death let him go. Was there anger in that sound, or pity?

With that his body melted into the ground, hot metal
being dissolved. He opened his eyes, and Margawt saw
darkness.

But it was not darkness, for the dark is the opposite of
light. This world had never known light. He was in the
earth's very bones.

His body arched and sucked in a breath, but there was no
air here. His lungs pumped in soil and rock. Thick, heavy,
filling his body. There was no pain. It was pleasant; relaxing
and thrilling at the same time.

On all sides, top and bottom, he was totally surrounded
by the earth. He was part of it. Weightless, free in a way
only a creature of the sea might understand. With that there
was . . . no, not light, something less. The particles of earth
went translucent. Margawt could see each individual grain.
A million, billion gems all glowing. Separate and distinct.
Alive yet inert. Immovable but active.

He could see, see through the earth for a thousand miles. He saw the roots of plants hanging down, gently waving in the flow of solid matter. Thousands and thousands of creatures swam about him. Some so small they showed as tiny sparks of life, others so gigantic his mind could not comprehend them, all dancing in the eternal womb.

He moved his arms. Easily they pushed away the weight that should have crushed him. He dived deeper and rode a current that he knew would bring him to his goal.

She waited for him. Even in this oceanic world She was astride her small dark pony. She appeared to him naked, long black hair flying in the breezes of rock and soil; her body was smooth; balanced muscles playing beneath the dark skin. Small, tapered hands beckoned to him.

Her face was indistinct, blurred like the soft outlines of a memory, but the eyes of the goddess watched him as if She peered through a mask. They were dark brown and overlarge for her oval face. At first they frightened Margawt, as if he stared into the eyes of a starving wolf, then something, something behind them, something soft and gentle, like the doe watching her fawn.

Her black hair wrapped about her body with caressing motions. She smiled, but he would not look. Perhaps her teeth were really fangs? She dismounted and stood before him, her body rocking with the motion of the earth. She was wild, abandoned. She was security and She was heart-binding lust. His useless loins ached with need and he felt a perverse shame at her maddening, demanding call.

"Few have seen me as I am, Lord Shee. But you will know me in all my forms. You are mine as no other creature can ever be, though all belong and are a part of me." They were words of promise, and of a darker threat he could not fathom.

"Lady, mother, I know you well and I shall serve you always and faithfully." The words left his mouth, stirring the translucent stuff about him and made their way to her.

*   *   *

"You shall try, my child. The power is yours now. You are the Morigunamachamain; you are my avenger. Mightier than all my creatures, faster, stronger, the most dangerous. One who has walked through the earth, will move in the air with speed that no creature can match. One who has turned from Lord Death shall be the most invulnerable, one who is given the curse to feel the world's pain shall be the most vicious of all."

Her words eddied around his body, caressing it, scratching and holding at the same time.

"Listen to the call of the earth. Avenge me on those who blaspheme my soul. Great harm, great evil has come, and even I was caught unawares." She moved toward him slowly, her steps a dance of beauty and perfection beyond mortal understanding. She kissed his forehead lightly, then each hand, each foot, his chest and loins.

"You are the weapon promised, the first morigu in 150 years. You, unlike the others before you, were born of blood and despair, and this is the gift you shall bring my enemies. Go, my assassin, go and kill, hunt and kill!" With that She kissed him full on the lips, holding him tight to Her small body. For a second he felt the great weight of the earth around him, felt it crushing him from all sides. Then She stepped away from him.

He longed to stay, but the pull of air drew him. He came through the ground as he went in, slowly and with no pain. He stood in a glade far from his home, naked, unscarred, and powerful beyond imagining. His hands clenched, savoring the incredible strength they now held. He sniffed the air, and listened to the earth's constant murmur.

"Blood!" he cried. "Blood and death!" They were east of him, a few miles away, no less, the murderers of his family, of his life. He would hunt them and kill, slowly. It would be the first of many such hunts. He was the Morigunamachamain and the earth called to him for vengeance. He would answer with joy and hate, he would answer and he would hunt.

And in a place that only She could be, a goddess cried alone and unheard by all that is. She cried, for where could She go for forgiveness? Such a gentle child, such a sad boy. She could have let him go free, let him escape. But She could not ignore Her need.

"My Son," She spoke aloud, "my lover, forgive me, forgive as those before you never could. . . ."

CHAPTER

One

Mearead, Lord of the Crystal Falls, stopped his pony and stared at the city ahead of him. Tolan, the capital of the empire of Tolath, was an impressive sight, even to the dwarf lord. The main wall stood some fifty feet high. Its thick walls were newly whitewashed and pennons flew from every tower. Mearead's sharp eyes picked out the two massive dragon skulls on either side of the gold-plated gate. He dug his hand into his plaited white beard and shuddered.

"My lord?" questioned his young nephew, Colin.

"Remembering." The king's hand pointed to the skulls. "The skull on the left, it belonged to the great worm Ruhti-vak. My father died fighting that beast and my ax took its life. . . ."

The young dwarf looked at the skull, visible even though they were still a quarter of a mile away from the city. He whistled aloud.

"I've heard the story a million times, my lord, but never did I realize the size of the monster."

Mearead did not answer; he strode the paths of his memory. Once again he saw the great beast rear in front of him, laying low the warriors beneath its bulk with fire and claw; his father, a small defiant figure standing amidst the smouldering bodies of his warriors; the red flame curling around Connal's form, piercing the power of dwarven magic. His armor melting, still the dwarf struggled to fight, his ax thrown into Ruhtivak's scaled chest. With one slash of his mighty claws the dragon tore the dwarf king in half, in front of Mearead's eyes.

All was a blur from there. Mearead could remember Dammuth appearing by his side, lightning flashing from the wizard's outstretched hands to splash against the dragon's bulk—and Mearead's own battle madness, his heart crying with the need of vengeance for his father's death. One great blow, all the strength of his magic behind it, and he severed the dragon's scaly neck. The black blood covered him and burned through armor and shield, but he knew, he knew as his consciousness left him, he knew that day he had had his vengeance.

The other dwarves of the king's entourage watched their leader, uncommonly quiet for their kind. Colin held his breath while watching the thick frame of his uncle shake with memories of a battle fought 150 years ago.

Mearead turned to Colin, smiling at the hero worship in the young dwarf's eye.

"He was a big bastard all right," he laughed, "and smell—eeeee, what a stench." The dwarves all laughed aloud. "By the way," Mearead continued, "do me a favor, will you, boyo?"

"Yes, my lord?" Colin's face filled with expectation.

"'Yes, my lord?'" Mearead mimicked. "Gods below, boy, cut out that 'my lord' crap. Don't you know that's for humans and those bloody elves? No self-respecting dwarf calls anybody 'my lord,' especially another dwarf."

He smiled as the youth's face fell. Mearead looked Colin up and down. He compared his nephew's gold-washed armor, purple cloak, sparkling boots and spurs to his own rusted chain mail; the simple, battered silver corset which he used for a crown, set on unkempt hair; and a sort of brown (once green) traveling cloak. The Lord of the Crystal Falls, Warrior of the Star, shook his head. "You can dress them up, but you can't take them out," he said aloud.

The dwarves broke out in loud laughter. Flann, the standard-bearer, twirled the king's standard in the air. Since Flann had been using the standard to stab the mud periodically, he splattered those around him with wet clods. "Three cheers for the fair, the noble, nay, the shining gem of the Crystal Falls, Lord Colin, master warrior, the greatest dwarf I personally have ever met." Removing a bit of mud from his face, Colin gave the standard-bearer an evil look.

"Leave me alone, you rat," he retorted.

"I guess he told you," a deep voice from the back said.

"Eloquence is the key word here," another shouted.

"Don't mess with Colin. Why, he could have killed a dragon with just one of his beautiful smiles."

"Or one of his incredibly scalding comebacks."

As the troop of two hundred dwarves continued their trek, their laughter rang across the plain. The subject of their humor huddled in his cloak trying to look noble (which his uncle would have told him is impossible for a dwarf with a mud-splattered purple cloak riding a fat little pony). The furiously blushing face didn't help matters much, either.

The dwarves rode up to the gate of Tolan. There, an honor guard of the empire's finest awaited them, fifty knights dressed in silver and gold. Flann muttered to Mearead, "Pretentious little peacocks, aren't they?"

"Give them a break, Flann. They like this sort of thing. It inspires them."

The emperor came riding up with his nobles. Trell'dem, emperor of Tolath, was an impressive-looking man. He wore a full suit of chain mail, a white cassock over the mail, and his greying locks hung well past his shoulders. His strong face broke into a smile.

"My lord," he nodded his head, recognizing Mearead as an equal.

Colin's face lit up.

"I am honored to greet the illustrious Lord of the Crystal Falls here under the skull of the dark dragon he overthrew in the great wars. I greet you in peace. My house is open to you and yours, now and forever."

Mearead smiled, and staring right into the grey eyes of the emperor, grandly gestured and boomed so all could hear. "You do me the honor of meeting me with these noble knights on their great horses, making me and mine look even shorter than we are. But that's okay, kid. It's nice to see you anyways."

The knights and aristocrats were shocked by this unseemly behavior, at least those who had never seen a dwarf before were. Could this possibly be the same dwarf who was commemorated with a statue in the great palace hall itself?

Trell'dem laughed. "Well, age hasn't improved your manners any."

"Nope, but then the years will do that to you. And I might add, son, it's a hot day and age *has* improved my drinking skills."

Trell'dem grabbed a flask from the saddle's pommel and threw it to the grinning dwarf. "You're all right in my book, kid," said the dwarf, taking a huge swig and throwing the flask behind him, knowing that one of the dwarves would catch it.

"Shall we go in?" asked the emperor.

"I think we shall," answered Mearead, and the two rode through the gates.

The next afternoon the emperor called a grand council; all the leaders of the Alliance were expected to appear.

The meeting was held in a large round chamber. It had five rows of seats ringing the wall, and looked like a miniature amphitheater. The two large windows at either end of the room let in the sun's light, bringing out the luster in the golden marble walls. The seats were covered with velvet cushions.

In the middle of the floor lay a relief map of the empire covered with troop markers, and by it stood the emperor still dressed in chain mail. He bowed as each of his guests entered the room and found seats. True to form, the dwarves were the last to arrive.

Mearead grimaced as he entered the chamber followed by

Flann and Colin. "This is not going to be a lot of fun," he stage-whispered to his nephew, even as he silently replayed the plan for the council that he, Trell'dem, and Dammuth had decided on the night before.

Mearead and the dwarves clumped up the stairs to sit next to the humans. He eyed the wine decanters set around the room. He nudged Dammuth with an elbow. "Do you perchance have anything stronger than that limpid wine your emperor is so justly renowned for serving?" The wizard arched one greying eyebrow and reached into his green robe. He deftly withdrew a flask and handed it to Mearead with a smile. "You, sir, are a prince," the dwarf mumbled as he took a long pull.

"Now that we're all here," the emperor looked pointedly at the dwarf king, who favored him with a big smile in return, "let us start with introductions."

He began with his own men: Lord Crane, warlord of the empire's armies; Fin, Laird of Dun Scaga; Mannon, Archduke of Ruegal; Baron Teague of Dulatia; and last of all, the Arch Mage Dammuth, whose unlined face belied his over two hundred years.

From the elven nation of Cather-na-nog was their Ard Riegh, Lonnlarcan; his sister's son Ceallac; Baibre, the sorceress; Lord Cainhill, his purple eyes troubled; and Lord Cucullin the Bright.

The people of Aes Lugh were led by their dark queen, Arianrood, the Ead, eldest of all the world's children, her beauty and nobility outshining all there. With her were her Warlord, Donal Longsword, the half elven; Lord Cartach, an elven mage; and Remon, king of the human land of Fiodha, which owed her allegiance. These with the three dwarves made up the council, and few times in the world has such an assembly of heroes been convened.

"Before we begin formally," stated the emperor, "I'd like to ask Mearead if he has heard from his cousins, the dwarves of Cardoc-nae-corond?"

The dwarf put his flask down at his feet with a dramatic

gesture. Then he leaned back in the seat and looked the others over one by one. Finally, he broke the silence, his glance eyeing the sorceress.

"Indeed, I had hoped not to start this meeting with talk of my morbid cousins, and frankly, I have little to tell. I've sent three messengers and only one has returned, with the news that he made no contact. The old entrances to their caverns were closed tight. What happened to the other messengers is anyone's guess. I had hoped perhaps the lady's magic could shed some light on this matter."

Arianrood's melodious voice answered. "You overestimate my powers, lord, and understate the importance of your news. Cardoc-nae-corond lies adjacent to the haunted lands of Maigull. Even in Fealoth's time my power could not pierce the veils that ring both lands."

"The fact that none from that mountain kingdom are here today is not a good sign, for, as you know, the 150th celebration of Fealoth's victories was to coincide with this meeting of all the kingdoms of the Alliance." Here, Trell'dem looked straight at Mearead.

"What can I say? My cousins have always been a depressing lot. For all I know, they could have closed the caves simply to aggravate the rest of us."

"Something must be done," added Dammuth. "The dwarves of Cardoc-nae-corond may be no fun, but they are one of the few peoples that possess any magic to speak of."

"Are you suggesting, my lord Dammuth, that we have need of magic?" asked the Archduke.

"There is always a need for magic, Mannon," answered the wizard.

"But," he persisted, "surely there is no need anymore. We celebrate Fealoth's victories, his defeat of the Worm Lords, and his ascension to godhood. The prophecies were complete. This is the Golden Age. There is no need for magic anymore."

"Yet your master seems to feel there is a need for armies," said Arianrood.

"A very great need," answered the emperor, "for, you see, the prophecies are wrong." There was hushed silence at Trell'dem's words, for they came close to blasphemy.

"Yes," he continued, "the prophecies are lies." Arianrood's eyes flashed. "I did not fight in the Dark Siegn wars as some of you here today did. As you know, both Arianrood and Dammuth were partially responsible for *my* great-uncle Fealoth's victory. And I think perhaps the fact that I was not there, indeed, not even born yet, gives me an insight that some of you have missed."

"What," asked Arianrood, her voice quiet, "do you mean by that?"

"I mean, my lady, that you have all missed something very important." Trell'dem gestured at the ceiling. "The prophecies are lies!" he shouted the word. "For twenty-seven years the Dark Lords fought the Alliance of Light in the Dark Siegn wars and they began to win. Then, in the greatest act of magic this world has ever seen, the Dark Lord himself was brought forth in corporeal form." He began pacing around the map, all eyes on him. "Then the prophecies came about. For if the Dark One should walk the earth, he who was pure of heart would be able to defeat the Evil One in mortal combat. The one so chosen was my great-uncle Fealoth."

"We know all this. We were there." Arianrood's voice was becoming cooler by the minute.

"Indulge me," snapped the emperor. "To give Fealoth the powers he needed, almost all the great artifacts of power were drained, and fourteen wizards and sorceresses transferred this power to Fealoth. Arianrood and Dammuth were two of these. Fealoth received and contained the power, becoming a god, a god with the power to destroy the Dark One, which he did, and before he ascended to his new place as godling, promised all creatures that peace had come and all evil had been wiped out of the world. Never would there be such a war again."

"I see what you are getting at. There is still evil in the world," said Mearead, watching the Ead with his dark eyes.

"But not such that could overwhelm us!" retorted Arianrood. Her hair floated in the air now, sparks of green flying from it.

"Dammit, Arianrood, quit interrupting me!" Even the elf king raised his eyes at this. 'Are they trying to bait her?' he wondered.

"It was a lie. I was born eighty-seven years ago, in this Golden Age, and I have seen combat steadily since the age of fifteen."

"All the goblins are not dead, my lord, even we in Cather-na-nog have been raided," said Ceallac, brushing the black hair from his forehead.

"Raided! Raided! A few tribes!" the emperor said. "My people have been steadily involved in larger and larger raids. But not just goblins; cave trolls, grey wolves, even the undead have assaulted us. And every year the evil of this world increases."

"A few skirmishes do not make a war," said Arianrood, her hair flying even wilder. Beside her, Remon, his face covered by his grey robe, shifted nervously.

"You are wrong, lady. This is a war whether you wish to see it or not. We shake off the fact that we hear nothing of the dwarves of Cardoc-nae-corond because this is the Golden Age. Well, tell me how I pass it off when I lose an entire fleet to a sea dragon?"

"What?!" shouted Donal. Remon put a restraining hand on the Warlord, but he shook it off, none missing his look of distaste.

"That is only part of it," Trell'dem turned to Donal. "I have had four villages burned to the ground, one small town sacked, and two hundred of my warriors fell in battle not a hundred miles from here—and that just one short month ago." Trell'dem signaled to Crane, who began handing out thick scrolls to each of the leaders. As they leafed through them he continued, "In there you will find a year by year

tally of encounters with the followers of Darkness. That
scroll documents the last thirty-five years, ever since I took
the sceptre. Each year of my reign, the encounters increase.
My great-uncle, whom you all love and revere so much,
lied."

"NO!" shouted Arianrood. "You profane he who was and
is your better. You know not what you speak of, boy."

"Oh, does he not, Arianrood?" Lonnlarcan stood up and
faced her. His eyes burned silver to match his hair. "I am no
mage of your or Dammuth's power yet I have power, too.
Can you honestly say nothing is amiss in this world of
ours?" Arianrood pointedly ignored the question. "The truth
is the portents are mixed and confusing. There are no prophecies as there were in Fealoth's time. The peoples of Pyridin
retreat further into their lairs and refuse even my summons."

"So, even you who were there turn your face from Fealoth's light?" Arianrood's hair no longer sparked her anger,
but her voice was soft and lethal. Ceallac's hand grabbed for
his sword, but Cucullin shook his head quickly. Ceallac
hissed between his teeth.

"Turn away from Fealoth? Be careful what you say to
me, my lady."

"You agree then with this, this *mortal*, that Fealoth lied?!
Such accusations will not, cannot, go unchallenged! Tell me,
my lord, do you agree with this," her hand pointed to
Trell'dem, "blasphemer?"

"Oh great," Mearead said to the wizard, "all hell's about
to break loose!" But a calculating smile belied his words.
Even as the men of Tolath leaped up to defend their emperor,
the followers of Arianrood stood to face them.

"Enough." The elven king's voice filled the chamber. "Sit
back down and contain yourselves." Under the power that
flowed from this voice, everyone sat down immediately. Except Arianrood.

"Your voice tricks have no effect on me, Witch King. I
say the mortal blasphemes. This is my right and duty. Do

you fear to admit you stand with him against the golden Fealoth?"

"Lady, you go too far." The king's hand chopped down. His eyes blazed at her. "None, not even you, have the right to speak to me as you have. Trell'dem speaks true and I do stand with him. So beware your anger, lady, for in me you have met your match!"

Arianrood smiled and with a quick motion of her hand she and her retinue were covered with a shimmering glow of green. "Threatening me is your worst mistake, Lonnlarcan, and one you shall rue."

Even as Trell'dem moved toward the two and Lonnlarcan made to answer, a loud crash shook the room and all turned to stare at the dwarf king, who had just slammed his ax down.

"Okay, everybody, fun is fun, but enough!" he roared. The elf king turned with surprise and looked down on the stout dwarf.

"What—" he began, even as Arianrood's anger turned on the dwarf.

"You impudent—"

Mearead stuck his tongue out at both of them. All stared, wondering if the dwarf was drunk. All except Dammuth, who had remained sitting, and watched the proceedings with a hint of a smirk on his face.

"Now, now, don't start threatening me, 'cause I got no patience for it." Suddenly, the dwarf's eyes went hard and a feral grin turned his face into the berserker's death mask. "I don't take it from anyone, see. So don't start it. Dwarves don't threaten. They act." Even Arianrood seemed a little daunted. At least she said nothing.

"Don't give me that 'wisdom of the ages' look, Arianrood. It isn't going to do any good. I didn't hear anyone accuse Fealoth of anything except for being wrong, something even gods are susceptible to, though it seems that's a lesson others could learn." He sighed and sat down. "Now, I'll admit the kid used some rather strong language, but I figure when your great-uncle is a god, you can say pretty damn near anything you want."

"You are aware that I am High Priestess to Fealoth?" said Arianrood. The green light died a little.

"I'm aware of a lot more than you think, darlin'. Such as the truth written in these scrolls." He smacked them against his palm. "I am aware of one more thing that Lonnlarcan was trying to get to." Everyone was quiet now. "It is not unknown to me, though it may be to some," he looked pointedly at Arianrood, "that evil is abroad and a helluva lot more than it should be. Don't forget who acted as Fealoth's herald. I alone of all in this room have seen and talked to the Dark Lord face to face."

He looked down at Trell'dem. "I know evil. I know its face, its smell." Though his voice was quiet it reverberated about the small room. "And," he continued, "I knew Fealoth best of all." He ruffled the pages, staring at nothing. "Evil? Evil. I don't know, it's too powerful, too much is going on. I know Fealoth had no idea the Dark Power would ever regain so much might." He sat down with a thump.

"I have no great magic of the elves, and the magic of men has always confused me. But I am Lord of the Crystal Falls, and the earth She speaks to me and her waters show me things. And I know what you seek to tell, Lord Lonnlarcan." He turned to Arianrood, one hand stroking his ax. "The Shee have returned."

"What?" said Arianrood, her anger flaming again. "Why was I not informed?"

The elves of Cather-na-nog exchanged quick looks, and all shifted a bit closer to their king. "We were not sure, Arianrood," Lonnlarcan deftly lied, "but there can be no doubt. Among the new generation of my people are those who are Shee."

"Surely," said Donal, "the question is not so much why, but why now?"

"Nay, my lord," said Arianrood. "The question is, why do you think the Shee can return without my knowledge?"

"Then it's true, Arianrood? You do not know of the return?" For the first time Dammuth spoke. His voice was soothing and the anger in the room seemed to visibly dissipate.

Arianrood looked at her old friend speculatively. It was by her hand he had taken his first steps to the power he now wielded. If she respected any here it was Dammuth, just as if she feared any it was the dwarf and his berserker power.

"Dammuth, surely you of all understand. Surely you see. Theirs is a web of lies and deceit, woven for what purpose and by whom," she turned to the elven king, "I do not know. I am the Ead, the eldest. There are *no* Shee." Cainhill rose to argue, but his king silenced him with one motion of his hand. Arianrood turned to the elf.

"I am the Ead," she stated again. "I train the Shee and none are born without my knowledge. Thus it has been since the world began. It is my sworn and sacred duty given unto me by the earth mother herself."

None spoke. The humans looked at one another. Even their emperor had no words. Arianrood was the eldest of all living things and the most powerful. To many, Arianrood was nothing less than a goddess. They shook their heads in silent agreement. There must be no Shee for she would know.

Dammuth spoke quietly, but all heard his words. "My lady, my teacher, you who have turned down the right to join the Bright World, who have given and sacrificed above all others," he looked straight into her eyes, "you are wrong." Anarchy took over the chamber as everyone sought to talk at once. Dammuth raised his hand. Strangely, the others quieted down. "It is true. I have met many of these young elves and I tell you with no hesitation, they are Shee!"

"You, too, Dammuth." The queen's voice held an edge of pain. "It cannot be, Dammuth; there are no Shee. It is a lie. I have heard too many lies this day. No!" she shouted as Dammuth sought to interrupt. "No. Hear me out. I have listened to blasphemy of the Bright One. I have heard outright lies. There is something wrong in this room. Pay attention, for I will not explain this twice."

She spread her hands and above the map a lifesize image appeared. It was of Arianrood in a glade. Trees towered over the glade, their trunks incredibly wide, colored a deep, almost black, brown. Their leaves were the bright green of sun through a forest, though it was night. Arianrood stood in the image, naked, her perfect body making all the men's hearts ache. Her arms were upraised to the starry sky and one shaft of silvery light was encompassed by her pale arms. The light shot straight into the sky, and inside there seemed to be a figure of silver, brighter than the shaft itself. Though they could hear no words, it was apparent to all that Arianrood spoke to the figure and that it answered her.

"It is true, then," Mearead said. His voice quivered a bit, in fear or envy none could say. "You speak directly to him."

"Aye," said Arianrood. "Did you think me some mortal, dependent on confused dreams for my lord's will? We speak, he and I. And I tell you direct from Fealoth, there is no need to fear. There is no resurgence of evil and there are no Shee!"

"What is this about, Arianrood?" For the first time anger was evident in the elven king's voice. "The Shee are returned. That blood flows almost as strong in me as it does in you. It is so!" He stood and faced her once more. His hands stretched toward her. "Don't you see, Arianrood? Something is amiss, deadly wrong. The Shee return. You know nothing of it. Evil is rampant and strengthening, yet Fealoth himself tells you there is no need to worry." He bowed his head. "My lady, look, see the truth. There is more to this than you think."

Arianrood stood up. Her body was surrounded by a green nimbus of flame. "Yes, there is something deadly wrong. I said I would not explain and I will not. Build your little armies, argue amongst yourselves. I care not. Fealoth has explained all to me. Listen or not. It is your choice. But beware, Fealoth remembers friends, but he is a god now, supposedly yours as well as mine. Remember a god's wrath!" With that she got up to leave the room, her lords following. Donal Longsword, though, looked reluctant.

"Perhaps," Lonnlarcan shouted at her retreating back, "you put too much faith in your god, lady. You forget the power of the elves is not dependent on any gods, no matter what power they claim."

Arianrood swung around. Her voice rose in fury. "You g too far, Witch King. You have marked yourself. The pay ment shall be made!"

"Arianrood," Dammuth's calm voice interrupted, "the power of the Shee is tied to the earth goddess, and though you are the eldest of us, She is the Ead of all. You warn us of a god's wrath. Forget not a goddess's jealousy."

"You presume too much. I have borne enough from you babes. Fret and worry like a bunch of old maids. I have not the time. Forget not my warnings and think of what I have said. Perhaps in time you will regain the wisdom that you once held." With that she left.

The room was completely silent.

"I assume," said Trell'dem, "that we who remain agree that there is a present danger?"

All nodded their heads. The dwarf stood up. "I think, my lords, it is time to adjourn this meeting. Do not doubt the dwarves. I say to Lonnlarcan and Trell'dem, continue to re-arm, but beware the lady's anger."

"And the dwarves?" asked Lonnlarcan.

"The dwarves as of now have no doubts. We consider ourselves at war and will take the actions necessary."

"Then we will adjourn. We will meet after dinner to begin to plan our defense and our next steps," said Trell'dem. With that, all began to leave the room. Lonnlarcan, the emperor, the wizard, and Mearead left together.

"The question is," said Dammuth, "if it comes to war, can we win without Arianrood?"

"That," said the elf, "depends on whether she fights not

at all, with us, or against us." The two left the room. Trell'dem looked down on the dwarf.

"I don't understand her reaction," said the emperor, "and I fear it."

"Well, all I can say is," answered Mearead, "I'll be damned if I would invite her to a party."

Lonnlarcan, Mearead and Dammuth stood up on the high wall of Tolan's main gate, the sharp early morning sun reflecting off the two dragon skulls to either side of them. Beneath them small figures turned south and rode away.

"And there she goes," Mearead mumbled.

"Aye, the Ead's reaction leaves me troubled." Lonnlarcan's pale hands clasped the battlements. "I find my heart at war with my head. Can we trust her or not?"

"You are right, great king, there is more here than meets the eye." Dammuth's soothing voice drew the others' attention away from the dwindling riders. "Still, Arianrood has promised her armies at our need."

"She was always proud," Mearead added.

"True, but then she had reason for it." Dammuth was the only one living who could call Arianrood friend. He alone truly understood her many sacrifices for the peoples of the world. "It may," he said, "just be a problem of perception. She has known life since the beginning. Time is different for her than for us."

"Perception," Lonnlarcan repeated, "simple perceptions." He sighed. "Time has no real hold on me or mine, but even to us the years Arianrood has seen are unimaginable."

"But it is a bad omen that the High Priestess of Fealoth will not be here at the celebration of the god," the dwarf king said.

No one had an answer for that. Dammuth glanced at Lonnlarcan, raising an eyebrow, and received a small nod in answer. The wizard cleared his throat and looked down at the dwarf lord.

"We have some news for you, Mearead," he said.

"Good news, I hope."

"That remains to be seen."

"We felt since you had divined the truth of the Shee," Lonnlarcan added, "that you have the right to know."

"By the gods, will you two quit being so cryptic and tell me!"

"There is a Morigunamachamain," Dammuth said quietly.

"Goddess," Mearead fingered his ax, "goddess, what does this portend?"

"He was chosen seven years ago." Lonnlarcan kneeled down to face the dwarf, his chain mail rattling. "Mearead, he is not like the others, he is . . ." He looked up at Dammuth.

". . . Dangerous," Dammuth finished for him.

"All the Morigu are," Mearead answered.

"No, it is more than that." The Ard Riegh's silver eyes held Mearead's. "The Morigunamachamain were always chosen from those of the Shee who served the earth with full hearts. Margawt, Margawt never knew that service. It did not take long years of training for him to come to his power."

"How can that be?"

"He will say nothing of it," Dammuth answered. "I found him six years ago after the goddess placed the knowledge in my heart. He will speak only to me, but I have gleaned little from him."

"He hunts as the old ones did," Lonnlarcan added. "He is as powerful as any of his kind have been, but he does not control his power well. He is wild, he cannot always tell friend from foe."

"We know raiders killed his family, and as might be expected of such, tortured him." Dammuth turned from the other two, his face hard. "He should have died that day, but he did not. The goddess transformed him and now he hunts the pathways of the world for the agents of the Dark One."

"The goddess will not choose any of the other Shee for her now." Lonnlarcan stretched to his full height, towering over the dwarf. "He is *the* Morigu, the only one there is, and I think the only one that will be."

"This is the last sign, then," Mearead said quietly. "It will be war." Dammuth just nodded his head, his back to the others. The Ard Riegh's hand closed on one of the battlements, crushing the stone beneath.

"We cannot know where, we cannot know when, but," he turned to Mearead, his form covered with a silver nimbus, "we do know it *will* be war!"

CHAPTER

Two

He raced through the trees, his form an unearthly blur of speed. He wore only a chain mail vest and armored girdle, stained black. Strapped to his shoulders was a one-and-a-half-handed sword. A long hunting knife was sheathed to his thigh. His chest was covered with white necklaces made from goblin fangs. Rows of the same hung about his wrists and his ankles.

He made no sound as he sped through the wood, his waist length warrior's braid streaming behind him. Even the sound of his breath was hidden by a powerful silence spell, one of the few spells he had mastered, and, as he often thought, the only one he really needed.

The earth cried to him: *Disease, Evil, Revenge!* And he answered the call. He was hunting and all his hunts led to one thing: death.

The goblins squatted around a large fire. This far from the elven kingdom of Cather-na-nog, they feared no creatures.

They were a dismal lot. Their coloring was a bizarre mixture of pink and grey, and though some had scraggles of hair on their dirty faces, all were uniformly bald. Though the goblins are humanoid, they don't resemble other races such as elves or men.

Their arms were disproportionately long to their bodies, ending in six-fingered hands with long fingers possessing an extra joint. Goblins don't have claws like their cousins, the gargoyles. Indeed, they have no nails. Their skin is very rough, like calluses on a human foot. The goblins are six-toed, the last toe on the foot ending in the only claw a goblin possesses. The claw is long and curved and very strong. They rarely wear any sort of foot covering.

Their faces are the grinning horror of a nightmare. The small skull slopes into a snout. The nose is really just two large air holes on the sides of the snout. They have no eyebrows, but instead a bumpy ridge of flesh that extends across the face. Cat-eyed, the goblins possess excellent night vision. They have no eyelids, but a rectractable clear membrane protects the eyes from damage.

Their ears are pointed and placed almost on top of the head. Both ears are independently movable to a small degree. As witnessed by a few half-goblins, occasionally, and always through rape, a goblin can conceive with a human.

There were eight goblins around the fire. One was tying a dirty rag around a small knife wound in his arm. He had received the wound from one of his comrades as an answer to a slur against the other's looks. Being an egotistical race, such remarks are considered the deadliest of insults.

Unknown to the goblins, they were watched. The hunter had found his prey. He sat in a tree some twenty yards away and watched the creatures with a mixture of loathing and glee. His name is Margawt.

He is the Morigunamachamain, the only one alive. His success as the earth's avenger is attested to by the necklaces that cover his body, the left fangs of every goblin he had ever killed. And the Morigu meant to begin a new necklace today. He silently climbed down the tree.

"Listen, parrot face, no more out of you or you get no grub," said the chief to the wounded one. In answer the other picked up his knife and looked at the speaker in front of him. He said nothing.

The chief reached into a bag of badly cured hide. He pulled out what looked to be a very mouldy human leg, without the foot. He pulled off a piece of rotting meat and spitted it, thrusting it into the fire. He tossed the rest to another.

Looking at the winner of the fight, he said, "Stab another one, stupid, and I might decide you wouldn't be such bad eating, good looks and all." This jibe was greeted by a barrage of hoots and insults.

"He's too pretty to eat, but we could take a chunk out of his arse!"

"A thigh for me!"

"Not likely. I'd rather eat my own arse than that slime's."

"You would, scumhole."

"Suck me, you little turd!" This went on for a while until two of the goblins tore into each other. With a lot of oaths and frequent kicks, the chief finally settled them all down.

"One more fight and I'm going to take someone's ears as a trophy, see?" He bared his large canines for emphasis.

"Ya can't blame 'em, Tuk. We've seen no action in a long time," said a smaller goblin as he sharpened his spear point.

"Quit complaining. We leave these lousy woods in another two days, then we'll join the others. Big war's brewing, plenty of action then," the chief answered. The goblins howled with pleasure at the thought, each crying out the vilest things they could think to do to a captured woman.

Not far from the camp, another goblin was amusing himself by breaking the wings of a bird he had managed to bag. The bird was making pitiful attempts to escape but the goblin had tied one foot with a small piece of leather.

"Going somewhere, my pretty?" he asked the bird. "Maybe to tell those vile elves where Noga and his mates are, eh?" With that he tugged the tether hard and the bird fell to its side. The goblin chuckled, showing its yellowed fangs.

Suddenly, two booted feet stood over the bird, and a powerful hand grabbed the goblin's neck and thrust him against a tree.

"So, having a little fun, eh, Noga?" hissed Margawt. "Sentry duty and a little bored. Well, if I didn't have to talk

with your 'mates,' I'd show you a little 'vile' elvish fun."
Margawt thrust a knife through the goblin's chain mail into
its stomach.

The goblin stared into the elf's black eyes. Noga knew
who he was looking at. Instinctively, he recognized the
Morigunamachamain. No goblin had described that face
since any that had seen it never liked to tell about it. Terrified by fear and pain, the goblin stood frozen. He tried to
scream but the air couldn't get past the iron hand around his
throat.

Margawt tore the knife up the goblin's chest.

"Missed your heart," he whispered. "Wonder if you'll die
before I find it?"

Back at the camp, the others were cleaning their weapons
and contentedly fighting with one another. Their weapons
consisted mainly of stabbing swords, spears, a few long
swords, one mace, and a couple of two-handed axes, along
with the various daggers and knives that so delighted their
kind. The weapons were tended carefully and were all razor
sharp.

One goblin screamed and fell back, clawing at a knife
sprouting from his left eye. Another fell into the fire, a small
throwing ax protruding from his shoulders. The remaining
goblins leapt to their feet, brandishing their weapons. The
Morigu was among them.

"Kill!" the earth cried to Margawt. He flew into the
camp, the pointed boss of his shield catching one goblin in
its face as his sword neatly chopped the arm off another.
Three of the goblins kept the fire between them and the
Morigu. A fourth lunged with his stabbing sword at his
thigh. In a blur of speed the elf's sword parried the blade
and the warrior stepped inside his opponent's guard. Margawt slashed the goblin across the waist and disemboweled
him. Following through with his motion, the elf bowled over
the goblin, who was desperately trying to place his intestines
inside his stomach. In two steps Margawt reached the goblin

whose face he had smashed with the shield. The shield flashed down and its sharp edge decapitated the creature.

The Morigunamachamain faced the three survivors across the fire. He smiled. The goblins huddled together. In less than two minutes the elf had killed or incapacitated five of them.

"No bird am I. I am your death," he said.

The goblins stared into his dark eyes. Tuk and another began to hyperventilate. Foam flecked their lips and with two howls of terror they leaped across the fire at their antagonist. Tuk reached the elf first and swung a mighty blow with his long sword at the warrior's head. Smoothly, Margawt caught the blade on his shield. The shield was at such an angle that it didn't catch the blow with full force but neatly deflected and diverted it so that it whispered harmlessly over his head. Even as the chief's blade hit the shield, Margawt's sword caught the goblin. It hit with terrible force and cut through the bottom half of Tuk's shield. The sword continued until it sunk deep in his thigh.

Margawt withdrew his sword in a fluid motion. His other attacker had reached him and swung an ax toward the elf's head. He took a step forward with his left foot and went into a crouch. The weapon missed his back by mere centimeters, as he knew it would. The goblin's ax was driven into the earth.

As the creature tried to regain his balance and weapon, he saw a blur to his left. Margawt had come out of his crouch doing a complete turn to his right. The sword which he now held two-handed cut through the goblin's elbow and completely through his body. Pinkish blood sprayed into the air as the bisected body fell to the ground.

The last of the raiders had had enough and turned and ran. Briefly, Margawt entertained the thought of chasing the goblin and cutting him apart piece by piece as it tried to escape him. But the earth cried for its vengeance and the goblin was going in the opposite direction that the Morigu needed to go. With five strides he caught the panic-stricken goblin and with one swift stroke removed its head in mid-flight.

Margawt strode back into the camp. He took out a rag and began wiping the thick, pink-green blood off his sword. He listened to the dying moans of those still left alive.

"Quit moaning, pigs. You'll soon join your master in hell and I promise that the pain you feel is nothing compared to what you'll face." Margawt smiled as anguished moans answered him. He was sorry he didn't have time to really make them moan. But there were other raiders in the woods, and the Goddess demanded Her due.

Unsmiling, he began to methodically relieve the dead and half-dead goblins of their left canine teeth. The cries of his enemies did not faze the warrior. He hated such as these with all his soul. Indeed, it was only because of his hatred that Margawt was alive.

The goblin that Margawt had hit in the eye with the knife tried to bite him when he went to remove its tooth. The elf pulled his knife out and slit its belly. In between its cries of pain, Margawt tore its canine out.

"Payment," he smiled in its face, "we all must pay. . . ."

Margawt knew many would despise his cruelty. He knew he could have killed all the goblins quickly and painlessly, but that wasn't his way.

He liked his enemies to feel some of the pain they were so quick to inflict upon others. He was the Morigunamachamain. What others thought or felt meant nothing to such as he.

He stood still among his fallen prey and cleared his heart and mind of the excitement of the hunt. A cool wind came through his legs from the ground, hollowing out his bones. He lost a sense of body and felt himself spread out through the soil like an overflowing lake. Then, contact! The tramp of marching feet. The dismay of the earth as these, her unfavored children, walked across her breast.

Margawt stood again in his body, a sigh escaping his lips

at the power flowing through vein and muscle. The goblin raiders were not far away. He would reach them by nightfall.

"Goddess!" he cried in love and despair as he ran off into the woods, the hunt calling him again. Behind, the fire slowly went out, as the life left the last of the still steaming corpses of his enemy, their crumbled remains mute testimony to the wrath of the Morigu.

Far away from the woods of Margawt's hunt the Ard Riegh of Cather-na-nog walked down the corridors of the great citadel of Tolan. The small page in front of him scurried ahead, not daring to talk to the awesome figure of the great elven king. The boy stopped at a thick wooden door, knocked once and scurried away. Lonnlarcan opened the door and walked in.

It was a small library covered from floor to ceiling with bookcases. The only furniture was a round marble table and two hand-carved chairs. Trell'dem, Emperor of Tolath, stood up to greet his guest.

"Thank you for coming at such short notice, your majesty." He nodded at the chair across from him. Lonnlarcan lowered himself into it. "I am sorry about the hour, but as soon as the sun rises I must go to the Temple of Fealoth to perform more of the ceremonies." Trell'dem could not hide a look of distaste at the thought.

Lonnlarcan smiled. "You forget, my lord, that I and my people have no need of sleep as you humans know it. You have not inconvenienced me in the slightest." 'But,' he thought to himself, 'you have certainly intrigued me.'

"Dammuth tells me your people have a spell that will keep secret anything that is said in a room?" He raised a dark eyebrow at the elf lord, and gazed steadily in Lonnlarcan's silver eyes. The Ard Riegh said nothing, but raised one hand in a casual wave. Trell'dem felt a peculiar tingling on his face and palms. He said nothing.

A moment later Lonnlarcan closed his eyes and said, "It is secure, my Lord."

Trell'dem sighed and reached under the table, withdrawing a map and placing it on the table before the two. Lonnlarcan said nothing, just examining the map quietly. It was of the empire and covered with tiny flags of blue, green, and white.

"The blue are representations of my troops that are at full capabilities," the emperor explained. "The green are troops that can be marshaled in one week, the white in one month." Lonnlarcan studied the board carefully.

He looked the emperor over, taking in the strong hands, the determined chin partially hidden by his neatly trimmed beard. 'In his man eyes,' thought Lonnlarcan, 'you can always see what is in a human by his eyes.' And what the elf king saw pleased him.

He pointed at the map. "This troop disposition, besides being considerably larger than those shown at the council meeting, are also placed in different parts of your empire."

The emperor smiled, showing thick white teeth. "Ah, my lord, I don't want you to think I am not a trusting man," he shrugged. "Dangerous times and all that."

"I suppose since the Lord Mearead is not here, that he has already been informed of this?" The elf cocked his head to one side. Trell'dem shifted in his seat, but no smile came to his lips. He leaned toward Lonnlarcan, his face hard.

"Do not take this amiss, my lord, but Mearead has known from the beginning of my plans." Lonnlarcan simply nodded. It was as Baibre had thought. The whole scene in the council had been carefully orchestrated by Mearead and the emperor.

"I understand," he answered, his musical voice giving nothing of his private thoughts away. "I think it has always been easier for dwarf and man to work together than for either races to deal with the elven kind." Trell'dem leaned back, letting his pleasure at Lonnlarcan's responses, spoken and unspoken, show.

"What are these?" Lonnlarcan pointed to the black circles that were strewn about the map.

"Caches of weapons, my lord. I have been building them up for twenty years now."

"Dwarven forged, no doubt."

"Even so." Trell'dem studied Lonnlarcan. There was no sign of what the enigmatic being was thinking. Lonnlarcan was truly the king of his people; he represented all that was best of the elves. He was tall, way beyond human stature, and though slim, well muscled. His features were of such great beauty that no human could hold the picture of the elf king's appearance in his mind. One was continually surprised when he came into contact with that unearthly beauty.

'Which,' thought Trell'dem, 'is not to say that there is anything feminine about him. It is like looking at the moving statue of a god, or as if one's flesh could take on the form of his soul.' To a human being alone in a room with one such as Lonnlarcan was nothing short of terrifying, and a bit humbling.

"Do you really expect to need such forces in the near future?" Lonnlarcan's voice brought Trell'dem out of his contemplation.

"Honestly?" Trell'dem leaned back in his chair. "No. No, but I do expect something, not this year, not next, but soon, sooner than we imagine."

The Ard Riegh's eyes swept the map once more. "So," he said, "I know now, and Mearead knows, but I expect few others."

"Dammuth, my Warlord Crane, the Archduke, Fin, a handful of Green Branch knights, that is all, good king."

"To hide it from your people, from your commanders, and allies, is no small feat." Trell'dem smiled his pleasure and pride.

"I've had help."

"Ah, yes, Dammuth is very resourceful, is he not?"

"Magic has many uses, my lord."

"Oh, indeed it does, indeed it does." Lonnlarcan was using his magic to try to grasp the measure of the man across from him, but the emperor was shielded, and the elf could feel the presence of Dammuth in that. So there was more, hidden, and considering Trell'dem's attitude, he doubted any knew the whole truth save the emperor himself.

"You have two sons, do you not?" he asked.

"I—yes. And no, they know nothing of what is going on." Lonnlarcan gave him a questioning look.

"My sons are good lads both. And well trained, but," Trell'dem's voice quivered with something like anger, "I must face the fact if the enemy should strike they would be prime targets. The less they know, the better for all. They must be kept safe for the empire."

Lonnlarcan did not bring up the obvious that if the sons were in danger surely the father was in more. Such words of caution would be wasted on this one.

"What does Dammuth say of all this?" Again Trell'dem could not hide his uneasiness. 'So,' thought Lonnlarcan, 'he does hide something even from Dammuth.'

"Dammuth, my lord, is the rock the empire is built on."

"But?"

"But, I do not know how to explain it. Indeed, it is partially for that reason I asked you here." Lonnlarcan just waited.

"Dammuth is changed. He has not the fire he once possessed."

"Dammuth," answered the great king, "is old for your kind, very old. But he is Dammuth." Trell'dem just waited. 'Is that all he wants?' the Ard Riegh thought, 'to be reassured?'

"Dammuth is the greatest wielder of magic with perhaps the exception of Arianrood. More important, though perhaps others have equal or more power, he is the best." Lonnlarcan's silver eyes burned in the dim light of the room. "Of all of us that walk the earth! *He* is the strongest, the most incorruptible. Every ounce of strength at his command is earned, not given.

"Your Green Branch knights have a saying in their honor code: 'No evil is powerful enough to corrupt the unconsenting.' Dammuth is incorruptible. He could not be turned. He could not consent for he never learned how.

"Whatever worries you have for that one, put them at rest," he continued. "Did not Dammuth destroy the most powerful of the dragons, Sessthon? I do not think any but the Dark Lord himself could conquer Dammuth, and even then only in death."

Trell'dem relaxed again, leaning back, placing his booted feet up on the corner of the table. "And if the enemy were to invade, what forces would you bring to bear, my lord?"

"Time, my good emperor, time is my enemy." The elf lord sighed. "It takes a great deal of effort to get a majority of my people in the same subjective time frame. And truly I can only do that if there is an apparent threat. I always have a thousand of my personal guard ready, but," he shrugged, "perhaps in first hosting I have say, two of your months, I can have 8,000 elven riders ready. All depending of course where the enemy strikes, and with what force."

Trell'dem started to speak but the Ard Riegh interrupted. "No promises from me, my lord. We will help where and when we can. Prepare yourself as best you may. We are true to the Alliance, as we have ever been. We will not fail in our duties."

"Believe me, my lord, I never doubted the elves of Cather-na-nog." He did not need to speak of his distrust of Arianrood, and Lonnlarcan did not wish to pursue that thought.

"There are many powers in the world, Trell'dem," Lonnlarcan said. "I do not believe we shall ever again face such a trial as we did in the Dark Siegn wars. Whatever failings Fealoth had with predicting the future, none can argue that he did bind the Dark One. Creation and destruction must ever be in conflict, in whatever form. But without the Beast, the enemy can never wield such a power again."

"To your eyes, my lord, I am sure this might seem an overreaction on my part, but," Trell'dem sat up straight, "there *are* many powers in the world, and some are more than a little troubled." Again the elf wondered what secret ally the emperor had made. There was no point in trying to figure it out, the man's heart was true, and, frankly, the thought that the emperor had a hidden weapon in his cloak was a comfort.

"I am not unaware of such concerns, Trell'dem." 'Should I tell him of the Morigu?' he thought. 'But, no, if Dammuth keeps it from him, then I will follow the wizard's lead.' Still it troubled him. 'So many secrets amongst allies. What fear was it that shook them all?'

"And I think," he continued aloud, "we both realize there are other powers that will hear the horn cry of war if need be." Trell'dem smiled. 'So,' he thought, 'Lonnlarcan had his surprises, too. Good! Perhaps I'm being overanxious, but treachery had ever been the enemy's greatest weapon!'

There was a muffled knock on the door. Lonnlarcan looked at it for a moment as if he could see who was on the other side. He nodded and made a brisk gesture with his left hand. Trell'dem hid the map once more. He felt the strange tingling as the spell was dismissed.

"Come in!" he cried. The door opened. A young knight in armor stood there and bowed.

"It is time, sire. The priests await you."

The emperor made his apologies to the Ard Riegh and left, following the knight.

Lonnlarcan sat there a moment, his mind slowly replaying the conversation. 'An odd man,' he thought, 'so confident, yet so cautious. What nightmares had plagued this emperor that he should fear so? The mortals were so confusing. For all that the other peoples of the world wield greater power, yet ever the humans proved to be the pivotal piece.'

He looked up at the ceiling, feeling the oppressive weight of the city about him. Angles and straight lines, the humans were ever enamored of them. But Lonnlarcan did not trust them. They sought to inflict rules and logic alien to the world. They sought to defeat chaos by measuring and defining everything about them. Even time. 'What a sad lot,' he thought, 'to be of the race of men. Children trapped in a world they cannot truly see.'

With that the elf king left the room, his thoughts on the tragedy and folly of the human race. Two guards stood on either side of the door, closing it behind the Ard Riegh and remaining on guard there. They both followed the strange elf with their eyes, both wondering how any being could move with such fluidity and power.

Neither of the guards saw the shadow, that was not a shadow, flit across the torchlit hall, or feel its presence as it slid beneath the door they guarded. Once in the room the shadow coalesced on itself, sick from the residue of the elf king's magic. Then it expanded and lay across the table, as if something humanoid bent over to examine what lie beneath.

It remained for a few moments in that position. Then with a sharp bark of victory, unheard by the guards without, slipped away. Through the door and into the freedom of the winds, to bring its masters its newfound knowledge.

Three weeks to a day after Mearead and his dwarves had entered Tolan they prepared to depart. But considering half were drunk and the other half were nursing terrific hangovers, it was easier said than done. Dammuth and Trell'dem stood before the gates as the dwarves scurried around, falling off their ponies, dropping things, trying to keep each other awake, while Mearead strode among them bellowing out incomprehensible orders. It seemed as if the whole population of Tolan had come to see the dwarves' departure, and considering the laughter, everyone was having a great time. The dwarves happily waved and danced for their audience, to the applause of the crowd.

Dammuth and Trell'dem tried desperately to look stately and calm, but both were biting their lips trying not to join the crowd and break up. Dammuth compared this scene to the elves' departure the night before. The silent ranks drawn up, witchlight glowing about the king and his people. The thunder of the hoofbeats as their great steeds took off into the night. He wondered what Lonnlarcan's reaction to this mess would have been.

"I still can't believe it," Trell'dem said for the fifth time.

"Think of it this way, sire," Dammuth answered, "you've made the lad a folk hero among his people."

"But right in the middle of the ceremony." Trell'dem watched as Mearead tried to break up a fight between four dwarves who all claimed the same pony. "But his own sister's son." Trell'dem shook his head.

Dammuth laughed. "It was pretty funny."

"Sure, they thought so." He pointed to the dwarves, now half hidden by the dust they were kicking up. The emperor faked a shudder as he remembered. At the last celebration of the Festival of Fealoth, in the middle of his speech, young Colin, who had been steadily getting drunk for the two days preceding, turned white all of a sudden, and then with a mighty heave, threw up all over Trell'dem. The humans as one gasped, the elves seemed to take no notice at all, and the dwarves fell to the ground in hysterics.

"I thought it was clever of Mearead to claim it was a good omen from the gods," Dammuth added. Trell'dem just smirked.

"I still can't believe it."

At that moment Mearead joined them, his face red from exertion, but a happy smile on his face nonetheless.

"Mearead, if I didn't know better I'd say you planned this." Trell'dem waved at the chaos in front of him.

"Ah, well, I'd like to claim credit," the dwarf answered, "but you know, this sort of fun just doesn't come from planning." He grinned up at the emperor. "By the way, son, I'll gladly pay to replace the robe Colin messed on." Trell'dem gave him a filthy look.

"Isn't it time you were leaving?" Dammuth interjected.

"Soon, soon. The boys are almost all together now." If anything they looked in a worse state than before. "Are you sure you don't want us staying for your fire feasts?" Trell'dem leaned down to stare at the dwarf king.

"Another week of this?" Trell'dem smiled and put his mouth to the dwarf's ear.

"Not bloody likely," he whispered. They both laughed. Mearead bowed.

"We'll be away in a few moments, your lordship. Please accept my sincere apologies for my sister's son. He is in no state, as you can imagine, to give them himself."

Dammuth clasped the dwarf's arm. "Get out of here, you old liar."

"And," continued Mearead, "if it helps you any, oh emperor, the boy will be remembered for that golden moment for all time by my people. Which, of course," he added, "means you as the major player in the grand event will also be remembered in song for a thousand years."

"Go away," was Trell'dem's only answer. With that Mearead wished them all a good day and strode into the middle of his ragged troop. It only took another half hour of shouting and not a few kicks and punches to get the band off, the people of Tolan cheering them the whole way. Trell'dem and the wizard watched until the last of the dwarves disappeared over a ridge.

"Our allies." Trell'dem shook his head.

"Well, they do liven things up," Dammuth answered. "Besides, there are no fiercer warriors than those of the Crystal Falls." Trell'dem turned to him.

"Dammuth, how much time do you think we have?" The wizard reached inside his cloak and handed the emperor a flask. "We have time, my lord, we have time." The two turned and walked away, Trell'dem still shaking his head. "I still don't believe it," he mumbled under his breath.

But there were other eyes that watched that day. Other eyes that laughed, though there was no humor in them. The report they brought back to their masters was received with the same fierce glee. And that day the final plans were made.

CHAPTER

Three

Tor, son Thane'dule, was bored, which wasn't that uncommon a thing for Tor to be. He had been bored in his home village of Teft. Farming bored him. His two brothers and sister bored him and his father was a son-of-a-bitch. All these factors led him to the army where he found himself stationed at Fort Venture, which was a pretty stupid name for a fort, he had always thought.

Venture was built right on the border between the human empire of Tolath and the ancient land of the Dark Seign. It was a wood and stone construction that could hold some three hundred warriors, but now housed ninety-four, officers included. Since it was twelve miles from Glen Cam, the nearest village, the most exciting thing to do was to get obnoxiously dunk and pass out, something that the 19-year-old Tor got bored of his first month at Venture.

He kicked a loose stone knocking it off the catwalk. To make it all worse, he thought, it was April 30th, the night before the fire feast. All through the empire people were preparing for the spring festival. He could picture it so easily, the food and bonfires, the young dancing in their green in the field.

"Dancing," he murmured, "dancing to the Night of the Stranger." The night when the young and unmarried met between the fires to worship the Goddess. And here he was stuck on guard duty.

Nothing, but nothing, was worse than guard duty at Fort Venture. And since all the fort guarded was a desolate wasteland, everyone at the fort figured it was all pretty much a wasted venture ("Ha! Ha!") to stay up all night looking at a bunch of bog. Tor slapped lazily at a mosquito and wondered if the other six guards on duty were as miserable as he was. Somehow, his visions of becoming an heroic warrior were fading away, and he found himself wondering if farming really was all that bad.

But Tor did see some action after all. He heard the beat of drums and a loud mournful wail of some bizarre horn. He saw the hundreds of figures rise from the bog. He didn't see the scaling ladders thrown against the walls or the looks of hate on the goblins' faces as they slaughtered him and his comrades. He didn't see Sergeant Mait's last stand where he killed the goblins' captain in single combat. Tor didn't see his best friend, Reck Tell, disemboweled by one swing of an ax. He didn't even feel the arrows that took his life. They hit him with such force that they killed Tor immediately as they sliced through his young body. The young warrior was dead and so was Fort Venture, and their mutual destruction heralded in the horror of a new war.

Trell'dem, Emperor of Tolath, sat in an empty room, his chair facing the whitewashed wall where a map of his empire hung. It was covered with tiny colored pins, each pin representing thousands of troops—most of the pins were black.

They covered the south of his land. They formed an arrow, aiming straight north, straight toward Tolan, straight toward him. Somewhere under that dark mass of markers lay the city of Dulatia and the proud castle of Meath. If either stronghold was still held, he was sure they would fall soon.

In the southwest a line of blue pins ran from the Dudny River through the Shamblin Woods across to Dun Scaga. But in the southeast, up to the mountains of Tevulic, there were none.

"An eighth," he groaned, "an eighth of our land taken in two weeks." He did not, would not, think of what it meant for his people, how many lay dead, or worse, in that once prosperous land. His face was lined, the skin stretched over the skull tight and hard. A thin tear raced among the folds of his face. Trell'dem started at the feel of it. In eighty-seven years he had cried only twice.

'Sean,' he thought, 'Sean, my son.' His eldest, so silent that one. Now lost, lost, for his heir ruled Meath castle. "At least Rhee isn't alive to see this," he said aloud. She had died in bringing Cathbad into the world. Somewhere his youngest was putting on his armor, and would ride with his father into the war to the south, to meet that black arrow.

"Enough!" he cried, jumping from his seat. "Enough! Am I not a man?" he yelled to the ceiling. "Am I not Emperor?! It is my destiny, my duty!" he cried. With one whirling motion he drew his knife and shoved it into the midst of the black pins, scattering them about the room.

"You came early!" he shouted at the map. "You came early, you scum, but I am ready, more ready than you could ever know!" He paced the room, his hands grasping for the sword that was not there.

"*I* knew, you swine. Oh, I knew you would come." He turned to the map, pointing one strong hand at it. "You and your black magic that overwhelms us, if it wasn't for that where would you be? Maggots! You kill my people like cattle. You *eat* them!" he shouted, his voice trailing into a wail.

He reached and withdrew the dagger. "But," he murmured, running the edge across his palm, "but we have cold steel for you black hearts, and spirit, strength, defiance that you could never know! Never understand . . ." He threw the knife into the map where it hung quivering.

"Fealoth!" he cried. "Fealoth," his voice echoed past the room, into the hills. "Fealoth," yet a third time and his people shuddered at the rage in that voice. "What are you, great-uncle? Where are you now?! How can you let them *do this*?!!!!!!!"

He stopped and took a breath. "You came early," he whispered, "you came early. But *I* have planned. *I* have surprises for you yet. I WILL NOT FAIL MY PEOPLE!!!!!!" He dropped into his chair, his hand tugging at the back of his hair.

"Ah, Sean, Sean, my darling son." He gritted his teeth. "I will not fail." His voice was hard and sure. But his eyes were soft.

A timid knock on the door interrupted his thoughts. A young page, new to the court, stuck his blond head in.

"Your imperial majesty," the voice quivered, "the council, the council waits." Trell'dem stared at the round blue eyes, the soft-cheeked face. He did not recognize the page, but they were all new now, the older ones having already joined the armies. He took a deep breath, feeling his lungs expand, the power in his muscles.

"Fine, son, be with you in a moment." He wondered if the boy had heard his emperor's rages. No matter. He turned his back to the page and picked up the silver crown of Tolath.

As he felt the smooth, cool metal, he smiled, his teeth flashing white. He knew, he knew he could do it, knew he could win this war. It was what he was born for.

But he wasn't the only one to think that.

The page withdrew a stiletto from his sleeve and drove it through the emperor's back. Trell'dem grunted, his mind incapable of deciphering what had happened.

He turned and looked at his murderer, only surprise showing in the emperor's face. The gloating eyes of his assassin, so innocent a moment before, clouded with fear as Trell'dem reached out and snapped the boy's neck with one convulsive jerk.

Trell'dem's legs numbed and he fell to his knees, unable to cry out. The emperor was an incredibly strong man; he could have survived the wound, if it had come from a clean blade. But the enemy was thorough and the poison was fast acting and lethal. He felt his veins thicken, his muscles bloat. He turned his fury on himself. Of all he had prepared for, this, the most obvious move, is the one he missed.

"Gods," he whispered through already cold lips, "I could have . . ." His tongue turned hard and he fell to the ground, the silver crown falling from his dead fingers. It made a ringing noise as it rolled across the floor, the quiet, unheard death knell of an emperor and king.

The great audience hall of Tolan was empty except for one lone figure. The massive room seemed to weigh the man down. He sat bent and grey on the steps that led to the golden throne of the empire. The marble floors and solid gold pillars reverberated with his slow breath. His frame shook as Dammuth tried to hold back the sobs. His enemy's blows had come fast and sure. And the wizard had felt every one.

He picked up the scroll at his feet, his mind trying to absorb the death the black lines dancing on the paper represented.

Twelve thousand warriors of the empire, all presumed dead. Civilian casualties: incalculable. Assassinated: Trell'dem; three imperial generals; two barons; one count; four captains of exceptional quality; eight mages, the most powerful, next to Dammuth, the humans possessed.

'Had possessed,' he reminded himself.

The week since Trell'dem's death had been worse than the weeks before. Trell'dem's eldest son had never been found, but reliable reports from the front claimed the Dark Ones used a young boy's head as a standard that looked remarkably like the prince. The youngest. 'Ah,' he thought, 'Cathbad.' He could still hear the boy's mad screams. Some spell bound the boy and wracked him with madness. A spell Dammuth could not break.

"It should not be," he told the empty room. "Who can bind a spell, immune to my strength?" He threw the scroll away from him. "It should not be. . . ."

To make it worse, with Trell'dem's death and the fall of

his sons, the reins of the empire were left in the old wizard's
hand. In the south, Warlord Crane tried desperately to slow
the enemy's advance.

Dammuth knew it was only a matter of weeks until the
Dark Ones were howling outside the gates of the capital
itself. He lifted his white maned head to face the mosaic
ceiling, his dark eyes glittering with unshed tears.

A loud boom shook the walls as a young warrior, armor
clinking, opened the door and approached the archmage.
Dammuth did not bother to try and hide his anguish. The
warrior's steady march slowed and faltered as he approached
the mage.

"My—my lord," he stuttered, "the procession awaits
you." Dammuth looked the other over carefully. Young, not
quite twenty-five. His black hair was long, tied into a horse-
tail braid. He was short with the partially bowed legs of a
born horseman, but his eyes were grey stone.

"Yes," Dammuth answered, "time to bury the emperor. . . ." He looked back at the ceiling. The other just
waited. After a few moments the wizard's sad eyes focused
again on the warrior.

"What's your name, boy?"

"Mathwei ap Niall, my lord."

"You've already been to the front?"

"I was stationed at the village of Glen Cam, ten miles
from the Dark Seign border, when—when it all began, my
lord."

"And you survived?" Dammuth's voice was gentle, but
the warrior shifted his eyes from Dammuth to the floor.

"I was lucky, my lord." His voice was a whisper.

"You're a captain, I see."

"Yes," a smile—quickly lost. "I was a sergeant two
weeks ago."

"And so . . ." Dammuth slowly stood up. He pointed to
the ceiling. "Captain Mathwei, do you know who that is?"
The young man looked up to the mosaic the wizard pointed
at. It was of a tall dark man, holding a sceptre in one hand

and a sword in the other. A surcoat of pure white covered his mail-clad chest. In the background lay the map of the empire.

"That's Lir, the Liberator." He turned back to the wizard, quickly adding, "my lord."

"Yes, the first emperor of Tolath. Father of Fealoth." The wizard shook his head. "He was hated in his day, you know —despised. He wasn't the Liberator then. No," he laughed, "they had other names for him then." His laughter stopped abruptly. "I was about your age when I joined his army. I didn't know magic then, just the sword."

Mathwei knew he should remind Dammuth of the waiting funeral procession—but he was Dammuth, the greatest wizard to ever live. And he was talking to him, only him. . . . The wizard walked down the steps, weaving one arm in a slow gesture in front of him.

"The land, the land was broken then, little kingdoms as big as the castle that ruled them, fiercely independent city-states, roaming bands of nomads." He smiled. "Lir always claimed he was divinely guided, that Lugh told him it was his destiny to rule all the human lands." He stopped to stare down at Mathwei. "They really hated the poor bastard." He turned away again. "But he was magnificent! I didn't care if a god told him what to do. I didn't even care if we did the right thing. I just loved that man. . . ." He walked back up the stairs.

"And his wife, the empress Ellawyn," he whipped around, "let me tell you, boy, *she* was his match. A warrior, too!!! I would never have wanted to trade sword blows with that one." He smiled down at Mathwei, his eyes lost in memories. "I loved her, too. Not just admired her. I loved her! Between the two of them they made me what I am." He sat down again. "I loved them so. . . ." For a moment he sat quietly, the warrior struggling to meet his eyes. Dammuth cleared his throat.

"What do you think, boy? Were they doing the god's bidding?"

"I'm not sure, my lord, I guess so." Mathwei shifted the weight of his mail coat. "I mean, he did build the empire, and if he hadn't . . ."

"Exactly! If he hadn't," Dammuth said, "then we would never have been able to face the Dragon Lords during the Dark Seign wars. They would have eaten us one by one."

"And there's Fealoth, my lord."

"Oh yes, Fealoth. One can't forget him." He put his head in his hands. "Do you follow Fealoth, Mathwei ap Niall?"

"Well," Mathwei wiped sweat from his brow, "I did, I mean I do, I mean, we all thought—"

"—that Fealoth had defeated the enemy for all time," Dammuth interrupted. "The Golden Age. Yes, the Golden Age. Do you think we were foolish to believe in the Golden Age, Mathwei?"

"It was promised, my lord."

"Yes, I know. But where is he, our mighty Fealoth?" Dammuth shook his head. "God or no, he was never the man his father was." Mathwei took a deep breath, his only reaction to the wizard's blasphemy. Dammuth looked up. He patted the stair next to him.

"Sit, boy. Come sit down." Mathwei sat reluctantly, keeping his distance. The mage Dammuth looked him in the eyes.

"Do I surprise you, Mathwei?" he asked. "Well, I'm old. Very old, you know. Seen a lot of things. And let me tell you—Fealoth, he was *my* friend. I helped to make him a god. After all, you don't go around doing that to people you don't like, do you?" He laughed. "Or do you?" He turned away.

"I have to leave this room, this silly, bloody hall and bury another friend. Trell'dem, ah Trell'dem. Now he was like the Liberator! But better, better. The best man I ever knew." He shifted to face the warrior. "He was incorruptible, you know." His voice grew quieter. "Power corrupts, even the best. Even those who should know better. But Trell'dem, he was *incorruptible*!" He shouted the word out. "Of all the men I have met, he was the best. The best that a human being could be. The world is a darker place without his light." He drew his robes around him, looking old, old. "The world grows darker and the shadows draw close to me, calling my name. . . ." He grew silent, seemingly forgetting the young warrior next to him. "I doubt that another like him shall ever come again, ever."

Mathwei did not move a muscle. The old man's grief was too much, what could he say? He felt so tiny, so ignorant. 'Dammuth, Dammuth,' he thought, 'I sit here next to you, you the greatest hero alive, and I can do nothing for you, nothing.'

"You can do something for me, boy," Dammuth answered quietly. "You can tell me, tell me what it's like."

"My lord?" The voice trembled.

"They killed him, they stabbed him in the back," Dammuth shouted, "the sons of bitches poisoned him!" The air grew static at the wizard's shout. Mathwei shifted further away, his skin dancing with the magic forces let free by the mage's anger. Mathwei could barely hear the other's voice. "Surely he deserved better than that. . . .

"Tell me, young follower of Fealoth," Dammuth stood up again and walked a few feet away, "tell me what you think has happened to your god."

"I don't know, my lord," Mathwei answered. "I think—I think he must be dead." He spat the word out. The wizard stared at the sitting warrior for a moment. 'So young,' he thought, 'sitting there with his hands clasped like some lad caught at stealing an apple.'

"I never followed Fealoth, never prayed to him," Dammuth said. "Never even went to one of his temples." He smiled again, a bright child's smile. "I prefer to be friendly with the gods, not their friends." Silence. Mathwei shifted nervously; even in his pain Dammuth was impressive. His dark green robes fit his body tightly, showing the strength in the slim body. His eyes were deep-set behind a thick brow bridge covered with a thatch of white hair. His face was

smooth except for the long mustache which still retained a
dark hair here and there. Remembering his duty, Mathwei
stood up.

"My lord, the others await you."

"Do they?" Dammuth smiled again, his child's smile.
"They're really too busy getting the carriage horses settled."
Mathwei looked uncomprehendingly at him. "Sit down, boy.
Magic has many uses and I am not yet ready to leave this
cold hall."

"You mean," Mathwei asked, "you bewitched the
horses?" Dammuth laughed. This time the hall rang with his
voice.

"Oh yes, yes. Sometimes it's a handy thing to be a
mage."

"Surely not the ones pulling the hearse?" Mathwei asked.

Dammuth laughed louder. "No, no, boy. Just an odd one
here and there." He sat back down next to the warrior, shaking his head at his joke. "Now, I have a friend," he said
confidentially, "he would have wanted me to tip the bloody
casket over. Probably would have insisted on it."

"My Lord," Mathwei could not hide his nervousness.

"Well," Dammuth answered, "he's a dwarf. They laugh
at anything, you know." He turned to Mathwei.

"You must understand, boy," he began, "I am old. Tired.
Death and I have become too intertwined. It is hard to face.
Another war—death—death everywhere. When humans
fought one another during the liberation, much evil was
done. It is an ugly thing for a creature to fight its brother, but
still there were the saving moments, the ones who said no to
the blood. The little acts of mercy.

"But the enemy, the enemy knows nothing of mercy!
Nothing of kindness." He ran his hands through this thick
hair. "I hate them for what they've done, for what they will
do, but it's not enough. I need more than hate, I don't know
—anger, revulsion . . . I just don't know." He waved at the
hall in front of them.

"I've heard all the reports, seen the refugees. But it's not enough. You want to help me? Then fill me with the anger and outrage of youth. That, that surety of purpose only the young know. Tell me, Mathwei." His voice became quiet, incessant. "Tell me, young warrior, what have you seen? What has it been like?"

Mathwei sat silent, the mage's power permeating the air, pressing on him, demanding to know. To see and feel what Mathwei had experienced.

"It is hard," he began, his eyes unfocusing as Dammuth's magic infused his memories. "I was at Glen Cam, a small village, barely 150 lived there," he coughed. "It was night time. Late, I don't really know, my corporal woke me up. I, I had been drinking all night at the fire feast. There was a rider with an urgent message. I got up. I, I thought, oh, I don't know, a raid maybe—there was no way to guess. My biggest concern was my hangover." As the spell strengthened his memories, his voice became a monotone. "I walked outside, and the night . . . it was light. The fires, from the border forts, lit it up." Dammuth's voice underscored the other's tale with a slow chant, his hands moving in complicated patterns. In front of the two a miniature tableau slowly formed. The dark shapes of cottages and huts outlined by the fires ten miles away. The scurrying of the people, confused. Their voices raised in fear as they pointed to the south. The rider, dirty, exhausted. Blood sliding down the young, pale face.

"He shouted at me," Mathwei continued. "'There were thousands,' he cried, 'so many—couldn't stop them. The others must be dead, have to be dead.' I thought he was exaggerating, he was shaking so much. . . . I sent him to the infirmary, had the captain woken up and called my squad together. God knows where the officer of the watch was, probably still celebrating." He ground his teeth together, his jaw muscles standing out in high relief. "We were saddled and riding in twenty minutes. Bits and pieces of what armor we could grab thrown on." The illusion wavered as the warrior took a shaking breath.

"We were riding a half hour maybe," he said, "fast as we could. We were all half asleep. But excited about the thought of some action. What fools! We didn't know. . ." He turned pleading eyes to the wizard. "We *wanted* a fight, but, gods, we didn't know." He felt the pressure of Dammuth's magic and turned back to the wavering image in front of him.

Eight horsemen reigning their horses to a halt on top of a small hill. Shouting incoherently at the sight before them. The land in front was level, the great road a straight arm thrusting into the night. And everywhere, covering the road, covering the land, the dark figures of the enemy army. They were backlighted by the fires behind them. The numbers were uncountable. And they were less than a mile away and moving fast.

"It was like," Mathwei's voice shook, "an incredible animal, black and dark. I don't know how to . . . It was terrifying! There were so many. And they were coming, coming for us! Even so far away we could hear their mad cries. And, and cries, screams of another sort . . . We knew there could be no survivors. And only us between them and the village."

The hall rang with the drums of the goblins, and one voice screaming in fear. One of Mathwei's soldiers, crying, "Mama, oh, Mama." Finally, a warrior knocked him off his horse. Mathwei turned away again.

"I had to shut him up, he wouldn't shut up." The wizard said nothing. "I had to shut him up," Mathwei insisted.

The wizard's spell gathered strength. The illusion grew until it encompassed the whole hall. Dammuth stared at the oncoming army, now seeming to march in miniature in front of him. Mathwei was unaware of his memories being played out on the marble floor. He saw it all in his mind's eye.

"There was just no end to them," he continued. "It was like looking down the mouth of some great ravenous beast. Devouring everything in front of it. All life, all the land, the light itself."

Dammuth ended his spell with a harsh Word of power.

His consciousness drifted from him, merging with Mathwei, melding with the warrior's memories. The two now became one, living the past as the present.

They rode together the fear-maddened horse, tearing through the night to the village. Time moved faster, images flashed by . . . a rushed report to the captain . . . the cries of desperation from the civilians . . . the conflicting orders being shouted . . . trying to get everyone up and out, away from the village before the enemy reached them.

A kaleidoscope of quick moments in time. A child crying for its parents. A woman's face, terrified, trying to pack an old mule with boxes and boxes of things. A horse running wild through the streets, knocking people down. A lantern kicked over, starting a small fire. An old woman begging them if they had seen her son, a guard at one of the border forts. And beneath it all the building sounds of the approaching army. The thud of drums, the wails of horns, and louder and louder the tramp of thousands of clawed feet shaking the very earth beneath them.

Events speeded up. A line of cavalry, twenty maybe, forming on the road. Sword flash and a quick charge into the enemy running wildly toward them. Loud clashes of metal! Nightmare faces! The "thuk" noise of his spear impaling a goblin. A quick retreat, not five left to race into the village. People everywhere, still trying to pack things, many running now. The first goblins through the gates. A few soldiers holding the short wall, then gone, covered in a wave of dark, shouting forms.

It was a nightmare, no, worse, no nightmare could encompass such horror. He shouted himself hoarse, having no idea what he cried. The goblins poured through the street. He and a few others fought a running battle against the invaders. The noise was deafening as the goblins began to destroy the village. Every creature they came across, man, woman, child, or beast, they slaughtered out of hand.

One man came flying out of his shop to run smack into a group of the enemy. In desperation he swung at a goblin's face. It just tore its fangs into the fist, severing the hand, and contentedly settled down to its feast as its companions tore the man limb from limb.

Down the dusty street the goblins came charging straight at the warrior. Unable to help the shopkeeper, he jerked his horse around and fled the main street.

On a narrow side way a goblin leaped from the roof of a building, unhorsing Mathwei. A desperate struggle as the horse ran off. Kicks and punches ended when he buried his knife in the goblin's throat. The pink-green blood of his enemy sprayed him. The smell overwhelmed him so much that as he came to his feet he vomited all over himself.

He heard a screeching cry behind him. Turning, he saw a young woman running toward him, followed by a mass of the invaders. Her right arm hung limp, the shoulder bleeding from a deep wound. Her eyes, insane, rolling to the top of her head, pleading with the warrior even as the leading goblin pulled her down. The others soon surrounded her, their laughter drowning out her screams.

"Noooo!!!!" he cried, but he didn't run to her rescue, even as he saw through the flash of fangs and limbs, her dress being torn off. There were too many, too many. He wanted to live!! Fealoth save him . . . he wanted to live.

He ran away as fast as he could, dropping his sword in his haste to get away. Run! his mind cried. Run—fast, away—anywhere, just run!!!

The images were stronger, the smell of blood everywhere. Dammuth could no longer define his being and the warrior—they were Mathwei, running. Running away.

The fires were spreading fast, he ran by struggling groups of fighters. He couldn't stop even if he wanted to. As he sped for the gate, he saw the captain, still holding some of the troops together, go down with two arrows in his face. Right at the gate he saw a single goblin impale a small dog with its spear, then bend down and tear the animal's throat out with tusklike fangs. The goblin turned to watch Mathwei run through the gates, its eyes gleaming wickedly in the firelight.

All he could see as he tore down the road was that goblin's face. The dog's blood dripping down its chin. The sharp teeth, yellowed and large, opening wider . . . wider, to swallow him . . . to drink his blood . . . eat his flesh. But worst of all was the evil in its nightmare face, the total lack of anything vaguely human in its features. He felt its dark soul reach out to him, laughing at him for running. It told him—forced him—to realize its contempt and its silent message, your time will come, I'll let you go, but your time will come!

Now the spell raced faster, too fast to hold any moment long enough to dwell on it.

The town burned at his back as he ran, running past people pleading with him to stop, or yelling at him to fight. But he kept going.

The days sped by. The organization of the army . . . new men to lead . . . the first real battle to be fought . . . the slow chilling of the spirit . . . the inner cry for something much more powerful than revenge, more terrible than hate.

Their desperate attempt to ambush the enemy's vanguard as it crossed the river . . . the terrible magics throwing the attack back . . . the Crash! of weapons . . . the Whisper of blood . . . the cries of the wounded . . . the faces of the dead . . . the army routed, devastated . . . another terrible retreat . . . but no fear this time, just the soul's cry of outrage.

Days a blur . . . cold nights . . . short rations . . . wounded everywhere . . . and always the people running, clogging the roads, trying to stay ahead of the enemy's advance, their faces white, tear-stained, empty.

Less than a week later another battle . . . two sides facing each other . . . night falling . . . cry of the horns . . . Crash! . . . and the screams begin . . . another defeat, this time an orderly withdrawal, with half the army left behind.

Then half a week of useless ambushes, the enemy always knowing where they are, how many. Another army formed two days away from Dulatia. The battle lasted a day and a night. Vengeance always denied; by the magic. The undead appeared but the warriors become immune to any new horror.

The images stop, focusing on an elongated picture of a priest of Fealoth trying to cast the undead down. The priest screams, more surprise than pain, as the zombies tear his flesh off him ... eating him alive .... staining his white robes with his own blood.

Another lost ... another retreat ... the warriors getting shabbier, but always more determined. They all began to share the soul bond inside of Mathwei ap Niall. Revenge was not enough, death not enough, only the annihilation of the scum will soothe their shrinking spirits.

Then a sharp stab in the side as a lance presses through mail and skin ... but the defiance welling up will not die! His sword crashing through the goblin's helmet, splitting the skull beneath, the blue-purple brains showering through the air a sight of ecstasy even as the blackness takes hold.

Time slows down. The cart ride to Comar. The hard ride —the wound aching—to be at the site for the great emperor's funeral. The quick reunion with his parents. Unable to tell them the horror ... unable to answer the question in their eyes, the ones they dare not voice ... unable to tell anyone.

"Until you made me," he said aloud to the wizard. Dammuth reached his hand out to the other's sweating brow.

"Peace," he said quietly, "peace, you sad, sad boy." He held the other in his arms, his voice soothing and gentle.

He kept the warrior in his power for a moment.

"I can't wipe away the memory, Mathwei," he said. "It is your right to remember. Your tragedy to learn to live with it." He placed his fingers on the other's temple. "But I can take away the self-hate. I can take away the lash your mind whips your soul with. That, boy, I can do."

Dammuth gently rocked the youth back and forth as his power reached into the young warrior. He felt the fear and hate like deep pools churning inside Mathwei, the acid of corruption and bitterness rotting away the many good things of the soul within. These he sucked into himself, these he eased and emptied, leaving the spaces to be filled by Mathwei's own needs.

The forces took physical form and two streams of putrid green corruption slid down the youth's face. From the wizard's eyes two beams of bright light shot into the other's eyes, making his countenance shine as once his god Fealoth's had. The liquid darkness hissed and disappeared, black steam rising from either side of Mathwei's face.

Dammuth let go of him and smiled at the warrior. Mathwei's eyes flew open.

"My lord?" He smiled back happy and free. He could not remember anything of what the spell had done. He felt curiously elated, content almost.

"I said," Dammuth stood up, "you can do something for me."

The other leaped to his feet.

"Anything, my lord." 'Dammuth,' he thought, 'wants my help!'

"Stand by me at the funeral," the wizard continued, putting his arm around the warrior, "and when things get particularly dull, I shall tell you some dirty elf jokes a friend of mine has forced me to memorize." Mathwei felt safe with that thin arm around him.

"My lord," he enunciated the words slowly, "can we win without the emperor?"

"I honestly don't know," Dammuth answered. "But we shall do what he would wish and try our damnedest." At last the two felt the stirrings of what they had both been seeking, not revenge, not hate, but hope. . . .

"You know," Dammuth's voice reverberated around the hall as they left, "you remind me of another young warrior." 'And,' he thought, 'I wish I could do for him what I have done for you.'

Mathwei hurried to open the thick wooden door for the

wizard. As Dammuth started to walk through, Mathwei cleared his throat.

"My lord," Dammuth raised an eyebrow, "I was wondering, I mean, the men have been talking." Dammuth said nothing. "Well, what I want to ask is, well, what about our allies?" The wizard looked into the young warrior's eyes, clearer now, he thought, a spark there again. He liked this boy a lot, but lying was never the path he chose.

"A good question, son." He shrugged. "What about our allies?" With that he left to face the crowds at the procession, the young warrior stumbling after him.

CHAPTER

Four

Mearead, Lord of the Crystal Falls, walked quickly, his sister-son, Colin, scampering to keep up. They entered one of the Caves of Making, the crash and clang of metalworking assaulting their ears.

The cave was vast, the roof hidden in its height. The floor was covered with forges and anvils and the thick shapes of dwarves moving about. The whole area seemed to be simply thrown together; there was apparently no logic in the placement of fire and forge.

Mearead smiled at all the chaos, waving at dwarves as he passed, swapping a quick joke or a pat on the back. It was not lost on Colin that the three hundred or so dwarves in the cave were all working on armor or weapons.

The red light of the flames cast great shadows on the walls, as if unseen giants mimicked the work of the dwarves.

"Kinda spooky, ain't it?" Mearead laughed. "Sort of picturesque. I guess this is how humans picture us." He turned away and picked up his pace before Colin could answer him. Mearead for once did not want to talk, and the young dwarf honored his uncle's wishes even if he was bewildered by them.

Colin had been arguing with Flann about the merits of an ax versus a mace in one of the many small libraries that dotted the caves of the Crystal Falls. Such conversations had become commonplace for the seldom serious dwarves as the rumors of the invasion of Tolath spread. Mearead had appeared out of nowhere and had ordered Colin to follow him. For the last hour and a half the young dwarf followed his uncle deeper and deeper into the interior of the caves. He had no idea where they were going.

Neither said anything as they left the Cave of Making and continued down through narrow tunnels seldom used. There was little light except from the occasional Duiarcsolus, the dwarf light stones, set into the walls or ceiling. The stones found here were of poor workmanship and their light was weak and discolored. The young dwarf got more nervous as the way became more gloomy.

He was surprised to find that at every bend or new hall there was a fully armored guard. It cheered him some to think about the impregnability of the dwarven caves.

"Maybe," Mearead said aloud, "maybe we're not as impregnable as we think." Colin stared at him, wondering if his uncle could really read his mind. Well, he wouldn't put anything past Mearead's powers.

"Who could invade us, my lord?" 'After all,' he thought to himself, 'the caves, for all their incredible beauty, had always been built for defense.' There was no dichotomy about this in the dwarf's mind; after all, his people were all born artists and warriors.

"Probably said the same thing in Cardoc-nae-corond," answered Mearead, his voice unusually quiet.

"You think that's what happened?" Colin asked. "That they were overrun?" He got only a shrug in response.

The way now became harder. The hall they followed was full of defensive works. Colin's trained eyes picked out the many traps and pits prepared for any would-be invader.

They passed a whole squad of guards who didn't disturb their card game to greet them. Colin had long given up his early dreams of introducing the human ideas of respect due to a superior. Mearead amused himself by shouting out one of the players' hands at the top of his voice.

They left the happily arguing guards behind them, stepping into a small, half-finished hall. They followed this path until it ended in a solid wall, and before Colin could ask a question, Mearead placed both his hands on the wall, intoning a Word softly under his breath. The wall, which seemed so impenetrable even to Colin's dwarven eyes, opened slowly, a thin, greenish light filling the small tunnel. He followed Mearead through the door.

They stood on a slim, uneven ledge. Some thirty feet beneath them lay the cave floor. The other side of the cave was lost in the distance. It was one of the largest caverns Colin had ever seen and it was filled with life.

Little streams meandered all about, watering a great mass of vegetation and fungi. Dwarves wandered about, pruning here, uprooting there. The shapes of the vegetation were bewildering. Here a great mushroom-type fungus rose ten feet off the ground, there a twisting vine roamed the stream's bank, oval red fruits hanging off it like giant drops of blood.

The plants radiated their own light. It was not a sickly, pale color, but bright hues covering the spectrum, miniature rainbows arching from one stream to another. The whole blended into a pulsating green light that beat with health and vigor. Colin whistled.

"It's huge!" He looked at his uncle. "Why, I didn't even know this place existed." Mearead stared at the vision beneath him, the light softening the age and worry in his face.

"There's much for you to learn," he said. "This is one of several gardens we keep in case the upper halls ever fall. This one alone produces enough food for half our population. Only those of our people who wish to work here know of its existence. There are always some who prefer to work with growing things instead of metal or stone." He turned and continued to walk along the path.

Colin followed him, silent in his wonder. He sometimes liked to work in the gardens, but for all the beauty of the ones he knew, none compared with this. The two trudged on, through another secret way off the ledge, deeper into tunnels dusty with lack of use.

As they went deeper the atmosphere became thick; not stuffy, but as if the air itself somehow gained weight. It made Colin uncomfortably aware of his own breathing. He could feel the breath going into his lungs, spreading through them like water. Sounds became muffled and Colin could hear little except his own beating heart.

They finally stopped inside a cave. It was a lonely place, dark even to their eyes. Giant stalagtites and stalagmites reached for each other, the smallest wider than a cart. Mearead led the young dwarf deep into the confusing maze. Colin soon lost his sense of direction completely, something that had never happened to him before. Mearead pointed to one stalagmite.

"There," he said, his voice sounding tiny and distant in the strange air, "there is our door to the heart of the mountain, deep, deep into the very breast of She who is Mother to us all."

He walked up to the stalagmite and stood in front of it. Colin waited to see a secret door appear, but nothing happened. Mearead just stood there with eyes closed for a minute, his mouth moving in silent prayer. He turned back to Colin.

"Once I told a friend that the dwarven folk and the Morigunamachamain were greatly alike." He pointed at the stone. "But I did not tell even him about this, our greatest secret. Only we and the Morigu can know this. The full embrace of the Mother, only we can become part of that which is all." He took the other's hand. "Fear nothing," he said, "where we go, none may follow"; and with that he stepped into the rock. Colin could not believe it, even as he, too, went through solid stone. It was like stepping into a liquid with a slightly warm temperature.

He could see, but what he saw his mind could not grasp. Here, all forms, all colors were one, and yet distinct and individual. His mind would recognize an image, a light, or the form of lines and shapes, but before he could focus on anything it would be absorbed back into the soothing darkness that was all.

He could no longer see his body, but he felt, he felt his hands, his fingers move in the fluid, or the fluid move by him—which, he could not tell. His lungs filled with the darkness all around him. He went deeper but could not tell if it was up or down; he just knew he moved. He could not focus even on the touch of his uncle's hand. He grasped harder, and though he thought he felt nothing, he could close his hand no further. He was stopped by something that was firm but not solid. His thoughts drifted as if he was about to sleep.

His mind retained no thought, yet it was aware, aware of the life above, below, around him: the dwarves busy in their caves, the horrors of the war in the south, the strange impressions from the mystical kingdom of Aes Lugh. But even this he could not hold. The outside world flowed away, leaving only vague emotions: the contentment, fulfillment in simply being, the erotic all that surrounded and infused him.

Then . . . Pain. Actually, his mind realized not so much pain as he knew it, no warnings of damage to the body, just the flush of renewed sensations, the nerves once more awake, aware. He felt strong hands holding him up.

"Take it easy, lad. It's always confusing the first time." Mearead's voice pained his ears, though the tone was soft. The strong arms wrapped around Colin's chest and grasped hard, forcing him to gasp for air. His lungs burned with the fire of breath, the pain the newborn feels. He fell into a cushioned softness, gasping and choking. Mearead lifted him to a sitting position.

"Open your eyes, boy," he said, "look, and see the heart, the womb of the Mother."

Colin slitted his eyes carefully, waiting for the pain of vision, but it did not come. The room was light, gentle, and warming, like the sun burning red behind closed eyelids. But there was no real color to the light. It was as if his eyes had a new ability, an ability to perceive that which did not need light to take visual form.

It was not a room that he saw, it was not a place. It simply was, it existed; it was warm, comfortable, safe. But it had no name, therefore it could never have a name; it just was.

There weren't angles or definitions of form to focus on. There was no sound except for his breathing and Mearead's. Movement rustled clothes, but there was no floor to scrape against, no ceiling or walls to surround. Yet the feeling of being somewhere—here—was present.

"Mearead," Colin's voice rasped, but the place absorbed the edges of the sound, "am I blind?" He dared not look at the other dwarf, not knowing what he would see or if he would see anything.

"No, lad," said a voice behind him, "you're not blind. There is nothing here to blind you, or for you to see. Here eyes are not needed, neither are hands or ears. But the Mother gives us breath here, gives us speech and hearing, but there is really nothing to see."

"I, I don't understand. Where are we? I mean, it is like nowhere, nothing, but it is." He stared down at his legs and rubbed his fingers back and forth on his shirt, concentrating on the rough texture.

"This is the soul's place, lad. Our bodies are no help here."

"What, what do we do now?"

"We wait." Still Mearead did not show himself. "We wait." His voice, quiet, was swallowed by that which never needed voices, never needed air.

Dun Scaga stood high up on a bare hillock. Its walls were hard and grey with age, its towers thrust toward the sky with a dogged determination that had daunted many a would-be invader. But for all that, the grand old castle's days were numbered and none knew that better than its master, Laird Fin.

Fin sprawled on the massive wooden throne that dominated the small audience hall deep behind the castle walls. His red hair and beard fit with his stout and powerful frame. He lounged indolently on the throne, fitting the picture of a Laird: independent and strong, born to rule.

His features were solid and undistinguished except for his left eye. There, a scar through the eyebrow lifted the corner of the eye and the edge of his brow. It gave his face an almost comical effect, as if he viewed everything with constant skepticism and a touch of humor. Many times had that scar served him well as an opponent misjudged him, only to fall to his elemental anger or razor mind.

Two warriors stood at either end of the small dais that the throne rested on. They, like their lord, wore chain-mail coats with odd bits of armor strapped here and there. Each held a heavy two-handed sword across their shoulders. The two followed Fin's lead and stood comfortably, their bodies angled as if any minute they would simply crash to the ground. But their weapons were sharp and their hands held the scars of seasoned warriors. None held a sword in Dun Scaga unless they were well-versed in its deadly magic.

Except for these three the hall was empty. On the walls hung the dusty battle flags that the clan of Scaga had been taking from their enemies' dead hands for three hundred years. Though there were larger and more powerful clans, it was known throughout the empire that there were none more deadly.

The nail-studded wooden door at the end of the hall ground open and an old veteran led in two figures. Both were draped with black cloaks that hid head and hand. The two figures were wide at the shoulders and their gait was bowlegged like a horseman's. Fin was not the only one to recognize them as goblins. Though none of the three figures at the end of the hall moved or shifted their positions, a tense edge filled the void between them and the figures moving toward them.

The old veteran stayed by the door, closing it behind him.

The two goblins walked the expanse of the hall alone, their soft footsteps the only sound. They reached the foot of the dais and bowed in unison, bowed deeply, a servant to his master.

"Greetings to the lord of Dun Scaga," said one, his voice remarkably refined. "We bring a message from our masters —meant, I might add, for the lord's ears alone." Fin said nothing. Staring at the two of them for a moment, he let the silence drag out until the one who had not spoken shifted in agitation.

"Your masters," he stretched the word out, "should have informed you that the *Laird* of Dun Scaga has more than one pair of ears."

"I see," answered the speaker. "Well, in that case, I bring you this." He gestured to the other who reached inside his cloak and withdrew a small pouch. One of the soldiers took it and handed it to Fin. Fin grasped it in his hand, feeling the small hardness within. His face showed nothing, he had expected this, but still. . . . He opened the bag, letting the signet ring fall into his palm, the small ruby flashing red in the torchlight. He inspected it for a moment, his mind surprised by the sudden heaviness of the delicate bit of jewelry.

"You recognize it, of course," the speaker said softly.

"Oh, aye, I recognize it," Fin's voice was equally soft, almost a snake's hiss. His grey-green eyes refused to look at the thing in his hand, staring at a point directly over his antagonist's head. "She was a lass of seventeen when I put it on her finger." His two warriors moved closer to their lord, their hands fastening around their sword grips. The two goblins ignored them.

"You will be glad to know your wife is in fine health, alive, unharmed, and," the goblin cleared his throat with a decidedly unhuman sound, "untouched." This last bit almost broke Fin's composure. He was no stranger to the goblins' desire for human women.

"Don't fool with me, scum!" He spit the words out. Both the goblins recoiled from the harshness of the words. "Tell me what you want, and tell me now!" The goblins could not help giving each other a quick glance. They were in the lion's den; getting out was not going to be easy.

"All know of the prowess of the Scaga clan," began the speaker. "Since the creation of the Green Branch knights the Clan Lord of Scaga has always been a member and usually several members of his immediate family. Both you and your son are members of that elite group, as is an inordinate number of your clan's warriors." He stopped for a moment. Fin could picture in his mind the goblin licking his fangs.

"Get on with it," he said. Another pause.

"The war, which the empire has brought upon itself by its unjust persecution of the goblin race, is a waste," the speaker's hand fluttered out; it was covered by a black glove, "a waste for your people and mine. We wish to end it as soon as possible. Once we have reclaimed land that right-fully belongs to us." He stopped for a moment as if he expected an answer. He got none.

"But, as I say, this war is with the empire, not with humans. We therefore do not wish to antagonize those who will soon be our neighbors."

"My lord," the youngest of the warriors turned to Fin, "must we listen—"

"Shut up," Fin silenced the other. He looked back at the goblin. "Finish."

"Well, as I was saying, we hold no claim on the land of Scaga. We have no fight with you."

"Ah, so that's why you kidnapped my wife."

"Detained, my lord, detained so that we would have a chance to speak with you, before, ah, blood was shed between your people and mine.

"After all, it is not unknown to me that your clan fought hard against the destroyer Lir. Your people quite rightly wish their independence. This is a quality both our peoples share."

"The terms," Fin's voice was pitched low.

"Your wife will be returned to you after we have

overthrown the harsh rule of the empire. In the interim none of the Scaga clan will take arms against us. Of course, we realize that you do not wish to fight your own kind, so all we ask is free passage of our armies through your land. Your people will become neutral, and have no doubt," he added quickly, "we will pay well for the right to cross your borders, very well. Furthermore, we will make a binding nonaggression pact between your people and mine, a treaty that will last until the end of time."

"My wife."

"Your wife will be well taken care of, treated as her station deserves, served by human women and guarded against any evil; she will be safe until Tolan falls. Once the city is taken she will be returned to you safe and unharmed. It is well-known in all the land the great love you have for your lady. We respect that, and in fact admire it."

"My wife," Fin continued as if the goblin had said nothing, "is dead." The two goblins went still. After a moment the speaker cleared his throat again; this time it sounded like a growl.

"I assure you, my lord, she is alive and well taken care of."

"My wife," Fin interrupted; he sat straight and stared at the two, "is also a knight of the Green Branch."

"That is known to us, my lord, and believe me, she is treated as such a noble lady should be." Fin sat back, massaging his eyes for a moment. Then slowly he got to his feet. He walked down the dais and circled the two goblins. He shook his head again.

"You do not understand," he smiled at the two. "Your information is remarkable, I'll give you that, and your assassins first-rate, though I suppose you noticed the head of the one you sent after me at the front gate. But," he sighed theatrically, "your masters are not as clever as they think they are. They think to use my love for Katherine against me, thinking that I would betray all my people to get her back. This I would never do, mainly because she would never forgive me. But that doesn't really matter, because she is a Green Branch knight."

The two goblins' orders were clear: if Fin did not agree, then kill him. They both raised their throwing daggers at the same time, but the two warriors stationed at the throne moved first. They threw the goblins to the ground. Several doors, unseen until now, opened and warriors poured into the room. Quickly the goblins were disarmed and tied, their concealing cloaks torn away. Their mouths were gagged, since Fin had guessed one could use magic. With their arms tied, their mouths gagged, and some mage from inside the castle sheathing their minds, their magic was as useless as their daggers.

Fin shook his head.

"I thought your masters more clever than this, to so underestimate me." He moved closer to the two, staring in their cat eyes. "You are certainly much more inept than your predecessor. He managed to give me a bruise at least." He drew a dagger and held it in front of him, its blade winking in the light.

"As I said, my wife was a knight," he continued, as if lecturing two truant children, "and all the knights of the Green Branch are trained with Tag-Aug-Neal, the chosen death. Even unconscious a knight can and will use death if he sees no other way. My Katherine was quick to see how you would seek to use her. She did the honorable thing, and since she is my wife, and since I am who I am, I knew of her passing; I felt her leave. I see by your eyes you do not understand. . . . Your kind never do." He turned away for a moment and surveyed the warriors in the room.

"I feel pity for your kind, you do not know love, you do not understand nobility, honor. You are destroyers and you serve those who destroy you. You know only death, never life. But my pity goes only so far," he walked up to the two, "because there is really nothing I hate more than liars!" With that, he cut the goblins' throats with two quick strokes. As their blood spurted across his boots, he just watched.

The warriors let the bodies fall, Fin feeling nothing as the bodies banged to the cobblestones. He reached one finger down to the blood and dipped it in the still steaming liquid. He lifted the finger to his face, staring at the bizarre pink-green fluid for a moment. It seemed thinner somehow than human blood, but it was warm, like all blood it was warm. . . .

He streaked the blood across his forehead, his lips forming a silent "Katherine." With that, the Laird of Dun Scaga left his hall. The blood of war called him and he eagerly sought its warmth.

Within the earth She felt her two children, their needs beating inside her. One—strong, curious, angry; the other—nervous, scared, yet in him She detected the steel core that She most admired in these, her most misunderstood followers.

She centered some of herself and sped it toward them, to bring the comfort they needed, even as her body shook in pain at the ravages of the Dark Ones.

Colin did not become aware of the Mother immediately, for as Mearead had said, sight was of no use here. He felt the blood inside of him change, go rich and strong, the heart beating hard and steady. His skin flushed with the warmth he felt inside and out. There was comfort all about him, as if some huge arms had held him close. Only then did he remember Mearead's words: "The breast, the heart, the very womb of the Mother." Then he knew She was there, and he was safe.

"Ahh," the voice soothed Colin, though he could not say where it came from, or how it sounded. It was not of sound, but of the physicalness of that which surrounded him, a hand brushing his hair lightly. "You have done well, Mearead. He is strong and full of such light."

"Thank you, Goddess," Mearead's voice seemed hoarse and jarred Colin's ears. "He is the son of my heart."

"Indeed, he may one day eclipse even you, my hard little warrior."

"Perhaps, Mother," the dwarf did not seem insulted by the goddess's words, "but so soon, he, all of my people, it is so soon for this test."

Colin felt the comfort remove itself a little. The air grew cool as he focused on the two voices, one behind, one around him.

"This is no test." Colin saw for a moment the gleam of a cat's eyes in firelight. "This is death, destruction—annihilation! For your people, for me, for all my children."

"It cannot be!" the king's voice shouted.

"It is, it is . . ." the Mother soothed again. "Old powers best forgotten walk the earth again, and dark things that were never mine dare to tread my breast."

"What is to be done?"

"Death, death, my children."

Colin glimpsed an old woman shuddering in the cold. There was silence for a moment. Slowly, the arms spread wide again, this time to hold both the dwarves.

"War," Mearead whispered, "true war." He went silent as he relaxed into Earth's warm embrace. "What of our cousins of Cardoc-nae-corond? Will they help, Mother? Do you know their fate?"

"I know the fate of none, not even myself. You know that they have turned from me and follow the Cold One." A sigh massaged their souls. Sorrow too great to stand, to comprehend, withdrawn immediately before it broke them with despair. "That one was my son, too, but he left me long ago, long even for me. Cardoc-nae-corond is no longer part of me. I fear they are all dead, or worse."

"Can you give us no words of comfort?"

"Comfort? No, I have none. . . . Beyond this land the Dark Ones have triumphed over and over. Much of my power has been sucked away. It is here, Mearead, here that the last battle shall be fought. If it is lost, all is lost, for us, for those who could have been, perhaps even for those long gone."

"Have we no allies? Do not others see the danger?"

"How could they not? But what those who could truly help will do I cannot say. I have felt stirrings, but of these I cannot speak." Again Colin saw a figure, but this one was small and dark, naked and fanged. He recognized the first face of the goddess, young and dangerous. "And of the gods," the Word was like acid upon the two dwarves, "they will do nothing, secure in their dream world, sure that nothing can truly reach them." A flash of a taloned hand raking flesh. "Fools! If Earth herself can die what chance have they?" Both dwarves froze. They felt as rabbits caught by the wolf. She turned to them and relented, but did not meet their needs again. They must know, they must understand.

And so She became physical in their sense of the word, and the two saw the third face of the goddess, the face of barrenness and defeat. She stood in front of them, naked, her skin wrinkled with age, her breasts abnormally long and thin hanging past her waist, her hair still rich, white, floating about her, her womb bald, empty. But both felt drawn to the eyes, pure black-brown orbs, rich as newly tilled earth, horrible as the dirt of the grave.

"See me, my children, see the face of your Mother, battered, beaten, ravaged." The nose jutted out like a fin, the jaw hung slack: the face of senility. But the eyes, the wisdom of pain, anger of time itself. "Listen well. They have killed, destroyed, but I still am! And I will be! It is not for them to choose my death. They shall feel their strength dry up, their sight blur, their purpose wander. You are the greatest of my creations for you are creators! Your strength will be a storm to crash upon them. All my children will rise and Death himself will shudder at their hatred. Life will burn the Dark Ones' bleak souls! There is no hell great enough to enact my vengeance!" The terrible power of her pain swamped the two like a great wave, twisting and turning them, no force could resist it. They screamed in horror.

And She heard, as She always did. She shook with guilt. She did not need to do this, this outrage had nothing to do with these, her favorite children. The tempest calmed and She held them, rocking them gently.

"Ah, my dears, my sweet boys, I am sorry, so sorry. I should have protected you from this. So much, so much has gone wrong from the beginning. This, all of this, is never what I wanted for my children. Death and life were meant to be so much sweeter, so much kinder. Even I have changed, and gentleness never moves me as it did at first, so long ago, so long ago when I held my first as I hold you, so long ago, so long ago. . . ."

The voice soothed the two and sleep claimed them. There were no dreams, no worries, no fear; all was calm. They woke the next day in their beds, warm and happy, full of strength and hope. The fear of the day before was gone, but the anger remained. Both arose to check their weapons before they did anything else. But her last words were for Mearead alone.

"I have sent him to hunt, my poor driven son. He is the Morigunamachamain! He is as the first were! And you, Mearead, in time, you, too, must hunt. . . ."

CHAPTER

Five

If there was one creature that understood the pain of the Goddess, it was the Morigu. He could feel the tread of the Dark Ones on the Mother's breast, feel their desecration upon the living world as a disease, eating through flesh, gnawing on bone, letting off a putrid stench that would consume all but the strongest.

Margawt sat perched upon a rock that peered down at the river flowing at its feet. Once long ago, in a life that he could remember only in momentary flashes, this had been his favorite place, his refuge. But now the rock was a magnet, drawing the anguish of the world, pouring up through the souls of his feet, burning his soul.

He leaped to his feet, brandishing his sword at the skies.

"Damn you, damn you to the darkest pit! Blood, blood, I will have your blood!!!" At his cry the woods about him grew quiet, the animals frozen by the sound of his outrage. He stood there, defiant, the sun flashing off mail and sword, but that light could not match the fire beneath his brows.

It was time, he knew it, felt it. He must go to the south, to the human lands. He shuddered as his mind formed a picture of the horrors the people of Tolath were enduring.

'Even the land,' he thought, a picture of goblins shredding and killing the very ground they walked upon. And of greater powers, the life of all things withering about them.

"Ayeeeee," he cried, "they even kill the land!" Somehow

he bore the agony, turning his thoughts to the battlefields in the south. He searched them, searched the living and the dead, for one man, one being.

"Dammuth!" he cried. "Dammuth, I am alone. Dammuth! I am alone." And he added in a small voice as he leapt from the rock, "It hurts me, it all hurts me. . . ."

But there was no answer for him, not from the wizard, not from anyone. There was only the need for revenge, the red haze of vengeance. He turned to the south, blocking out the worst of the land's pain. He ran off with a hard smile on his lips.

There was one remedy for the pain: kill those who caused it. He raced on, he knew the elves of Cather-na-nog would form an army to help the allies. They would expect him to join them; they would be waiting for him, for his war. The war was not just his anymore.

"I am coming," he chanted, "I am coming." But whether the words were for his enemies or his would-be allies, the Morigu could not say.

Dammuth swore as he counted aloud, ". . . one hundred and fifty-four. By the White Light, why did I put my sanctuary in this damn tower?"

Dammuth continued grumbling as he climbed the dark tower stairs. And it was dark, pitch dark. Even a dwarf would have been hard-pressed to find his way in that blackness. "Dammit." Dammuth stumbled up the last stairs. He raised his right palm outward and made a series of quick gestures with his left. "Let me in. I'm tired," he chanted in a monotone.

Slowly, lines of light formed a doorway which opened grudgingly. Dammuth strode into the brightly lit chamber, the door closing after him. A white owl flew to his shoulder and Dammuth gave the bird a big smile.

"I bet no one will ever figure out the words to open that door, eh, Shorty?"

Frankly, Shorty thought the joke a little thin. After all,

Dammuth had used the same words for over a century now, ever since he had made the tower his sanctuary.

The room was lit by four globes suspended from the twenty-foot ceiling. The rest of the room was a clutter of benches, tables, a full goblin skeleton, various vials and pitchers, a ripped and tattered wall hanging showing a forest scene, and some rush mats. It looked like what it was: a wizard's workroom.

Near the far corner of the room stood a pedestal with a half globe of water. The water was not held by anything. It simply formed itself.

Dammuth moved to the water wyrd and stroked the surface gently. He stared at the water for over an hour, periodically intoning a Word or making small motions with his hand. Finally, he gave up and sighed. He sat down heavily on a bench and peered out the only window in the room.

"Ah, Shorty, I'm still blocked! None of my scrying spells will work. What power keeps me blind? Who has the strength to resist me? All is unclear and this should not be."

Dammuth sighed again. 'The weight,' he thought, 'the weight of the empire presses me down.' His mind replayed the encounter with the young warrior, Mathwei, the terror the boy had faced already, and the horrors that lay ahead for all the people of the land. His mind heard their silent thoughts: 'Dammuth will save us, Dammuth has the strength, Dammuth has the power.'

He walked to the south window of the tower, his witch sight focusing on the dark clouds of red war. He almost could see the tiny figures of struggling forms. He could see, smell the evil, dank and hot, covering the empire, the land dying beneath the strength of that swollen maw.

"I should have known," his hand banged the ledge with such force the stone cracked. "I should have known! I should have felt it!" But there was no answer to his cry, except the tiny voice in his head. 'You should have known,' it whispered, 'Lonnlarcan should have known, Arianrood should have known, Mearead should have known, the gods, the gods should have known. . . .'

'Ah, yes,' he thought, 'the gods. Where were the masters of the Bright World? Dead like Fealoth? Where was the Goddess? What happened in the rest of the world, so much vaster than the tiny empire? Were the people of the whole world under attack? Was earth herself the prize the Dark Ones lusted for? What had they been doing for a hundred and fifty years? What?!'

And again the voice answered in him, 'Killing, dying.' His imagination formed the pictures. He saw flames, and blood, stretching across the Mother like a leprous growth. In his heart he knew the answers to his questions, but he turned away from what he saw there. The knowledge that the enemy had been smarter, faster than he had ever feared in his darkest dreams.

He knew, he knew then.

It was a war of genocide against all the followers of the Light and those who might yet reach for the Bright World.

A great cry shook the tower as Dammuth let out his fear and hate. His witch sight pierced the veils of the enemy's magic for a moment. He took in the dark hunger that craved to devour a world, and was succeeding. He heard the terror-filled pleas of a million living creatures. His soul cried in rage and his magic shaped that power, and hundreds of miles away the smoke from the fires of war coalesced and formed into a great fist a mile high.

All that walked the earth—man, beast, god—froze and turned toward the sky as the great fist descended faster than thought, straight into the land of the Dark Seign. It smashed into mountains, shattering stone, and thousands of the Dark followers died beneath that onslaught.

The vibrations of Dammuth's power ripped deep into the Bright World, but there was no answer to Dammuth's plea. No being, god or other, returned his cry. They hid, the doors between the worlds slammed shut.

But for a moment he heard laughter, the laughter of the

insane, of the tortured, of the victim. And he felt more than saw a deep place darker than darkness, beyond madness, and heard the rattle of thick, world-heavy chains.

He turned from the window fighting despair. Crackling shards of magic flashed about his form. His eyes burned with a blue, harsh light. He had his answer, he had it! He shook with the knowledge, as a tear slid down his face. It was the war, the last war, the clash of chaos against the walls of life.

The gods would not answer, for to reach to Dammuth, to reach to the peoples of the earth was to open the doors, the doors to the infinite night, the ending of all. The tear fell to the floor, staining the stone red. He had the answer. Men, elves, dwarves, all the followers of Light, would get no help from the Bright World.

He stared sightlessly at the walls of his tower. 'Alone,' his mind cried to him, 'we are alone. . . .'

Did he imagine the laughter that answered his despair?

He made no movement as he stood high up in his tower of wizardry. His mind slowly unfolded the tale he had lived, the glory, the defeats, the loves gained and lost. The familiar followed the pathways of the old wizard's mind. It felt a new emotion inside itself, one it had never experienced—fear. Fear for the mage who had called it forth to this plane, who had given it three-dimensional form, and through the years taught its soul the meaning of freedom.

The despair the wizard felt was palatable in the room so attuned to magic. It took the form of sad shadows haunting the corners and a faint odor of decay. Shorty could barely retain its owl form in the leeching magic that surrounded it.

Its mind struggled with the new experiences, the great thrust of Dammuth's magic that had formed the spectre fist. This was power even it had never known the old one to possess, and if he did contain such power and was still blocked, then the enemy was greater than any imagined. . . .

That was what Dammuth's mind tortured him with—magic, always the magic. That would be the undoing of them all. Even with the enemy employing all the power that they had, they should not be able to block Dammuth's as they were.

The wizard, with Arianrood, was the last of the Shields of Light, the fourteen sorcerers, wizards, and healers that had gifted Fealoth with his godhood. Only those two had survived the awesome act. Only she should have the ability to block him, for next to the Ead and the gods themselves, Dammuth knew he was the most powerful of all beings that walked the earth, the greatest wizard man had ever produced and probably ever would.

"And I feel so helpless," he whispered aloud. It was not a feeling he was used to experiencing. Surely, if nothing else, his imagination would be a potent weapon. But his mind felt so sluggish, as if a cloak covered his thoughts, blunting them.

He thought of Margawt; the power of the Morigu could and should count as something. But what was a Morigu? And what was this one, the one all the earth things called *the* Morigu? A boy, by elven standards, little more than an infant. His power, born of desperation and rage. Could any soul survive such a burden?

A phrase from the Green Branch code of honor flashed in his sight for a moment: "The honorable man knows strength is earned, power given." Did Margawt earn his strength? Was he existing on power the Goddess had infused in him? Power that wasn't truly his?

So much would depend on the boy, Dammuth was sure of it. Hadn't the Goddess herself said so? Dammuth cared for Margawt, he felt it keenly, a heavy pain in his heart. Must he lose another? Death was no friend to Dammuth, but they knew each other well.

In some ways Margawt reminded Dammuth of Mathwei, the two so different, yet young, full of passion. Who carried the greater burden? One with great power, the other with so little. . . . Did either stand a chance? Or were they both, as Dammuth feared, doomed? Perhaps they all were. . . .

"No!" he shouted. "Enough old man! Fight back, you are Dammuth, the people depend on you! Fight back!" And with that he knew what he must do. A magic, a dark magic he had never dared use. He remembered another phrase of the ancient honor code: 'No evil is powerful enough to corrupt the unconsenting.' He knew in his heart hell itself could not conquer a man, and he knew it was hell he must now face.

"Well, Shorty, if I must, I must. . . ." He ruffled the familiar's ears and turned to the side wall with the bookshelves. The bird flew to a nearby table and shot a question at the wizard.

"No, little one, you would risk yourself needlessly, and if I should fail, I would not have you fall with me." It crossed his mind that perhaps he should tell someone of his discoveries of the nature of this war, but no, there was no time.

"You must be my messenger should I fail," he said to the owl. "Warn Arianrood first, then find Margawt." He left the rest unspoken, for both knew if Dammuth was killed the Morigu would revenge the death of his only friend.

With that Dammuth turned back to the bookshelf. Intoning words of power softly, his hands danced a graceful pattern as he shaped his magic. He ended the chant with a Word terrible and strong. With a loud crack and an inrush of air, a four foot square of the books vanished. A bluish glow came from the opening. Without looking back he stepped through. The opening closed with a snap and the owl stared at the returned bookshelf. It waited, not daring to blink at the closed door. If it had a heart its beating would have surely resounded within the room.

The room Dammuth had entered was a shadow. There was no clear definition of walls or ceiling. It wasn't really a room, since no angles existed there; only soft blue shadows, with a dark red pentacle on what might be called the floor. Next to the pentacle lay a brass chest with a little pile of leaves scattered around it, the only physical things in the place.

The mage walked carefully around the pentacle to the chest. His steps were slow and deliberate, carefully and evenly placed. Yet some steps took him closer to his goal, while others just led him to the very place he started from.

Dammuth reached the chest and stepped behind it. Intoning a Word, he took a small sliver of wood from the chest hinges. Throwing it into the air he cried aloud, like the hunting call of a wolf.

The sliver twirled slowly in the air. Each twist it took it became larger until at last it quivered point down in front of the wizard. It was a grey shaft of wood some five feet in length. Taking the staff in his hand, he struck it against the iron padlock on the chest. The padlock fell and burst open. Five black candles and five white fell onto the floor.

Dammuth picked them up and carefully placed the black ones on the points of the pentacle. Then he retreated some fifteen paces. He seemed to be standing about three feet above the pentacle. Now he drew another, smaller pentacle using the point of the staff. The lines of this one were edged in the same blue that the shadows about him were. Dammuth then placed the white candles on the points of the new pentacle.

'Careful, careful, old man,' he thought as he stepped inside the small pentacle. Here he sat down cross-legged and placed the staff across his knees.

"Never have I used such dark magic," he said aloud. "May the Gods of Light forgive me, but I need to know what we face."

The wizard chanted to himself under his breath. He raised one finger. "Omet," he cried and a breeze blew one of the leaves from the pile near the chest into the air. The leaf caught fire and lit one of the black candles.

"Terasma," and another leaf lit another black candle.

"Jum, Ferut, Cardeem," and all the candles around the red pentacle were lit.

"The die is cast, oh mighty Lugh, look upon me with favor. Stretch out your arm and give me your strength. Imadium, Carfirt, Massuemanum," he cried aloud. The ends of his staff seemed to melt into the shadows around Dammuth, and the five white candles burst into a piercing white-silver flame.

"To the nether regions let my call be heard, let the voice of Dammuth, the will of Dammuth, the power of Dammuth become awake. I call. I will be heard. Listen, Dark Powers, and heed me. My call is to you, Methrasdemondium. You cannot resist. The bridge is made. Come to me, blacksoul. I call and I will not be denied. Dammuth, Wizard of Light, Dragonslayer, Warrior of the Star, Dammuth calls, you will heed! Come to me *NOW*!!!"

The red pentacle burst into a red wall of light and then a cry was heard. Inside the pentacle a shape took form. It was at least nine feet tall. Its feet were those of a bird, tapering off from powerful thighs covered in a dark, short fur. Its chest was human with powerful arms ending in surprisingly small hands. The demon's face was oddly angular and covered with a mesh of dark scales. Two ragged holes where the nose was supposed to be were overshadowed by a very prominent brow ridge. Its eyes had no pupils or irises. They were completely white as if it was blind. The hairless head possessed two ears that were pointed at the tops and the lobes. The demon bared its lipless mouth to show brown, stunted teeth.

"This cannot be," cried Dammuth. "Begone, foul one, you are not who I called!"

"That is true," answered the demon in a sibilant hiss. "The one you called was told to stay. I chose to take his place."

"You chose!?" the wizard's voice cracked. "I chose, dog! Leave before I choose to destroy your black soul!"

"Fool! You do not tell such as I what to do. I am the master here!" The demon's gash of a mouth split into a macabre smile, the face of a nightmare.

"By the Light, a Prince, a Demon Prince. It cannot be. . . ."

"Oh, but it can, old man. I am here and you will do as I say." The demon moved toward the pentacle's boundaries.

"No. You have no power over me." The wizard stood up and placed his staff in the center of his pentagram. "By deeds, by thought, my power banishes thee, to the darkness bought."

As the wizard finished his chant, the black candles belched forth a dark smoke that entwined the demon. "Really, Dammuth, I thought you could do better than that," laughed the demon.

He cupped one hand and the smoke gathered in his palm. Crying words of power, he threw the ball of smoke toward Dammuth. The black globe smashed against the barrier of the confining pentacle. The black candles burst into flame and consumed themselves.

"So much for your demon cage, dog. Resist me no further and I might have pity." The demon crossed the lines and moved toward the mage.

Dammuth lost all sense of fear. Now had his time come, the confrontation he knew he must one day face. He saw in the demon's eyes his own death. He felt its mind and dark soul reach to him. Simple spells would not defeat such as this, and now with the confining pentacle destroyed he had no chance of sending the demon back to its own plane. He must destroy it.

At first the battle was silent as both strove with the most elemental magic, attacking one another with will and force of thought alone. Slowly, the shadows took the shape of creatures of all kinds, clashing physically against one another. Both knew this was Dammuth's best chance, since this small area was a plane of existence he alone had created and it responded best to him.

The magic formed into small and giant beings of blue and black. The wizard's power crushed the darker aspects one by one. The demon felt the pressure as a physical thing. For a moment it knew fear; the old man was so much stronger than it had anticipated. It redoubled its efforts, creating a thousand monsters from the depths of darkest imaginings. But each was countered by Dammuth and destroyed.

Out of the pores of the demon dripped a black fluid that burst into flame. Soon it was covered in a sheet of flame, and for the first time in eons it felt the fires of hell upon its flesh.

Dammuth knew his enemy was weakening, he could taste victory. Though there was no time here, he knew in the world the sun was going down, the night called and if he did not finish the demon would be able to regain strength from the shadows of night.

The demon felt pain, an acid pain that swelled its limbs. The old one was so powerful! It felt a sharp lance of light plunge into it, and though night was here, the wizard's power had not diminished. The Prince's magic was such that he could last only another day, and annihilation would be its due. There would be no rebirth for the demon, even the tortures of hell would be lost.

Dammuth's shadow fighters had turned red as victory drew near. They formed themselves into great armored knights, charging on warhorses that dwarfed the demon. Its power crumbled beneath the onslaught, its magic diluted into a thin, grey shield that blood red waves slowly pounded apart. There was only one chance, and even though the payment would be great, it was still preferable to the true death facing the Dark One.

It waved its burning arms, fanning a black flame, howling in a language no human was meant to hear. Beneath its feet a great roar built up, then an explosion of fire and molten rock. Deafening screams shook the room that was not a room, and the Gate of Hell opened.

The stench alone nearly overthrew Dammuth. His magic crumbled as thousands of dark and evil forms flew from the hole at the demon's feet and toward him. The twisted and demented shapes of the demons were so grotesque that Dammuth felt bile rise in his throat, choking the words of power stuck there.

The dark vomit of Hell smashed upon the walls of his protecting pentacle, trying to overwhelm it. The shadows turned brown and extended indefinitely as thousands of demons expanded its boundaries. They devoured one another in their desperation to reach Dammuth. Now, on all sides, up and down, he was surrounded, a globe of blue light the only thing between him and their diseased talons.

Even as his mind struggled for sanity, his soul fought back. Great streaks of power shot out from the protecting globe, skewering a hundred of the lesser demons. He called a great elemental of wind that thrust them away, only to be overwhelmed by hell fire. But in its place earth elementals rose, pounding the demons into a thick slush. Fire elementals fought fire with fire, burning dark forms by the thousands. Even water elementals sought to wash the stain of darkness away, and still the demons came.

Incredibly, with the whole might of Hell arrayed against him, the old man stood up. Holding his staff above his head he slowly got to his feet. Within his small globe of power he stood, his shoulders held back, the brilliance of his soul shining about his form, his eyes so deadly that the demons that faced them withered away.

Dammuth knew, he knew his time had come. He felt the incredible vastness of the power arrayed against him, and he did not falter. He called his allies to him, great beings of earth, sky, and water, beyond the spheres was his power felt and many raced to his aid. Luminous beings a hundred feet tall attacked the demons, creatures of rainbow brilliance no bigger than a thumb swirled in mortal and immortal conflicts. Old gods long forgotten raised their heads and wielded their lightning. The battle spread and spread, a conflict as had never taken place before, as one old man defied Hell itself.

The Gate widened, the infinite darkness spread, and one by one the Demon Lords rose and made war. Apkieran, Lord of the Undead, wielded his bleeding ax; Roella, the Fire Lord, followed by his burning minions; and others, great

vast shadows, insectlike horrors, shapes of leprosy and
nightmares, for here Hell revealed all its might. There was
no constraint, no fear of the last battle, and they were win-
ning.

The cries of the tortured deafened all sound, the stench a
physical weapon, and in the middle Dammuth stood, un-
bowed, his magic flashing from him as lightning, as fire, as
pure bolts of energy, and Death himself shuddered at the
horror and madness of it all.

And on it went for what could have been days, though
there was no point in trying to understand that battle in time.
It was endless and over in a moment. Even as the wizard's
allies died they rejoiced in the sheer ferocity and daring of it
all, for many had feared their deaths and saw them in the
war that embroiled the world, but here, now, the enemy was
defined and clear, the battle lines easily drawn, and though
the outside world knew nothing of this battle, surely there
were many there who would join if they could.

And so one by one they fell, and though Dammuth's
power seemed only to increase, how could any stand against
that unrelenting force of squalid despair? He laughed in the
faces of his tormentors, his lips blistered as the Words of
power he never thought he could contain rolled out. Never,
not once did his frame shudder, even as wounds began to
break from his flesh, even when he stood alone again, alone,
alone, and all Hell crying for his blood.

Finally the globe of power shattered. Its radiance
smashed into a million glowing fragments, but did not Apkieran himself fall before that burst, back to the pit of Hell?
An old evil, dark and nameless, reared itself up, towering
over the undefended wizard and fell before Dammuth's
magic. The demons crowded to reach him, crowding in
triumph, only to be cast back again and again. Dammuth's
heart rejoiced, for he had hurt the enemy! He had destroyed
much of its power! He had fought the greatest battle any
man born of woman could ever conceive of and as he fell to

his knees he knew in his soul that though he died, he had won.

The dark rolled back from the kneeling wizard, his life force still so strong. They retreated from this old man that had done more damage to them than anything in all the eons had ever come close to.

The great Prince stalked to the old man, the power of Hell at its back.

"It is done. Now you are mine." The demon's hoarse laughter filled Dammuth's ears.

"It is not over yet," Dammuth's voice was a whisper. He broke his staff in two and from the break a green beam of light shot forth and struck the demon's legs.

"Oh, such power!" the Prince gloated as its talons reached for the mage. But then it shrieked in rage and pain. Such was that cry that its followers fell away from it, cringing in fear.

"With this act," shouted Dammuth, daring to look straight in the demon's eyes, "I defy you! With my heart and soul, with my life, I defy you! With all that I am and ever could be, I defy you!"

From the demon's legs, through its skin, sprouted leaves. It howled in agony, for the magic desecrated its very soul, impossible for it or any of the creatures of Hell to understand. Dammuth, in his last act of magic, had created life within the body of he who personified unlife, creation not only from chaos and death, but from nonexistence.

The Dark Prince howled and so did all of Hell, shaken to its core. What could not be done, had been done. With one voice they cried to their master chained beyond the night, and he heard. He spoke a Word, so terrible that even his own nonsoul shook at it, so powerful that many of the lesser demons who heard exploded in agony.

They took the Word and the million glowing eyes turned to Dammuth and shouted it at him. He cried aloud as bone and sinew shattered. He was lifted and pushed down at the same time; his flesh became a prison of red pain.

The Demon Prince was covered by the power of the Word. A fire of sludge and mucus covered it, dissolved into it, and destroyed the seed of life inside its corrupt flesh. The pain lasted a true eternity, a pain so great that even he, the greatest of all save the Dark Master, barely survived. He felt each atom of body and black soul torn asunder, then re-knit in a raging fire of agony that no creature had ever stood.

The demon opened its eyes once more to find itself in the small blue room that was not a room. No sign of the epic battle remained. The Gate was closed. He knelt at the body of its enemy, surprised to see the simple form of a dying man, torn and shredded, the blood steaming into a red haze.

The Dark Prince shook with wonder at his own survival, at the power and grandeur of his defeated enemy, at the change inside, the loss of power but increase in strength. He stared at the old man for a moment, wondering at this creature—so frail, so brave. For a moment, for the first time in its long unlife, it felt doubt about itself, about its destiny. The demon reached his hand out to the wizard, feeling the life still beating in that devastated form. The hand hovered there for a moment as the demon fought with its very essence, and almost, almost he reached toward Dammuth with a caress.

But then what it was reinforced itself. The demon remembered its eons old battle to be the Only, the most powerful, to become all that is. And he felt, he felt inside the terrible hunger for power more demanding than ever. He had become more and his form shimmered as he tried to contain the newly won magic. The dark one howled in joy at his survival and strength.

Dammuth felt it all, the demon's struggle and its failure of the test, the last the demon would ever have. The mage's tongue was destroyed, his throat a ruin. So it was his thoughts and not his voice that reached the demon.

"No evil is powerful enough to corrupt the unconsenting." For a moment all was silent as the demon looked upon Dammuth. He knew the meaning of the mage's words but was unaffected by his sorrow. He laughed at him, at this silly old man, who could have been so much—who could have rivaled them all! But instead chose death. . . . He laughed at his own pain and the pain of Hell beating upon it. Like some giant larva the Dark Prince reveled in that agony, his being infused with unholy joy and madness.

The demon's eyes turned red.

It's hand, snake-fast, struck at Dammuth, ripping the wizard's chest open. Somehow Dammuth was able to scream as the demon pulled his still beating heart out.

"You've lost, little man," the demon sneered, "and with your heart I will make great magic!" The demon shoved Dammuth's heart into the ruin of his face. But it could not block out Dammuth's thoughts.

"No, you won't." Unbelievably, the thought voice was gentle and sad. "You have lost for all time and you shall never even know it."

With that thought, Dammuth, Wizard of Light, Warrior of the Star, Dragonslayer, died. The heart imploded and a glowing blue fluid spread across the demon's hand. The Prince looked at it in surprise. Suddenly, he shouted in pain once more as the glowing blue fluid that had been the wizard's heart dissolved the demon's hand like acid. In seconds, it was totally dissolved. Crying with rage, the demon lifted his good hand in the air and was enveloped in a sheet of flame, already working to forget the wizard's last words.

All that was left in the room of shadows as proof of the great battle, of one man's ultimate defiance and victory, was a few melted candles and the mutilated corpse of an old man.

A door of light brightened the shadowed room and the scruffy owl flew in. Slowly, it took in the mangled body of its master, the melted candles. It breathed the gangrenous smell of the Dark Ones. The owl flew to the chest, its yellow eyes focusing intently on the inside lid. Small, three-dimensional figures formed and replayed the battle for the owl's sad eyes. The eyes turned a piercing green.

The images focused on the dead body of the wizard for a moment, and then the whole chest misted over and dripped to the floor as if it had been formed of water. The owl/familiar flew to its master, to its friend. Slowly, it bobbed its head, once, twice, three times, then flew from the room.

The owl flew out of the tower and headed toward Aes Lugh. The enemy had killed the last great wizard. Except for Arianrood and what magic the elves and dwarves had, there was nothing to stand in the Dark Ones' way. Armies weren't enough. Murdering Dammuth was a smart move, as Trell'dem's assassination had been.

'Smart,' thought the owl, 'except for one thing, the one thing they don't know: Margawt's love for the old wizard. . . .' A grim purpose stirred the spirit's soul. 'We don't possess great magic, but we have the greatest Morigu that has ever lived, and you've just killed his only friend, you bastards.'

But when Dammuth's anger had formed the mighty fist, not all the powers turned from him as the gods had. For there were other powers, powers that Dammuth had forgotten, that the Dark had forgotten.

One stood above the destruction Dammuth's magic had created. He stood tall, taller than the sky. His hand was vast and touched all living things. But such was he that none, god or man, dead or undead, could see him if he did not wish it so.

He had heard Dammuth, he heard the thousand cries of war. For as long as he could remember, as long as anything had lived, he had heard these cries, and he had answered.

But now, this time, it was different, it was wrong. He laughed though there was none who could hear. Not even the Chained One could hear his laughter. . . .

'Wrong,' he thought, 'wrong. And am I not blamed for all that is wrong? Am I not the great enemy?' With that his laughter died. 'No, I have known sympathy. My touch has not always been unwelcome. Not all spurned my gift, not those who know, not those who understand. I am the equalizer! I am the doorway!' A light began to burn in the pits where his eyes hid.

'But the doorway, all doorways, could be shattered in this war, the true war, the war that has existed since before time had begun. . . . Would he be broken? Dwindled? Corrupted? Or even'—again his laughter shook him, 'die?! Should I fear?' he asked, but there was no one to answer him. He *was* the answer.

He was not like the other humans called gods, he was as nothing else, singular, the only being truly alone in all the many universes. And he did not know fear, could not know fear, for he was fear. . . .

"I hear," he cried to the millions upon millions that could not hear him. "I hear, I see, I know." And he detached himself from himself. He coalesced into another form, a heavy grey shadow. And he stood, upon the highest of all mountains, a being that none could see.

"I shall break my bounds," he said, and all things that lived upon the mountain died at the voice he let them hear. "I shall do that which I was not meant to do! I shall take sides! I shall fight! I, I will make war!" And he laughed again, and though his laughter killed, it was the music and beauty of that sound, not its deadliness, that mortal souls could not bear.

"I shall reach for him! The Dark Lord will feel my touch! I shall do that which I am incapable of! For who is the greatest warrior if not I?" He took in the whole world with his sight, even as his hand continued to reach across the globe, across the universe.

"Yes, I shall do that which I have forbidden myself. And who," he asked, "who shall say me nay. Who shall judge Death?"

But even as he, Lord Death, dared to test his very being,

the wizard cast his magic and the demon Prince answered.
And Death, Lord Death, fell silent. He watched all, he
claimed the fallen, but still was he silent. He heard the great
wizard's last thoughts, and he did not turn from their wisdom.

"I did not need this sacrifice," and with these words he let
the gods know his thoughts. But they did not understand
them. Death knew, he knew that even in the golden realm,
sides had been taken. And Death was not one to warn an
enemy, though in truth he was hard-pressed to remember a
time when he truly had an enemy. Those that defeated him
were not often in his disfavor.

Finally he touched the wizard, and the cord was unbound.
Lord Death shook his giant head, his feet straddling the
world. He watched Dammuth's soul leap and dance to the
beyond.

'Unbelievable,' he thought, 'few humans are strong
enough to be accepted in my halls, but this one has leapt
over my domain and gone on . . .' He watched silently the
laughing souls following Dammuth, those who fell fighting
Hell.

"Hell! Can you imagine?!" He shouted. "Fighting Hell
itself!" The audacity! The glory! He took one more look at
the great multihued radiance of all that was the wizard,
wondering where it went. He was the door, but even he was
unsure where those who passed him went. And this one,
who knows? If Death cannot say, who could?

Such a tale—his mind spun with the music of it. Such a
tale, but it was not his to sing. In the fullness of time Dammuth's fall would become known; it was not for him to tell.
There were limits even Death could not break, and though
he would have refused Dammuth's death, he could not . . .
though he wished to sing the tale, who was there to hear? It
was impossible for him to talk to mortals on the world's
plane; they were so fragile.

'A shame,' he thought, 'this would inspire them so. . . .'

"The glory," he shouted to the multitudes who did not hear him, "is this not true glory?! Is this not what life and death are meant to be?" But there was no one to stand at his side. He sought through to the world. 'There,' he thought, 'there. My brother can hear, my brother can see.' With that he separated again and called his golden chariot to him, racing to the world, racing to war.

CHAPTER

Six

The last day in May should have been a bright morning, but the sun was covered by sullen clouds, concealed by the fires of war and the magic of the Dark Ones. It made the light mute and thin, dusk instead of dawn.

The leaders of Tolath's Third Army, surrounded by their officers, stood upon a low hill facing the battlefield layed out at their feet. The warriors were massed in three groups. The right flank, mainly foot soldiers and archers, held the bank of the Dudny River. The left held a small area of woods and rough foothills; there was stationed a like force with a small cavalry brigade in support. The center was held by the empire's finest. The foot soldiers were set on a low ridge, their shields locked, their spears placed. In front of them waited the cavalry of Tolath, some 2500 strong, led by three hundred knights of the Green Branch.

The Warlord Crane looked up from his camp stool.

"General Ernet," his voice was harsh, "you have the right flank." The general bowed and with his officers behind him, mounted and rode off. "General Fintan," the slim warrior saluted, "the left." Fintan nodded and did the same.

"That leaves the center to me, eh?" Laird Fin smiled down at the Warlord.

"Afraid so." Crane reached down at his feet and picked up a wine flask, taking a deep drink. He offered it to Fin, who just shook his head no.

"Ah, well," the commander said, "for once we have chosen the field, for once we have a chance." Crane sucked his teeth as he remembered the many defeats already. "We have to hold them, Fin. If we don't, all that's between them and Tolan is Comar, and we could never hold that city against them."

"Aye," the Laird answered, "they took Dulatia in two days. They'll take Comar in one." Both thought of Baron Teague who had fallen along with his city. The three had been friends for twenty years. Neither mentioned their dead comrade. There were too many deaths to remember.

"It's up to you, Fin. They'll throw everything they've got against you." The Laird of Dun Scaga looked out at the advancing army. They held no ranks, just marched as one dark mass. He grasped his sword hilt.

"The magic," he said quietly.

"The magic," Crane rubbed his eye with a scarred hand, "and without Dammuth. . . ." Again there was silence between the two. Both wrestled with the same question. Less than a week ago the wizard had disappeared. Was Dammuth dead? Or did he, like so many, betray them? Without the Arch Mage the empire had few magicians left, and none with the power to openly confront the enemy.

"It will be the Green Branch that decides the day," Crane said abruptly.

"Perhaps," Fin pulled his mind back to the battle, "perhaps, we have some small magic of our own, and we can resist the enemy's power better than any of the others."

"It's you, Fin, you and your knights. If you falter, it will be another rout, another slaughter."

The Laird of Dun Scaga reached out and grasped the Warlord's shoulder. He thought of his son, Fergus, left to hold his land and his castle. He thought of his dead wife, of all the many dead. He gripped Crane so hard, the Warlord could feel the pressure beneath his mail coat.

"We will not fail, not this time." Fin's voice was pitched

so low Crane had to strain to hear it. "Not this time. . . ." With that the clan Laird left to take his command.

The Warlord sat on the hill, silent as the enemy army moved closer. For the first time in two months his heart felt light. They had lost Trell'dem and Crane was sure the Dark Ones had killed Dammuth. Half the high command had been wiped out in those first weeks, but still, there was Fin. There were others, but most of all, he thought, there was Fin.

He got up, calling his officers to him, his mind filling with a hope, with a phrase pounding in his blood—"Not this time. . . ."

Mathwei ap Niall shuddered as the beat of the enemy drums reached his ears, his horse dancing beneath him. He touched the little vial of poison hanging around his neck. All the warriors of Tolath's Third Army wore the poison. No one had any intentions of being caught by the Dark Ones.

"Captain," a young orderly tugged on Mathwei's stirrups, "Sergeant Kai says all the men are in position."

"Fine, son, now you get behind the lines," replied Mathwei, little realizing the youth was but six months his junior. The orderly took off running for the rear.

"He's the lucky one," Dak, the standard bearer mumbled. Mathwei pretended not to hear. His mind raced over his orders as the enemy came into view. He led the cavalry on the left flank. He was to move, strike, retreat, keep the enemy off balance so the warriors behind could hold their positions.

"Damn," he spit, watching the horde move closer. In the front ranks of the enemy were gibbering, dancing goblins. Though goblins were strong, they were slow. Mathwei knew that in a fair fight his warriors could demolish goblin foot soldiers. But there were no fair fights in this war. This was the fourth major battle since the invasion and it looked to the cavalry captain that it would be the fourth to be lost.

The Third Army of Tolath consisted of what was left of the First, all the troops of the Southern March, a couple thousand free men, some four thousand reinforcements from the north, and the three hundred knights of the Green Branch. All told, some twelve thousand warriors, but it was not enough.

The invaders had at least fifteen thousand goblins. Scattered among them were a few units of black dwarves, some dark cave trolls, gargoyles, etc. But by far the worst were the undead. Zombies, the walking dead, many who had once been warriors of Tolath. Now they were the enemy's most feared fighters. The zombies were weak, but nearly impossible to defeat. If a man was bitten by one he would bloat up, turn black, and die within a week. There was no cure for the deadly plague.

"Damn," he said louder, "how do you kill the dead?" He inspected the enemy carefully.

"Thank Lugh," he sighed in relief. No dark wizards or undead faced his men.

He wiped the sweat from his eyes and turned to look at his warriors. Every one of them was a veteran. In this war, surviving one battle was enough to make one a veteran. Their swords were nicked, their chain-mail shirts dirty and battered. Many had lost their helmets and only a few retained thigh guards. Each man carried an eight-foot spear with a crossguard between the foot-long blade and the shaft, long swords, round shields of embossed wood, and short stabbing swords.

Mathwei sighed at the sight of the goblin heads at the ends of spears, saddles, belts, and even pinned to shields.

Noticing his look, Dak spoke up. "You can't blame them, Captain. It's been too much, sir, too damn much. They've watched their friends butchered, wounded, tortured, and gods preserve us, how many times must they watch that?" Dak pointed to the grisly tableau before them.

A score of goblins stepped out from their ranks. They carried a large reinforced pole and a struggling human. Quickly, they surrounded the human, and a pounding, followed by cries of pain, was heard. The pole was raised, the man dangling from it. Early in the war, the goblins had taken to using crucified men as their war banners.

On Mathwei's right, a shower of arrows rose from the Bantry archers stationed there. Predictably, a wall of flame intercepted the missiles. Not one reached its target.

"Damn, damn, damn," Mathwei swore over and over.

"Lugh protect us, save us Lugh." The murmur passed through the ranks as the victims' cries reached a new crescendo. No one prayed to Fealoth anymore. His priests were ineffective against the undead. It was Fealoth who was supposed to stop just what was happening. Mathwei sighed. "Fealoth," he murmured.

There was only one answer. Fealoth had been overthrown, destroyed by the Dark One he had defeated 150 years ago. Now everyone turned to the old gods. The young god, Fealoth, was dead. There was no help there.

Mathwei signaled to his bugler. "Advance, Walk," was sounded. The warriors kicked their mounts and moved into the waiting dark embrace. He turned to Dak and smiled, his smile engraved in a pale face. "Dak, pass it down the line. The first order of business is to kill that poor bastard on the pole. There will be no retreat unless I command it. Anyone found running, I'll spit on my sword. One more thing, Dak," he leaned over the horse's neck, his eyes sharp as his weapons, "pass along the line: Today, Mathwei ap Niall collects his first goblin head."

Dak angled his horse to the troops behind, his only answer an inarticulate shout of defiance.

The two hosts clashed with a great roar. The horde of Darkness howled its hate. The army of Tolath cried its outrage. Fireballs exploded into the humans, bursting with great gouts of flame. Lightning bolts arced from the sky, and darker magic killed by the score.

At one point a wind elemental appeared in front of a cavalry charge. In minutes, half of the cavalrymen were dead or dying. The rest ran for their lives.

All across the four-mile battlefield it was the same. The human units would defeat the enemy, throwing them back only to be routed themselves by some arcane blast of magic.

The few humans left with any knowledge of magic dared not use their powers in contention against the dark ones. They used what power they had to heal the wounded and to keep supplies fresh. This was enough to tax them to their limits.

The warriors fought stubbornly on. Too many times had they fled and listened to the enemy's laughter. No more, each man told himself, victory or death. The cry was taken up. Soon the chant was picked up by the whole army. "Death. Death." With one voice the warriors cried, and for the first time since the war had begun, the evil hordes knew fear.

And He heard them, He heard them cry His name. He rode his chariot with the humans, silent, unseen, except for those who felt his touch. He spread his power and gave strength to the warriors' arms. He heard them and answered as only He could.

The humans pressed on, deserting their positions across the field. No leader could stop them, even if one had been inclined. The battle madness infected them all. This day, this day they would be the reapers, this day they would have revenge.

Dak, Mathwei's sergeant, was the first to reach the crucified soldier. With one quick thrust he ended the man's life. Seconds later, two javelins pierced Dak's armor. He pitched off the horse and knew he was dying. "I'm glad I was the first," he told the blood-drenched earth. "It was worth it."

Magic or no, the enemy could not stop the empire's advance. Goblins died by the thousands. The humans fought like madmen and even the undead held no fear for them.

The knights of the Green Branch led the advance. They kept three lines of horses. The first would charge and break off, then the second would charge and break off, the third, charge and break off. Already a hundred of the feared knights were down, but still they kept their lines, charge and break off, charge and break off. The enemy, folding underneath the relentless pressure, turned and ran.

The Dark Ones' magic began to go awry. A fireball meant for Tolath's cavalry destroyed its casters instead. Concentration was broken in the midst of a spell, their power became misdirected, as simple mistakes began to kill their own troops. They couldn't understand it, couldn't fight it, and the leaders began to join their army in flight.

And above it all, heard only by the dying, a wild laughter filled the field, and a golden chariot trampled the fallen.

Mathwei led his men in a crossing pattern, slashing at the fleeing goblins. He tried to shout his triumph but his dry throat would only let out a gasp. For a moment he became separated from his men. Dark forms rushed by him, running, running. But one stood and waited for the warrior.

It rode a skeletal horse with eyes of green flame. The rider was pale, bloodless, its eyes bulging and red veined. The vampire bared its fangs at Mathwei.

"Die," it hissed, drawing a wicked scimitar. Unhesitantly, Mathwei kicked his horse and charged the apparition. The two swords clashed with a shower of sparks, but the spectre was too powerful for Mathwei. Before he could withdraw, the scimitar darted beneath his guard and slid through the mail chest, even as a clawed hand ripped the throat of Mathwei's mount. Man and horse collapsed in a heap.

Mathwei rolled away from the animal's death throes and jumped to his feet to meet the attack that would surely be his last. The ripped tissue in his chest tried to respond, but the pain was too much and the warrior fell to his knees.

"Death." He tried to shout at the vampire, who wheeled his mount around, its eyes turning red in bloodlust.

Lord Death heard that cry, so small amongst all the sounds of the battlefield. He had read Dammuth's soul as the wizard departed. He had seen this young warrior in Dammuth's heart. This he could do, this he would do.

A wave of a shadow hand, a burst of wind deflecting an arrow, the missile sticking the vampire through the neck. It fell from its mount, and was covered by a wave of retreating goblins. Mathwei's men rode up, surrounding their captain, bringing him from the field. As the pain overcame him and Mathwei felt healing sleep numb him, he heard a voice, sad and silent.

"Twice have I let you go, young warrior. The third time you must join me in my halls."

And all across the battlefield the goblins and their allies fled in terror. They had lost the battle and wished only to save their lives.

A mile away from Mathwei, three figures of horror stood. The tallest stood some eight feet. It was a vaguely human skeleton with bits and pieces of muscle and flesh holding the bones together. The skull had two sickly yellow-green luminous worms spinning in endless circles where the eyes should be.

"We have lost." The voice was a whisper of branches cracking beneath a heavy foot. "They still have spirit." But he felt uneasy. There was something else here. Something that was more a threat to him than to the others. He was Lord of the Undead, but the humans' chant of "Death" had unnerved him. There was something more, something more. . . .

The second figure was about six feet tall. It would have looked human except for the albinic flesh and hair and the extended spinal ridge along its back. The demon was a hermaphrodite and displayed its oddity with perverse pride. It raised a three-fingered hand.

"Yes, lost, but not defeated." The voice was cool, soft. "Still, the master will be displeased." The figure shifted and moved forward with its back to the battle. Its reddish eyes, slitted like a snake's, stared at the burnt grass where its feet stood a moment before.

"The fortunes of war," said the first, its laughter made weirder by the hollow rattle of air through bone.

"Still," continued the second, "still, I think those over-zealous Green Branch knights are most to blame. I think it is time they were withered. Yes, withered." It turned its back to its companions and began an incantation in a high-pitched voice.

The third figure sighed. He was less worried about how the master would feel. They would win the war. Who cared about a few thousand goblins, more or less? 'A gesture does seem in order, though,' the demon prince thought.

He was less than three feet tall. He looked to be a rather insignificant imp. The red scaly skin was highlighted in yellow and his wings looked too weak to carry his grossly overweight body. He jumped off the giant rat he had been riding, patted him affectionately on the back, and watched the hermaphrodite with interest.

The skeleton shifted its attention to the imp. If there was any doubt as to who was the leader here, one had only to look in the skeleton's eyes as he watched the diminutive figure caress the rat. The glowworms turned a purple-greyish color. They cast a violet shadow on the creature's face. There was fear in that glow, fear and terror.

"Well," said the imp in a pleasing and melodious voice, "I think I need a new mount." With that, he patted the rat once more. At his touch it squealed in a human voice and thrashed around on the ground, trying to dislodge the large larvae that had appeared on its back and were even now digging into its flesh.

The skeleton shivered and said no word.

The imp watched the rat dispassionately for a few minutes. The hermaphrodite shrieked a word and a red streak flew from its hand straight toward Tolath's army.

"Yes, you are right. Some gesture is in order here. And I think Warlord Crane has enjoyed his victory long enough." The imp made several quick motions in the air and a blot of blackness, a tear in the very fabric of reality, appeared from

his brow. It was slowly moving toward the victorious army.
"Yes," said the imp, "a new mount would suit me fine."

The evil army fled the field losing all order. Behind them
they left nearly three-fourths of their comrades. For miles,
the dark shapes of goblins, trolls, and wolves dotted the
countryside in the twisted shapes of defeat, and lying next to
them were the dead and dying of Tolath's finest.

Fin, Laird of Dun Scage, emptied his canteen over his
head. The lukewarm water did little to relieve his exhaustion. All around him the knights of the Green Branch tried to
collect themselves and bind their wounds.

"Fin, get off that horse and have a shot with us," a knight
called across the clearing. The knights had found a clearing
relatively free of the dead. Some of the younger warriors
were decapitating the few enemy corpses around.

Fin looked at the knights who called to him and slowly
shook his head. A shadow seemed to stand near him and
whisper that it wasn't over, that he shouldn't dismount. He
longed to throw off his armor and weapons as the others
had, but the voice was incessant. 'Ridiculous,' thought the
knight to himself, 'I am hearing voices now.' But he stayed
on his horse. A lonely sentinel, battered and weary, but he
stayed on the horse.

One warrior leapt to his feet, the sudden movement star-
tling the others. "Arm!" the knight cried. "The Dark Lord
reaches for retribution! The trees crack, the leaves wither.
Beware, the Sword itself melts!" The knights leapt to their
feet, grabbing weapons, the pump of adrenaline in them a
palpable force as the men threw off their exhaustion. Fin
shifted his grip on his lance. All the knights searched for the
attack they knew would come. The warning had been given
by Malachai, and all had learned to heed his witch sight.

The men stopped their frantic arming as a sound rose in
volume all around them. It was the sigh of a great animal, a
storm on the ocean, and it was coming to them.

"Woe," cried Malachai, "the Fire Lord calls us to Hell.

The Green Branch is withered." Fin's mind raced as he tried to decipher the warnings.

"What," he mumbled, "what attacks us?" He heard a soft whisper, the fall of leaves in a silent forest: *salamander*.

Even as Fin registered the whisper the sighing stopped, and with a crash the fire elemental landed in the midst of the knights.

It was at least twelve feet in length. The upper part of its body was human and colored a deep black. The human torso flowed into an elongated tail with no legs. The tail ended with a wicked-looking pincer and was covered with red scales. The creature radiated a terrible heat, its tail flicking fire as it thrashed about. The four knights it landed amongst burst into flame, their cries reverberating across the clearing.

Immediately, the others attacked the demon. The few who made it close enough to the creature found the weapons useless against the salamander's flesh. In minutes, the air was full of the smell of burning flesh and molten metal. Weapons were melted, men were crushed by the slap of the awesome tail, eyes burned before a warrior could strike, arrows charred to cinders as they struck the creature. But still the knights attacked.

The demon was meant to destroy them, and they knew that there was no running. It was a personal challenge, and though the men shivered with fear as their comrades died in agony, still they fought.

Fin moved his horse around the salamander. He knew why he had been chosen to fight this creature. He had several small salamanders at Dun Scaga. They had been given to an ancestor by a wizard before the Dark Seign wars. In Fin's great-grandfather's time, one of the elementals had escaped and was finally killed by his great-uncle Don. The story was told and retold in the family. Fin knew there was only one way to kill a salamander. In the cleft where the creature's human back merged into the red scales of the tail, there is a raised vertebra. Between this vertebra and the tail, a weapon could be driven into the monster, here and only here. Unless one had magic. "Which," snorted Fin, "we have woefully little of."

Fin tried to shout this knowledge to the others but the sounds of the battle were too loud. Already a score of warriors were down and Fin realized he had only minutes before the creature finished them all off.

The salamander was not twisting and turning around as most of its kind do to protect its one weak spot. With a thrill of hope, Fin realized the salamander was sure of its strength and was not protecting itself at all.

He rode the horse toward the monster. One part of his mind wondered at the horse; it should not be moving toward the fire demon. Though as well trained as a war horse could be, its fear of fire should make it bolt, even as all the other horses had already. Fin kicked it into a gallop and a cry of triumph burst from his throat.

As he approached, the salamander turned to face Fin. It was too late to stop the charge. His chance was lost. All would die because he failed. Fin's soul wailed in desperation. So close, so close. . . .

As the monster's heat began to bring out blisters on Fin's metal-encased hands, a cry broke to his right.

"Scaga!" He heard his ancient war cry and Malachai charged the salamander from the other side. His hand flew up and a bottle burst against the creature's snout. The whiskey, ignited by the creature's own heat, flamed up and momentarily blinded it. It turned toward Malachai and lunged at him. With a mighty blow, Malachai chopped at the hand, his sword splintering and melting at the same time. The black hand grabbed the warrior around the waist and as his body caught fire, Malachai drew his dagger and stabbed at the demon's eyes.

Fin spurred his horse into a gallop and he lowered his lance. The salamander's entire attention was on Malachai. The ridged back and flashing tail filled Fin's entire vision. The ride took forever, but Fin knew he would make it.

Though heat still radiated from the creature, Fin could stand it. It was using its full powers on Malachai.

The horse's mane began to singe and shrivel. Everywhere that metal touched Fin's flesh, it began to smoulder. But he didn't care. His whole being was centered around a six-inch square of black flesh. The salamander dropped Malachai's burning body and began to turn toward the sound of hoof-beats, but two more knights recklessly attacked it from the front, and even as it tried to decide what to do, the lance pierced its flesh.

Fin and the horse were one creature, and their weight pushed the lance through the demon with terrific power. The lance sunk four feet of its length into the salamander, push-ing out through the other side in an explosion of fire and black blood. The creature arched with a high-pitched scream, the only sound it had made throughout the whole battle. A spasmodic thrust of its tail sent Fin and his horse reeling through the air. He crashed into the ground some twenty feety away. The air seemed incredibly cool, but Fin knew he was dead, his lungs were burned, shriveled, his face a ruin of melted flesh. He opened his left eye—the right didn't seem to work at all—to stare up at a shadow.

Fin knew it was time and reached his hand to the shadow, but it shook its head, and kneeling down, touched the war-rior's chest. His body was filled with a cool wind that whipped about inside him. As the wind healed his flesh, he realized the agony his body had been suffering. He let out a scream without knowing it. But as his body arched in the pain of healing, his mind laughed with joy. For Fin, Laird of Dun Scage, knew he wouldn't die this day. And he heard a voice answer, "Not this time. . . ."

Warlord Crane sighed and took another sip of his wine. He sat on a camp stool, surrounded by officers and aides. The younger ones all had the flushed look of the victorious, but Crane felt none of their elation.

"Very good," he sighed to the officer that had just given

his report. "Take as many men as you can and help search for the wounded." The officer saluted and left.

Crane stretched his greying body and moved his bulk on the flimsy stool. He stood over six-four and though his body was beginning to lose its tone with age, Crane was a massively imposing man. "Fintan, Ernet, send the others away."

The two generals dismissed the other officers and squatted down around the Warlord. Crane looked the two over. 'Good men, but damned young to be officers. So many,' he thought, 'so many assassinated, murdered. And here I am, one of the few left.' He looked at the two expectant faces and took another sip of wine. 'An old alcoholic with rheumatism. Damn.'

"Well, gentlemen, your assessment." The two looked at each other. Ernet shrugged, and tracing his dagger in the ground, spoke, his eyes downcast.

"A week, maybe two, my lord, before they reorganize."

"Aye," said Crane, "and they'll bring a larger army probably."

"The men think of it as a great victory. They won't like us retreating again, my lord," Fintan spoke. His voice was slurred, one side of his face a ruin of scars, the memory of a fireball. He still woke up screaming at night.

Crane watched a trail of saliva drip down the ruined side of Fintan's face. The general had no nerves there and consequently no knowledge of the drool. For some reason it fascinated Crane, and he felt almost disappointed when Fintan licked his mouth unconsciously. 'God, I crave some whiskey,' thought the Warlord.

"No choice, son," he said aloud. "We've decimated their army but we can't establish an offensive. If we can field half the force we had today in two weeks, we'll be lucky.

"Still," said Ernet, "it is our victory, the first, and we can keep the people from knowing how many we really lost."

'Damned fewer than we should have'; Crane kept his thoughts to himself.

"Yes, morale, my lord, at all costs we must keep up the morale," Fintan added.

"We retreat in two days. We'll leave a strong garrison at Comar, make our stand in Tolan, and pray the elves and dwarves get there in time."

"Volunteers, my lord, at Comar, only volunteers," said Fintan. Crane looked over at Ernet.

"Aye, my lord, the city will never hold, but we can slow the advance some."

"Time is what we need, lord, a good defense to hold them as long as possible and make them pay a price." Fintan stood up and stared his leader in the eye. Fintan's grey eyes showed no emotion. He reached up and rubbed the scars on his face, his right hand burned and misshapen. Three fingers emphasized his next words.

"The dreams, my lord, they get worse. The pain never ceases."

"No," said Crane quietly.

"My lord, someone must lead the men. We must hold at Comar. You must give me the command."

"No," but the conviction wasn't in Crane's voice. "You're too valuable."

"My lord, I have fulfilled my duties well but I am no great tactician. The pain. The dreams. The drugs the mages give me are habitual. It takes more and more to stop the pain. Soon, very soon, nothing will ease it. I can hold Comar for days, perhaps even a week. You must allow me."

Crane looked at Ernet, who averted his eyes. None would survive Comar. Yet, to ask for volunteers, Crane must give them a leader. 'A damn good one,' Crane thought. He must, there was no choice.

"Wait till the army bivouacs at Comar, then ask for volunteers." The words choked in his throat. "The command is yours, General Fintan."

The doomed general's eyes filled with . . . what? Relief? 'Gods damn this war. It is killing the best, always the best.'

Crane cleared his throat once more, refusing to look at

Fintan. "We didn't win this battle, you know. They did." His hand made a vague motion to the army around them. "We were in a good defensive position. We could have inflicted incredible damage on the enemy, but something took over them." Crane shivered as he remembered that deep chant of death reverberating around the fields. "I don't understand it. We lost all control. The original plan would have worked."

"But," said Ernet, "we would've had to retreat. We would never have hurt them like we did."

"Dammit!" shouted Crane. "They could afford it! We couldn't. We lost too damn many." Crane's angry tirade stopped as something caught his eye. A red flash. "What the hell?" He leapt to his feet pointing, "A fireball?"

They all followed his finger. Cries of battle drifted on the air. The red flash seemed stable. Around it, scurrying black shapes could be seen. All the officers on the hill moved to the edge to peer down.

"Laird Fin and the Green Branch are down there, sir. I don't know what it is, but," Fintan added, "it is no fireball."

Crane looked at him and called to his aide. "Glasny, get some cavalry down there immediately." He called after the warrior, "Send those archers, the Bantry men."

He turned to Ernet. "There's some regular infantry down at the foot of the hill. Form a shield wall, and send a battalion on to that clearing now." The general turned and ran to his horse. "Fintan, call to arms. Get the men in position. Their armies are done, but they still have their stinking magic." Fintan grabbed two other officers and the bugler. Even as they mounted, a new cry came up and Crane saw a blot of darkness angling from the skies toward him. He leaped up and drew his sword.

"'Ware," he cried, "the bastards send a parting shot!" His men made a concerted rush to his side, but they were too late.

The blot headed straight for the Warlord. He swung with his sword and staggered as the thing hit him full in the brow. Instantly, the general's body was covered by a black shadow surrounding him on all sides. There was a tearing noise and the general dwindled inside the black shadow as if he was falling down a hole. Then the shadow was sucked inside itself. The shadow was gone and so was the Warlord. The officers stared at the place their leader had stood and wondered what black magic the enemy had employed.

"No!" cried Ernet. "Oh, no," he moaned, "not him, too."

It seemed to Crane that he had simply closed his eyes, for all he could see was darkness and little dots whirling around him. 'As if,' he thought, 'I was closing my eyes to sleep.'

Then he felt the firm earth beneath his legs and found himself facing three horrors.

"Welcome, Lord Crane," said the imp. "I'm glad we finally got the chance to meet."

Crane looked them over, the skeleton, the pale hermaphrodite, and the fat little imp. The rat still writhed in agony, the maggots burrowing deeper and deeper.

"You," Crane's voice was fierce, "are the leader?"

"Oh, allow us to introduce ourselves. This is Roella, the Fire Lord." The imp made a gesture toward the hermaphrodite, whose attention was still on his salamander. "This is Apkieran, Lord of the Undead." The skeleton's larva eyes just stared. "And you may call me Dubh, if you like, my lord." The imp sketched a satiric bow. Crane noticed it sought to hide the fact that it was missing a hand.

He drew himself up and stared down at the imp. "Well, halfhand, it's a good day to die, eh?" With that, Crane brought his sword down with full fury on the imp's head. With a clang, it shivered apart in his hand.

The imp smiled and looked straight into the Warlord's eyes. Crane fell to his knees, the pure evil in that stare overcoming him.

"You shall pay for that, my little warlord," said the imp. "And you shall rue the halfhand remark for all eternity." He touched the Warlord's brow, and Crane cried out once and passed out into merciful unconsciousness.

He did not feel the pain as his body shivered and contracted. Bone, muscle, and flesh spewed from knees that separated from the legs. The dark mess fused into hooves even as the hands contracted and went hard doing the same.

"A new mount indeed," laughed the Demon Prince. Just then Roella shouted as his salamander was pierced by Fin's lance. Roella turned to the others, his eyes erupting in flame.

"How?" he shouted. The imp just shrugged, petting the still convulsing form of what was once Lord Crane, Warlord of the Empire.

Apkieran made no sign, standing silent. He was close, close to figuring out 'Something,' he told himself, 'something more here.'

A grey shadow watched the three demon princes. And He laughed. . . .

CHAPTER

Seven

Fire flew from the hooves and mouths of the two black stallions that pulled Death's golden chariot, their eyes burning with a pale blue light. He guided them across the pathways of the world, where no god or man could see his passage.

He veered them toward a dark cave, the grey stone of the opening covered with green lichen. They galloped through at the speed of the wind, following a long winding tunnel. Cries and howls and glowing red eyes followed them down, but Lord Death never slowed his pace. Finally, the passage ended in an ancient cavern, and Death reared his steeds to a halt. They screamed with human voices, their hooves pounding the ground.

A shadow lifted itself from the corner of the cave, its form human except for the two staglike horns that sprung from its brow. Red eyes burned beneath.

"Ah, grey man," it approached the chariot, "you always were dramatic."

Death laughed; a hollow sound. "I have come looking for allies, brother."

"And does Death make war?"

"He does." The two faced one another, the air cold about them.

"Why do you come to me?"

"Of all the gods," Death hissed, "only you are like me,

117

and you are the only one who would dare to take sides in this war."

"And which side do you take?"

"Don't insult me, scavenger!" He leaped from his chariot to stand face to face with the other. "If you have betrayed yourself and joined the Dark One, then this day you shall feel my touch!" Neither moved, the only sound the fire snorting from the steeds. Then the second shadow laughed, the harsh sound of the god's voice echoing about them.

"Dear brother," it said, still laughing, "it is long, long till your cold touch shall reach me." It held one hand up, the form wavered, sometimes a paw, sometimes a human hand. "But do not doubt me. I have chosen my side, and I have chosen ere now."

"When?"

"Ah, thirty or so human years ago did I begin to plan."

"So," Death's voice was sibilant, "so, do—" but he stopped at the sound of approaching hooves. The Hunter turned to watch the entrance, as another shadow danced into the cave. It was of a great steed, its substance somehow more vibrant than the others. It knelt on one knee before them.

"Ah, my son," said the Hunter, "I don't believe you have met our guest."

"Not lately," said the newcomer. "I hope this doesn't mean that unbeknownst to me I have tripped and broken my neck?" All three laughed, though Death's laugh was shrill.

"So, Trickster, you, too, have joined our little war."

"War has always been a favorite sport of mine," said the horse-form, though the look from its flashing eyes belied its words. "I fought in the Dark Seign wars, against the dragon kind."

"Yes," answered Death, "with Dammuth, I believe," but he said no more.

"If the goblins and their masters tread the world again," said the Hunter, "I wonder can the dragons be far behind?" None had an answer to that.

"I was hoping you would be here, Trickster," Death turned his pale eyes on the horse-form. "There is one who could use such a mount as you."

"No offense, but I hope it is not your cold shanks you wish me to carry."

"No, but the Morigunamachamain."

"Feh!" he swore. "I have heard the earththings murmur his name, but I thought it was a wish for a defender, just a rumor."

"No, my son, it is so," answered the Hunter. "I have watched him. He is perilous and wild. The earththings call him *the* Morigu. As if somehow he embodies all the ones that went before him."

"You choose a sad partner for me, Lord Death."

"He needs a directing force," came the answer. "He has been called to the elven war council of Cather-na-nog, but he does not go."

"He feels the agony of the earth as no other before him," the Hunter added. "The pain in the south is too much for him to bear."

"Alone," added Death. The Trickster bowed his noble head.

"I will do what you have asked. I will find him and do what I can." The other two nodded.

"Good," Death said. "Now, what do either of you know of the elven lords of Cather-na-nog?"

"The same as you," the Hunter answered, "they plan within the heart of their kingdom. They will ride when they are ready, and when that is, no one can say."

Death turned to the south. "The humans are hard-pressed. The Dark must be stopped in the empire, or the land will be split and eaten piece by piece."

"I have been to the Crystal Falls," the Trickster added. "Mearead and his people have been attacked and many have fallen." Death sighed.

"I know. Have I not freed so many of the valiant in those bright halls?"

"I have planned," added the Hunter. "I have other allies. They are not as prepared as I had hoped, but they will add their power to the empire." Death said nothing, his hand tapping his sword hilt. The other two waited.

"I rode with the humans," he said quietly. "I have broken my bounds, but I cannot show my full strength lest I crack the world in two."

"My allies are my followers, brother," added the Hunter. "They are humans."

"I did not know humans still prayed to you, scavenger."

"I had help." A flash of fangs, a rare smile from this god. "A man turned to me on his own. He saw before any others. An emperor."

"Trell'dem," Death's shadow-form turned black. "Even now he mourns in my halls, begging me to let him go back to his land, to fight again."

"Feh," the Trickster stamped his shadow hooves, "that was no way for such a one to die."

"I had to take him," came Death's harsh answer, "it was his time. I could not postpone it."

"You have others." The Hunter's voice was harsh; even a god may grieve.

"I know, but to let him live would have been no boon to any of us. It would have tipped the balance too far."

"And your hand too soon," added the Trickster.

"Yes," the Hunter whispered, "I have kept my involvement unknown, but soon my followers will reveal themselves. And when they do . . ."

". . . the Dark One shall turn his thoughts to you," Death finished.

"If I may, Lord Death," the Trickster said, "why have you chosen to join us?"

"Join you?" Death laughed again. "I am Death. I join nothing, nobody. . . ." He turned from the other two. "There are reasons, many. And there is the memory of one man I cannot forget." The other two nodded, thinking he spoke of Trell'dem.

"He was a good man," added the Trickster, "but in truth I thought it was Apkieran that would have forced your decision."

"The Undead Lord!?" Death spat. "Did I raise my might against him when he desecrated the world during the Dark Seign war? No! You are young yet, godling. All things have their opposite—even death. . . ."

"But," insisted the other, "his minions walk the earth in increasing numbers. He flaunts his power and expends it wildly."

"The last days," added the Hunter. "They strive to destroy the world itself and suck the power of that destruction into themselves."

"And turn against the Bright World!" shouted Death, and the others shuddered to hear that sound. "But the gods, in all their glory, hide their heads. For fear of the last battle. But I tell you now, if we and the peoples of this world fail, the gods themselves are doomed and the Beast will tread upon the thrones of the mighty." He turned to the Trickster. "Go. Find the Morigu. We need him. Find him and bring him to war." He slammed his hand on the chariot. The sound of the blow reverberated about the cave—Doom! The horse-shadow bowed once and sped out of the cave.

"We have little time, scavenger," he said to the other. "The gods even now seek our thoughts. We must plan and—"

"I have a question first," the Hunter interrupted, "a question only you can answer." Death turned to him. "Has Dammuth fallen?" Death said nothing. A glowing dot sprung from his brow landing in the other's paw/hand. From this piece of Death, the god learned of the life and fall of Dammuth, Arch Mage of the land. He held it to his heart.

"Ah, so rare," he whispered, "so rare." He looked up, facing the pale eyes of Death. "You always were more gentle than I." He sat down, staring up. "Why did you not tell the Trickster? They were friends. He had a right to know."

"As you say, I am gentler than you, little brother, and I

am more used to war." Death squatted down across from the god. "Dammuth was the Morigu's only link to the Light. If he learned of the mage's death he would seek for the demon and ignore all other duties. Even if he overcame that black soul, the enemy would be aware. They would know that only I could have known of Dammuth's death so soon. In one act we could lose the whole war."

The Hunter reached out, touching his brother on the knee.

"It grieves me to see you so," he said. Death shook his head.

"When the whole world cries in agony, who are we to turn away?" He stood up again and entered his chariot. Without looking back, he whipped the horses and raced out of the cave, saying no more.

The Hunter stared after him, speaking softly.

"And should not the whole world tremble, my sad brother, when Death himself fears?"

Margawt stood staring at the south, his mouth twisted in confusion. He let his soul sink and merge with the earth and followed her veins, down one branch after another. Seeking, seeking for the Goddess, but all he felt was the pain of war. He shuddered and returned. His body shook spastically, his mind whirling with needs he could not understand.

The Goddess had withdrawn her attention from this part of the world. He was unsure where to look for her. Though he felt the elven king's call, he resisted. Each step south was like walking on a lake of fire. He warred within himself, wishing for the balm of the hunt, yet unable to stand the thoughts of the terror ahead.

Then he felt a new current, cool and soft. His name was wrapped in it. He could detect no deceit, so he followed.

In less than half an hour, Margawt found himself in a quiet glade. Magic was strong here, earth magic and something more. Though the sky was overcast, the grass and trees gleamed as if washed in moonlight. He felt another tug and stood still, looking around with eyes and power. But nothing registered. He was alone.

"Margawt," said a voice. He turned quickly, his sword out of the sheath and pointed straight at the intruder. It was a large beast, its dark blue coat turning black where shadows played on its hide. Its mane and tail were a deep earth brown color. The hooves and spiraled horn, jet black. Red horns protruded over its eyes that burned with an orange flame.

"Unicorn," it was almost a question, "how is it that you can surprise me?"

"You do not know me?" came the answer. Margawt shook his head trying to detect wrongness in the being, but he could not. 'Though,' he thought, 'perhaps it could hide that from me, as it hid its approach.'

"Trust," came the earth's answer. He almost shouted to hear the Goddess' voice, but she turned from him again. He looked back in the unicorn's eyes, realizing he had been called here to meet this odd creature.

"Well met, earth avenger," said the unicorn. Its mouth did not move and Margawt realized that it somehow used its horn to communicate. The horn sent out the proper rhythms in the air but it had a curious effect since the voice Margawt heard had no inflection, timbre, or volume.

"You may call me Anlon, if you like," it continued.

Margawt put his sword away and approached the beast.

"You are here to help me in my battles?" he asked.

The unicorn nodded once. "You're a serious one, aren't you?" Margawt ignored him.

"Am I to ride you?"

"Feh, no, I ride you." He stamped his hoof in irritation.

"We leave now, then." As Margawt approached to mount, the unicorn shied away.

"We leave when I say, Kondo-s," which means 'intelligent.' "I am no beast of burden. I am here to fight and to teach. Lesson one," he moved closer, staring in Margawt's dark eyes, "where do you plan to go?"

"I, I have to go," he pointed to the south. "I must . . ." but he made no move to mount the unicorn.

"What do you fear most, Morigu? The pain of the war, or the pain of being with other creatures?" He got no answer.

"Dammuth said you were a tough one," 'but,' he added to himself, 'Dammuth never told you of me. Does that mean he doesn't trust you?'

"You know Dammuth?" asked Margawt, for the first time emotion touching his voice.

"Ah, so you do care for the old man. Yes, I know Dammuth, and he and I talked long about you. We both had the feeling that I would come to you one day."

"Come to me?" said Margawt. "I thought the earth sent you?"

"Sent me?" Anlon snorted. "Not likely. You were sent. I decided to come."

"The Goddess, She . . ." Margawt lost his thoughts.

"She wars, too, little one," the unicorn said gently. "The dwarves of the Crystal Falls are hard-pressed, their own mountains turn against them. She is there, because—"

"I will go there," Margawt interrupted.

"What doom sense keeps you from the south, avenger?" asked the unicorn. "There is where your destiny lies. You and I must await the first hosting of the elves and then we must ride with them. Come, mount me." He moved to Margawt, who unhesitatingly leaped upon the unicorn's back.

"We have some time. I will help you," the unicorn said. But his thoughts were dark. Could this one already be insane? "The Light has need of you," he said aloud.

"But the dwarves, the Goddess . . ." Margawt's voice got stronger. Somehow, on the back of the unicorn, the pain from the south did not reach him in such strength.

"The dwarves and the Goddess will take care of themselves. You and I must learn more about one another so that we, too, can play our role."

Margawt marveled to feel the unicorn's strength, and his heart lightened now with Anlon's words.

"The enemy does not know you, Avenger," Anlon said. "The Ard Riegh hopes others of the Shee will be chosen to become Morigunamachamain, but Dammuth is convinced that even though you were born in blood instead of service to the earth, that you could be trusted and that much hinges on you. So do not wonder why I am here. After all, some-one must keep an eye out on you, Kondo-s." The unicorn reared to his full height, and with an incredible burst, gal-loped in toward the south. The wind roared by Margawt and he marveled how the unicorn could possibly move so fast and yet not touch a branch or bend a blade of grass.

"You and me, Margawt, we are a spear aimed at the Dark One's heart!"

With that they moved even faster so all was a blur to the Morigu. He could hardly believe that any creature could move faster than he, but the unicorn left him no doubt. They flew off into the night, and the enemy did not know that they were coming.

Colin signaled to the waiting troops behind him. He heard the other dwarves mutter under their breath as, with a clang of armor, they took what comfort they could from the cold floor of the cavern. Counting Colin there were sixty-four warriors, all from his clan. They had been trooping through the lower halls, seeking their enemy for over two hours, with no success.

One of the warriors slid over to sit next to his leader. He lifted his helmet mask off his face, his armor echoing weirdly in the small chamber.

"Anything?" he asked. His face was unlined, but a pure white beard hung to his waist.

"Nay, Math." Colin pulled his wolf mask from his head, dropping it at his feet. "My powers have grown in the last weeks, but whatever force attacks the caves blocks my clair-voyance." The other nodded gravely. It was not a good sign. Colin, as sister-son of Mearead and heir to the throne, should be able to search through all the caves and caverns of the Crystal Falls with his magic, detecting any wrongness in the rhythm of life in the dwarven kingdom. Math reached up over and patted the younger dwarf on his mail-clad shoulder.

"Don't feel bad, lad, even Mearead's power has been blocked and the lore masters are hard-pressed to perform the simplest of rituals."

Colin did not answer. Sighing, the other left the dwarf lord to his thoughts. Colin unhooked his ax from his silver girdle. He stared at the sharp edge of the weapon, his mind wandering.

It had been three weeks since the first attacks. The dwarves thought it likely the Dark Ones would move against them, but they had thought the enemy would try to storm the gates. But evil was smarter than that and more powerful. Somehow, the enemy had bridged the ancient magic that protected the Crystal Falls, and attacked from the lower halls.

In the first surprise the enemy was able to capture and hold many of the older and less used caverns, using them as a staging area to press their advantage. Hundreds had died trying to recapture the lost territory. Finally, with a combination of magic and weapons, the dwarves had overrun all the enemy camps. But the cost was high. Two of the twelve lore masters died along with three thousand warriors. And Mearead himself wounded.

That was a week ago, and things had only gotten worse. The dwarves discovered hitherto unknown caverns, passages all through the lower regions of the Crystal Falls. Mearead thought the enemy must have been digging them for years. Many of the passages ran parallel with the ones the dwarves had carved, and no one knew when next a wall would crumble and the enemy would pour in through the breach.

It was impossible. What power had the enemy to do this thing? It was sacrilege and desecration. Since Mearead had introduced Colin to the Goddess he had become more aware of her and her power. He knew that in Her own way, She, too, fought in the caverns, 'But,' he thought gloomily, 'She isn't doing very well either.'

The cavern the dwarves sat in was not very large, barely a hundred feet by forty, the ceiling a scant ten feet above their heads. No passages led out of it, though a wide passage had led the dwarven troop here. The cave was obviously not natural. In its crudity it could be seen it had never been shaped by dwarven hands.

They had searched for some sign that the enemy had been here, but there was nothing. What purpose did it serve? One small riddle in a world gone mad with them.

Colin lifted his head for a moment to peer in the pitch-black cave. He felt something. There! There it was again. He pulled off his gauntlets and placed his hands on the ground. The floor felt distasteful, unpleasant, like no stone had ever felt to his touch. It was like touching a corpse, for here the stone was dead. . . . The riddle was answered!

"'Ware!" he cried, jumping to his feet. "To the passage! It's a trap!" The others leapt up, brandishing weapons. But even as the first few headed toward the opening, a loud crash was heard, and the rock wall furthest away began to flake apart. At the same time, the thud of running feet came toward them from the passage.

"Close ranks!" Colin yelled, even as he tugged his gauntlets and helmet on. "Form a wedge facing the far wall!" A weird howling filled the area. It was unlike anything Colin had ever heard. It was low-pitched, but hurt his ears like a high-pitched shriek. It continued for a moment and then stopped as the first of the enemy piled in from the opening.

They were cronbage, creatures barely the height of dwarves, brutish and fur-covered. For a moment the dwarves just stared. Up to now all they had fought had been goblins. The cronbage shouldn't even exist. They had been the troops of the Fomarians, the elder dark gods of ages gone by.

"Damn, damn!" Colin swore. One more riddle. What were these creatures doing here? The ancient enemy of the dwarven folk. They were supposed to be long dead. They smashed into the dwarven ranks.

The cronbage wore little armor and relied mostly upon spears and maces, but for all that proved to be hardy fighters. Five dwarves fell in the first rush.

Then the opposite wall crashed down, a mass of the hairy warriors rushing through the dust into the waiting dwarven ranks.

It was a bizarre battle, there in the depths of the mountains. Neither dwarf nor cronbage made any sound. The cave filled with grunts and cries of pain, but no war cries, no calls to heroism, just the grim business of survival.

As the dust settled from the fallen wall, the dwarves let out a shout of dismay, for the wall had hidden a cavern of immense size. So large that neither roof nor wall could be seen. And the whole area was covered with a blanket of the cronbage.

The warriors of the Crystal Falls held their ranks. Their enemy falling at their feet two and three feet deep as the superior armor and weapons skill of the dwarves began to take its toll. But as Colin's ax swept off the arm off one of the fanged cronbage, he knew it was useless. The enemy's number was endless, and already one third of his men had fallen. He wiped blood from his mask's eyeguards, his mind losing all concerns. For some reason, this day, this moment, seemed familiar, and death held no fear for him.

Another crack began in the wall behind them, and Colin knew it was over, even as he formed his men in a rough circle so they could face this new threat. The weird howling began again, but the note was different, and for a moment the enemy pulled back in confusion. Colin knew this was their only chance and ordered the dwarves to make a break for the passage. As he began shouting his orders, a new voice interrupted him.

"For honor! For the Crystal Falls!" a great voice yelled, as the second cave wall gave way. This time it was dwarves who rushed through, hundreds, thousands, with their king, Mearead, leading the way.

The cronbage were swept away and Colin and his men, with the new forces, pushed the enemy back out of the first cavern into the larger one.

Colin stopped as the dimensions of the cavern before him became apparent. It was fully a mile long in all directions and its roof hung two hundred feet in the air.

Mearead strode ahead, five lore masters to either side of him, white fire streaming from their hands, burning the enemy before them. The dwarves pushed further on, as the enemy scattered in confusion, the front ranks trying to retreat, the warriors in the back trying to move forward to fight.

Colin cried, "For Mearead and the Crystal Falls!" and plunged into the battle, seeking to fight his way to his uncle's side.

The fighting became more fierce and the cronbage answered the dwarves' challenge with inarticulate cries of their own. In the larger cave the dwarves could use their bows to devastating advantage on the poorly armored enemy. The cronbage gave way, grudgingly, leaving hundreds of their fallen to be trodden by dwarven boots.

Then a third time the strange voice howled, but this time all the dwarves heard the hatred in that sound. Streaks of red power flew from the enemy's ranks to smash into the dwarves, and the room was lit by strange colors as black magic met dwarven strength.

On the far back wall a large, dark shadow took form in the witchlight. It was long and bent, as of an old woman, and its eyes glowed red. Colin could see now that the cavern was dotted with openings and from these poured enemy reinforcements. Large goblins dressed in grey, and giant trolls, their wicked fangs gleaming white. And more cronbage, most armed as their fellows, but some units marching, covered in armor as the dwarves, poleaxes and halberds dancing over their heads.

The dwarves pushed on and Colin realized not all the cave openings were held by the enemy as dwarven reinforcements joined the fight. The crash and roar of the battle was deafening in the cavern. Smoke stung eyes and nose from where bodies burned from magic flames.

Colin fought his way to his uncle, his armor covered in the blood of his enemies. Mearead turned to his nephew, his eyes glowing behind the dragon mask he wore.

"Well met, lad," he cried above the battle noise.

"Well met, indeed!" Colin laughed. "What took you so long?" he added.

"Damn wall was thicker than I thought." Mearead grabbed the lad's shoulder. "I need your strength, boy. Whatever that thing is," he pointed at the shadow, "it's stronger than anything I've ever encountered." Colin nodded once and sat by the king's feet, as their warriors pressed by the two.

He closed his eyes, cutting out sight, sound, and smell. He focused on his uncle's face, the dwarf king's laugh and, like a sword slipped into its sheath, followed with his magic the power of Mearead's spells.

He opened his eyes again to see the battle with new eyes. The individual warriors blended into shades of light and dark. Above, around, and through them multicolored lines and shapes slashed at one another, as the magic light and dark fought with grim determination.

Colin burned with his power. He directed it to strengthen Mearead's magic, thickening a line here, widening a formless shape there. He felt the enemy's counterstrokes as a pressure on him, a weight, and when an attack was particularly strong, a slash along his insides. When that happened the pain was such that he would shout in agony, trying desperately not to lose his concentration.

All sense of time was lost to him. At first the battle went back and forth. Once he felt the death agony of a lore master as the strange shadow's power cut the old one to ribbons. Another time Colin had to leave Mearead's spell to throw a shield about himself as a fireball crashed into his body. But slowly the battle turned. The enemy's magic was strong, but even the least of dwarves has some ability to resist. The berserker strength of the dwarves that made them immune to pain and inhumanly strong, beat back the invading army.

One by one, the dark wizards were overcome by magic or ax blade. The cronbage and their allies died by the thousands. And magic or no, weariness and simple survival forced them to retreat. Mearead pushed his strength to the limit as he tried to break once and for all the enemy's power, to bring wreck and ruin on the Dark One's army. But his strength and Colin's was giving out.

Colin saw with his witch sight a glowing form pull itself from the cavern floor. It spread and the luminescence became unbearable, and with long arms it reached toward the shadow. The shadow thing contracted itself and fled. With that the dwarven magic could be turned on the enemy army alone and what would have been a retreat in good order became panic.

The dwarf power cut deep into the ranks of troll, goblin, and cronbage. What few wizards they had retreated as quickly as they could, leaving the warriors to the mercy of the dwarven berserkers.

The Dark Ones threw down their weapons and fought one another to flee through the narrow passages. They were chopped down from the rear, and as many as had died up to that time, twice as many fell now. With a gasp Colin allowed unconsciousness to take him as his strength finally gave out. But his ears still filled with the savage cries of the victorious dwarves. . . .

He awoke to the soft light of an oil lamp by his side. It took him a moment to realize he was in his own room. Colin smiled and stretched luxuriously in the cool sheets, his mind already working to dull the nightmare images of the battle.

"Well, good morning to you." Mearead pulled a stool up

and sat by the bed. His dark eyes unclouded, throwing the light of the room back.

"Ah, uncle," Colin just beamed. He felt light-headed, his whole body fresh and healthy. Mearead touched the other's hands lightly.

"You look good, boy."

"I don't know. I don't understand, I feel so, uh . . ."

"Better than a good drunk, huh?" Mearead laughed. "The Goddess's gift to you, boy. You fought well in the cavern." Colin pushed himself up on the pillows facing his uncle.

"What happened after I fell?"

"You can guess." Mearead's mouth went hard. "We hunted the scum down, slaughtered them like pigs. Even now our warriors track the Dark Ones through the bowels of the mountains."

"How long?"

"A week." That shocked Colin. A whole week lost is hard.

"So long," he murmured.

"You pushed yourself, boy. The trance you were in is a subtle trap for the uninitiated. It can lull you, and hold you tight, killing you before you know it." He brushed a lock of Colin's hair. "Partially my fault. I drew a lot off your power. I was pretty unmerciful about it." He sighed and looked away. "You were closer to death than you could imagine."

"We won. That's all that matters."

"Oh, aye, we won, and we had to. It was our only chance to catch the enemy together, to break them. Otherwise we would be fighting them in our halls for the next three hundred years." Colin was quiet for a moment.

"Uncle?"

"You should go to sleep, boy." Mearead started to stand up, but the young dwarf caught his arm.

"I've slept enough, thank you," he said, though even as the words came out he felt a deep weariness in his bones. "Just a few questions, then I promise I'll go to sleep." Mearead snorted once, but sat down.

"First, where did you come from?"

Mearead laughed, but his eyes were hard. "These are our caves, our mountains, Colin. And I am king. Somehow the enemy was able to build those tunnels and caves without my or the Goddess's knowledge, but," he held up a finger, "but it is still ours. It wasn't hard to find them once we thought about it. That cavern we fought in, it was humongous. Could I not feel the enemy's breath in all that space?"

"Okay, but how did you show up then, right when we needed you?"

Mearead put both hands on his knees, his long beard swinging. "That breath I felt was heady and foul. The enemy could not hide it from me. I sent you down that tunnel while I followed right next to you." He smiled. "The passage we went down was finished only the day before."

"You knew," Colin sat up straighter. "Why, you old bastard. You never even told me."

Mearead looked at Colin as if he studied something not particularly bright.

"Boyo, you have power, and one day maybe more than I wield. But," he emphasized, "you're still new to it. If I told you the plan, then the enemy could have picked it from your brain."

"So I was the bait."

"Yep." Mearead looked well-pleased with himself. "They did not know we knew that the cave you were in was right next to their main stronghold. We also knew they, whoever they are, could not resist the chance at attacking the heir to the throne."

"Why didn't you just attack them? Why did you need me?"

"Simple. We had to hide ourselves from their magic. If they were busy doing the same so you wouldn't find them, that was less strength they had to search for me."

Colin slapped his knees. "Well I'll be damned. Simple, direct, and absolutely brilliant."

"Oh, I could get to like you, boy," Mearead laughed.

"The cronbage . . ."

"Ah, yes," Mearead said, "the cronbage. You know what they are?"

"I know who they are, but not why."

"I really can't answer that, Colin. The cronbage were supposed to have been killed long years ago, when the Goddess and the Hunter fought the Fomarians for the rule of the world." He tugged his beard.

"We were young then, we dwarves, the only people to take part in that war. And," he shrugged, "the cronbage were our enemies, like the goblins are for the elves and humans. They were like us, but unlike us. Opposites. Long before ever a dragon dreamed of dwarven holds, the cronbage fought with us for the caverns of the mountains."

"They were supposed to have been wiped out when the fomarians were cast down," the young dwarf added.

"Yes, they were. The story goes that the Hunter tracked the few that survived and slaughtered them one and all."

"Then you think the Hunter . . . ?" Colin left the thought unsaid.

"Ha! Not that one. The cronbage are Fomarian slaves, heart and soul. Nope, the Hunter would never have anything to do with that lot."

"So who?"

Another shrug.

"Perhaps that duiraglym, that howling shadow."

"That's another thing. What the hell was that?"

"If I only knew." Mearead got up and walked about the bed, his hands emphasizing his words. "Whatever it was, it was a power! A great power. Unknown to me or any of the loremasters. Perhaps Arianrood or Lonnlarcan might know, maybe even Dammuth, but I have no idea."

"It ran from the Goddess."

"Yes, but I didn't detect any fear in it as it fled. At least no mortal fear." Mearead watched Colin's pale face. "Did you?"

Colin thought for a moment. "No, it was afraid of something, but not death, not of a trial of strength."

"Exactly. It was afraid." 'His eyes are too bright,' he thought.

"It was afraid," Colin repeated, going over bit by bit the whole of those last moments of consciousness, "it was afraid of Her. No, not of Her, but—Gods! It was afraid of the Goddess touching it, therefore knowing it . . . !"

Mearead slapped his hands together.

"Good, lad," but his smile quickly faded. "It has great power, Colin. Whether enough to contest the Goddess or not, well, She is constrained from true battle." He shook his head. "No, it was afraid She would recognize it, and let us know what power we faced. Frankly, that thing could be almost anything. Something the Goddess would know, perhaps from an earlier time."

Colin felt his strength leaving him and his body crying for sleep."

"Mearead, the cronbage."

"Aye, lad, the warriors of the Fomarians. If they are here could their master be far?"

"If that thing was a Fomarian . . ." he stopped, mumbled.

"Don't worry, lad." Mearead touched Colin's brow and sleep held the young dwarf tight. The king fixed his nephew's covers and gave him a light peck on the forehead. But his mind was elsewhere.

'If that thing was a Fomarian,' he thought, 'and the elder gods walk the earth, then surely this is the last war. . . .'

CHAPTER

Eight

That same night, a thousand miles away from the dwarven caves, another battle was being fought, and being lost. A tall man stood on a slope, silent. Around him his warriors muttered amongst themselves as the red flames a mile away lit the night sky.

Niall of the Long Arm wiped the sticky sweat from his face, grinding his teeth in frustration. He watched the destruction of the fort that had been his command, making no sound except an occasional swear when the cries of the men trapped behind reached him through the thin air.

He stood six feet six, his short, cropped blond head towering over his men. He wore scale armor, and strapped about his heroic frame was an awesome selection of weapons. The second son of the Archduke of Ruegal, Niall had been trained for war since birth. He had never been trained for defeat. All his strength and knowledge had been useless in the face of the enemy horde.

Six days earlier, he had with five hundred warriors prepared this place against the invaders. The completely controlled south plains and the mountains of Trulic were the only barrier between their continued advance and the lush farmlands of Ruegal.

Lying on the south side of the mountains, the fort had seemed like a perfect base of operations for raids against the enemy's strung-out supply lines. The fort was a wide vale a mile in diameter surrounded by the sheer walls of the mountain. An underground stream bubbled up to form a small lake. It was protected by one great wall across the only entrance to the vale.

The wall stood some thirty feet high and fifteen broad. Made of carefully placed rough-cut stone and possessing no gate, it had always proved impregnable. The enemy had captured the wall in three hours. . . .

The sides of the valley reached to incredible heights. The only way into the vale was through the wall, or so Niall and his war band thought. Somehow, the enemy had come behind the fort's defense, and only by the dint of Niall's fierce valor did some of the warriors escape. Escape to be trapped against the mountain's foot.

Niall counted some eighty-odd men with him, all that survived of his command. Not a one, including himself, was without a wound. They listened with anguish to the sounds of the rape of the vale. Soon, the enemy would seek them out, and here, with nowhere to retreat, the small force would be wiped out.

Any other leader would despair. But not Niall. He felt only anger. He had an unshakable faith in his own capabilities. He knew he would find a way out, and his fanatically loyal men waited in the sure belief that they were not defeated as long as their lord survived.

A small band of goblins warily approached the humans. A few arrows were enough to send them running. 'Now,' thought Niall, 'they will attack in earnest.'

"Sergeant, form the shield wall. Whatever archers are left, in the middle. I will take point." The sergeant nodded once, looking like a dwarf next to his lord. Quickly, the men formed a wall of swords. They made two lines like a 'V,' the ends right up against the mountain's sides. Hardly had they taken their positions than the invaders were upon them.

Like a great black wave, the goblins threw themselves on the men. There was a crash, screams, howls, and war shouts. The enemy withdrew in five minutes, leaving one quarter of their number behind. Quickly, the humans dispatched the enemy wounded. Only six of theirs had fallen.

A large goblin chief urged his troops on. Now some two hundred faced Niall's men. Quickly, the goblins were on them. The humans were so pressed that their long swords were useless. It was shortsword, dagger, and spear work. The enemy fell by the score, but exhorted by the chieftain, they continued to press, with others running up to join the battle and continually taking the place of the fallen.

Niall knew his men could not last. He stepped back from the front ranks. Immediately, two of his warriors took his place. The line of the shield wall held, but few reserves were left to close up any gaps. Niall's mind raced for an answer. He spotted the goblin chieftain and without a conscious thought, took action.

"Out of the way!" he yelled, moving through his warriors. Niall barreled into the enemy ranks. He had drawn his longsword again, and with a great two-handed blow, cleared a path to his enemy.

The chieftain was fast for his kind. Quickly, it threw a short-shafted spear at the approaching warrior. Niall turned it easily on his shield. The goblins raised a war ax to strike at the human. Without even slowing his rush, Niall held his sword two-handed straight ahead of him and thrust it deep in the goblin's throat. Leaving the sword there he withdrew his long dagger, and with maniacal fury charged the nearest enemy.

Four goblins fell and Niall received only a scratch on his thigh. None would face him and the whole group turned and ran. Niall's warriors pursued them a few yards and then worked their way back to the hill, making sure all the enemy on the ground were dead.

Now, barely fifty humans survived. Niall had the men collect the wounded warriors and drag them to the middle of the thinned shield wall. The goblins regrouped at the foot of the slope, screaming insults and waving their weapons menacingly. They were frightening to look at, with the light of the burning buildings at their back mixing with the dark shadows on the lake. But for all their taunts and ferocious mien, none approached the hill.

Niall walked up to his wounded. "I can't leave you to the swine, my bravos," he said. The warriors said nothing but stared back as bravely as they could. Quickly and painlessly they were dispatched by their lord, not a one making a sound of protest. Niall never hesitated in the grim task, but he felt each knife thrust in his own breast.

He stood wiping the blood from his hands. He had no intentions of dying here. He knew another leader would give the goblins courage and this time his men would be butchered. But the only emotion the war leader felt was anger. Aye, a warrior's death for him, but not now, not in an insignificant skirmish. . . .

A commotion in the enemy ranks caught his attention. From the midst of the enemy walked a large creature. Even in this light, Niall's sharp eyes could make out its features.

"A cave troll," he murmured. He frowned, taking in the great barrel chest, the two-jointed arms ending in three shovellike fingers. Now he understood how the enemy had breached the vale. He walked to the front of the ranks. 'More time,' he thought, 'more time.'

"Well, worm!" he shouted. "You look big enough to give me a half decent row. I dinna think your bonnie lasses have much stomach for this fight! Perhaps you and I should become a little better acquainted." Niall bared his teeth and rattled his weapons.

The troll growled, a wicked light burning in its shark eyes. Slowly, ponderously, it walked up the hill. The goblins shouted encouragement, breaking out in grotesque dances. The humans wondered if even their lord could defeat such a monster. Niall just waited.

The troll stopped three yards away. Niall's warriors moved away at his curt hand signal. Though his adversary stood only a few inches taller, it outweighed the man by four hundred pounds.

"Feth, manthing," growled the troll, "rip thy flesh, eat thy bones, this is good food for troll people." The creature had an apelike snout, but the top of its face angled back, giving it a bizarre appearance unlike anything Niall had ever seen.

"Och, now you have me shaking, you big turd," he answered. "Come now, my pretty, I tire of Niall Long Arm. Trollsbane fits me better." The creature gasped something in its guttural language and baring its two tusks, charged the human.

For all its bulk, the creature moved fast and its first rush nearly did Niall in. His hastily swung sword was easily blocked. The troll's powerful arms opened up to sweep him into death's embrace. The warrior feinted to the right and then dove between the troll's legs. He did a quick roll and before the slow-thinking monster could react, was on his feet behind it.

A bellow roared out of Niall's throat as his sword flashed at the troll's neck. With a thunk, the sword hit, but the creature's thick hide protected it. The sword barely cut an inch into its flesh. A brown liquid leaked out. The creature grabbed Niall's shield and threw the warrior ten feet to the side.

Niall smoothly rolled and met the troll's advance with a stop thrust. This time, the monster's inertia did what Niall's strength could not. The sword buried a foot of steel in its gut. The troll made no sound, but grasped the weapon around where it stood out from its chest with one hand, while the other gave Niall a terrific backhand that knocked him into the air and cracked his wooden shield.

The monster pulled the blade from its body and contemptuously snapped it in two. More brown fluid stained its midsection, but it showed no sign of weakening.

Niall withdrew a throwing dagger from his boot, and with a quick motion sent it at the troll's head. The dagger scored a long gash in its face, but again it took no notice. Niall barely avoided the troll's swing. He felt a burning pain along his arm. The creature had bitten through the mail and scored a painful, if harmless, wound.

The warrior backed up against the mountain's wall. In one hand he held a small throwing ax, while in the other he held a wide parrying dagger. The creature rushed again. This time Niall met the attack. He parried both arms with knife and ax while his helmeted head butted the troll viciously in the snout. It backpedaled a foot or two. Niall delivered a vicious kick to its knee. That kick would have broken bones in a bull. The creature gasped, but no crack of bone was heard.

Pressing his advantage, Niall swung the ax into the snout and simultaneously stabbed the knife under the creature's armpit. The knife stuck and the ax ruined the troll's face. But it retaliated with a clawed swipe that tore the man's helmet and sent him smashing into the mountain's side.

The creature's wounds were beginning to tell. Niall went for the face with the ax but was blocked. The troll's left hand raked into Niall's side. The armor shredded and Niall heard ribs crack. In desperation, he chopped at the small knee and this time was rewarded with a bitter snap. The troll shook its head, drunkenly slipping in its own foul-smelling blood.

Niall smashed the knee again and with a jerk straight up, drove the pointed end of the ax two-handed into the underside of the troll's snout. The troll punched the warrior's shield, demolishing it and nearly breaking Niall's arm. Once again he smashed into the mountain wall. The troll made a wild swing that Niall easily ducked. Its fingers ripped a deep gash into the stone behind his head. With a wordless shout, Niall swung the ax into the creature's snout. Such was the force of the blow that the ax handle broke and the creature fell like a tree newly cut. It did not rise.

"Trollsbane," chanted the warriors. "Trollsbane." His men took up the chant and turned on the already retreating goblins. They had no more wish to face this fierce warrior and once again took up their position at the foot of the slope.

Even as his warriors rejoiced in his victory, Niall finally faced the thought of defeat, for now at the foot of the hill were some four or five hundred goblins and more were streaming in to join them.

He shifted his great weight on the pile of his treasure. His mind roved in and through the black caverns. He felt the troll's hands dig in the wall. His mind flowed through the gate entrance to touch the welter of emotions beyond.

"Humans," he thought. His mind expanded further out to explore and identify all that happened in the vale. "It is early," he thought, "but this is a golden opportunity."

His thoughts swiftly centered on the doorway. "Someone knocking," he thought. "Impolite not to answer."

Two warriors helped Niall discard his ruined shield and placed a splint on the damaged arm. Another bound his wounds in dirty bandages. From behind, Niall heard a loud cracking noise and all four of the humans turned.

Where the troll's hand had torn the rock a thin line was seen. This line widened and as it did, three inches of rock facing crumbled and a bizarre doorway was revealed. Slowly, the door opened. It was shaped oddly in a disjointed geometric figure. Behind was only darkness.

Niall glanced down at the goblin hordes. There was no hope there.

"In," he gasped, "everyone in. Whatever is behind this doorway canna be worse than what waits for us here." Inwardly, he rejoiced. He knew this was a way out, knew he would not die this day. "Trollsbane," he mouthed silently, "Trollsbane."

The warriors shambled into the waiting darkness, trying to shield their movements from the enemy's eyes. With a great cry the goblins began to charge up the hill, but by now all the humans were within the door.

"We must close the damn thing," said one. Then as if in answer, the door quickly swung shut, fitting perfectly into the mountain face. The warriors stared about. They were in pitch blackness.

The goblins hammered at the door in a futile attempt to open it. Two cave trolls approached to try.

"Hold," came a voice. A rider garbed in a complete suit of black plate mail rode up on a skeletal horse. A helmet entirely covered his features. About his frame a purple haze shimmered. The goblins shrank from the figure.

"They have not escaped." His voice was harsh and scarcely human. "There is doom behind those walls and yours if you seek to follow." The goblins withdrew, leaving just the dark rider. He dismounted from his skeletal steed and approached the wall, stretching his fingers across the doorway. He assumed a position of listening and held it for a few minutes. A weird yelping sound echoed from the helmet, perhaps a laugh. With that he rode off into the black vale to enjoy what entertainment he could muster from the few captured humans.

Niall struggled to see in the darkness about him. The floor beneath his feet was smooth and free of debris. They seemed to be in a long, low tunnel with barely room for two men to walk abreast.

"Crohan," he called out, "you take point, laddie, and see you dinna fall into some great black hole." The young warrior edged past the others and slowly felt his way along the tunnel. The road took a slight downward trek but there was nothing on the floors for anyone to stumble on. They continued downward for some twenty minutes.

"Ye better clasp belts," cried Crohan from in front. "There's a bloody great cavern down here." The warriors carefully joined the man, all straining to catch a glimpse of their surroundings.

Suddenly, a great light burst in front of them. Momentarily blinded, the warriors struggled to assume some sort of defensive position. As their eyes adjusted to the light, they saw drifting in front of them a small flame. It floated about five feet off the ground, flickering and weaving in the still air. The flame made no move to attack, it would just float toward the men and then dart away about three feet.

After studying this odd behavior for a few minutes, Niall's mind clicked.

"Whatever it is, it wants us to follow," he said. "Our choices are limited. We either follow this wee bit of flame, or stand here like a great bunch of idiots. Or I suppose we could wander around aimlessly seeing who could get lost first." The men put on stern faces and followed their lord, the flame leading the way.

They went through ancient caverns, catching glimpses of statues, ornate pillars, doorways, and stairs. The flame led them deeper and deeper into the mountain. All recognized the place as some sort of dwarf dwelling, though none had ever heard of any of the wee people living in these mountains.

After more than an hour of walking, the men found themselves on a great thoroughfare wide enough for carts and horses. A sparkling was seen ahead, answering the tiny flame's bit of radiance.

As they approached, the sparkle became a bright sheen and the men were led to a great hall. It was full of treasure of unimaginable splendor. The roof was lost in the shadows above. Around the huge hall were lighted torches spaced every twenty feet or so.

"Visitors, oh welcome, welcome," came a voice from the chamber. The warriors warily walked through the great double doors that none had missed were made of beaten silver.

"This is so exciting," continued the voice. "Oh, do come in. Don't be shy." The voice emanated from the largest pile of treasure. Atop it was a wooden chair where an indistinguishable figure sat. It made vague motions to the men.

"Come, come, let me see you," it said.

Niall led the men in, carefully walking over the foot-deep treasure. His eyes noticed that all the treasure seemed to be curiously crushed, but could think of no reason for it.

"We beg your leave, my lord," he began, but the figure cut him off.

"No, no, no," it said, "I'm no lord. You got it all wrong, dear me." It seemed to lean forward toward the men. "Eyes aren't what they used to be, nope, not anymore. My, you are a big fellow, aren't you?"

The little flame stopped floating above the figure's head, which the humans could now see was an old man. He wore a dirty, frayed robe that might once have been white. A long scraggly beard reached to his waist. A hooked nose amid a million wrinkles was counterpointed by dark eyes that sparkled in the flame's light. In his hand, the old man held a staff that was so time worn it looked like it might crumble at any minute.

"My, my, *people*!" he shouted the word with joy. "Ah, goodness, by the flame, it has been so long. No one here, you know, 'cept me of course. Ah, yes, just me. Not even a little bitty rat or a big bitty rat." The old man crooned with delight. "Must have our jokes. Not much else to do around here, it is such a gloomy place."

Niall did not know what to make of the old man. Lugh only knew how long he had been here. His face was open and his obvious delight at seeing humans was apparent. He had the look of a wizard, albeit a senile one.

"We dinna mean to invade your hall, grandfather," Niall said. "We were trapped and we—"

Again the old man interrupted. "Yes, yes, I know. Nasty, vicious creatures those goblins, but I opened the door. You're safe, you know. I can show you right to the other side of the mountains. But," he added hesitantly, "you won't leave me here, will you?"

"Of course not," said Niall, his heart warming to the old one. "You have saved us, and, to be sure, we are glad for your company." All of the warriors had climbed the pile of treasure and stood in a loose circle about the chair. This pile was easily twenty feet high.

"Young man," the old one's voice cracked like a whip,

"you put that down this instant." In the back of the warriors one grinned with embarrassment and dropped a jewel he had picked up. "This isn't yours, you know, so don't any of you hulking warriors touch it! Bad things happen to those who try to take it . . ." Niall noticed a red gleam in the old man's eyes, a look that was quickly hidden.

'There is more to this one than appears,' he thought. But he was too tired to try and follow that thought.

"Now, you may call me Oidean," the old man continued, "and really, it's time for us to go. I really can't bear to stay a moment longer. It's so gloomy, don't you think?" Niall laughed and forgot his momentary doubt.

"My men are tired and hurt, friend Oidean, but in truth, we would all like to get away from these great black caves."

"Of course, of course," said Oidean. "I heard your fight with that awful troll. Good show, I say, and again, good show!" He got off his chair and fairly skipped down the pile of riches. "Trollsbane, a mighty name for a mighty lord," he said. "Off we go now and do see you don't disturb anything. One, two, three, people, people, people," he laughed.

The men followed after their new companion. The way was long and the old man talked constantly, his voice reverberating across the unseen caverns, the little flame seeming to dance with joy in front of them. The men shared grins; they couldn't help but laugh at the old man's antics.

Oidean informed them that he really wasn't sure how long he had been in the caverns or why he was there. He did proudly state he was a wizard after all.

"A fire wizard, you know," he said. "Oh yes, yes, I used to blow things up all the time, but my, my, so long ago. I really don't remember what I blew up. But I think it was fun, you know. Don't you think it would be fun to blow things up? Not to hurt anyone, of course, just blow things up." Niall solemnly agreed he thought it would be great fun.

The trip was marred by only one thing. While walking through a vast cavern, a stalactite fell and killed the man who had picked up the jewel. Oidean shook his head knowingly but said nothing. Carefully, the warriors bundled their dead comrade up and continued the journey.

Finally, they came to a blank wall and a crack was heard. Another oddly shaped door opened and the warriors found themselves in a little valley. They threw themselves down in exhaustion, the door closing behind them. Oidean turned to Niall.

"Don't worry, the Dark Ones will never use that passage. The old dwarven magic keeps them out." Before Niall could answer, a warrior tapped him on the shoulder.

"I know this place," he said. "We're not two marches away from Ruegal Keep." Niall ordered three warriors that were in the best shape to seek a nearby village and get help.

The wizard happily offered to light the fire and lived up to his word. He blew a great hole in the earth. The old man nearly burst into tears at the thought of killing the grass and insects and Niall was hard-pressed to calm him down. In spite of himself, Niall, who was usually cold to others, found himself liking the old gentleman. And, he noted, anyone that could blow a hole into the ground could be a help in this war.

Three days later, Niall and his men with the wizard approached Ruegal Keep. The keep was built on a great plateau that was really a series of five plateaus. Each was at a different level, getting higher in progression, forming a giant five-step circular stairway. It was said that once the Gods of Light themselves lived there and that it was they who created the plateau stairs. The keep was the largest city of the empire next to Tolan, holding some thirty thousand people.

Niall held up his horse to take in the magnificent sight of his clan's home. Great walls surrounded the city on all sides and on the last stair a giant fortress of red marble looked down on the world at its feet. Niall's heart swelled with pride. This was his home and, though he was the second son, he was sure he would be the next duke and rule this glorious citadel.

At the foot of the bottom plateau stood the first great gate. Here, one of his father's lords escorted Niall and the wizard to the top. People and soldiers shouted greeting to Niall, the cry "Trollsbane" ringing in his ears. At the door of his father's court, he was given a bright gold-worked cloak and a ceremonial sword. The wizard had long since been given a new white cloak.

The bronze doors swung open and the court, jeweled and dazzling in the splender of the Empire, bowed as one to the two travelers. Niall's father, Mannon, Archduke of Ruegal, sat on a throne of the same red marble that covered the walls. On his brow was a silver circlet. Niall's brother stood at his sire's right hand while a stranger stood on the left.

The Archduke's hawklike features were blunted some by a golden beard, now greying a little. He got off the throne and hugged his son in his bearlike arms.

"Honor and glory you bring to our house, Trollsbane," he said in a gruff voice. "Sure and it is glad to have you back I am." Mannon turned to the old man and smiled. "Och, now this is my son's savior, eh? My house is at your service."

The wizard's face turned a bright red and he mumbled, "It's nothing," his smile shy and happy.

Niall's brother, Shiel, approached his brother as if he was approaching a wild bull. The two clasped arms, if not warmly, at least with mutual respect.

"It's a great deed you have done, my brother," said Shiel grudgingly.

"Thank you for your praise," answered Niall. "And sure it is good to be home," he said to his noble father.

"We'll have a grand feast tonight," said Mannon, "to celebrate your return."

"And the war," said Niall, "how does it go?"

"Ah, tomorrow we'll talk of it. Tonight is a night for enjoyment, not talk of war." Niall did not say he preferred to talk of the war, but gave a graceful bow.

* * *

The next morning, the two brothers joined their father in his study. Both were a little worn around the edges after the night's festivities, but were friendlier thanks to an all night drinking binge. As they entered the room, Niall was surprised to see the same warrior who had been with his father in the court.

"Niall," said the Archduke, "this is Colonel Mathwei ap Niall," his son smiled at the name, "of the imperial cavalry," finished Mannon. Niall looked over the other. Mathwei was pale, his eyes hidden. He bore newly won scars, but still he gave the others a friendly grin.

"Colonel," Niall nodded.

"The Colonel was at the battle of Greenway," Mannon said.

"I'm sorry I missed that one," Niall answered. Mathwei's grin disappeared, and he said nothing.

"It was a great victory," added the duke, though his voice was quiet.

"We lost a lot of men," Shiel interjected, his voice deep.

"What's happened in the last week?" Niall asked. He and his brother sat at the table with the others.

"A force was to be left at Comar, to try and hold it," Mathwei shrugged. "I was ordered here on the fifth, so I don't know whether it's been attacked yet."

"The latest dispatches," the Archduke added, "suggest that Comar will be attacked within a matter of days." He reached for the goblet in front of him. "And to be sure, they know the city can't be held."

"Then the enemy will reach Tolan?" asked Niall.

"Without a doubt, boyo." The Archduke waved toward Mathwei. "The colonel here has been sent with important orders."

"Lord Fin of Dun Scaga, at the request of General Ernet, has been chosen Warlord of the West." Mathwei didn't look at any of the others or touch his wine. "General Fintan holds

Comar. Your father has been named Warlord of the East. In his hands is the defense of the whole empire from Brest to the Tivulic mountains and across to the port cities."

"So." Niall said nothing more, his mind trying to picture the strategic situation.

"By the end of the month," Shiel added, "the enemy will be at Tolan's gates. It's there that the next major battle will be."

"Two Warlords," Niall murmured.

"If Tolan falls, the empire will crack like a bad egg," Mannon said.

"We hope the elves will reach us in time to help, but with the elder people, one can never be sure. So we need to gather all the men we can." The faces of Mathwei's three sisters flashed through his mind. "We must hold Tolan!" All were surprised by his vehemence.

"With the emperor dead, with one son lost, the other insane," Mannon said, "and Dammuth missing," Mathwei winced at that, "there is no other leader to hold the empire together. Without the elves we may end up isolated, cut off from one another, laddie."

"All of the empire's troops have been given to Warlord Fin," Shiel added. "It's with our own men we must hold the East."

"You have been given a commission in the army," Mathwei handed Niall a scroll, "with the rank of general. The imperial troops still in the East have all been gathered here. They are your command. You are to bring them to Tolan immediately."

"Mathwei is your second-in-command," the Archduke added. Niall looked at the other. So young for such a command, he thought, forgetting the fact he was barely five years older. His father caught his look.

"The colonel has been in every major engagement of the war," he said. "He's still alive. Listen to what he has to say, son." Niall smirked.

"Shiel will take a force to the east to keep the enemy

behind the mountains." The Archduke reached out over the table and grabbed his son's hand. "We may be separated for the duration, lad," he said. "Sure am I you'll add great deeds to the book of Ruegal."

For the next two days the plan was finalized. It was decided that Oidean should go with Niall; perhaps in time he would remember his magical powers. "If he has any," added Shiel. But Niall was glad to have the old man.

That night in camp Oidean lay still in his cot. His consciousness flew back to its rightful home. He sighed happily to feel the strength and power of his true form. A chuckle escaped through his lips; he had been so clever, so devious.

Luxuriating in the steam and heat of his chamber his mind wandered back to a few weeks before. He had been sleeping for a long time, long even for his kind. Then the pressure of a demand had built in his mind until he could no longer ignore it. He woke. He listened. He made his pact. And he planned as only he, the last of his people, could.

The deception was well thought out, he had been quick to take advantage of circumstances. His illusion was strong; only Arianrood was powerful enough to break it, and he didn't have to worry about that one. And he had not lost the magic of his words.

He was clever, clever, and the game had only begun. Before he was done there would be surprises for everyone involved, oh, yes, everyone. He opened his mouth and consumed some of his treasure, the creative energy that had formed his meal infusing him with revitalized strength. This horde would last him long, and soon there would be new additions to it. He laughed again, silently, contentedly. Oh, yes, this was a good game, a fine game. Blouie! And his laughter filled the caverns.

CHAPTER

Nine

Lonnlarcan, Ard Riegh of the elves of Cather-na-nog, struggled with uncharacteristic exasperation. For three hundred years he had ruled his people and never had it been such a burden as now. A month and a half ago, Tolath had been invaded and since the first day of the attack, Lonnlarcan had been trying to pull his armies together to assist his human allies.

The king sat in his great hall of Dummo Sorcha. It lay underneath a green hill covered with Richliess, the silver flowers of elfdom. No one could say how large that ancient hall was since the dimensions changed constantly.

There was no ceiling. Above the great king the ancient night sky loomed. The bright, multicolored constellations revolved around each other in the slow dance of life, as they had before the sun had been born. It is said the sky roof is really a doorway into the first times. It is true that in this hall the Ard Riegh controlled time, so a day could seem a month or a year or a week. Since the invasion, the king and his advisors had been planning in the hall for one long day.

The throne of Lonnlarcan is formed by a great root, a piece of the world tree that binds all that is living. The floors and walls were made of mosaics and tapestries that constantly formed and reformed to present marvelous tales of the first people. Behind Lonnlarcan's throne lay the ancient tapestry of Cuin Finnen which can predict the future or futures to come. Now it was strangely blank. No answers came from that corner.

In the hall, tables were placed in a seemingly random plan, though to elvish eyes it surely had some meaning. On the floor at Lonnlarcan's feet, a great world map sprawled, all bright and glowing colors, except where Darkness ruled. In these areas, a black stain covered the land. As the elves watched, the darkness spread across the land of Tolath.

"It will be at Tolan," said the king. At his words the map glowed a deep red where the city lay. "We ride at the rising of Dahy Dryw."

"My lord," spoke one of his advisors, the mage Fiachra. "We will be able to bring only three thousand if we leave so soon, four thousand counting your guard."

Lonnlarcan stared at the other's long golden hair, fingering his own silver locks. "Nevertheless, we ride." Fiachra's purple eyes showed a hint of defiance. "There is no choice, my friend. Tolan will fall if we are not there."

"With only four thousand, it may fall anyway, my lord," added another.

"No time, the Aislinneenna slows us at every turn. The people fear and indulge in the dream world more than they should."

"You could stop them, my lord," answered Ceallac, the king's cousin.

Lonnlarcan gestured to the other's mail-clad body. "War is too much to your liking, cousin. You are too fierce to fear as the people do. My power must be saved for the coming war. I'll not waste it in trying to control the uncontrollable."

Silence came to those about the king. In the way of the elves they opened themselves and shared their souls with one another. It was not telepathy, but a type of empathy that allowed each to be the other for a moment or a lifetime.

"Then it is agreed. Let the blood horn be lifted and the hosting begin." Even as he spoke, the horn was sounded and a great wailing filled all the elf nation. Those that were to respond knew and prepared their weapons and horses. Fire and magic ran through the elves and burned them with a fierce delight as they prepared for the hosting. Only a people who had no fear of death would respond so—only the elves.

"And, my lord," said Fiachra, "who will lead the army?"

In answer, Lonnlarcan rose from his throne and walked behind it. In that moment, all the elves of Cather-na-nog held their breath. At the foot of Cuin Finnen lay a scabbarded sword. The king grasped the silver handle.

"No!" cried the elves in the hall. Lonnlarcan started to withdraw the blade. "My lord," cried Fiachra in despair, "never has an Ard Riegh led the first host. Never does he leave this hall except in the worst of circumstances. Never since the elves have been has the Ard Riegh ridden in the first hosting!"

Underneath the Cuin Finnen, Lonnlarcan was a proud shadow amongst the beauty of the hall.

"Never has the enemy possessed such power in so short a time . . . I will ride. I will lead. And I *will* reap!" As the chant was voiced, the king's form filled with a bright light. He drew the sword and the hill shuddered. All that was evil in the world from the highest to the lowest felt a cold wind of doom and knew fear.

And in the darkest of all dark planes, in a place that ate and destroyed life, a patch of darkness raised itself up and a black chain rattled. A voice, a voice that would kill if any heard it, a voice that was all evil and more, spoke for the first time in long ages.

"You show yourself too soon, Witch King." And all that was evil and that had allied itself to Darkness shook once more and grew brave.

Moments after the blade was drawn, a naked elf dismounted and walked to the edge of a small lake deep in the heart of Cather-na-nog. The water was a rich and deep blue, but gave off no reflection. The elf was Cucullin, and with the Ard Riegh, Ceallac, and the warrior maid Breeda, was the greatest of all the elves in war. His naked body was proud and unbending. His compact muscles flowed across his tall frame.

In his mind's eye, Cucullin saw himself in golden armor, the great ax, Kervalen, slung across his back. In the Dark Seign wars, his father had lost the armor and the ax to the demon, Apkieran. For a hundred years Cucullin sought to recover that which was lost. Finally, through the power of the Aislinneena, he relived his quest and succeeded. The power of the armor and the ax were the elf lord's as any who stood against him would find.

The elf's beardless face (none of the elven kind, and very few of the half-elven, can grow facial hair of any sort), boasted a great scar that ran from chin to brow line. Cucullin's golden hair was braided in one long braid that reached his waist.

He knelt to the water and breathed once.

"Sister of the first people," he said quietly, "it is I, Cucullin. Come to me and speak of what only you may know. Come, sister, and touch your servant with the hand of wisdom."

For a moment all the green land around was quiet. No birds or animals moved. None of the fair people, the brown elves, sang or laughed. When their land of Mai Methra was destroyed in the old wars many of that people sought refuge in Aes Lugh, but there they dwindled. Here in this valley and the hillsides surrounding it, the greatest of those who had survived came to be with she who was their goddess, though they marched to war no more.

The dark green lake stayed calm. No wind ruffled the waters. Then, the lake contracted and bulged up at its center as if a blanket was picked up by its middle. The water receded inches from Cucullin's hand. The newly formed water spout glistened in the light and formed into a beautiful elven woman. Her pale body was entwined by green-gold hair that floated on the breeze lightly as if she lie under the water still. Her body was curved and rounded, soft and sensuous. Oversized eyes stretched far across her face. There were no pupils or whites, just a deep and changing blue. Her ears were pointed as the elves', but larger. They would seem to detract from her beauty, but added instead.

"I know why you have come, warrior, and I do not want to give you what you seek." Her voice was so soft it was barely audible.

"Sister of my people, I must know," he said. He went down on bended knee. "Apkieran has come to the world, has he not?"

"Ah, leave it, Bright One, the universe is lighter for your honest loyalty."

"I cannot. My father's death is the blackest sin the world has ever seen." Tears filled the grey eyes of the elf.

"Ah, Cucullin, you are not meant to be a warrior. Vengeance has been the undoing of so many. Must you fall, too?" Still she stayed and he knew she would answer him.

"Lady, lady, vengeance and justice are separate. Of all the elves that have been, only my father has been totally destroyed, died in a way that even mortals cannot. Body, soul, and spirit Apkieran took. He will pay for this." The elf raised himself up and faced the prophetess across the expanse of water.

"Of all that have come to me since the war, few could I help. Lonnlarcan himself came, and though I respect him above all others, I have not the power to answer the riddle of this war." Her eyes filled with the sight of the elf before her. "I know the question you would speak and it is a black deed that I must answer."

"Tell me," cried Cucullin, "can I find him? Will I meet him? Once I faced him, once I nearly defeated him. I must have his life." The sun blackened over the two and the air became chill at the elflord's words.

"Listen, Cu, listen to one that cares for you as a lover. The power of the Aislinneena cannot take what I have, the answer you seek cannot change even with the full power of the elves."

"Tell me," he urged.

"Of all the elves, you have used the Aislinneena the wisest, remembering your father's death, going through pain after pain in order to grow stronger. Once only have you used the dream power and it will be your bane. I am not the only one who can defeat the Aislinneena, not anymore."

The elf didn't know of what she was speaking. In all his long life, Cucullin of all the elves had only used the Aislinneena once, and of course could not remember doing so. He had no fear of any who could destroy the power, though a part of him reeled in the revelation that one existed besides the lady who could defeat the Aislinneena. Whoever had such a power must be cast down or all works of the elves could be undone.

"I have paid a price willingly, that all my people have shunned. I have trained to be the strongest I could so that the black life of the Undead Lord would flow through my fingers. Now I must know. Will I meet him in this war?"

A sigh escaped the lady like wind across the water. Her eyes filled with crystal tears. "You have asked three times and I must answer. In all my days never have I despised what I am, my power, as I do now. Ah, Cu, you could have joined me in time, a lord of the Bright World, a god to the mortals who seek gods so desperately. Ah, Cu, such brightness to the sad world you could have brought. . . ." Once more she sighed and the land around her lake was browned as if fall had come; here, where it had never been before.

"Here is my reed, Cucullin. Great deeds will you do and your power shall be a pillar that upholds the Light. Not the least of your deeds shall be the undoing of the Lord of the Undead, should the two of you meet." The elf's heart leapt at her words. "But Cucullin, warrior prince, shall not grace the world long with his bright soul, for though he brings the demon down, it shall only be at the price his father paid before him and the demon's death shall come at the hands of another. Apkieran shall die with the sacrifice of Cucullin. Apkieran shall be destroyed by he who is the master of all things of this world."

At these dark words, the elf felt no fear, for though the price the prophetess named was terrible, to his warrior soul it was worth the destruction of his enemy.

"I thank you, my lady, and though I know I could never hope to share your world with you, always will I remember that if things had been different I could have been yours." With a deep bow, the elf withdrew and mounted his horse.

"It is not too late, Cu." Her voice wrenched his noble heart. "You could turn from your revenge and we could become one."

"What must be done, must be done, most beautiful of all," he called back. "One soul for the defeat of such evil is never too much of a price to pay and I will pay it happily." With that he left.

"You are wrong," whispered the lady, "it is always too high of a price." With that the lake became still and smooth again, though now it was grey and all the land around it lost its elven spring and became bare and empty as if winter had struck where it never could. The animals and all living things left, until only the bare trees and a grey lake were left, a monument to the despair and pain of a goddess.

In the valley of Ogan, the elven army gathered. The valley was surrounded by giant trees that have no name. Their bark glistened with a silvery light and the branches were all a light orange shade. The leaves were a riot of colors that all blended in a beautiful tapestry of lights and darks. The valley itself had no growth except a thick carpet of green moss.

The stars burned larger and brighter here than anywhere in the world, but no moon was ever seen in the valley of Ogan. Underneath the daybright stars the elves rode singly and in groups, arranging themselves in a chaotic profusion of order. Underneath that magic light, the elven eyes burned.

They all rode the great elven horses, giant animals, deep of chest and muscular. Many of the steeds, under the influence of magic, were colored as no other horses could be.

The colors ranged the full spectrum of the rainbow and in hues that no mortal eye can perceive.

They were saddled with gold and silver, and though they all had stirrups, not a one had a bridle. The elves did not rule the horses, they fought as partners. And for all the color, braids, and jewels, none would mistake these animals for anything but great beasts of war.

The elves were no less a wonder than the horses. They wore full body armor, all silvers, greens, and golds. Each wore a torc of silver around their necks with a priceless gem set within it. Many wore more jewels around brow and hair. The weapons glowed and glittered, each a deadly instrument of death. If the stars themselves gathered in the valley, the elves would outshine them.

Lonnlarcan looked across the host. Everything that met his eye was beautiful and deadly. Power flowed through that valley, wild and strong, and it infused everything it touched.

"It is beautiful, is it not, my king?" said Ceallac. He was covered in ebony armor trimmed with gold, matching his black hair and golden eyes. Ceallac's eyes were maniacal as the soul within delighted at the thought of war.

"Ceallac, this is no war of glory we face. It is the blackest hour of the world. I see nothing beautiful in it." Lonnlarcan's silver armor shed a light of its own.

"Ah, cousin, if you saw with my eyes. . . ." His face glowed with magic. "I doubt not your words. The greatest threat of all is what we face. And though you may not understand, it is in that that I rejoice," he answered.

"Am I not the first in war, Driven One? I understand better than you could now." As Lonnlarcan finished, Fiachra rode up with several elven knights. In his hand he held a golden spear covered with runes of deep red.

"Kianbearac, my lord." Reverently the old elf handed his king the mighty spear. Lonnlarcan took it and gingerly held it in his hands, studying the runes.

"Old One," he addressed the spear, "mighty are your

deeds and never have you failed the people in need. Now I need you more than ever."

"My magic is not what it once was, my lord," said Fiachra, "but two warnings I give. Draw the elven sword as a last resort, for it is doom and salvation." He turned to Ceallac. "And to you, warrior, I give this warning: to fight and strive you were born but such deeds should always be the last resort. Be not so proud of your strength for the enemy knows the lure of pride and is aware of all weakness."

"Fiachra, my cousin I'm sure understands your words, but all I hear is the promise of battle. It is for battle I live and breathe. Nothing can change that," answered the warrior prince.

"Into your hands I leave my kingdom," said Lonnlarcan to his advisor. "Only three of the Shee do I bring with me. The others I leave to your care. The battlemaid Breeda will stay with you and help train them for war. Keep them well, Fiachra. Much will depend on the young ones."

"As you will, my lord," Fiachra answered with a bow.

Around the leaders the elven host was singing, some dancing on their horses' backs. All who were to come were present and they only awaited the king's desire.

"People of the trees! Warriors of the stars!" began Lonnlarcan, and as he spoke the elves became silent. "I lead this first hosting because we must strike deep into the enemy and off-balance them so we may have time to build our strength." He lifted Kianbearac in his hand. "The greatest danger faces us. Fight and reap, my warriors, fight and reap!"

With that the air filled with a multitude of horns rising up in one great note of defiance. As one, the elves wheeled the horses around and rode from the valley in silence. A mortal a hundred yards away might have felt a vague misgiving, but no sound would he have heard and no elf would he have seen.

Fiachra and those left behind headed back to the king's

hall, not a one doubting that they must prepare for the bloodiest war the world had known.

The next day Cucullin caught up with the elven host as it neared the borders of Cather-na-nog. The silent warriors flowed around him as he waited for the king. Lonnlarcan slowed his golden mount. Ceallac joined them and the three rode in the rear.

"The lady weeps in her caverns, Cu," said the king.

"Aye, my lord, and would that it could be otherwise, yet I must follow my destiny."

The king shook his head sadly. "Your father said the same once."

"Friend Cucullin, what is it that has so torn the Goddess?" interrupted Ceallac.

"Ah, would that I could feign misunderstanding," answered the warrior. He then told the others of all that had passed at the lake.

"This bodes evil for our people," said Lonnlarcan. "If the enemy possesses the power to defeat the Aislinneena, much of our strength will be useless."

"And the pyridin, my lord," said Cucullin, "such a power would destroy them with ease."

"We must find who or what controls this power and defeat it quickly," added Ceallac.

"There is no choice, such a one is our greatest threat. Ceallac, ride to Teague and Baibre. Have them turn our mages to the quest of finding who wields this power. Also have a message sent back to inform Fiachra." Ceallac rode forward in a burst of speed.

"Cu," Lonnlarcan turned to the warrior, "will you not turn from your black path?"

"Nay, my lord. There is nothing you can say, no command you may give that can dissuade me. Whatever else happens, I will be the bane of Apkieran." The king's witch sight saw the dark nimbus surrounding the warrior and knew that this pledge could not be broken, the doom light shone bright around Cucullin.

"As you will," he said quietly. "Wait." He stopped his horse. Suddenly a creature appeared in front of the two elves. It stood about four feet tall and though humanoid, was impossibly skinny. Its skin was a dusky grey, a perfect match for the deep-set grey eyes, split like a cat's.

The creature was apparently sexless and though it bore no weapon, it projected an aura of danger. From the corners of its slanted eyes two thin filaments of skin or hair projected to the tips of its pointed ears. Its fingers were abnormally long and ended in black talons.

It shifted uneasily from foot to foot, its body making odd jerking movements as if it were unused to standing still for any period of time. It bent sideways at an impossible angle in a parody of a courtly bow. Neither elf missed the fact that the bow was to Cucullin.

"Dorrenlassarslany," Lonnlarcan named it, "I am glad for your help."

"No choice, witchlord. Need great elf things to fight deepest unhealth in land." The creature looked sullen. Its voice was oddly flat and dead. It turned to Cucullin, its voice changing to an excited high-pitched twitter. "Pyridin peoples know of Lady Orlaith's words of choices to you. Great and good from us, for your choice is well made and honorable. Less gods, more dead unthings, is our will."

"I thank you for your words, Dorrenlassarslany-s," answered Cucullin. "More choices to your people is a boon that I hope my quest will fulfill."

The pyridin danced around more at these words and smiled to show cracked and browned fangs. "Choice, choice," it sang, "that is the good thing. But," its voice went dead again, "unthings narrow, destroy choice. We help great elf things. They help us." It looked up at Lonnlarcan. "Great unmaker must be called. Unthings know of elves' plan. Kill and rend instead."

"The Morigunamachamain knows of the hosting. He will come when it suits him," answered the Ard Riegh.

"No, no," it squealed. "He is with a maker, but the unmaker must ride with elves, to rend. Great dark master wait for elves, must have unmaker, must rend."

"Ambush, and we need the Morigu to face it," said Lonnlarcan. "I will call the Morigu, the unmaker. I cannot say whether he will come."

"Will, must come," it sighed. "No choice for unmaker, steed wait, must come."

"Stop, make a circle," said the elf king. Immediately the elves returned to him and the silent army encircled the two. Ceallac, Baibre, Cainhill, and Teague joined Lonnlarcan and Cucullin. Ceallac gave the pyridin a disdainful look.

"Why do we stop, cousin?" he asked, making no attempt to hide the irritation in his voice.

"Somehow the enemy knows of our approach," the king answered. "The pyridin know of an ambush ahead, but insist we call the Morigunamachamain."

"Margawt," muttered the lord Cainhill.

"Aye, I trust not that one, but he is the only one there is." Lonnlarcan dismounted his horse and the others moved away from him. With no further discussion, he squatted down and touched the ground lightly, chanting softly. He then took the spear Kianbearac and touched its tip to the ground. The king's voice grew louder as a silver aura covered his body. Soon, one word could be made out.

"Brestalo, Brestalo." The chant became deeper and the spear began to pulse to it. It was the pulse of a heartbeat and the word punctuated the rhythm, "Brest-alo, Brest-alo." The grass began to undulate with the beat and soon the ground rippled away from the spear as if someone had thrown a rock in a pond. The chant continued for a few moments until it met resistance, a wave hitting a ship.

The Ard Riegh continued it for a moment. "Brest-alo, Brest-alo," again and again impressing his message. Finally, an answering shudder shook the spear. Lonnlarcan stood up, the silver light immediately winked out. The pyridin appeared in front of him and bobbed its head once.

"I was not sure he would answer. The power of the elves does not reach into the earth's veins. The trees and grass are our domain."

"He heard," said the little one, his voice now gentle and friendly.

The others joined the two. "Now," said Lonnlarcan, "what great dark master dares to try and ambush my people?"

The creature seemed to lose its size and began to bound about, practically running in circles. "Great less god." It fell flat on the grass, twitching. Quietly it said, "Fomarian."

The elves as one gasped. Fomarians were demigod. Once they had in the twilight years been among the chief powers of the world. Now they were less, but their power was still great.

Lonnlarcan looked down at the twitching creature. "I must have a full explanation of this, Dorrenlassarslany. Ceallac, call the war council." Ceallac bowed once and rode off. "Lord Cainhill," the warrior turned his purple eyes to the king, "take your people ahead to the border." Cainhill saluted and turned his mount around, riding off in a burst of unnatural speed.

A chair was brought for the king and he sat quietly, waiting for the council to all appear. His eyes were blank and roamed in a place far and away from elves and men. For the first time in his memory, Lonnlarcan was unsure.

The Morigu felt the Ard Riegh's call and at first was not inclined to pay attention, but then he felt the High King's insistence. He wondered at that for Lonnlarcan knew Margawt was coming to join the elves. The Morigu sat on the ground and extended his knowledge. Quickly, his perception flew to the elves. They were not hard to find. The land's acceptance of the elves always verged on ecstasy. Wherever there was an elf, the land was cleaner, healthier. Few elves had the taint of wrongness and those that did had so little it was infinitesimal compared to what the other creatures of the world usually possessed.

The Morigu knew the pyridins' fear and discomfort and realized it was because of this that he was called so urgently. He went past the elves, beyond the borders of Cather-na-nog. His body jerked once and he felt his stomach churn with distaste.

"A Fomarian," he said aloud. Somehow the enemy had revived the monster and it led a large army. How it got past the humans and so near the elvish border he could not guess. Once again, Margawt was amazed by the Dark Ones' incredible power.

He leapt to his feet. "Anlon!" he cried with voice and magic. The unicorn appeared behind him.

"Yes, I heard the call, too," the unicorn said. Margawt spun to face his comrade.

"A fomarian," Margawt's eyes were wild. Anlon bowed his head once.

"Yes, the Goddess' ancient enemy." He snorted black fire. "Who has the power to unbind them? Why does the Goddess remain at the dwarven caves? She should be here to fight her old enemies."

"Unless," Margawt shuddered at the thought, "there were others freed. And one attacks the Crystal Falls."

"Margawt, this is black news." Anlon danced nervously on the broad lawn. "There were seven of the Fomarians left after the Goddess and the Hunter cast them down. Seven to be bound until the end of time. But someone has freed them. How can this be?"

Margawt ran a hand through his thick hair. "Maybe, Anlon," he said, "maybe no one freed them. Maybe they freed themselves."

"Impossible."

"Perhaps, but it could be we are not at war with the Dark

One, but with the Fomarians. Perhaps they have come to claim the world once more." The unicorn's red eyes stared at the sky as if the answer would be written there.

"I don't know, Margawt, I don't know. It makes sense but I doubt it. They could never have attained the power they once had." Again Margawt felt the cry of the land, far away, as the Fomarian shaped it with its magic.

"There," his voice was weak, "are still raiders, Anlon."

"You must go, Margawt," Anlon answered. "You are needed with the armies."

"So you've said over and over these last weeks." The elf turned away. He tried to cut off the rush of magic through his feet. "The others," he made a vague gesture about him, "the others, sometimes they are wrong . . . sometimes I can't tell what is a danger, what is wrongness to be attacked!" He pressed his fingers into his forehead.

"Margawt, you must," Anlon moved closer, "you must ride with the Ard Riegh's army." He struggled for words. "The, the enemy does not know you exist. You are our weapon, maybe our best."

"Weapon!!" screamed the Morigu, his voice breaking. "Oh yes, the promise." He bit his lip, drawing blood. "A weapon to wield vengeance, that is what I am. The sword of two edges. I cut both ways, Anlon. . . ."

"The Fomarians are ancient evil, Margawt." Anlon's hooves stamped. "You must fight them."

"Goblins are evil," Margawt turned to the other, his face purple with his anger, "I know that. I know what they do. I've seen what they do. I've . . ." his words failed him.

"Margawt, goblins are the slaves of such as the Fomarian. Cut off the head and the body dies!"

"I know that," the elf laughed a hard sound. "I know all about that!" He withdrew his knife and slit his hand across the palm. Staring at the blood he whispered, "I bleed, too. We all bleed, but we don't all die. . . ."

"Margawt," Anlon's voice was gentle, "it is your destiny."

"Some say," he turned pleading eyes to the unicorn, "some say Dammuth has betrayed us."

"How..." Anlon shook his great head, "where could you have heard such a lie!"

"I can hear almost anything, anywhere I want, Anlon." The unicorn's eyes widened at that. This was a power the elder Morigunamachamain never had. "I can hear the cries of the newborn, the curses of the dying. I have heard this said. I have heard it said by many."

"It is a lie!" Anlon's fire from his nostrils burned the grass at his feet. "A lie!"

"It is said!" Margawt shouted back. "Who could free the Fomarians? You say they could not do it themselves. Dammuth could. We know that Dammuth could!"

"There are other powers."

"Other powers," the elf spat, "always other powers." He walked away again, saying nothing. Finally, he turned back. "So be it," he shook his bleeding fist, "so be it. If Dammuth has turned, I will kill him. KILL!!!!!" The shout turned to a wail—stopped suddenly. "I have to," he finished quietly.

"Margawt."

"No. No more," he gasped. "I must go. I must fight this thing." The unicorn's fierce features somehow showed his pity for the Morigu's plight.

"On my back, Margawt," he said, moving to the other. "I have not found you to desert you. It is time the Morigu went to war." Margawt leapt on the unicorn's back. All his mind, his thoughts, chaotic as the need of the earth increased.

"Kill!!" he cried, though he did not know he said anything. Anlon took off, forgetting the threat ahead of him as his heart filled with pain for the poor, mad boy.

He wasn't unaffected by the power of the Morigunamachamain. He could feel the earth magic reaching through his body to grasp the soul of Margawt. It was unbearable. 'Mother,' he thought, 'how could you be so cruel . . . ?'

The Morigu drew his sword, screaming in bloodlust, urging Anlon on. And lost in the wind of their great speed as the two rode to war were their tears, one shed them from pity, the other from pain.

CHAPTER

Ten

Lonnlarcan reined in and turned to Ceallac. Pointing ahead he said, "See cousin, the hills seem to narrow through here. Our scouts say the whole land is shaped like a funnel, a downed tree there, a rock slide there. It is as the pyridin has said. The Fomarian seeks to have us follow the path he has laid down, follow right into his powerful arms."

"If we had not been warned," said Ceallac, "we would've ridden right into it."

"Aye, we will circle around and trap the monster, but surprise will not be enough. The fomarians were once the earth gods. Only the Goddess could face them. Then the Hunter joined her and the young gods against the fomarians. Our people were in their youth then and had not the power they now possess. Fallen god though he is, the Fomarian will sorely test our strength."

"How, my lord, did he get to our borders without the empire's knowledge?" Cucullin asked as he rode up and joined the two.

"I do not know. He must possess much of his old earth power." Cainhill, Lord of Ionaltraye, rode up. He wore blue-washed armor, his long white hair held in a horsetail braid at the top of his head. His purple eyes did not focus on the others as he spoke.

"The pyridin have found an approach for us, my lord."
Cainhill's voice was gruff for an elf. "The fomarian has conjured some sort of creatures made from the earth itself."

"How many?" asked Lonnlarcan.

"A thousand, maybe more. They are hard to see even for
the pyridin."

Baibre joined the warriors. She was tall and her hair was
a bright red reaching to her knees. She was clad in a full
mail suit, its mirror polish reflecting the red hair and eyes.
She, with Teague, was the foremost of the wielders of magic
the elven host contained. In lieu of a spear she carried a long
oaken staff.

"The mages are ready, lord," she bowed to Lonnlarcan.
"One quick attack against the Fomarian is planned. After
that we will focus our magic on his troops. It is in your
hands to defeat him." She made it clear by her tone and
gesture that she felt it was her power that should be matched
against the earth god.

"Do not look so, lady," the king rebuffed her. "The Fomarians have always been very resistant to any sort of magical attack. It has always been the warrior's lot to face them."
Lonnlarcan lifted Kianbearac to eye level. "Weapons he will
feel, not magic." He turned to Cainhill. "Get the host in
motion. You will lead the attack against these earth creatures
the creature has." The elf lord lowered his head, not
pleased with the thought of missing the chance to fight the
monster. "Ceallac, you will lead my guard in a straight
charge to cut a way to the Fomarian. Cucullin and I will
follow and seek to engage it." Ceallac began to protest.
"After the way is clear, my cousin, join us. We will need all
the help we can get."

The necessary orders were given. The elves wrapped the
surrounding lands in a concealing mist, and then moving
even more quietly than before, they left to meet the Fomarian.

* * *

The battlefield was a place of hill and stone. The Fomarian waited for the elves in the end of a small valley, his armies ranged around the valley's sides and mouth. They were creatures of earth magic, conjurings of the demigod, made of earth and stone, badly shaped, some humanoid, some four-legged, some unrecognizable. Their deformed and stunted limbs dropped loose earth and stone to the ground as they waited. They were all large, some bigger than a horse.

As a mist filled the valley the Fomarian allowed himself a moment of pleasure. He could dispel this magic fog easily, but didn't wish to expend his power. He knew it would be needed against the elves. Neither he nor his army were dependent on eyes to see. Suddenly, the land filled with the wail of elvish horns. The creature turned in confusion. 'They come from behind!'

The elvish charge caught the enemy completely by surprise. The Ard Riegh's knights burst through the thin skin of earth creatures and rode straight toward the Fomarian.

He was an impressive sight. His twelve-foot frame was impossibly thick. His muscles were knotted cords of power. From a distance he looked entirely human, except for his pure massiveness. Then as the elves came closer they saw the third arm of the Fomarian. It was sickly looking and attached to a second shoulder that jutted out from underneath the giant's right arm.

The demigod was covered in a breastplate, greaves, shin guards and shield all formed of stone. In his right arm, the good one, was a massive mattock. With no hesitation he moved to meet the elves' attack.

Five lights of power burst from the elves to intercept the Fomarian. His sickly right arm thrust forward. In the palm of the hand was a dark eye. The magic rays hit the eye dead-center.

The eye closed its eyelid and then opened it. From it shone a single grey light that shot at the advancing warriors.

The light hit the ground in front of them and the earth formed a great wave that enveloped the whole front rank.

Lonnlarcan followed his knights. Even as the magical attack began one of the fomarian servants rose in front of the elf king. His horse plunged two hooves into the man-shaped thing. Both legs went through the creature and stuck. Its arm clubbed Lonnlarcan, throwing him to the ground. As he rose to his feet, two other creatures barred him from his mount. With a shout he thrust Kianbearac into one of them. The monster shivered and shook itself apart. Its comrade, looking like a mudpie dog, leaped at the king.

Lonnlarcan said a Word and from his eyes a sunburst flew and the creature melted to the ground as if a downpour of rain had dissolved it. The king moved toward his horse and freed it from its assailant.

Ceallac was covered by the earth wave the Fomarian had created. As the weight of the land settled on him he heard his horse's neck crack. His shout of anguish was muffled by a mouth full of dirt.

It was Cucullin that was the first to reach the giant. The sounds of the battle goaded him on as he jumped his horse over the area of the buried knights. The Fomarian smiled through its thick beard as the elf approached. He showed more stunted, browned, twisted teeth as he realized he was being attacked by a naked elf.

Cucullin and his horse nimbly evaded the demigod's mattock. The horse reared to its hind legs; its two hooves hit the fomarian's shield. Cu followed through with a swing of his Aislinneena ax, Kervalen. The Fomarian stumbled back in surprise, looking at the great chip of its shield that had flown away at the waving of the elf's arms.

The elf continued to advance. He had to dive off his horse to avoid being crushed by his foe's great shield. He rolled to his feet and gave a great chop at the creature's legs. The Fomarian bellowed in pain as a great slice was taken from his left calf by a creature that bore no weapon.

The demigod's third hand thrust forward again, the eye

opening. Cu burst into a bright incandescent flame, but the armor the Aislinneena had provided him with kept the flames from doing any damage.

He held his ax two-handed and with all his might chopped into the Fomarian's stone chest armor. The power of the blow made the Fomarian stumble a step but the damage was negligible. Cu's vision was now hindered by the flames that still covered him and he did not see the mattock come down at him.

The elf lord was hit on the left side, his shield splintering and bones breaking. The warrior was thrown by the blow twenty feet away and he smashed into the ground with terrible force. He did not move.

An elven knight's charge at the demigod was stopped cold as the third arm caught him and lifted him from his saddle. In seconds the pulped body was dropped to the earth. Two more knights fell to the mattock before Ceallac freed himself from the death's embrace of earth and stone. His war shout carried above the din of battle.

The monster turned to face this new threat. It was the bull fighting the wolf and both joined the fray with fury and savagery. But this time, the bull was ready.

For all his speed and agility, Ceallac could not pierce the Fomarian defense. Similarly, the monster could not hit his taunting foe. Ceallac darted about. Finally, his sword scored his enemy's right hand. The bright red blood that flew from the wound hit him in the face. It was like being smacked with liquid metal.

Blinded, his face burning with pain, still Ceallac managed to avoid the mattock. As he strove to fight the pain and clear his vision, a great weight fell on his back and Ceallac went down, one of the earth creatures striving with all its might to split his back.

As the Fomarian lifted his mattock to crush the warrior, a red sunburst blew up in his misshapen face and Lonnlarcan stood against him.

The monster recognized his new antagonist and for the

first time spoke. "Die," he said, and the rocks split at his booming voice. Lonnlarcan's horse stumbled to its knees, blood rolling from its ears and mouth. He went flying at the Fomarian's feet. The mattock crashed down to crush the elf to the earth. But this was Lonnlarcan, Ard Riegh of the elves.

The king lifted his spear two-handed above his head. The mattock crashed into it. Incredibly, the spear withstood the blow though the elven king's feet sank four inches into the ground. The elf became a being of pure silver light, a light that hurt the eyes of the demigod, and all the earth creatures within twenty yards of Lonnlarcan fell to the ground lifeless.

The third eye was open again and a dark liquid flew at the king. Lonnlarcan's shield intercepted it. The liquid splashed against the imposed barrier and covered the shield. Quickly the shield rusted and fell from Lonnlarcan's arm, destroyed and useless. Great gaps in his armor appeared wherever the liquid had touched. Undaunted, the Ard Riegh charged his enemy.

From the eye the liquid came again. This time it was the point of Kianbearac that met the attack. The two met and the spear blazed a deep red. The liquid solidified and fell to the earth, a dark harmless mass. Lonnlarcan evaded the mattock easily, and rammed the end of the spear into the already bleeding calf of the monster.

The great stone shield caught him a glancing blow and Lonnlarcan tumbled away. Ceallac, freed and revitalized, attacked again. He cried to the heavens and swung his sword with all his might. It smashed against the stone shield. Both shield and sword splintered, a jagged edge of stone penetrating deep into the elf lord's side.

At Ceallac's cry, Lonnlarcan turned to him. In that instance the mattock crashed into the king's back. The Fomarian shouted in triumph. Lonnlarcan rolled over on his back trying to gather strength to resist the blow he knew was coming. But he could not gather his thoughts.

His ears filled with the cries of his warriors killing and

being killed. With the death of each elf the Ard Riegh shook
with pain. He could feel their last moment, filled with surprise or anguish. Some died in rage, some in confusion, but
they died, and for the one moment he needed to collect his
thoughts and spirit all the king could do was listen to the
elves die.

Another blow smashed into Lonnlarcan's undefended
body. A half dozen elves sought to protect their lord, but the
eye opened again and all fell to its power. The Fomarian
lifted his mattock again. He called his magic to him. The
end of the mattock began to glow with the accumulated energies. The attacks of the eye increased; none could with-
stand them. All around the giant the grass withered as he
withdrew the earth's power. His mind burst with triumph.
Then, in agony and shock, he buckled to his knees.

For the bull had forgotten the wolf. Covered in his own
gore, Ceallac had risen to his feet and driven a dagger deep
into the fomarian's already wounded knee. Ceallac fell to the
ground, depleted. He had used his remaining strength to
mask himself from the demigod's awareness.

Lonnlarcan felt the Fomarian's power dissipate as its concentration was broken by Ceallac's blow. He struggled to his
knees in time to see a red bolt of pure power hit the giant
square between the eyes. The Fomarian reeled and sought to
gain its feet. 'Bairbre,' thought the king, and grasping Kianbearac, he rose.

The giant smashed the mattock to the ground, the blow
seeming to give him strength. Facing him was the silver
flame of the Ard Riegh's anger. Spear and mattock met,
their eyes locked in combat for the other's will.

The great fist of the demigod's left hand missed Lonnlarcan by inches. The spear pierced the hand. The eye sapped
the king of moisture. A silver flame scarred the Fomarian's
face. So great was the power of the battle that none could
approach for fear of being destroyed by the energies being
released.

But for all the power of the Elven King, he faced a demigod, one who had been an earth god of incredible power. A jagged edge of the mattock tore mail and flesh. No blood ran for the eye continued to sap all water and fluid from the king. A backhand broke a nose that could not turn red. Lonnlarcan began to die.

They came at last, even as the Ard Riegh began to fall. Never had any creature run as fast as the unicorn. Never had a Morigu been tortured by the earth's cries as Margawt had.

Though the earth rocked and split, the unicorn did not lose its footing. The mattock was easily evaded, the eye had no effect. Horn and sword pierced the stone armor at the same time and the horn burned. The Fomarian bellowed in a deep voice, so deep no human could hear it, but the elves could.

The cry was not of fear or pain, but of pure hate and rage. The Fomarian felt the bite of the She who had once defeated him, and no emotion could match his devouring hate for Her whom he considered betrayer.

The eye blazed a burning red and unicorn and rider were thrown to the ground. The weight of the world seemed to press them down deep into the earth. The unicorn floundered and sought to fight back as he was pressed deeper and deeper into the earth. But the Morigu dove into the ground as if he dove into a pond. Again he saw the crystal earth, the light that was no light, again he rode the warm earth currents, and again he heard the land's cry of pain, and again he sought to kill.

The Fomarian gasped, this time in pain; he was nearly spent. As Margawt swam toward the surface, having avoided the eye's hold, he saw the withered arm thrust into the ground. The eye opened and the earth around him froze and encased him in a great block of crystal. He began to sink in the unsinkable.

Kianbearac burned red and gold in front of the demigod, Lonnlarcan a being of pure flame behind. The Fomarian stamped his great foot once and the earth shook with an earthquake. Great fissures swallowed elf and earth thing randomly. The unicorn sunk deeper. Lonnlarcan fell to his knees.

The Fomarian stamped again and his creatures burst asunder, raining earth and stone among the elf host. Still the king strove to rise to his feet.

The Fomarian stamped a third time, and the earth revolted. Great geysers of dirt flew into the air. The rocks were blown apart from the inside. All that was green and alive died. The air held more earth than air, but Lonnlarcan rose.

The great spear Kianbearac flew from his hand, a javelin of red and gold lightning shot forth by a silver inferno. Through stone and flesh the spear flew, ripping muscle and bone. The monster grabbed the spear, though his hand smouldered, and pulled it from his chest. The ground heaved even more at the anguished cry of a demigod. The first cry of fear he had ever voiced.

Great waves of rock and soil, bashed against the elves. A huge one reared in front of Lonnlarcan and swallowed him before he could call the spear back to him. 'The Fomarian isn't dead,' he thought. 'It escapes.' And though he struggled against the earth's storm he had no more strength and he thought no more.

The next morning the elves were encamped about the battle-field. The concealing mist had been dispersed and the camp sparkled with the rising of the sun. Many elves wandered around in seemingly aimless patterns seeking to repair the damage to the earth the Fomarian had caused. A quieter group prepared the mound to bury the two hundred plus that had died in the fighting. Others brought out the litters of wounded so that they might feel the warmth of the morning sun.

The Ard Riegh's tent sat right in the middle of the encampment. It was an impossible affair of reds, yellows, and greens. Inside, the leaders of the host assembled.

"We have no choice," said Cainhill. "The king cannot move for a few more days and the people will not leave him here."

"Aye, there's no other choice. The Fomarian didn't defeat us, but we need time to heal ourselves," said Cucullin, his arm hung in a sling of white silk. "Many of the weaker have fallen into the dreamstate. Only you, my king, will be able to return them to this place."

Lonnlarcan shifted carefully. He lay in a bier, his Warlords ranged around him sitting on stools or standing. The reddened bandages about his naked torso stood in high relief to the golden pillows that supported him.

"Ah, the curse of the elves," he sighed. "I dare not split our forces now. If the pyridin had not made us aware of the trap we would have been decimated. Four days, no more, then we ride again."

"Four days!" Margawt exploded from a darkened corner. "The earth groans with her rape. There is no time for this weakness!" All the elves except Cainhill gave the Morigu a wide berth. Cainhill just stared.

"Watch you mouth, warrior," the elf lord spat the word out. "For all your vaunted power you did little good against the Fomarian."

"The Fomarian is an abomination, the greatest betrayal by the enemy! He must be followed and destroyed. Such cannot be allowed to exist!" The Morigu turned to Cainhill. "And you beware, elfling. The wrongness eats around you. I am watching."

Lonnlarcan headed the confrontation off. "Enough. There is no choice, Margawt. It is all our war now. We must fight together." His silver eyes burned deep into Margawt. "We leave in four days. I suggest you use that time to help our mages in trying to trace the Fomarian down, and find out how he was freed from the Goddess' hold."

"That, noble king," a voice boomed, "we can ascertain here and now." In walked the unicorn. Even among this assembly his beauty and power were awesome. "Cucullin,

Baibre, restrain the Morigunamachamain." Both quickly moved to either side of Margawt. "Now, our answer." The tent flap opened and four figures moved in.

With a cry, the Morigu lunged at the creatures but was quickly grabbed by the two elves. He turned in confusion. The wrongness of one of the creatures was piercing pain to him yet he could not lift a hand against either elf.

The creatures moved in front of the unicorn. One was Dorrenlassarslany, looking more nervous than ever. Two more of his people restrained a creature between them. The creature was barely three feet tall. It had the body of a goat with the armless torso of a human, its face looking like an idolized satyr. Around its neck were two grass ropes, each in the hand of one of the pyridin.

One was a fat hairy creature with an angular face set upon a remarkably flexible neck. The other was a petite female standing a foot and a half, its fragile beauty ruined by an evil, wizened face. Both jittered and hopped even more than their leader, but they never let go of the goat creature's rope.

"What is it?" asked Cainhill.

"A sending," answered the enchantress Bairbre. She did not let go of the Morigu. "A sending of great power. It is a creature of another plane, a plane that only the greatest wielders of magic can reach. None of our people have the strength."

"The sending," said Anlon, "was captured by the pyridin just as the sun rose, when its power was weakest." Two knights moved to hold the creature. The unicorn waved them away with its horn. "No, you could not hold such. It would vanish as a mist. The power of the pyridin alone may bind it."

Margawt shook in his need. The earth died beneath the hooves of the sending.

"Kill it, give it to me. Wrong, it is so wrong . . . It kills the ground it walks upon!" In a blinding move he freed himself from the elves and unsheathed his sword before any could act . . . except the unicorn, who leaped into his path.

"No, Morigu, it has knowledge that we need. Control yourself," said Anlon. "No," he turned to Cainhill. "Say nothing. You do not comprehend the agony this creature is to the Morigu. Forget not, he is the Earth Goddess' chosen."

"It watched and spied on us, did it not, Dorrenlassarslany?" asked Lonnlarcan.

"Unmaker," Dorrenlassarslany addressed the Morigu, "understand eating aways. Unhealth is worse to you than lack of choice." It turned to Lonnlarcan. "Witchlord, you fought, defeated less god, but not destroy. Must destroy this Binneckgasdaintehly, this unhealth-blight-disease-thing. Watch, follow elves, guide less god, to elf things. Evil, corrupt, pyridin peoples take, no choices, for unthing. It no master, but mastered. Sickness of creature, others decide, for it, make its choices." The little creature said this as if it was the most horrendous of things. It bobbed and danced its disbelief. "Worm mind, larva soul. Take its choices, Unmaker. First, though, ask it, find its master."

"Dorrenlassarslany speaks wisely as always," said the king, smiling down at the pyridin. "Bring that thing to me."

The creature was led to the king. Its apparent passivity was belied by its wildly roving eyes and the drool and excrement it constantly deposited on the ground.

"Allow me," said Anlon. "No evasions, Dark One. Who sent you? Who freed the Fomarian? Who?" The horn of Anlon burned with black sparks. He brought it closer to the creature and it screamed in fear and pain. The Morigu grasped his hilt two-handed and shook in agony.

"Cannot speak, bindings too powerful." The sending's voice was rich and disturbingly female.

The unicorn reared and his two front hooves stamped the ground; his horn vibrated, the waves from it shaking all there. From the horn strands of some black filament flew deep into the breast of the sending. The creature buckled to its knees, its eyes going blank and unseeing. Slowly, the strands still connecting it to the horn, it rose to its feet. It looked unseeing at the unicorn and spoke in a husky whisper.

"The Ead," it said.

The tent went quiet in shock as all tried to digest this.

"No!" cried the Morigu. Moving at blinding speed he reached the creature, his sword severing its head in one swift cut. The head flew into the air, dark gore splattering everyone. Before the head hit ground, the Morigu dug his hand in the sending's breast and withdrew its still beating heart. He ground it deeply into the earth.

A wave of his hand dispersed the threads from Anlon's horn. His hand continued through the earth into the ground.

"Blackest betrayer, the Goddess understands now! Earth shall have its blood due! Arianrood, feel the call! I am coming." He stood and faced the shocked group.

"The creature spoke truth. Its disease is eradicated." He began to walk to the entrance.

"Hold!" cried Lonnlarcan. He stood up with a quick motion. "The dwarves, their army was to meet with Arianrood's and together march to the empire!"

Black fire snorted through Anlon's nose. "Blackest betrayal, they walk into a trap unknowing."

"Even," added Cucullin, "as we nearly did."

The Morigu looked at the dark gore on his hand. "She will pay and the dwarves will be warned!" He looked at Anlon who shook his head in agreement. Quickly they left.

"There is more here, my lord," said Bairbre, "than meets the eye."

"Indeed," he answered. "The Ead turns and the earth will repay her, but what, I wonder, is Fealoth doing?"

In minutes Anlon and the Morigu were galloping to the east. Anlon continued to snort black fire in anger. For hours the two rode unspeaking at the incredible pace of the unicorn. In midstride he reared and stopped.

"Damn!" he swore. "Oh damn!"

"What is it?" asked Margawt.

"The dwarves, oh Mother, I forgot," he groaned.

"What?" cried the warrior.

"Don't you see? The elves know that the dwarves were to meet Arianrood's host, but their time is skewed. Gods, the dwarves were to join the betrayers in two days. We can never reach them in time!" With no other word the Morigu leaped off the unicorn.

"What are you doing?" asked Anlon.

"The dwarves are creatures of earth magic. We cannot reach them in time in person but I can warn them through the currents of the Mother." With no further word Margawt dug his hands in the earth and went into a trance. For long moments no noise was made as Anlon stamped around impatiently.

Then Anlon felt a tingling in his hooves, a tickling, burning pain the like he had never in his long life experienced.

He saw a red shimmering travel up the Morigu's arm. Margawt jumped to his feet slapping his arms as if a thousand flies had just landed there. He cried like a wolf, the red shimmering flashing up and down his arms.

"Aieee! Foulness tries to infect me, the vermin of Darkness reaches for me!" The Morigu was berserk in rage and disgust. Anlon reared up and knocked the elf to the ground. His horn sparked again and he touched it to Margawt's arms. A silent battle was fought between the red and black energy while the Morigu writhed on the ground.

Finally the black won out and Margawt calmed himself.

"Oh Mother," he wailed, "such desecration." Once again he dug his hands into the earth, this time for apparent relief. Anlon waited patiently.

"The caves of the dwarves are infected. Death and plague run through the mountain veins. I am blocked from them." Margawt's face was lined with the agony of his ineffectualness.

"The Goddess will defend her children, Margawt. We will not reach them for days yet," Anlon spoke quietly.

"There is more, unicorn." Margawt looked into the burning red orbs of his companion. "I was attacked by the earth power itself."

"The Fomarian?" Anlon was stunned.

"Like him, less powerful but more diseased, more wrong than even that one." The Morigu stood up and looked to the east. "Arianrood heard my challenge. Her answer uses the very paths of the earth. It comes, it comes for us."

Anlon stared at the warrior, his erect figure framed against the midday sun. He looked around, grassland all around and no sign of habitation anywhere. His feet jittered at the memory of the taste of what had attacked the Morigu. He did not like the idea of facing anything that could attack the Morigunamachamain through the earth.

"Well, great," he snorted. "Not only do you tell the bitch we're coming, you also just happen to mention where we are."

Margawt looked at him in confusion, not understanding the unicorn's anger.

"I did what I must, what matter the creature knows we are here? It must die, we must destroy it. This thing is worse than the Fomarian." He turned to the east again and folded his arms saying quietly, "I must kill it."

"Did you ever consider it might not be so easy to kill?" The Morigu did not deign to answer.

"Okay, Margawt, hop on." The unicorn nudged him in the shoulder. "We might as well go meet the bloody thing instead of standing around looking brave." Margawt mounted.

He patted Anlon's muscled neck. "Anlon, this is the way —my way. One on one, no doubt about what is right to do." He gave a war shout, "I hunt! I hunt!"

"Great," Anlon mumbled. "Great, we go, you madman, right into the embrace of our enemy." With that they rode off into the west.

CHAPTER

Eleven

Mearead banged his hand into the stone wall in frustration. The fist sunk deep into the wall as if it was clay, not rock. He stood in a large, dimly lit cavern ringed by the stone statues of his fathers. Facing him were the old ones, loremasters of the earth magic, their faces shadowed by the cowls of their grey cloaks. All that showed were their white dwarven beards.

"Mearead!" cried the eldest, "you hurt the mountain with your anger. Control yourself lest you earn its wrath."

"Its wrath," he cried, "its wrath! The mountains of our people have turned on us!"

Cries of outrage came from the shadowed masters. "This is not so. Sacrilege!"

"Silence," said the lord of the Crystal Falls. "Warn me not of sacrilege. The people die from poisoned waters, dark creatures from the mountain's bowels attack us in our halls! Sacrilege, why I'll tear this bloody mountain apart piece by piece. The spirit of this mountain better beware my wrath!"

"It is not the mountain as you well know, lord," said the eldest. "It's some attacker without that has broken through the earth magic of the Crystal Falls."

"That Duiraglym," another added.

Mearead slumped down at the foot of a statue. "Aye, what you say is true, but by the Goddess, how can it be?"

"We are the loremasters," spoke the eldest, "but you are

the lord here. Never in the history of the caves has such an attack taken place. We have no words of comfort for you, Mearead." The old one leaned heavily on his staff made from a rod of brown-green marble.

"I cannot and will not leave the caves while this cancerous siege takes place. Colin must lead the armies we send to Tolath." Mearead shook his head. "The lad is young but possesses more strength than he knows."

"It is the wisest course, lord." The old one sat next to the distraught king. "Our power would be halved if you went to Tolath and Colin is a worthy successor."

"Ah, Trell'dem, can you see us now? I cannot ride to help your kingdom and I send less than a third of the force I had once promised you." Mearead stared up at the dark cavern ceiling. To his dwarven eyes it was as clear as daylight. He traced the runes and magnificent sculptures that covered every inch of rock. "Oh, Dammuth," he said quietly, "what went wrong? What is Fealoth doing?" He stood up.

"Fealoth is dead," said the old one. "The Dark Lord has returned. It is the only answer, my lord." Mearead studied the ancient master for a moment and then looked at the others, a peculiar expression tugging at his face.

"Is it?" he said, then bowed and left.

He walked up the caverns toward the living levels. His people hailed him quietly and with respect, but they could not hide the fear in their hearts. Though a few tried a feeble joke, the emptiness of laughter in the dwarven holds was the clearest proof of the despair they all felt.

'The lorewardens tell me nothing I do not know,' he said to himself. 'It is not their fault. Have not half their number fallen in the battles of the pit? The earth power leaves me. I can feel it draining from me like a river damming up, but what can stop the earth power?' With these black thoughts as company, the stout dwarf continued.

Usually when walking through the caverns, the dwarf king would stop to admire a piece of sculpture or one of the beautiful mosaics on walls and floor. Often he would stop to speak to the artisans at work, which could be any dwarf since all were free to embellish the caverns at will. But there was precious little work being done these days and what little was done was not to his liking, the pieces generally being morbid or depressing. Why, twice in the last month Mearead had to cancel work for it was marring the caverns, something most of his predecessors had never had to do in their whole reigns!

Mearead stopped in front of a door fancifully done up in the shape of a lion's head. It glittered and sparkled with jewels and precious metals. That door alone could ransom a kingdom (not that a dwarf would care; such figuring was more in the minds of men and their ilk). Mearead drew a deep breath and put a smile on his face. The door opened of its own accord as he approached it.

The room was opulent and dazzling, the light just bright enough to give everything a sheen and hint at the wonders the place possessed. Across the room a dwarf in full battle armor turned at the entrance of Mearead.

Mearead took in Colin's black beard, now streaked with grey, the reddened eyes for want of sleep, and the fierce possessive hold on his war ax. 'The lad grows older, and much faster than a dwarf should,' thought Mearead.

"Ah uncle, that happy-go-lucky air about you does not fool me. I felt your anger in the Cave of Remembrances," he said.

'He comes early to his powers,' thought the king. Aloud he said, "Colin, I do believe you are becoming a bit on the dull side." His voice was shocked in outrage.

"And as an actor, my leader, you stink." They both smiled and embraced warmly.

Colin stood back and poured wine for both of them. "I take it from your cheery attitude you are to be rid of me for a while?"

"Your speech has always been stilted, whelp." Mearead took an appreciative sip of the wine. "But it's true, you will lead the armies to Tolath." He collapsed into a chair.

"I had hoped with the defeat of the enemy's main army I would be able to march to Tolan," he shrugged, "but the Duiraglym still haunts us, and raiders still hide in the mountains." Colin looked down at his wine, jiggling the cup to swirl the dark liquid.

"Do you think the enemy can attack us from the caverns with such numbers again?" he asked.

"No, we've found most of the entrance caves they made and sealed them," Mearead answered. "It's not their armies we have to watch out for, it's their magic." Colin dipped a finger in his wine, smiling as he licked the drops off his finger.

"We could use the Morigu," he said. "He would be able to hunt down what is left of the Dark One's armies easier than us."

"You've learned some hard lessons, lad," Mearead smiled. "You never were one to think before."

Colin snorted, "Ha, ha." He sat down across from his uncle, searching the other's eyes. "Mearead, I've thought on it. I'm sure the Duiraglym is a demigod." The older dwarf just waited. "I mean, it will take everything we have to deal with a demigod."

"That's an understatement," Mearead said. "But as for the Morigu, forget him. He will fight with the elves if he fights with anyone."

"But he is the Goddess' own, and I feel her presence here. Surely She will call him to us."

"Maybe, but will he get here?" He bit his upper lip. "Colin, our enemies have outfoxed us time and time again. They are crushing the empire, and have nearly ruined us. Whatever part the Morigu will play, it won't be here. We are on our own." He laughed hoarsely. "No, we're the ones who are supposed to send help to the others."

"The elves of Cather-na-nog will go to the empire's aid," Colin said.

"Oh, they already have, and the Ard Riegh leads them."

'That's hard news,' Colin thought. 'Things are desperate

everywhere. The king of the elves never rides with the first hosting.'

"Listen," Mearead interrupted the young dwarf's musing, "whatever it is that is infecting the mountain, we will cast it out. The war won't be fought in our caves. I will follow you with a great army, lad, in a matter of weeks, I am sure." Colin answered with a tight smile.

"So, we're on our own." He stood. "Well, I best be getting ready. We must meet the elves of Aes Lugh in two days at the valley of Morhalk."

"Aye, listen to me well, Colin. I trust not Arianrood's flighty elves. They are not of the ilk of those of Cather-na-nog. Watch them carefully."

"Surely you do not think they will betray us?" said Colin.

"I don't know what to expect from them. Arianrood has a fierce pride and I don't comprehend what goes through that weedy little brain of hers."

"Uncle, you speak of the Ead!" Colin's voice was shocked.

"Yah, right. Nonetheless, watch your back and trust only dwarves, understood?"

"Of course, uncle." Colin downed his glass with one swig. Wiping his lips, he smiled at the king. "I will be off to inform the commanders. See you at dinner tonight." He walked to the door, then turned around. "You know, Mearead, you haven't aged well. One could almost say you were getting to be a bit of a pain."

"And," answered the old dwarf, "you are getting duller by the minute. Now off with you so I can find someone to talk to who won't put me to sleep." Answering grin for grin, Colin left. Mearead dropped into a chair with a grunt, suddenly feeling much older.

Two days later, Colin and his troops marched into the valley of Morhalk. They were five-thousand strong and presented a fierce sight. All the dwarves wore thick mail coats that reached to their knees. Mailed and plated legs with elbow, back, and breast protectors made them practically invulnerable. On their hands they wore cleverly jointed gauntlets that encased them in metal. They also carried short, round warshields which they generally did not use since their favored weapons were mace, ax, and mattock. Their helms were all individualized and tended to cover their faces completely. Some even had jewels for eye guards. All that could be seen were their long beards hanging down, and even these were often plaited with metal.

The valley they entered was rich with green life. Flowers, shrubs, and bushes all greeted the solemn sight of the dwarven horde. Remembering his uncle's warnings, Colin stopped the march and sent in scouts ahead. They soon reported that there was no sight of the elvish army. Knowing the elves' disregard for time, this did not worry Colin unduly, but he warned his officers to be on the alert nonetheless.

The dwarves had for the past two days been full of laughter and jokes. For once they enjoyed getting away from their caves and looked forward to venting their pent-up fears on a foe they could face in an honest fight.

Colin positioned his men around some low hills he found in the center of the valley. Once there, he ordered all to prepare themselves for battle, just in case. He then ordered scouts to the ridges of the valley. He drew a pipe and a glass of ale, sat, and waited.

A war horn came from the east ridge and Colin turned to see the army of Aes Lugh approach. The huge army was a bizarre-looking group. Donal Longsword led the host riding a giant black war horse. The leaders were all elven or half-elven lords looking to Colin to be a bit overdressed for the occasion. Following them were a great number of Brown or lesser elves; the little people they were sometimes called, not quite elves and not quite pyridin. They were descendants of the once great nation of Mai Methra, though they were less than their ancestors had been. Following them came a host of men who owed allegiance to the elven queen. They were led by a black-cowled rider that brought an uneasiness to the dwarven lord.

The host began to spread out along the valley floor. There were many more than Colin expected, something he was not sure he liked. They outnumbered his force at least four to one. In the very back of the elves there was a hazy flickering cloud where figures moved and gamboled about. And that was something he had definitely not expected.

As the army of Aes Lugh continued to pour in and form ranks, Colin got up. Turning to his lieutenants he said, "Flann, unfurl the banner and come with me. Noghor and Feohors join us." The dwarves were all nervously handling their weapons. "Math," he spoke to the old dwarf, his armor battle-scarred, "you're in charge. Anything goes wrong, don't stand and fight. Retreat back to the caves." Math nodded once and the four dwarves marched out to meet the elves.

"Colin," said Flann, "this doesn't strike me as a party sort of crowd."

"What does that hide, I wonder?" Pointing at the magic cloud in the rear, Flann spat.

"With our luck, Cronbage." With oaths the others drew their weapons.

"Hey, look," Colin pointed to their right. The others turned but saw nothing.

"What is it, lad?" asked Feohors.

"I don't know. For a minute I thought I saw a chariot, with a figure on it."

"More black magic?" Flann growled.

"No, I don't know. Just my eyes playing tricks, I suppose." But his heart knew different. The chariot of Lord Death was not a sight unknown to the dwarven race.

Donal rode forward to meet them alone, but the dark rider moved up and joined him. There were words between them but the rider continued with the Warlord. They reined the mounts in front of the dwarves, the cowled one giving a savage tug that was not lost on any of the dwarves.

"Well, friend Longsword," said Colin, "it's an impressive group you bring before us today."

Donal's face twitched with a quick grimace. "It's not me you need to talk to, friend," he said, "but Lord Remon here." His hand twitched toward the cowled rider.

"Ah, Colin, I had thought Mearead himself would be here." The cowl covered the man's face entirely; no hint of features showed, his voice cajoling and well modulated. "But I suppose his lordship's busy in his caves, eh?"

"Look, tough guy," said the dwarf, "I don't know what's in Arianrood's head to give her armies to you and not her Warlord. Nor do I care for your stupid insinuations. So I'll make this meeting brief." He turned to the half-elven. "You're an honorable man, I know, Longsword, though your choice of company has declined since times past. But be that as it may, our armies are supposed to join up and move to Tolath, but I find your people making mine a little uneasy. So move them to the other side or we withdraw."

"I assure you," said Donal, "there are no ill intentions."

"Oh, be quiet," said Remon. "Listen, little man, your posturing and insults mean nothing to me, but I am ordered to give you a chance. So, hand me your ax and surrender or I'll wipe you and your people off the face of this planet!"

"What are you talking about, you maniac? These are our allies!" cried Donal.

Colin noticed the elves were moving closer and his own men were forming ranks.

"They were our allies," corrected the rider. "I was to use you to catch them by surprise but I have no time for games. Well, dwarf, yield or die."

"You know," said Colin, "I'm beginning to think you have a personality problem." Slowly his face was becoming harder as he began to call up the berserker in him.

Donal drew his sword and pointed it at the rider's neck.

"You, friend, are relieved of command," he said through grinding teeth.

"No, fool, you are." With that the mage raised an arm and his form dissolved to mist. At the same time the host of Aes Lugh took up a cry and charged.

Colin turned and raced to his men, his dwarves following. He called behind his back, "Looks like you're screwed, half-elven. You better come with us." The huge Warlord sat still, watching the army that was his attack him. With an oath to Lugh, he turned and raced with the dwarves toward their positions.

The warriors made it just ahead of the onrushing attack. Donal jumped off his mount. "Colin, I swear I know nothing of—"

The dwarf interrupted him. "Enough. We've no time," he said, placing his war helm on. "Listen, we'll try to retreat but we've little chance. Take that great beast of yours and ride. Mearead must know of this betrayal."

"No!" cried the half-elven. "Perhaps I can stop this useless attack."

Again Colin broke through. "Listen, we've been betrayed! Arianrood's betrayed us!"

"NO!" Donal shouted.

"Yes!" Colin said. "Yes. Mearead suspected it and now this is proof. Take your horse, man, and run. Get to Mearead or he may never learn what has happened." Just then with a crash the first ranks fell upon the dwarves. Colin grabbed the warrior's arm and shook.

"Look, you great hunk of meat," he said, "we're doomed. They're too many. Mearead must know before more are betrayed."

Donal took a breath and nodded his head once. "The ones in the rear," he said, "in that mist, I know not what they are, that's your great danger. No elvish lords of great power have ridden with us." He had to shout now over the fighting. "The little ones," he continued, "are vicious but lousy fighters. Concentrate on the men and elves." He turned to the dwarf, tears streaming down his face. "The black one's a sorcerer. Kill the son-of-a-bitch." Colin's face was covered by his helmet which was made to look like a wolf. The eyes behind the faceplate matched the fierce visage.

He held the half-elf with an imploring look. "It's not your fault," he said. "Don't fail me, warrior. I'll die better knowing I will be revenged." His voice was husky with the battle fever that comes to all his kind.

"Die well, warrior," said the half-elf. He leaped upon his horse's back. Yelling over the sounds of the battle, he cried, "Listen well to the oath of the Longsword." He brandished his namesake. "Arianrood will pay." He kicked his horse, his voice hoarse for betrayal and tears. "Gods, she shall pay!" And with the sounds of battle ringing in his torn heart, Donal rode away.

As he turned away from the retreating figure of the half-elven, Colin saw a bright golden flash to his right. He turned to see the figure in the chariot raise one shadowy hand in salute. Colin just stared.

'So,' he thought, 'this is what I felt at the battle in the caverns. It is my time to die, and Lord Death waits for me.' He thought briefly of his mother's and uncle's pain when they heard the news, but he had no fear. A savage thrill came to him as he thought what Mearead's reaction would be. He ground his teeth together, the only sign of his inner turmoil as the Dwarf Lord moved to the front ranks to join his warriors in killing and in dying.

And unheard by all, Death howled his anguish. For in this fight he dare not take part—too many powers had turned their attention that way and he was not ready to reveal himself. The most he could do was hesitate a bit to take the dead so they might strike once more with ax, mace, and mattock. It was not the first nor the last time that Lord Death cried for the fallen.

Meanwhile, Donal Longsword raced his great steed toward the mountains, his thoughts bitter and cold.

It took him a day and a night to reach the caves of the

Crystal Falls. He stumbled up to the main gate battered and bleeding. His horse had died during the night in the talons of one of the sorcerous creatures that continually attacked him. Donal had run and fought for thirty miles on foot, and as he saw the guardians of the gate running toward him he collapsed in a haze of weariness and pain.

Donal awoke stretched out on four dwarven beds that had been placed together to hold his giant frame. Tending him were several young dwarven women. Donal smiled to see the small yet attractive women tending him. Then the reality of the past days crashed on him and he groaned in anguish.

"Ah," said one of the little women, "you just lay there, lad. You've been through a lot you have." She smoothed his hair gently.

"I am in the caves of the Crystal Falls?" he asked.

"That you are."

"Then get Lord Mearead. I must speak with him." He sat up. Before she could press him back down, a deep voice boomed.

"I am here, Warlord." Mearead walked in, his face one grim line of anguish. "And I've guessed much of your news already."

"Arianrood," Donal spat out, "she has betrayed us all."

"She'll pay in rich, red blood," said the king. "Tell me the story from the start."

Donal told the king everything, from the mage-king Remon being given the army, to the addition of the sorcerous army in the veil. Mearead said nothing the whole time, his eyes blank and devoid of emotion. When Donal told of Colin's last words, the old dwarf simply sighed and waited to hear the rest of the warrior's tale. When he was finished, the king shooed the women away, telling them to bear the tale to all the dwarves. He then poured a goblet of wine and handed it to Donal.

"Well," he said, "this is a black tale and never have my ears heard worse." He stared at the Warlord for a moment and then said, "She's been in this all along, damn her black soul."

"But she is the Ead," whispered Donal.

"Aye, it was the perfect shield from our doubts. Whatever changed her, she has joined our enemy." He sighed. "I suspect it is she who has reawakened the Darkness that attacks the earth power. She is the most powerful of all." He shook his head and stood. Turning his back he whispered one word to the dwarven shadows: "Colin."

"What will we do?" asked Donal.

"Do, do!" The old one's voice shook with his anger. "We will give Colin his vengeance. That, Warlord, is what we will do!"

"How?"

Once again Mearead turned his back. As he spoke, his size seemed to grow until his presence filled the room. "My armies have their hands full with the creatures that attack the caves. I can spare no more warriors to help Tolan. But I can have the blood of that witch." On the last word, Mearead's voice boomed and it seemed to Donal the room shook with the king's anger.

"You have been abed a day, Longsword," he spoke quietly. "Colin's and the others' death rites have been done. We cannot retrieve their bones now." His face still void of any emotion, he said, "I am told you are healed. Dwarven women are well skilled in such arts. I go to the namesake of this place to start my quest."

"Quest?"

"Aye, lad. My armies cannot strike back now, but I can." He started to leave the room. "If you wish, someone will bring you to the Crystal Falls and you may join me."

"In what?" said Donal. "I still don't understand."

"It's simple enough." Mearead spoke carefully and slowly. "I am going to kill Arianrood!" With that he left the room.

CHAPTER

Twelve

As Donal and Mearead spoke three hundred miles away, Anlon reared to a halt at a small stream. He and Margawt were deep in the borderlands. For miles around all they could see was rolling grassland dotted with an occasional tree.

"How far away?" he asked.

"Not far now," answered the Morigu. "Whatever it is it will appear anytime," Anlon sighed. Margawt's sense of distance was as accurate as the elves' sense of time. They had been moving west for five days with no sign of their unseen enemy, and Margawt was still blocked from communicating with the dwarves.

That, Anlon knew, was the worst threat. The enemy knew about the Morigu now and they were preparing something for both of them. Margawt's daily attempts to contact the dwarves only told the enemy where they were, and trying to explain this to the Morigu was useless, whose sense of tactics was only rivaled in its ridiculousness by his sense of distance.

To make it all even more annoying, Margawt announced at least three times a day that their enemy would appear anytime. Nor did he have the grace to be upset when his predictions proved wrong.

"We'll wait for it here," Anlon said aloud. "The running

water of the stream may help us." 'Actually,' he thought to himself, 'I'm just thirsty.'

"Not against this one," Margawt stated. But Anlon raised his head at that. There was something different this time, in Margawt, or himself, some warning of danger.

"Can you feel the creature's presence?" asked Anlon, his eyes scanning the horizon for any sign of the enemy.

"No, it masks itself now." Margawt bent down to take a sip of the water. Still on one knee, he turned to the unicorn. "You have never told me of your dealings with Dammuth," he said.

Before the unicorn could answer, two large and skinny arms rose from the water and wrapped themselves about the Morigu. The arms were followed by a head. It was twice the size of Margawt's.

It was the face of an old woman marked and ravaged by time and evil. The grey straggly hair tangled itself around Margawt, and with powerful arms sought to draw him under.

Margawt's reaction was instantaneous. He drew his dagger and drove it into the withered breast. At the same time he shifted away from the blow and freed himself. He rolled to his feet with his sword out. Even as he turned, the hag disappeared into the water just as Anlon dove at her.

The unicorn stamped the stream bed in anger.

"'Ware!" he cried. "It is the Hag of the Elder Night, a Fomarian and perhaps the most dangerous." Margawt went on bended knee, staring at the ground as if searching a lake for fish.

"She is beneath us," he said. "She defiles the earth and blocks its power from me." There was a whooshing noise and the Hag appeared on Anlon's right flank. She came halfway up and raked five talons across the unicorn. Margawt dove toward her but her other hand unleashed a dazzling red beam that hit him full in the chest and threw him to the ground. Even as she sank into the ground again, Anlon's horn tore her right arm, and as quick as that she was gone.

Margawt rose to his feet. He could see that the unicorn had taken a bad wound, but Anlon showed no ill effects.

"Arianrood's power is greater than ever to have freed this one," said Anlon, his head wagging back and forth looking for the hag.

"Aye, we now know what attacked the dwarves in their caves." Margawt wiped dust from his mouth. "The Ead has much to pay for."

The hands reached through the ground and grabbed Margawt's feet. He was pulled up to his knees into the earth. He felt a sharp pain in his calf and plunged his sword deep into the ground. He was rewarded by freedom for his legs. He leaped and rolled, standing up once again, his left calf bleeding freely.

"She bit me!" his voice was full of outrage.

"We must kill her quickly, Margawt," answered the unicorn, "or the poison from her talons and teeth will kill us."

The Hag reared in front of Anlon. She was at least ten feet tall, her naked body withered and diseased. He rose to his hind legs and stabbed at her, but a terrific blow from her fist sent him stumbling into the dirt.

Margawt was there before she could withdraw again. She swiped at him, but he avoided it. His sword went straight between her sagging breasts, lying open an anemic chest. As his sword drove through her she laughed and a red shimmering aura danced up the blade. Before it could reach Margawt, the unicorn was on its feet again.

"No!" he cried, his horn smashing and breaking the weapon. Margawt fell to his knees, his arms numb from the blow. The red shimmer wrapped around the horn of the unicorn. Anlon cried with pain and danced away.

Margawt rose to his feet and dived away from another swipe. The demigod sank again. He made his way to the unicorn, who continued to shake his head as if trying to rid himself from an irritating fly.

"Don't touch me," he gasped, "it is plague and pestilence she has set on me. You must kill her yourself."

As if she had been conjured, the Hag appeared behind Margawt. He rolled away from her blow, but not the unicorn. A huge and decrepit fist smashed full into his muzzle. Blood and teeth flying, the unicorn fell to his feet.

Margawt dived barehanded at the Hag, but again she sank into the ground. He picked up the broken sword. It still had a foot and a half of steel attached to it. He dared not send his senses into the earth. The Fomarian had infected the ground for hundreds of yards around him. Margawt stood by the unicorn feeling pity for the first time since he had become the Morigu as Anlon struggled to his feet. His horn was almost buried in the shimmer of disease and the ground was soaked with his blood.

"I have her magic." Blood streamed from the unicorn's mouth. "You can defeat her with physical weapons," he gasped.

Again the arms came through the ground, this time grabbing the unicorn's back leg. Anlon cried out. A gruesome crack—the leg snapped and bone showed through the dark hide. Before the hand disappeared, Margawt's sword severed three fingers from the Hag's left hand. There was a ghastly howl beneath them. Quickly, Margawt fell to his knees and dug his hands deep into the earth during the reprieve his blow had provided. He called his power to him, and a small island of healthy earth formed around the two. The Hag strove to break it but could not.

She reared in front of them and waved her arms across her chest. Even as Margawt dove at her, his ears were pounded and he was pressed to the ground. The Hag sank into the earth again. Anlon gasped for air, but there was none. Somehow, the demigod had created a vacuum about the two. Margawt's island of salvation became a tomb.

Margawt's bark of desperation was not heard and with a backward glance at the suffocating unicorn he dove into the ground as smoothly as if he dove into a lake.

This was unlike any trip into the earth he had ever taken. There was no crystal radiance around him. The earth shivered and moaned, trying to throw off the fever of the Hag. Though he could move in the desecrated ground he could not see well. Margawt tried desperately to sense the Hag, but before he could, she came behind him and grabbed him about the neck seeking to choke him to death.

Margawt moved in a blur of speed. His right elbow slammed into her chest. He brought his legs straight up as far as he could, and levering with his left arm flipped free of the Hag. His body popped half up out of the ground. He felt his legs grabbed but the hold was unsure due to the loss of fingers on her hand.

He reached down and grabbing an arm held it while his sword flew through air, earth, and unholy flesh. He had severed her arm. The Hag sank deeper into the earth, her arm floating to the top as if they truly did fight in water.

This time, Margawt centered on her evil and dove toward her. He could see well enough so that he saw her remaining arm point and a Word of tremendous power usher from her lips. He gasped in pain, his left breast feeling as if a sledge-hammer had hit it. The force of the magic threw him out of the earth and onto its surface. He stared incredulously at his breast. It was torn completely, muscle and tissue hanging as if it had blown out from the inside.

The Fomarian appeared in front of him and sent his blade spinning from his hand with one push. Matching savagery with savagery, Margawt leaped upon her chest and one hand sent a blow to her chin that threw her to the ground. She could not marshal enough willpower to sink into the ground. Margawt's knees pressed into her shoulders. He smashed his left elbow into her toothless mouth as his right hand dove stiff-fingered into her throat.

She lifted herself into a sitting position but could not attack, for Margawt gave her a vicious head butt. As her head snapped back, his hands clapped either side of her ears. If she had eardrums it would have popped them. As it was, she swooned nearly unconscious . . . but Margawt knew he was weakening fast and must finish her now.

Again, his right hand went deep into her neck. This time he grasped the neck bone and pulled it straight through the neck. It broke and the Hag of the Elder Night, making no sound, bleeding no blood, died.

"At last," Margawt heard a whisper but he could not tell where it came from. Unseen by him, Lord Death straddled the dead Fomarian's body. In his hand he held a shimmering green and black bit of light. He laughed, juggling the demigod's soul from hand to hand.

"I curse you," he whispered to the soul form, "I curse you with all my power. Wherever you go from here, black one, the curse of Death will haunt you till you find final annihilation." He cast the evil thing from him watching as it sank into the earth. He smiled. No rebirth for that one, except in Hell. He stared into the many worlds, daring any to gainsay his right. But the gods in their fear still kept their eyes turned from the world. And none of the enemy saw his gesture.

'Soon,' he thought, 'soon,' and he was gone.

Margawt rolled off the stinking corpse and dragged himself to the unicorn. Anlon's bloody form made no movement. The red shimmering was gone from the horn. The blue-black coat was covered with deep red as the ground all about Anlon was stained.

Margawt tried to call the earth power to him to help himself and the unicorn, but the disease of the Hag remained and blocked him. The pain in his calf and breast built until even he could no longer bear it. He collapsed next to the unicorn, their blood mingling and spreading in pools about them.

For three nights the Morigu lay on the battlefield. He tried desperately to draw on the earth power to awaken, but it was too diseased. Corruption entered his veins and ravaged his soul. He wished to die but the call of the earth was too great. Then, he felt himself lifted and placed on clean earth. With a surge of joy, he drank in the health of the land, but it was not enough. He could not awaken. Grimly, he fought on as his life's energies drained away.

Two hours after speaking with Mearead Donal Longsword followed two dwarven warriors down a sloping path. He still could not believe the king really thought he could kill Arianrood and though he knew it a mad, futile venture he was determined to join the dwarf.

Donal's mail had been replaced with a full suit of dwarven chain mail. It was remarkably light and made no sound as he walked. It was a dusky brown color. "So," said the dwarf who presented it to him, "in shadow where you will walk no sound or sight will this mail give." In his hands he carried the two-handed longsword he was named for. It was unsheathed and in his heart he pledged never to sheath it till it drank the traitoress' blood, a vow he knew to be impossible but one he pledged to a brave dwarf lying dead in the valley of Morhalk.

Now Donal could hear a tingling as of wind chimes coming from ahead. He entered a great cavern filled with dwarves. His guides led him to the front, where Mearead stood by the falls.

The first thing that caught Donal's attention was the fact that this cave, unlike all the others he had seen, was untouched and left in its natural state. The falls came from the tremendous ceiling fully three hundred feet above. He had thought it would be a powerful flood of water. Instead, it was more like a stream, not more than a foot in depth and two in width. All along its straight path, imbedded in the wall, were beautiful glowing jewels that refracted the light off the wall, covering face and stone alike in a dazzling and ever-changing dance of colors, some that only one with elven or dwarven eyes could see. And the only noise the falls made was gentling music. Donal stopped and stared until a dwarf tugged him along out of his trance.

The fall came to land in a shallow pool. Where the water went after that he could not say. The pool's bottom was

covered with small multicolored stones that had been placed
there for thousands of years by dwarves seeking solace. In
this beautiful pool stood the king up to his waist in the
water. About him were seven cowled figures chanting in a
deep monotone.

The chanting stopped and Mearead spoke to the assembled crowd.

"All here know the news and the betrayal." He spoke
quietly but the cavern carried his words to everyone. "I leave
the kingdom in the worthy hands of my sister, Sorcha." The
woman bowed her head silently. All that Donal could see
was her blond hair. "Long has it been that any king has
called for the blood price. Now, I do. Despair not for me,
my friends, but for the fall of Colin and the dwarves, the fall
planned and executed by the black witch." Donal could feel
the hate and anger raging from all the dwarves. 'There must
be thousands in the cave,' he thought.

"We cannot march and burn her land, but we'll have vengeance and I will be the instrument." With that he turned to
the cowled ones. "I am ready, fathers," he said. He took off
his shirt, and with muscles rippling in the light held out his
hand. In it a knife made of pure crystal was placed.

"You claim the blood price?" came the deep voice from
the cowls, all chanting as one.

"I do."

"To strive until thy enemy dies beneath thy hands?"

"I will."

"To overcome all that stands in thy way until blood is
paid?"

"I can."

"To make the pact with earth and bone?"

"Earth and Bone."

"Blood and muscle?"

"Blood and muscle."

"Soul and spirit?"

"Soul and spirit."

"Life and destruction?"

"Life and destruction."

"Through all paths, all doors?"

"I will pass."

"And death?"

"Cannot defeat me."

"And pain?"

"Cannot reach me."

"You claim the blood price?"

"I will."

"You claim the blood price?"

"I do."

"You claim the blood price?"

"I have."

A sigh passed through the crowd. Now one of the cloaked dwarves stepped into the water. He took the blade and shrugged back his sleeves, revealing bare arms. With one hand, then the other, he cut long lines down his forearms. The blood flowed and was absorbed by the crystal. Quickly the cuts healed. The crystal seemed to be made out of liquid blood. The blade was handed back to the king.

"This is the blood of your people," said the cowled dwarf. "You have claimed the blood price as is your right. Do with it as you will." He stepped back out of the water. His robes were not wet.

"Blood price," said the king and he drew a long scarlet line across his chest. His blood did not go into the crystal but flowed down his chest to the water that slowly turned red.

"What is the price?" came the chant.

"The price is blood eagle." The dwarves shuddered as one, from fear or anticipation Donal could not tell.

"The price," came the chant, "is accepted." The pool was completely red now. Donal lifted his head with all the dwarves as, incredibly, the blood flowed up the falls. When it reached the top the whole cavern was cast a lurid color. All the dwarves seemed to be bleeding. The caverns and ceiling dripped the blood. The floor became a thick pool of red. Donal checked his arms. None of the strange light even reflected off his skin.

"The price is accepted," said the king. With that the seven figures melted to shadows and were gone. As quick as that the falls were clear and the cavern was its normal colors. Donal was covered with sweat and he knew he would never forget the cavern of blood he had seen. Mearead held the knife to his heart and the wound healed. The crystal returned to its normal state. He reverently placed it at the bottom of the pool. He came up to Donal and clasped his arm.

"We must begin," he said.

Mearead and Donal left the Crystal Caves a few hours later. They were in full armor and because of the properties of the camouflaging dwarven mail, wore no cloaks over it. For the rest of the day they walked without saying a word. That night they made a cheerless camp wedged among a large growth of bramble. Donal watched quietly as the dwarf reverently wiped and polished his helm. The helmet covered the dwarf's head and face completely. The front was designed to resemble a dragon. It was cleverly made so that the dwarf's beard seemed to jut out from the dragon's chin.

"Mearead," Donal said tentatively.

"Aye, lad."

"I've noticed that your helm is unlike any I've seen," he said awkwardly. "I mean, I've never known your people to make a dragon helm." Mearead said nothing. "What I mean is, I thought there was a great hatred for dragonkind among your folk." The old dwarven king's heart was brought from the dark plain of vengeance where it had dwelled for so long. He could not help but like this elf/man, bumbling his words around like some boy. He place his helmet down and lit a pipe.

"Well, lad," he started, "the dragon folk are the worst of all creatures. People think they are greedy. They are, but not in the way you imagine." He took a puff. "They desire gold and jewels, it's true, and hoard it, but what use have they for it? After all, they aren't going to go buy clothes now, are they?" He favored Donal with a smile.

"No, lad, it's not wealth they crave, but creations. He stabbed his pipe at the warrior. "That's why they are ever at war with my folk. For, of all thinking beings we are the most creative. We are artists born and revel in the making of all things."

"But why," asked Donal, "do they crave such works?"

"How is it, lad, that you were Warlord of Arianrood and know not of the great worms?"

"I was born during the Dark Seign wars. I became Warlord after the armies of Aes Lugh defeated the last of the old sorcerers."

"Ah," said Mearead, shaking his head at dark memories. "You mean Roinoin of the Third Eye. He was a nasty bastard. Well, I'll tell you, Longsword, the dragons don't eat as you and I. They get their strength from the destruction of others' work. The creative force remains in all things that are made, especially if they are dear to the heart of the creator and to others. The dragon consumes them and leeches that force as sustenance. Let that be a lesson to you, lad. Evil, by its nature, can never be creative. It can only flourish by destruction and seduction."

"And the helm?"

"Well, that's obvious, isn't it?" Mearead took a long puff and smiled to see the other's interest and expectancy. "Dragons can reach full maturity quickly if they have the hoard to devour. Consequently, great size does not denote age, but cunning and strength in acquiring and destroying hoards. So," smiled the old dwarf, "if there were any of their kind left, wouldn't it irritate them to see a fine large fellow like myself dressed to look like them? My, they are pleased to fatten up their obese ugly bodies." He chuckled at his own bravado.

He stopped abruptly and pointed his pipe at the Warlord. "Now, Longsword, I have a question for you," he said. "What do you know of the Duiraglym?"

"Duiraglym?" Donal asked.

"That's what we call it, the Howling Shadow. It is the power that has attacked us in the caves."

"I do not know of such a being, my lord." Donal placed his sword on his lap. "Why do you ask me? Do you not trust me?"

"Hmm, well, for the first question," Mearead leaned back, "the Duiraglym withdrew from our caves the night Colin left. But—and this is the strange part—it did not follow after Colin, but went to the east."

"How do you know?"

"I could feel it, boy. It is more than evil, that thing. It left a trail behind it of dead and diseased earth, like the slime of a dragon." Donal said nothing.

"I think it's a Fomarian. Colin was sure it was." Mearead sucked on the pipe. Donal rocked back and forth on his heels.

"No!" he said. "No. It is too much, too much." Mearead could see now that for all his strength and size, the Warlord was young, too young—as Colin had been.

"Well, it's no concern of ours right now," he relented. "As for the second question," he patted the other's knee, "dwarves see many things, Donal, and their King sees the most of all. I trust you implicitly." With that the dwarf wrapped himself in a cloak and went immediately to sleep.

Donal watched the small figure for a while, his mind dancing along the paths of elven dreams. Elven blood runs strong even in generations of dilution, but Donal was a half-elven and like all his kind was more elf than man. Sometimes, unlike true elves, he slept, but not tonight. For he knew that in a few days he would watch the sun rise over the battlefield he had been forced to leave. He shuddered to think about Mearead's anger when he saw the dead army.

Two days after leaving the caves, the companions approached the valley of Morhalk. All morning they had seen the scavengers flying through the sky, the heralds of Lord

Death. The two had become closer during the march. Mearead entertained Donal with a never ending catalogue of
elven jokes. But there were no jokes this day.

They walked into the battlefield and Donal choked back
his breakfast at the sight. The dwarves had died to a man.
The valley floor was covered with poles displaying dwarven
heads. The bodies had been torn and shredded until they
were unrecognizable lumps. Mearead said nothing, but trod
resolutely forward. They noticed at the top of the hill where
the dwarves had made their stand were several large, dark
shapes. When they reached the top, Donal lost his breakfast,
for, nailed to great poles were the bodies of Colin and Flann.
They were naked and mutilated. Mearead moved closer and
examined their bodies.

"They died fighting," he said, his voice more tired than
anything. "It took a lot to bring these two down. They died
fighting."

The field was also full of the enemy dead. The dwarves
had taken a terrific toll of their enemies. Mixed among the
men, elves, and brown elves, were grotesque and evil-look-
ing creatures which Donal now knew had hidden in the sorcerous mist. Neither said a thing as they took down the
crucified dwarves, and working the afternoon away made a
mound of stones and laid them to rest.

Donal stood shaking with his betrayal. His whole life and
his family before him for a thousand years had served the
Ead.

'And it all led to this,' he thought. He went back to the
pole and with a mixture of water and dried blood made a
thin red fluid. This he mixed with dirt from Colin's mound
and smeared it on his face. He no longer cared for the whys
or how comes, the Ead must die and that's all he knew.

"She must die!" his voice rose among the scavengers,
causing them to flap into the air. Mearead said nothing. He
withdrew six crystals, and juggling them in his hand walked
the edge of the battlefield depositing them equidistant from

each other. He came back to Donal and pulled him along with him. They moved to a higher ridge.

"You'll see some true dwarven magic now, lad!" Mearead spoke quietly. He held another crystal in his hand. He opened his mouth and from it issued a deep sound. Donal thought it sounded like 'Molin,' which means 'dwarf,' but he could not be sure.

For fifteen minutes the sound continued, and then the crystal began to glow. It sent out rays of different colored light to each of the other crystals. They in turn began to glow a red-orange, perfectly matching the sinking sun. The glow stretched from each crystal to a band of quivering light surrounding the battlefield.

"Blood price," whispered Mearead and his fist closed on the crystal. Instantly, the others flared and the whole field was covered in a fiery nimbus. The bodies took fire and burned away in minutes. When all that would burn was consumed and wispy grey smoke rose to the twilit sky, Mearead turned to the half-elf. Donal froze at the other's face.

It was totally unlined and held no emotion. The eyes were pure black with a speck of red, as if Donal were looking down a very deep tunnel with a small fire at the end.

"Her blood is mine," came the monotone chant and then Mearead walked away toward Aes Lugh. Donal hitched up his pack and followed. He began to think the dwarf might succeed in his quest.

CHAPTER

Thirteen

Eight nights after the battle with the Fomarian, the elf host rode into the plain before the capital of the empire. They had been joined by human warriors from Tinnafar and Teffit numbering about two thousand. The whole plain was covered with all the warriors of the realm that Tolath could field, their fires the glowing eyes of the beast in the night. The elves were picketed quickly and Lonnlarcan, Cucullin, Ceallac, Teague, and Bairbre with the commanders from the humans went into the city. There they met with Tolath's high command.

The meeting was adjourned in the same room that the alliance had met three long months ago. The emperor's place was conspicuously empty, and Lonnlarcan's heart ached when he saw no Dammuth. On the right hand of Trell'dem's empty seat stood Fin, elected Warlord of the West. His red beard bristling out from his chin, he shifted his great form uncomfortably in his chair.

Ernet, General of the armies, introduced everyone and began the conversation calling each to give their tales of the last weeks. Niall, Mathwei, and Oidean all sat together at one end, Niall looking sullen and angry, while Mathwei did the talking for these three.

"My lords and ladies," the whiplike Ernet bowed to Bairbre, "I will make no speeches. The enemy will move against us tomorrow." His intelligent eye was bright. "I suppose it's clear we need to win this one?"

"Our total force is?" asked Lonnlarcan.

"Nearly sixteen thousand, lord," answered Ernet, "containing your host."

"And the enemy?" Ceallac's voice was tired, his handsome face drawn.

"At least twice ours, maybe three," came the quick reply.

"It seems to me," stated Fin, "our main problem is can we offset their damnable magic?"

Lonnlarcan looked over to Bairbre. She stood up, her red hair and eyes looking wilder than ever. "That, my lords, depends upon their leaders." Oh, her voice was silk and steel. "We have five among the elves that may be called mages, myself included. Teague is our most powerful though he could never match the likes of Dammuth. The lords Cucullin, Ceallac, and Cainhill can match powers with nearly anything the enemy can throw against us, though they are mainly warriors. My Lord Lonnlarcan can fairly match magics and weapons against great powers." She sighed. "We have three Shee, but they are unlearned, fresh to their powers. They can do little. That, plus the normal elven magic, well, it adds up but it still depends upon their leaders."

"And we can safely assume," said Ernet, "that most of their power will be directed against us." He took a sip from his mug. "Dammuth is lost to us. Whatever has happened to him we cannot hope to see him again."

"And what other magics have you?" asked Lonnlarcan. The humans said nothing and shifted uneasily. Finally Niall leaped up.

"We have Oidean," he cried. The old man mumbled something and sank low into his chair. "He is a fire master and though he forgets much of his power, has helped us." The elves looked incredulously at the old man.

"It is true," added Mathwei. "We were ambushed on our

way to the city. Though Oidean has no subtle magics, he can command small fire elementals and create fireballs of no little strength." All perked up at this information and Bairbre eyed the old one thoughtfully.

"Is that the sum of your magic?" she asked.

"Aye, lady," said Fin, "the rest of our magic is used to heal. There is no great war magic in the empire anymore."

"Perhaps not," said Lonnlarcan, "but you have had help from some power in killing the salamander, Lord Fin, and perhaps such help will come again. And there is the Morigu and the Unicorn. They may return in time to help us."

"Perhaps," said Ernet, "we should withdraw behind the walls."

"I counsel against it," said Lonnlarcan.

"But surely," said Mathwei, "we cannot defeat the enemy on an open field." Lonnlarcan said nothing for a moment, sizing up the leaders in the room. He found he liked what he saw.

"I have learned one thing in this war, my lords. We must defeat the leaders of our enemies. So, though we may lose in the field, we need to draw out whatever powers the enemy has and seek to destroy them." After more discussion, all agreed on Lonnlarcan's plan and a few hours before daybreak the disposition of the forces were placed and the orders were given. The army waited.

They were spread across the plain. The main force of elves nd human knights held the center led by Lonnlarcan, Cainhill, and Fin. The left flank was held by the rest of the elves and a large force of human cavalry led by Ernet and Cucullin. The right flank was made up of Niall's troops and the knights of the Green Branch. Ceallac was given command of the Green Branch knights.

Ranged behind the mounted troops were the human foot soldiers bolstered by light cavalry and archers. Many great war machines were dragged from the city. And on a hill in the middle of the host, Teague, Bairbre, the three Shee, and the other mages of elfdom prepared their spells. In silence they awaited the rising of the sun.

It never came. Great black storm clouds billowed across the field heralding the approach of the Dark army. Their numbers filled the plain and the great army of Tolath seemed a tattered and tarnished sight compared to the black horde.

Ghastly fumes came from the Dark Ones. Crazy silhouettes danced among the witch lights. Moaning and screams, black chants and terrible war horns filled the air. And then Arianrood rode out.

She was surrounded by a nimbus of ghastly green light. She wore magnificent golden armor bedecked with jewels, her long black hair flowing free. Next to her walked the great Fomarian, his tread making the ground shudder. And then, riding on a beast of pure flame, the hermaphrodite Fire Lord. Next to him, riding a great bearlike shape, was a being of blackness and fear.

"The Shadow Lord," murmured Lonnlarcan.

"Another fomarian," Cainhill added, drawing his sword.

Then, last of all, striding behind the others, dripping horror and evil, Apkieran, the Lord of the Undead.

At the sight of him, Cucullin gave a great cry, but was restrained by Ernet. "Wait, lord," he said. "You'll have your chance." The story of the elf lord's hated of Apkieran was legendary.

The five horrors stood midway and the Fire Lord continued after a few words with Arianrood.

Lonnlarcan turned to Fin. "They seek to parlay." He shook his head. "Gods, the powers they bear against us."

Cainhill spoke, his voice tightly controlled. "Allow me, my lord."

Before Lonnlarcan could answer, the small figure of Dorrenlassarslany appeared.

"Great elf master," he said. "My choice, for honor of my people." He looked at the Ard Riegh imploringly.

"I had not thought your people would join battle," said the king.

"I am here. Choice is mine."

"Go, then," answered Lonnlarcan. The pyridin made to leave. "It is a good choice, a right choice you make, Dorrenlassarslany." The pyridin turned and whistled his pleasure and then was gone.

He appeared in front of the demon prince. The Fire Lord's mount had a human face that continually screamed in agony. It was the face of Fintan, general of Tolath.

"Well," the demon's voice was sibilant, "they have honored me by sending their greatest to talk, eh?" He smiled wickedly.

"Not impressed, unthing," answered the pyridin, for once standing straight and tall. "Talk fast before I decide eyeballs good choice for next meal." Dorrenlassarslany bared an impressive pair of fangs.

"Your time is up, little pig. Your people will be ground into the slime they are," answered the enraged demon.

"Bad choice to insult pyridin, unthing, say words." He just glared at the hermaphrodite.

"Tell your masters," Dorrenlassarslany hissed at that, "they may give themselves up. We will allow them to rule their people, under our guidance, of course. All they must do is deliver Lonnlarcan and his gang of cutthroats and their pathetic little Morigu."

The pyridin's form shivered for a minute. "Unmaker will mark you. You are undone, tell your masters," he spat out the words, "choice is stupid. You have chosen to be unmade. Leave, or all your choices will be taken from you by my hand!"

The Fire Lord felt a thrill of fear, not from the pyridin, but from his promise of the Morigu's wrath. He contemptuously spurred his mount, which cried in a horrible voice.

Dorrenlassarslany returned and told Lonnlarcan of the conversation. Then before anything else could be said, the little creature announced in a pout it would find a way to

make the unthing pay. It appeared in front of Cucullin minutes later.

The pyridin bowed low. "Great maker, choice you had,
god killer, you chose to be, no choice, understand need, for
my people great one, kill that Nullack (freak), make the
choice."

Cucullin stared down at the little creature who showed
none of the fear its kind was continually subjected to. He
realized it was an honor he was given, for Dorrenlassarslany
had admitted he could not kill the Fire Lord. It was a choice
he could not make; now he was asking Cucullin to make it.
The elf lord knew if he did not try the little one would pine
and die, not being able to face that a choice was denied to it.

"You know of my pledge and my word is given for the
life of the undead lord." He looked out at the battlefield
seeking his quarry, but the leaders had been swallowed up by
their army. He looked down at the pyridin, his eyes hard. "If
I can meet the Fire Lord before Apkieran faces my wrath,
rest assured, little one, I will kill him."

"Praise, good choice," the little creature danced. "Take
its choices and pyridin will always choose one to help elf
lords. It is fairly done, a good choice," and he was gone.

Ernet cleared his throat to catch Cucullin's attention. "My
lord," he said, "can you kill the demon?"

"I can," came the grim answer.

"Then I urge you to restrain your vengeance. You have
for long years. Kill the Fire Lord, Lord Cucullin, for the
help of the pyridin is not something we can afford to give
up."

Cucullin's green eyes filled with a pain the other could
never understand.

"It will be done," he said. How could a mortal understand
the pain in that choice? A quest of a hundred years, at last
the chance of its fruition and the elf lord postponing it for the
good of others? Such is the heart of the noblest of elven
kind.

Apkieran took up a position at the center of the host. The
Fomarian took the left flank and the Fire Lord led the right.

Arianrood and the Shadow Lord retreated to the rear to send spells against the humans and elves. A cry of a single horn was heard, and then, with growls, oaths, and battle cries from a thousand throats, the dark host moved toward the waiting allies.

The war machines of the empire fired as one. Great holes of destruction appeared in the enemy's front ranks, but it didn't slow them. In answer, fire and lightning hit the center of Tolan's line, but it did little damage to the elves there.

Lonnlarcan caught one bolt of lightning in Kianbearac and contemptuously flung it back. As the evil horde reached halfway, the human and elf horses charged. In the gloom of the storm clouds, the elves were easily picked out, for whenever one rode, a silver, clear light shimmered.

The war machines, enhanced with the elf magic, offset the enemy's usual advantage of battle magic. The air became full of smoke and fire, the smell of ozone and brimstone, blood and burnt flesh. Like two great leviathans the armies crashed together, howling their hate of one another.

For hours the two armies crashed while the onlookers in the city watched in fear. The horses and cavalry of the elves and men charged and reformed time after time, but each charge was lessened by empty saddles.

Fin pushed his way to the rear and climbed the hill where the elves slung their spells. The earth was scorched and torn and two of the elven mages had fallen. Of the twenty war machines, eight were totally destroyed and still destruction was hurled through the skies.

The elvish and human leaders tried desperately to engage the enemy leaders in personal combat but the three avoided every attempt. Step by step the army was pushed back toward the city.

Oidean cut a path to the Fomarian with a salamander of five foot height, but neither Ceallac nor Niall could reach the demigod to fight it. It threw a wall of earth to barricade itself, for it had its orders.

Fin led all the reinforcements to the left flank where Cucullin and Ernet were making some progress. The added manpower was enough for a counteroffensive to start.

Ernet and Cucullin rode at the front. All the elves charged as one and the enemy's line in front of them collapsed. Into the breach rode the two commanders, their warriors following. A great wall of fire appeared in front of them. Ernet was in the lead and was caught in it. His horse burst into flame even as he threw himself forward. He rose with drawn sword to face the Fire Lord. As the goblins moved to take Ernet, the demon's voice rang sharply.

"Leave this one to me." Ernet braced himself as the dark prince rode toward him.

The right flank of Tolan's host was completely stopped by the Fomarian's earth power. They stood firm but could not advance a single step.

The center was likewise caught. Facing them were hordes of undead and though the elves could not die by the hands of vampire or zombie, not so their allies. Lonnlarcan shouted encouragement and, with Cainhill on his right, wreaked mayhem upon the enemy. A deep cry of "Feth" was heard and a large wedge of trolls rammed into the center. With an audible groan the line held, but elf and man fell in huge numbers.

Cucullin's horse reared from the flames, but the elf lord encased the two in a golden aura, and unharmed they rode through to help the human general, but it was too late.

Ernet held his ground where many brave hearts would have given up. He heard a shriek of agony, and looking at its source was horrified to see Fintan's face wreathed in flames. In that moment the Fire Lord's blue-flamed sword took off the General's head.

Cucullin's cry of rage rose from the wall of fire, and, before the demon could retreat, Cucullin charged him.

Lonnlarcan spurred his horse at his adversary's. An explosion of silver fire from Kianbearac devastated the trolls. Cainhill followed, his violet eyes burning. He rode at Apkieran.

The right flank began to crumble as the Fomarian added his earth things to the goblin attack. Fighting every step, Niall kept his troops orderly, but he had no choice but to retreat. Mathwei, having lost his shield, fought at his side with a long dagger and a parrying knife. But his weapons did no harm to the creature that knocked Niall off his horse with a smack of its trunk. Two warriors grabbed the General up and pulled his unconscious body to the rear.

The firewall collapsed as the Fire Lord turned all his attention to the naked elf. The elves rode to support their lord and kept the goblins away from the fight. As Cucullin and his foe met, their sword and unseen ax sang as they clashed together. But Cu dived off his saddle and pulled the Demon Prince to the ground. The Fire Lord rolled away and stood facing the elf. Cu cried to his men.

"Kill that poor creature and give it its freedom." He pointed to the fire that was Fintan. The demon's sword crashed against Cucullin's ax as if to add emphasis to his words, as two elves ran the creature through with lances. The elves were hard-pressed to hold the enemy away as more goblins attacked.

The hermaphrodite's eyes burned red and two jets of flame splashed against the elf lord's chest, but it did no damage. Cucullin just showed his teeth. Enraged, the Demon Prince was forced on the defensive as the unseen ax beat against shield and sword. The demon cried in a great voice and his form was turned to fire. Now, in his true form, he could perceive the ax of the Aislinneena. Great rents appeared beneath the elf's feet and gouts of flame enveloped them.

Cucullin strode through them as if they were nothing but a light rain, his form encased in a golden light. The demon quailed at the sight of the armor and ax he could now perceive, recognizing them and Cucullin for the first time. A great ball of blue-white flame came from his brow but again no harm came to the elf.

"You put too much emphasis on your little fires, dog," said Cucullin, "and not enough in good blade work." His left hand contemptuously pushed the demon's thrust out of his ax's path. It came down in a silver flash. It clove through the demon's head and split it in two. From the cut a blue-black flame sprung and a wailing of terror was heard in the field. The charred body fell to the ground.

In the center of the field, Lonnlarcan desperately tried to get to Cainhill's side but he was cut off by a fresh attack. Cainhill's sword had twice breached the defenses of Apkieran, but it seemed to do no damage. His shield was beaten into uselessness by the great bleeding ax. Cainhill held his sword two-handed, crying spells desperately, throwing all his power at the demon.

Apkieran did not even try to defend himself from the spells, knowing his death could never be accomplished by magic. Cainhill's latest spell caused the grass to grasp the skeleton around its feet, but as soon as the grass touched skin or bone it withered and died. The great ax chopped down and Cainhill's sword shivered apart. He fell to his knees.

Apkieran picked the elf up with two hands.

"You have bitten off more than you can chew, little lordling." With that he bit deep into Cainhill's chest with his tusklike canines. At Cainhill's cry of anguish, Lonnlarcan cleared his path with a silver flame from Kianbearac. Apkieran dropped the elf and turned to meet this new attack.

"Not now," a sibilant hiss said in his ear. "Don't show your power too soon." Apkieran nodded to the unseen speaker and lifted his hands above his head. At his cry a hundred great bats enveloped Lonnlarcan and his mount. By the time the Ard Riegh freed himself the undead lord was gone. The elves grabbed up Cainhill and the retreat began.

* * *

It took two hours for the forces of Tolan to retreat inside the city. They had done great damage to the enemy, but their own hurt was tremendous. Fully a third of the army lay upon the field in front of the city. Only four of the war machines had been saved. Among the fallen were Ernet, their General, two of the elf mages, one of the Shee, and the lord Cainhill.

The enemy surrounded the city, but their forces were not endless and they were spread thin. But there was no force to break through the siege and free those within. It looked as if Tolan would fall.

The Dark army attacked all through the night. None of the attacks were too serious. They were used mainly to keep those in the city off balance. Lonnlarcan joined his magic with the three remaining elf mages to ward against the enemy's spells. Both Teague and Bairbre tried to get some much-needed rest. Lonnlarcan wished to use his power to heal the wounded, especially Cainhill, but the sorcerous attacks continued and he had no choice.

Cainhill's body was racked by fever. His skin turned a sick yellow and he was covered with black putrid sores, especially around the area where Apkieran had bitten him. Elvish healers worked grimly to save his life. But Cainhill was dying. Slowly, painfully, he was dying.

While the weary defenders of Tolan prepared for another assault, Donal and Mearead entered the woods of Aes Lugh. The dwarf led the way through a tangle of hanging moss, the pale growth clinging to his shoulders and arms. Donal was having an even tougher time of it, his large frame working against him. They made their way into a dismal clearing.

"It is not the Aes Lugh of my memory," said the dwarf.

"Evil clings to her, lord," answered Donal. "Hardly can I believe this is the place of my birth."

"It's hard to believe you saw none of these dark changes," questioned Mearead.

"I think I did, but my loyalty to the witch closed my

eyes." Donal never called Arianrood anything but 'the witch' now. "Many of our greatest lords have disppeared in times past. She always answered my queries with a curt explanation." He sighed. "I suppose they were the ones who had seen clearly. They must be dead or worse now."

"Wait a minute, lad, you might have hit on something." Mearead sat down with a thump. "This bloody forest is endless and to enter Arianrood's city would be suicide." He drew his pipe out, the picture of unconcern here in the hold of his most dire enemies. "I can find no trace of her. So what if she didn't kill off everyone who opposed her?"

"What do you mean?"

"Try using your head, lad, that's what it's there for." Mearead lit up, puffed, and sighed contentedly. "Oh, some must have seen even as you say. She could not convince the great ones to join her, so she had to get rid of them, kill them or otherwise."

"I see." Donal's face lit up. "I see. She'd have to imprison them, and one of power could not be imprisoned in her city. Too much of her old magic would be there to draw on. She'd have to place them elsewhere."

"Aye," Mearead's voice was excited now. "And aye again, lad. The bitch is not here, that I'm sure of. Even her power could not mask her from me. But if she were elsewhere, distance could do what no wall or door could." He withdrew his pipe. He stood up and cocked his head as if listening. "There's nothing about that can interfere."

He knelt down and dug in the soft earth for a while. Finally, he brought out a small jagged stone. "Like calls to like," he mumbled. He closed his eyes, his hands rubbing the stone, softly. As if brought out by his touch, a small glow appeared from the stone as if a light were inside it. Donal thought he could peer into the stone and see a small heart beating.

Mearead placed the stone on the ground, placing either hand opposite it as he bent down and breathed on it once. He sat back with a look of pleasure as the stone continued to glow. It moved a bit, as the earth underneath it popped into the air. A small squirt of water shot out, then more. It made a pool, bubbling quietly. Then the earth on one side bent back to form a furrow. The water flowed down it and in moments a tiny stream formed and flowed to the south.

"This will lead us to the witch?"

"No, but to her prison," Mearead answered. "Tightening the straps on his backpack, he began to follow the stream.

"Mearead," Donal could not hide his exasperation, "Aes Lugh is hundreds of miles wide. We could be following this thing for weeks."

Still walking away, Mearead sighed. "First, Arianrood would have to have made her prison far from the heart of Aes Lugh."

"I agree with that," Donal caught up with him, "but wouldn't she put it in Fiodha, Remon's land, or at least near it?"

"Maybe."

"Besides, even if we find the prison and free whoever's there, how does that bring us closer to getting her?" Mearead stopped and stared up at the seven foot giant.

"Arianrood is most likely in Tolath." He raised his head. "I know that because she's not here, so I can't reach her now. What I can do is get information, and perhaps allies."

"We could—"

The dwarf interrupted, "It has to be close now, or my magic wouldn't be able to find it easily. Try to be a bit more patient." He marched off. Donal shrugged in resignation and followed.

But Mearead was not as unconcerned as he pretended. In the back of his mind he heard a voice: "And in time, you, too, shall hunt. . . ."

CHAPTER

Fourteen

Two days later the Dwarf King and the Warlord still hunted. They were deep in the land of Aes Lugh now, but in all that time they had stopped only briefly to eat. Neither had slept or rested since leaving the valley of Morhalk. Such was their strength that despite their grueling pace neither showed any signs of fatigue.

Mearead's stream led them on, avoiding any path or place of habitation. Twice they had left the stream to attack patrols, but they got no information from their captives and killed them all.

'It is getting time to eat,' Donal thought. He and the dwarf rarely talked now. They had argued over the killing of the captives. Mearead insisting they could leave no trace behind, the Warlord grieving for the hard cruelties of this war.

As he walked he became aware of a pressure in front of him. Every step he took it became stronger, as if he was trying to walk through water that was slowly hardening to ice around him.

"I can feel something, Mearead," he gasped, wiping sweat from his face. "Some magic slowing me, stopping me. Gods, I can barely move!" Mearead stopped, placing his hands in front of him.

"We've found it." His voice was gruff. "There are bindings here, powerful ones."

"Yes," Donal took another sluggish step, "they are stronger than any I've ever encountered." Mearead drew his ax and looked up at the half-elf.

"Aye, Longsword," he said, "I doubt you can go any further. Your name is tied in this spell. Whatever the bitch has hidden here, she does not want you to find it. I'll go on alone."

"Nay, I go with you, Dwarven King," Donal answered, taking another step though his limbs quivered with the strain.

"Now, lad, there's nothing there to harm. You can only get through by breaking the magic and if you did that, her holiness would be alerted." It took more convincing, but Donal finally gave in after Mearead promised to call if he needed to help.

"I can get through without breaking the bindings, lad. It's the only way." Mearead lit his pipe and handed it to Donal. "Keep yourself busy," he admonished and with that he was gone.

As Donal tried to figure out what he was supposed to do with the pipe, Mearead made his way toward the place of power. As he went, he chanted. He would go ahead a few feet, step back one, move to the side and go a further step. The binding was made to stop all living things. As soon as it became aware of Mearead he would call his power to him and where there had been a living being there now became stone. The spell could not cope with this subtlety and Mearead broke through after an hour.

He walked into a clearing. It was a clearing because all that had been in this area had died. Great trees lay on the ground stinking of rot and putrefaction. There were bones of animals, still covered with strings of grey flesh, lying in grotesque heaps. Grass and vegetation were completely destroyed with bits and pieces of twigs strewn about. A memory of the life that was once here.

The area was about thirty yards in radius. It was bounded by a wall of grey shifting mist. This spell wall became dark smoke at the top and covered the prison in a dark and eerie dome. Chained to the trunks of dead trees were a dozen forms. Those nearest to Mearead were unmoving. He went to the closest and inspected it.

It was the mummy of an elf, probably a great lord by its size. He or she had been wrapped in a glistening chain. Mearead had never seen the like of that metal. The body had obviously been tortured and somehow all the fluids withdrawn; left was only parched skin and bone. The whole place smelled like a slaughterhouse and Mearead's eyes watered from it.

"Thus ends all your loyalty, friend," but his mind was on Donal and Colin. His voice came out dead and empty. 'As if one of these poor creatures could talk themselves,' he thought. Then he heard a moan. For a minute he started thinking one of the mummies had answered him, then he saw a movement from one of the further bodies. It was accompanied by the rasping of chain. He went over to the noise.

Bound to this stump was a human. She was naked and bruised, but all things considered, not bad off. Her tiny breasts fluttered with some movement.

"It's all right, lassie. I've come to free you." He grabbed hold of the chain. He dropped it with a curse. Somehow it had cut him. Though it seemed smooth, it was like ground glass to the touch. Mearead noticed the woman was bleeding wherever the chain touched her. He growled. 'That metal should be made so!'

He went around to the back of the tree. Lifting his ax he brought it down with a great bang. Nothing happened. He lifted his ax again, this time crying, "Naud betth!" When his ax hit, it cut deep into the chain. It lodged halfway while the chain went through a transformation.

The links glowed white as if with heat and then turned a metallic black. Mearead drew the ax with a grunt of satisfaction and grasped the transformed chain with two hands. He pulled it apart with one jerk, its loud snapping a dull thud in the dead air of that place.

Swiftly he went around and caught the girl. He was noticing a fatigue growing and realized it was the place itself that leeched the others of their life. It seemed to him the more powerful a person, the quicker and faster he was drained.

"I'll have you out of here soon, girl, as soon as I see if there are any others."

"There are no others alive here." She spoke through a haze of fatigue and weariness. "Take me away now. I can't last much longer." Her hand grasped him, but there was not strength in that grip. "Please," she whispered. Her eyes rolled white and she fell unconscious.

Mearead picked her up in his arms, and headed for the boundaries. Surprisingly, he could leave easily. The chains must have restrained the others until they were too weak to escape. Many spells were this way, all their power directed one way or the other. It was just a matter of finding their weakness. 'And,' thought Mearead, 'that weakness can always be found.'

As he left that place he felt his strength and vitality returning. He reached Donal and with a curt explanation began to tend the woman. As he left Mearead hadn't noticed a weak glowing on the farthest edge of the prison. There a little glowing spiral was encased in a glass prison. It bounced itself off the walls of its prison but could not escape. Its pitiful cry was not heard. And thus was it that Shorty, Dammuth's familiar in its true form, remained in the prison that Arianrood had trapped it in.

The next morning the girl awoke. Mearead, having become convinced there was no more point in remaining in Aes Lugh, had led the march east. They had walked all night, Donal bearing the woman the whole way. Even Mearead was impressed by the ex-warlord's strength. They stopped by a brook and revived their new companion.

She awoke with a start and stared up with sea-grey eyes at the dwarf and the hulking shadow that was Donal. "What?" she mouthed. Mearead gave her some water and in a soothing voice explained who they were and how it was that she was freed. She asked no questions but listened carefully, fondling her dark brown hair absently. Both the half-elf and the dwarf were well-skilled in the art of healing and since the woman had been more drained than damaged, she awoke almost to her full strength.

"So, lass, that's the tale," said Mearead. "And now who are you and what can you tell us?"

She turned away, lost in dark memory for a moment and then a quiet voice answered.

"I am Bronwen, lord. Bronwen ap . . ." she shook her head fiercely. "Well, that doesn't matter now. I am the daughter of the betrayer, Remon." Her hand dug at the ground. "Five years ago he joined the Ead and turned our land into a place of evil. I and others fought his power but his magic increased and all were killed save me, including my four brothers. *She* promised to keep me alive. I suppose one day he thought I'd join him," she turned away and spat. "It matters little now. We are on the same side, lord, and I will help you in your quest. Gladly will I help any who would contend with that black traitoress!"

"It's information we need the most," added Mearead.

"Aye, and I can most assuredly help you in that." She rose to her feet. "I fought them for five long years. Only weeks ago was I finally captured, for, my lords, I had help."

"Help?" asked Mearead.

"Oh yes, help." She turned and glared at Donal. "Surely the Warlord," it was a slur from her mouth, "has heard of the huntress?"

"You!" exclaimed Donal.

"Me!" she said, challenge in her very stance.

"Ah, well, that's grand," said Mearead, "absolutely grand. Suppose you two pups tell me what the hell you're talking about?"

"The huntress," Donal pointed accusingly at the woman, "she was a thorn in the witch's side. An assassin in the night, killing and murdering all who served the Ead."

"Well, that's certainly a good recommendation if you ask me," Mearead said.

"Well, it would be," said Donal, "except that it was said that she served that dark god, the Hunter!"

"You've got a lot to learn, Warlord," was the girl's swift and angry reply, "if you think the Hunter serves the dark!"

Mearead cut off Donal before he could reply.

"Hold now, hold now," he said. "The Hunter, eh?" She nodded her head. "How is it that you know of that one?"

"He came to me in those first few days, he taught me the ways of the hunt," she spoke proudly. "He told me of Remon's betrayal and that he thought Arianrood was behind it, but he was not sure. He dared not contest her openly to find out. He said he was preparing for a great war that was to come and I was to be one of his weapons."

"One of his weapons." Mearead sat down and rubbed his chin. "Oh gods, that is the best news I have learned of in long ages." He looked the woman over carefully. "If what you say is true, if the Hunter has truly given up his long neutrality, then welcome you are to our company!"

"My lord," cried Donal, "if what she says is true then she is surely not on our side!"

"Donal," said Mearead in a quiet but firm, very firm, tone, "quit calling me 'my lord.'" Donal looked confused. "I mean it. It aggravates the crap out of me. And, my brainless friend, consider if you would your sources of information." Donal had nothing to say to that. "For your information, the Hunter was once the husband of the earth Goddess herself. Long years ago he fought by her side to bind the Fomarians." He gave Bronwen a searching look. "Lass, the Hunter did not help in the Dark Seign wars. Why would he help in this one?"

"I do not know, my . . . Mearead," she said. "But you could ask him yourself."

"Why, how?"

"I will call him."

"You will call him," Mearead shook his head, "and he will come just like that?"

"He always has, my lord . . . Mearead." She glared at Donal. "I did not call him often, but he has always come."

"Well, call, lass, call!"

She smiled at him and turned to the west. "Hunter," was all she said. Then she knelt down by the brook and began to wash herself.

"Oh really, Mearead," exclaimed Donal. "'Hunter'! And he comes. A god! He comes when you just call his name?"

Mearead looked at the girl calmly washing her face. "That's it, lass?"

"Yes. He will come if he wishes to when he wishes to," she stated matter-of-factly.

Mearead shook his head. "Well," he said, "you're either crazy or you have a humble god, girl." He took out his pipe and tobacco pouch. As he filled it Donal snorted in disgust.

"By the gods!" he said. "This is a little too much, don't you think? We have serious things to do, Mearead. We can't sit around waiting for this woman's fantasies to appear."

"Why not?" said Mearead. "After all, she might be telling the truth."

"You're just going to sit there and smoke your pipe?"

"That I am," Mearead smiled up at him. "If you have a problem here, lad, don't hold it in. Get it off your chest."

"Gods!" Donal sat down in disgust.

"We'll see," answered Mearead.

"I am not a humble God," said a voice. All looked in surprise at the figure that had joined them. With no warning or noise, He had come. He stood seven feet tall, a grey shadow. His outline was human except for the two stag horns that came from His brow. There were two dark patches where His eyes should be. Other than that they could make no features out. He was like a silhouette of a shadow against a wall, except He had substance.

"And," He added, his voice deep and possessing a threatening and frightening quality to it, "I do not serve the Dark. I serve nothing save myself."

Bronwen went on her knees and bowed. "My lord," she whispered. Donal bowed in awe, despite his misgivings. Mearead just looked up.

"Now I'll be damned," he said. "You of all, I am honored." He made a little nod with his head.

The shadow knelt on one knee in front of the three of them. "Great praise from you, Mearead," He said chuckling. "I always wondered why your kind worshipped the Mother and not I."

"We worship none," bristled the dwarf. "We just, ah, tend to be on better terms with the Goddess."

"Indeed," said the God. The three felt a peculiar tingling in their bones and a refreshing clarity of mind. Only in this way did the Hunter manifest His divinity.

"Well, Bronwen, glad I am that you have been freed at last!" She smiled delicately and sat back on her ankles, water dripping down her chin. "And Warlord," said the God. Donal looked defiant, if a little worried. "Arianrood chose you knowing your loyalty would blind you longer than the others." Donal looked crestfallen at this latest disclosure. "But she made a mistake. You've proved to be a good ally and a fierce enemy."

"Then, my lord, you are going to actively join us in this war?" asked Mearead.

"I already have. More than you think. You've gathered by now this war is more dangerous than the Dark Seign wars?"

"Indeed, I'd begun to think along those lines."

"Dwarf understatement again." If a shadow could smile, then He did, though it was a feral grin. "There is more here than even I know. Much is hidden from me. There are no prophecies or true knowledge. This war was not supposed to be."

"Well," said Mearead, "that's life!"

The shadow chuckled again. "Aye, Mearead, life has surprises even for Gods! Now I cannot remain long or other powers will know." He stood up, looking over the others. "Arianrood is in Tolath. She leads the armies against Tolan. The battle has been going on for days there." Mearead's eyes went bright and he grasped his ax. "I'll get you there quick but you must do me a favor." Mearead nodded once.

"The Morigunamachamain has fallen wounded along with my servant. You will revive the Morigu with your powers, Mearead. Then the four of you will go there." He touched Mearead's forehead and a flash of a route, a path leading to a sanctuary was placed into his mind like a recalled memory. "There you will find others who are my followers. With them you will go and join the battle of Tolan." He pointed and behind Bronwen a blue oval appeared. "That is your doorway. Step through and you will reach the Morigunamachamain. Mounts wait for you to bring you to my temple. They await your arrival." Mearead and Donal quickly packed up.

"Mearead, kill her." The Hunter's voice was harsh. "She must die. Beware, though, I fear that they seek to free the Dark One. Stop them. If he rises, no God may contend with him and the last battle will begin. And Mearead, there is no time or power to create another Fealoth." Mearead stepped through and disappeared. "Bronwen, huntress you are and huntress you will be. I am well-pleased, my daughter." And she was gone. Donal made to go through, but the God's hand grabbed his shoulder. Donal spun around. "Fear me not, Longsword."

"I am sorry for my words, lord," he stammered.

"Many have been hurt in this war, you not the least." The God's hand reached into Donal's chest. Donal was filled with an ecstasy, a pulsing of his own strength and joy to be alive. "Ah, it is rare, young one, that I may touch the heart of honest loyalty and true honor." The Hunter withdrew his hand and held it out. "Your sword." Donal placed it pommel first in the God's hand.

"A good blade." His other hand traced the sword. Black runes were left etched in the blade. "Stay with Mearead, protect him with your life. Only he may destroy the witch. See that he has his chance." Donal nodded slowly, his face filled with awe. "The Morigu has been filled with wrongness. The enemy will seek to corrupt him. Befriend him, Donal. Teach him your honest vision of the world."

"By my sword, my lord, I will do as you ask."

"I am the God of the Hunt, Donal. God of blood and chase, fear and pain, savagery and quick death. I do not give my blessing often. You have it." Donal bowed long and deep and then with no further words between them he stepped through the hole.

Even as he disappeared, a great shape stepped through to his side. A third shadow joined them. This one was smaller than the others but it radiated immense power. It said in a gentle voice, "They are well-picked."

"Are they enough, great one?" said the second shadow.

"They must be," it answered.

"Our time is limited," said the Hunter. He turned to the second shadow. "We must move quickly. A dragon has risen."

As Bronwen woke, the defenders of Tolan prepared for another day of siege. Two forms broke from the enemy encamped at the front gate. One was tall and thick, his sickly third arm moving spastically at his side. The other rode a strange saurian beast some fifteen feet in length. The rider's features could not be seen. His form wavered in size from six to sixteen feet, though it was always vaguely humanoid.

The two fomarians stopped beneath the gate, staring up at the massive wall. Even as Lonnlarcan and the other leaders were rushing to the scene, the eye of the three-limbed Fomarian opened.

A beam of colorless power shot from it to encase the whole gate, and as it did the gold plating began to melt and run. The gates buckled as if they, too, were melting, though they were made of stone.

The young Shee, Geaspar, recklessly threw a spell down at the Fomarian assailing the gate. His power was weak and the spell was a simple one of force meant to knock an opponent to his knees. It did no damage and the giant ignored him, but the Shadow Lord rode out and pointed his finger at the youth.

Geaspar was immediately taken by a fit of shaking, his whole body twitching convulsively. Bairbre reached him and tried to dispel the magic, but it was too late. The young elf's body shook at an incredible rate, his head banging on the stone till it bled. Then, with a terrible squelching noise, his eyes, eardrums, heart, and veins all popped at once.

Bairbre rose with a cry and a sheet of red power flew from her outstretched body. It hit the Shadow Lord, knocking him off his mount. He rose to his feet to retaliate when a loud rending was heard and the great gates of Tolan fell to the ground, crumbled and useless. As the dust settled a mounted figure stood at the gate. It was Lonnlarcan, Ard Riegh of the elves. Everything was silent. Only the 'clop clop' of his horse's hooves were heard.

"I know your name, Flannlarc ap Laiche." Lonnlarcan's voice was low and dangerous. "Oh, it was a powerful spell that blinded your name to me, but not powerful enough." The giant waved his mattock threateningly and advanced a step.

"This way is barred. I am now the gate you must pass through!" The Elven King's form seemed to grow until he overshadowed the Fomarian. The Shadow Lord mounted and retreated into the mass of goblin soldiers.

The second Fomarian, Flannlorc ap Laiche—which means cruelty, son of spite—moved no closer to the Ard Riegh. No threatening gestures were made; the two antagonists just stared at one another. Slowly, sullenly, the demigod turned and walked away. The walls burst out in cheering as the giant disappeared in the quiet horde of the enemy army.

The defenders of Tolan surrounded Lonnlarcan, congratulating him. The elven king just shook his head. He knew the siege would start again and soon. How could they hold with no gate?

Later, as he was discussing his worries with Fin, Teague, the Lord Mage, entered. He bowed his old white head to the king.

"My lord," his eyes were gold to Lonnlarcan's silver, "I can bar the gate."

"What?" exclaimed Fin.

"It is a magic, a powerful magic I learned long ago," he explained. "I cover the gateway with a magic barrier and infuse myself with it. It will be impassable."

"But Teague," said Lonnlarcan, "if you do that we shall be that much weaker in our defensive magics."

"Aye, that's true, lord," the mage shrugged, "but if I don't do it, the city will surely fall. No barricade will stop the fomarians and the others."

Fin said nothing, leaving it to the elf king to decide.

"It will be done," sighed Lonnlarcan.

Many of the soldiers of both armies gathered at the gate to watch the elven magic. Teague approached the gate slowly. Across the entrance, wagons, beams, and loose rock had been piled to form a flimsy barricade. Ten paces from it the elf stopped.

He raised both his hands and spread them wide. From each finger a red line of thin filament flew out, like the web of a spider. The lines reached the sides of the gate, then raced across the entrance to meet. Teague's hands and fingers, starting at the tips, began to glow red.

"He says no words," said Fin to Lonnlarcan.

"Aye, this is a magic of the will," answered Lonnlarcan. "It is his very essence that creates and binds this magic. A lesser mage might need to accompany such a feat with gestures and words of power, but in this Teague needs no ritual."

The lines continued to thicken and now the onlookers could see that Teague's body began to blend into the lines. Already his hands were gone, just thick strands shot from his wrist to the gate. The process sped up.

First the elf's arms then shoulders melded into the gate, his body glowed and transformed into a coruscating shimmer of bright red power. In minutes that, too, was gone, and all that there was to see of Teague was a thick shield of red covering the gate from top to bottom.

Lonnlarcan walked over and picked up the elf lord's tunic and cloak that had not transformed with him. He held the clothes in his hands a minute, then not looking at the gate walked back toward the palace. Slowly the crowd broke up until only one figure remained.

It was Dermot, the last of the three Shee that had joined the elf hosting. Her brown hair was a fierce tangle that matched well her proud dark eyes. She was wearing a tattered piece of mail and had a single sword. She stared long at the barrier that was Teague.

It bothered her that anyone could do such an act, giving up all movement, thought, and feeling to protect others. She wondered if she were capable of such a gift. She thought not.

While the weary defenders prepared for the next assault, Donal, Mearead, and the huntress Bronwen all stepped from the grey doorway the Hunter had created. At their feet lay the battered Morigu, his breath coming in ragged gasps. Mearead bent down on one knee and began to tend him.

While Donal fetched water, Bronwen wandered around. She saw a great pool of dried blood right near where they had come through the portal. Investigating, she looked to find any sign of where the Morigu and unicorn had fought the Fomarian. But there was nothing but the blood stain.

It took Mearead half the day to revive Margawt. As far as Bronwen could tell, all the dwarf did was sit there and stare at the fallen warrior. Donal, more sensitive than she, could feel the earth strength rush through the land into the Morigu's body. The ground began to shake a little and both watched incredulously as the tissue of Margawt's breast was rebuilt, muscle by muscle, the old flesh falling away like so much dead meat.

Soon all bruises and cuts were gone. Margawt's eyes fluttered and opened. He stared impassively at the trio.

"Thank you, old one," he said to Mearead. Bronwen gasped as he rose to his feet; except for his tattered mail, none the worse for his ordeal. He walked over to the battlefield but not onto it. For a moment he studied it then he turned back to the others, his face handsome and hard.

"The unicorn?" he asked.

"You were the only one here, lad," answered Mearead. He stood up slowly, his body one ache. "We were sent to help you, Margawt, and all four of us were given another task." Quickly he made introductions and shared his story. The Morigu told of the fight and how he came to be here. As soon as he learned Arianrood was in Tolan, he made to go off but the dwarf restrained him.

"Mounts will be provided. You could learn some patience, warrior." The Morigu glared at him, but he did wait.

In minutes their mounts came. They were four great wolves, but not like wolves any of the companions had seen. The animals were pure white, a sickly anemic white. The only thing about them that wasn't white were their red eyes and tongues. They trotted up, five feet at the shoulder. They just stood there. The companions approached them warily.

"The hounds of the hunt," said Mearead. "Never have I heard they bore riders."

"They are not evil or wrong," said the Morigu, "but there is a taint about them I do not understand." Bronwen looked at the strange elf trying to decipher his words. She placed a hand on one of the wolves. The fur was soft, softer than any fabric or fur she had ever touched. She mounted the wolf.

"Come, my lords," she said. "The war awaits us." With

that she and her mount turned and took off at a fantastic pace.

"Almost as fast as fallen Anlon," said the Morigu. He mounted and waved once to the battleground. "I will remember, great one," and he was gone.

Donal and Mearead looked at each other. "Well, you better help me up on this nasty beast, lad. No other choice for it." Donal helped him and then mounted the last wolf. They tore after the others, with the wolves making no noise.

Donal cried over the rush of the wind. "Quit calling me 'lad,'" he said. "I am a hundred and seventeen years old."

"Right you are, boy," came the answer. They both laughed as their mounts sped them into the east.

CHAPTER

Fifteen

At Tolan the siege began again as soon as night came, the enemy assailing walls with soldiers, wills with magic. Nothing they brought to bear could break Teague's barrier at the main gate and the fomarians assailed no other doors.

Late that night as the attacks were intensifying, Donal, Mearead, Margawt and Bronwen rode their bizarre mounts through a strange land. It was not dark, but there was no sun where they traveled. They rode upon one vast empty plain.

"Mearead," Donal shouted through the rush of the wind, "this is not Tolan."

"No," Mearead clutched the fur of his mount tighter, "this is no land that I know."

"It is a door," Margawt offered. "We ride the pathways of the gods."

Bronwen moved her mount even with the other three.

"Can't we stop?" Her face was white with fatigue.

"No," Margawt answered. "This land is not meant for the touch of mortal flesh. You would die if you dismounted." He urged his mount on, and the giant wolf leapt ahead of the others.

"Cheerful guy, huh," Mearead shouted over to Donal, but the Warlord said nothing as he desperately strove to keep his long legs from touching the ground.

They continued for hours, though time has little meaning

in the nameless land. Finally, they saw a thick wood ahead. The wolves did not slow their reckless pace and all four concentrated on staying on the mounts. The woods became a little hillier and the wolves slowed down.

"Smell that!" Mearead yelled, taking a deep breath in his lungs. "This air, real air. Wherever we are, we're back in the land." They all shouted to feel the sun on their faces.

The travelers cleared the woods, and straight ahead, not a hundred paces, was a sheer face of a small cliff. Their mounts ran straight for it. All four riders tried to stop them but before even Margawt could leap off, the wolves plowed straight into the wall which wasn't a wall. The four found themselves riding through a pitch-black cave which even dwarven eyes would be hard-pressed to see in. Margawt and Donal felt the presence of watchers that were quickly left behind in the mad rush of speed. Then, just as quickly, the four found themselves out of the cave and in a small valley.

Looking behind her, Bronwen saw that there was a cliff wall behind them. It is a masking spell, she realized, one that covered the entrances to the tunnel.

The valley they found themselves in was tiny. It was all rock and dirt with no trees in sight. A path led up the side of the valley, where a structure could be seen. It was comprised of a wall with four grim towers, and a single gate that was lowered over a chasm of two hundred feet. All they could see inside the walls was a large grey dome that peeked over the side walls.

The wolves raced up and stopped at the lowered drawbridge. Quickly the four dismounted. The wolves turned and sped back the way they had come, making no noise. Three figures stood at the other side of the bridge. They were cloaked in grey and seemed to blend into the walls behind them.

"We have waited for you," said the tallest one. "We bid you welcome to the temple of the Horned God." The three bowed.

"Well," said Mearead, walking toward the mysterious figures, "no doubt about it. This is the place."

On the fifth morning of the siege the sun once again could not break through the barrier of clouds. The smoke from fires and magics created a dense second layer that made the day even gloomier. Arianrood, High Priestess of Fealoth, Queen of Aes Lugh, Ead, stretched her bare arms to the solemn sky. She stared at Tolan, her eyes two green beacons drawn to the red glare of Teague's barrier. Even she could not pierce that barrier. 'But there are ways,' she said to herself, 'there are always ways.'

"General," she called. A creature all brown scales and fangs walked up to her. He towered over her, his armor made of stretched human skin. They stood on a stark scorched hill, a small stunted and burned tree their only companion. Arianrood stared up at the demon, her naked body pale and ethereal in the dim morning haze.

"Tell the Fudiaacha (ravisher) to go to the main gate, and assemble a strong force there."

The demon bobbed his head. He took a step back. "But mistress, the gate is . . ."

Her hair sparked with green. "I know about the gate, fool. I will banish the spell that protects it." The creature made a hasty retreat. "And general," she called, "tell him to kill Lonnlarcan if he tries to bar his way again." She watched the shambling monstrosity make a hasty retreat. A smile formed on her lips. 'One day all creatures will fear me so,' she thought. She heard the rattle of a dark chain in her mind. 'All creatures,' she emphasized.

A moment later she felt the quiver in the air that meant her sorcerers were renewing their attacks against the city. She watched as lines of power arced toward Tolan shattering uselessly against the dome of power the elf lords maintained. She saw a grey mist hundreds of yards across drift slowly toward the south side of the capital. Immediately new lines of power, this time from the city, raced to intercept the mist. It slowed, but continued. Arianrood nodded her head. This was her signal to begin her magics for the Shadow Lord had begun his attack.

She squatted down, her hand tracing the foot-long piece of stone that lay there. It had been taken from the wall of the city. This was her key to destroying the barrier. Next to it lay a bowl filled with a dark red gore. Dipping in it a bone that had been whittled to a quill, she began to trace designs on the rock. Her voice rose up in a singsong chant as she began.

In the city, Bairbre, the three remaining elf mages and the Shee, Dermot, sat at a round table. Their hands were clasped and their eyes closed. On the table was a circle of nine black candles surrounding a circle of five white candles which surrounded three translucent candles, and in the middle of the candles was a miniature of the whole city. The miniature rested about five inches off the table and was surrounded by a transparent globe like a soap bubble. This was the power shield that had been placed completely around Tolan. Tiny flashes of color above and below the miniature city showed where the enemy tried to break through. The attacks were intensifying and all five of the elves were drenched in sweat as they fought to keep the barrier intact.

At one place a red glow showed faint and in perfect perspective on the miniature. The bubble's ends turned in at the point and met the red barrier, for the red was Teague and his power was melded with the other elves.

Deep in the emperor's castle's bowels a man crept silently. There were no guards here. All were needed on the walls. The man, bent and grey, moved to the end of a black corridor where two great doors stood. These doors had no handle, no way of opening. He rested two hands against them for a moment, then the hands pushed through as if they were going through a fog. The body followed until the figure stood on the other side of the doors.

He took a long shuddering breath at the sight that met his eyes, the sigh of two lovers when first they confront each other's nakedness.

The room was full of statues and paintings. Draperies, rugs, wall hangings of gorgeous design cluttered every inch of space. The intruder danced down the long aisles. Here were neat stacks of precious ores, there a chest of jewels and diamonds. The room was filled with incredible wealth. It was the storehouse of the empire. The man laughed, the sound reverberating about the gigantic room.

He began to talk to himself as he touched first one and then another treasure.

"Oh, so crafty," he hissed, "so sly." His hand caressed a statue. "Want my help, eh, no, demand it! Well, not so smart Black One because this time I will outsmart you all." He cackled to himself, rubbing his hands together like some demented miser counting his monies.

The intruder continued along until he found a hall filled with doors. He went to the end of this and entered the last door as he had entered the great chamber before. Inside he found a room some fifty by twenty feet.

"Perfect," he whispered, though there was no one to hear. "Perfect." He closed his eyes and flew to his consciousness so many miles away. There he gathered strength and re-formed as the bent cowled figure.

He reached inside his cloak and withdrew a large object some three feet by one. It was egg-shaped. The color was ebony streaked with white lines. That the intruder had hidden the large object in his cloak was an indication of his power. To change dimensions for a material object is a dangerous and costly magic and therefore seldom used.

This room was filled with paintings stacked against the wall. Almost all the floor space was covered by old statues. The figure, still holding the black object, walked to the door and placed the object down gently. He reached out and twisted the handle of the door. Three darts shot from the door and passed harmlessly through the figure. He picked up the object again and walked into the large room.

There he chose a chest full of precious rubies and emeralds. He placed the object on top and returned to the smaller room bearing both effortlessly. He deposited the chest in the far corner of the room. He took out the black object and scooped up much of the chest's contents. Then he placed the object inside. He covered it completely with the jewels. The intruder closed the lid of the chest then intoned several words of power over it. Covering the chest with paintings the figure stood and observed its handiwork with delight.

"Sly," he said aloud. "Very clever. Stupid bastards, I'll have you this time." The creature retreated to outside the room and closed the door behind him. Once again he intoned words of power, this time with visible results, for where once an iron reinforced door had stood, now there was a grey blank wall. Chuckling his delight, the man left the great chamber leaving everything the way it was, except for the room where the egg lay.

In a tower far above the treasure chamber, Lonnlarcan stared at the reposed body of Cainhill. All evidence of the wounds had disappeared and his chest rose slowly with breath. Cainhill's eyes stared sightlessly at the ceiling.

The Ard Riegh rubbed his eye. Though the elf lord yet lived, who knew what the bite of the undead lord would do?

Cainhill's skin held a sick yellow hue, but the healers had assured Lonnlarcan that his cousin's body was completely cured. Yet Cainhill made no response to any of them. The king shook his silver head in sorrow as he left the room. So it was that he did not see the elf lord's hand twitch and his head cock as if he was listening to a voice no one else could hear.

During the next day the magic attacks continued, though the dark army itself did little. A few catapults and such had been built outside the wall and were fired at the city with little result. All day long, Arianrood stayed upon the bleak hill working her magic. As the sun set, she stood up and had in her hands the piece of stone covered with runes. She held this up to the night sky and spoke in a harsh tongue.

"Rock to stone, muscle to vein, like to like." Her body began to sway back and forth. "This is the Fuiea Fulteak of the Ead, time has passed, time will pass, time for stone and flesh." The stone in her hand began to glow white and red. "Feel the age. I name you *Ageriach*! Feel the age, *Goister-ass*!" The stone began to crumble at the edges.

"Age, time—it makes you brittle. It saps your blood. It drains your soul. *Sierrach!*" she cried in a loud voice. "It is your time! *Seaetheadfay!*" She screamed the last word, and as she did the rock in her hand crumbled to dust.

All along the frame of the great gate, the rock that formed it began to crumble and fall to the ground. Teague, in his no-feeling, no-thought state, did not know what was passing. The barrier that was him spread to the firmer parts of the wall, but they too crumbled. Faster and faster until two feet on either side had already fallen and the top of the gate began to deteriorate from underneath.

In the tower room where the elf mages sat, they felt Arianrood's attack on the gate. Opening their eyes, they looked in horror at the miniature as the red glow of Teague's barrier spread itself thinner and thinner. Bairbre called for her lord with no voice and Lonnlarcan came.

In a moment, he took it all in and tore toward the front gate. The others intensified their efforts at fortifying the walls, but they were already tired and the other attacks from the enemy continued unabated.

By the time Lonnlarcan made it to the gate, eight feet on either side had crumbled and a bare five feet remained over the top of the gate. Mathwei, Niall, and Oidean skidded to a stop and stared up at the gate barrier that was thinning every moment.

"My lord," Mathwei was out of breath. The Ard Riegh

did not even turn to him. "We, Oidean and I, felt the attack. Can we do something?"

Lonnlarcan turned to the warrior; his elven eyes saw the potential of magic in him. The old one seemed to be a red burning flame. It quickly passed the elf king's mind that he meant to question that one further, but there was no time.

"We must stop the walls from crumbling or Teague will be torn apart." Several elf lords came running up. 'What I would do for a dwarf now,' thought Lonnlarcan.

"Hudden," he said to one of his lords. "Take the colonel and this old man and all the others you can find. Do a simple reinforcement spell on the stone and use their energy to fortify it. I will try to bring Teague to consciousness, before he is destroyed."

Mathwei and the others raced for the stairs as Lonnlarcan placed Kianbearac point first next to where the red barrier touched the ground. He went on one knee and sent his mind through the spear into the barrier to retrieve Teague's consciousness.

The others reached the top and at the elf lord Hudden's instructions placed their palms upon the battlement floor. Quickly he spoke a spell and all there felt a tingling in their palms and a tugging. The crumbling beneath them slowed, but did not stop.

Below, Lonnlarcan slowly gathered the elements of what was Teague. He only needed a few moments and he could free the mage from his own spell. The upper walls and all along the top of the frame had almost completely stopped their deterioration, as more elves hurried to add their strength. Niall strode up and down before the gate, sheathing and unsheathing his sword in agony over the thought that he could do nothing.

In the tower room Bairbre had taken full control over the whole barrier except where the gate was. The other four directed their power there. Suddenly one of the mages cried out.

"Another presence, it is. . . ." And then she cried in agony as she burst into flame. The bubble around the miniature shattered as the four remaining were blown across the room.

At the top of the gate some thirty figures knelt on the floor, their full attention to the task of willing strength to the stone.

They did not see the two great dragon skulls on either side of them begin to burn inside, or the empty eyeholes turn a fierce red. They heard the creaking as the two skulls turned to them but took no notice. The heads pivoted on their great poles that held them until they faced the group of warriors.

Mathwei felt a cold draft on his left side and turned inquiringly to Oidean, but the old man was engrossed in his task of mumbling words of power. Over the old one's shoulder, the warrior saw a red glow and looked with horror into the red pits of the long-dead dragon. He leapt to his feet and saw the other one likewise watching.

"'Ware the dragons!" he cried. All turned at his cry even as fire began to appear in the skull snouts. Hudden lifted his arms and a shield of golden light surrounded all there. It was just in time as flame poured from both the mouths. It covered the shield and the heat of it pressed all there to the ground.

Beneath them, Lonnlarcan was nearly through with his chore when he felt the crumbling of the stone begin again. He cried with despair as he felt Teague's consciousness torn from him as the spell forced the elf mage to try and close the gap.

Above, the other elves joined their spell barriers to help Hudden, even as they felt the floor shifting beneath their feet.

Niall, who had headed toward the top to see if he could help, froze in fear when he saw the dragon skulls attack. He could see that the elvish barriers would never hold against the dragon's fire.

"Hah!" he shouted, "Trollsbane!" He raced up the final steps toward the nearest skull, and brought his great two-handed sword down on the eight-foot snout with his clan's ancient war cry.

"Ruegal!" Such was the blow that the sword splintered and the great mouth was forced shut as it sought to release another great breath of fire. The skull exploded in flames, destroying it completely, the explosion throwing Niall through the air and almost over the lip of the battlements.

The elves were able to direct their waning spell barrier against the other dragon skull. They made a scramble to safety before the stone about them gave way, sending them to their deaths below.

Lonnlarcan cried with anguish as the top of the gate frame finally collapsed. The red barrier tore, reforming into Teague's flesh shredded into pieces. In a quirk of fate, Teague's head had completely reformed to fall at the Ard Riegh's feet.

With a great crash, part of the wall and the top of the gate frame fell to the ground to mix with the bloody remains of Teague, mage of the elven kind, and with the aged and destroyed rock fell Hudden, the elf lord, and the three others of the elven kind, and the great skull of Ruhtivak was no longer animated, crushed and destroyed like its brother had been by Niall's sword.

Even as the whole mess crashed at Lonnlarcan's feet, the Fudiaacha, Flannlorc ap Laiche, the Fomarian, led the Dark host toward the great gap that was once the gate of the city. But the charge halted before the rubble of the gate, for there stood Lonnlarcan with the elf host at his back. There was the wrath of the elven kind in their eyes. Behind them, the city took to flames as the Dark Ones' battle magic bombarded the undefended city.

Mearead and his companions followed their mysterious host into the keep. Inside the thick gate the dome they had glimpsed before stood before them. This, except for a few outbuildings, was the only structure the fortress held. None missed the obvious warlike preparations of the few people they saw. All were cowled like those the companions followed, yet all were heavily armed, and none said a word.

They followed the three figures into the dome, passing through a thick stone gate. Inside, all was gloom. The few lights were torches set high in the wall of the passage they entered. The passage snaked around the dome structure. Many of the turns were abrupt and held defensive works.

Mearead was impressed. Even dwarves long used to fighting in cavern and cave would be hard-pressed to breach these defenses. Every hundred feet or so a passageway would lead off the one they took and the dwarf could see in the dim hallways figures of shadow moving about.

The hallways went on a long time, and through a steady incline and steep stairs the passage wove its way deeper down into the cliff.

After nearly an hour of walking the tall figure stopped and spoke.

"You are about to enter the shrine of the Horned God. It is his will that you be shown this secret that you may know us for what we are." He turned and led them further down, and then he pressed his hand on the left side of the wall. A door appeared and opened at his touch. So cleverly had the door been made that not even Mearead's dwarven eyes had perceived it.

Again they entered a corridor, this one only wide enough for each to walk singly. This passage had several single steps, each about a foot high, and placed every ten yards or so. Mearead smiled to himself. Such a passage could be held indefinitely against an army. At last the party stopped. Before them stood two great doors, one silver, one of gold.

"One door leads to death, one to the shrine. They change constantly. Only the Stalkers may know the proper door at any given time," said the one who had spoken before. All three of the cowled figures bowed their heads once and then the tall one pressed the door of silver with one hand. It opened easily and he stepped aside to allow the others to pass. The companions slowly filed in. All was pitch blackness. As Margawt, the last to enter, stepped in the door behind him slammed shut and the companions were left alone.

"I can't see a bloody thing," Mearead said. His voice reverberated and echoed.

"It is obviously a large chamber, wherever we are," Donal added. He dug through his pack to find something to light.

"Is it a trap?" asked Bronwen.

"Not hardly," answered the dwarf. "They could've taken us anytime along in those passages."

"It is as the blackness of the earth. Not darkness, but the total opposite of light," said Margawt. His figure became outlined in a thin pale light. "It is an impressive place," he stated to the others who could not see a thing.

"You should be honored, Avenger," answered a voice. It was the voice of he who had led them earlier. It came from in front of them. "It is a mark of great favor that the master should allow any of Her servants into His shrine."

"How 'bout a little light, pal?" said Mearead.

"The darkness of the womb, the nonlight all living things share," said a new voice. It was quiet and reserved. "It is a rare thing to experience with lack of fear."

"Right," said the dwarf, "how 'bout some light?" The room lit up as Mearead finished. No noise was made, just light. The chamber was huge, the roof domed. At the very end of it, furthest from the companions, stood the three shadow figures.

They were upon the dais of a statue that was at least forty feet tall. The statue was made of pure silver that in the light seemed almost black. It was of the Hunter, the Horned God. He stood naked, his body human and flawless. But his face held no features and from his brow two antlers thrust. The room was otherwise empty. The light came from thousands of small, darting, flickering lights dancing around the ceiling.

The tall figure pointed up at the lights. "Will-o'-wisps," he said, "children of the night." He turned to the companions and gestured to the figure on his left, who took a step forward.

"This is the Hunter," he said. The figure bowed and dropped his cowl. He stood about five-ten, his shoulders broad, tapering to a narrow waist and powerful legs. His face was shadowed, only great black brows and the dark flicker of eyes could be made out. He was covered in leather which at chest, neck, arms, hands, loins, and thigh was covered with a flexible grey material that looked something like plate armor. His black hair was long and held a horse-tail braid at the top. He wore no weapons.

"The Hunter," continued the other, "can find all living things. Nothing can escape from him. He embodies all the abilities of the animals of prey." He motioned to the other.

"This is the destroyer," he said. This figure likewise stepped forward, bowed and dropped his cowl. He stood six-feet one, and was made of solid, fluid muscle. His entire body was covered with the grey material the hunter sported. Even his head was covered in a mask. A longsword and shortsword were tied to his back. On his arms were strapped throwing daggers, and in his buckskin boots, the handle of a long knife showed. Both his hands were gauntleted with the grey material which formed cestus. Along the upperside of each arm were five crystals, blood red. That these were some sort of weapon Mearead did not doubt.

"The destroyer," said the speaker, "can find a way to defeat all living things. Nothing is invulnerable to him. He embodies the abilities to kill in all creatures, especially man.

"And I," said the speaker, "am the maker." He threw back the hood of the cloak. The companions were surprised by how young he seemed. His features were strong and handsome. His hair was long and yellow-gold. The maker stared at them through bright blue eyes that did not seem so young.

"The maker," he said, his voice gentle, "can know all living things. Nothing is incomprehensible to him. He embodies the abilities to create. The passion in all living

things." He bowed to the companions. "You need not introduce yourselves. We know of all of you and your deeds. You
are welcome and we are honored." Four cowled figures appeared at the side of the dais. "These monks will take you to
quarters so that you may refresh yourselves. Later tonight,
we will meet to discuss our next move." He bowed and the
light went out with his gesture. The four, holding candles,
led the companions away, politely refusing to answer all
questions.

As they followed through the halls Donal whispered to
Mearead. "Can we trust them?"

"Do we have a choice?" answered Mearead.

"They are followers of the God," Bronwen added. "They
are our friends." The three continued their hushed conversation. But Margawt said nothing.

They were close, close to the enemy. He could feel it.
And he must go . . . He must hunt.

"Kill," he murmured, and the others went silent at his
harsh voice.

CHAPTER

Sixteen

The host of the Dark powers stood quiet, facing the wrath of the elves at the gate of Tolan. The Fomarian growled once and shifted his feet, waiting for the city's defenders to do something.

Lonnlarcan looked down at the blood covering him. He could hear no sound, smell no smell, but the anger of the elves at his back was like a physical force, a furnace pushing against him, through him, in him. He raised his eyes to the Fomarian and saw the dark spirit residing in the gigantic body. He could feel it confused, but still gloating, gloating at the death and blood—the destruction.

Lonnlarcan focused on the anger of his people, soaked it into his body, flaming his spirit. He concentrated, forcing the emotion into a ball, pressing for release. He held it until it became a razor pain, then opened his eyes, allowing the ball of power to spread through his arms into Kianbearac, holding it again for a moment, focusing it into an even greater power, combining it with the magic of the spear. He then let it out.

"Die," he sighed to the giant and a great silver light poured from the spear, hitting the giant full in its chest. The Fomarian stood firm, though his rock armor shattered like glass. His third arm stretched out to meet the power. The eye absorbed it for a moment, but then the hand blew apart and the arm shriveled. The silver light continued on through the demigod. His spirit tried to flee, but could not escape. In seconds, the flesh was stripped from the bones, and for a moment the skeleton stood, ragged streaks of flesh floating in the power of the elves' desire, but it, too, was blown apart. And the demigod's spirit was shredded to nothingness.

The ground buckled and the whole host behind the demigod fell to its knees, but the elves stood and their magic ripped through the Dark One's ranks, destroying anything in its way.

"Arianrood," the elves chanted, their eyes bright with silver vengeance. "Arianrood," and the power searched, a thick light of power. She heard their call, and atop the blasted hill she waited. The light reached the foot of the hill and two of her bodyguards were turned to ash. It reached up the hill but met her defense. A green fog dimmed and blurred the figure upon the hill as the silver light strove for her life . . . but it was not enough.

Kianbearac danced in Lonnlarcan's hands, scarring them with heat. He had to let go; the spear could hold no more. As quick as that the light was gone.

The elves stared across the plain, the dark path of destruction leading to the hill that was bright with the power of Arianrood. And though they could not see her or hear her, they knew she laughed.

In the fortress of the Stalkers, the companions rested in a large stone chamber sparsely furnished. Here they were served food and water—no wine, much to Mearead's disgust—and then led to separate rooms where they relaxed in hot, soothing baths. At no time were they left alone to discuss what had transpired.

They were all refitted with hunting leathers. Mearead's and Donal's armor had been taken away to be cleaned. Margawt's was ruined and the monks promised to replace it. Their weapons were left intact.

The four sat around the round wooden table that dominated the room. The four monks bowed and left.

As the door closed behind the retreating figures, Margawt leapt to his feet screaming in a high voice.

"Aiiee!" he cried. "The ravisher! The elves seek their betrayer! Aiiee, how the cleansing flame burns!!" He leapt about the room, biting through his lip as he convulsed.

Mearead and Donal grabbed him at the same time and tried to restrain him. The Morigu said no more, but his cries continued. They were animal sounds of pain and of pleasure. Bronwen backed into a corner and stared horrified at the three rolling on the floor.

"Hold him still!" Mearead yelled.

"I'm trying." Donal grabbed the Morigu in a choke hold. "He's too strong. I can't hold him!"

"Goddess, help me!" Mearead cried. His back and arms arched back as he felt a power flood into him. He smashed his fist into the Morigu's breast with a great blow. Margawt went limp.

"What was that all about?" Donal pulled himself up.

"Don't ask me." Mearead shook with the waning of the Goddess' magic. "He was in pain, I think, but hell, with this one who knows?"

Margawt sat up, the other two turned to charge him again, but he held one hand up. "Learn," he whispered. Then he reached into each of their minds, sharing his knowledge as the elven kind can. They saw the fall of the Fomarian, and felt the hatred of the elves.

For Bronwen it was a process beyond understanding. She tried to escape from it, but the Morigu held her. He did not show his pain, or joy—he did not explain his reaction. Donal reached over and helped him back to the table. All sat around it again. Bronwen turned away, Mearead watching Margawt wipe the blood from his lip.

'I understand the joy, lad,' he thought, 'but since when does elvish magic hurt a Morigu?'

"Well," he said aloud, "the death of the Fomarian is good news, and no mistake about that."

"Add that to Margawt's defeat of the Hag of the Elder Night," Donal said, "and the odds turn a bit in our favor."

"A bit," the dwarf said.

"If I understood Margawt's sending right," Donal looked over at the brooding elf, "then Tolan is in danger of being taken soon."

"What about these monks?" Mearead turned to Bronwen. "What do they want of us?"

"We," said the maker as he entered the room, "want nothing more than to assist you." They all turned to the maker. He smiled and handed a jug to Mearead.

"Trell'dem had mentioned to me your renowned thirst on more than one occasion." He smiled as the dwarf sniffed the wine appreciatively.

"You knew Trell'dem?" he asked, pouring himself a cup.

"Trell'dem was well known here. Did you not know he was a follower of the Hunter?"

"I find it strange," said Donal, "that the descendent of Fealoth should follow another god."

"Oh, he had his reasons," came the reply. "Trell'dem was very conscious of his duties. He did nothing without a purpose." He sat down. "In the third year of his reign, the Emperor was approached by the Hunter. Though young and new to the throne, Trell'dem was aware that things were not as they should be. It was with his help that this sanctuary was built." He smiled at Donal. "The Hunter had long had His suspicions that things were not as the prophecies had foretold. Much of the old magic had been used up in the Dark Seign wars. Thus it was that the God decided to build a new magic, a new power to help if things should go wrong. Thus were the Stalkers born."

"Stalkers?" asked Bronwen.

"Yes, we are all the Stalkers here, trained in the ways of the hunt, of war, and of magic."

"Magic . . ." said Mearead. "What powers have you?"

"Our powers are still fledgling, even the God was caught

by the rapidity of the enemy's return. But we have many who are near the mage level."

"You mentioned new magic," asked the dwarf. "What new magic?"

"The Hunter's way. Our forms are similar to elven magic in that it depends little on the help of gods or other powers. However, it is similar to the magic of the dwarves and men in that much is really just a twisting and bending of the laws of nature."

"Illusion," stated the Morigu.

"Yes, precisely. By the masters' powers—that is, myself, the hunter, and the destroyer—you could deduce that we depend not on pure power as on imagining, the power of thought."

"I don't see how I'm supposed to deduce that," mumbled Mearead.

"Simple," the maker answered. "The hunter uses the cunning of the animals to find his prey. The destroyer empathy and reason to find his enemy's weakness. And I, well, I just depend on intuition you might say, sort of spur of the moment things."

"Well great," said Mearead, "but let's get back to Trell'dem. How come he didn't tell any of the allies about you?"

"He couldn't. By the time we were established and coming to our power, the enemy had already approached and corrupted many, whom we did not know. Even the great wizard was under a powerful spell. He was not aware of the influence so his caution and curiosity were blunted."

Margawt looked up. "Great Wizard?"

"Yes. Dammuth."

"You knew Dammuth?"

"No, I never met him." His blue eyes gave Margawt an annoyed look. "Listen to what I say. We could not tell Dammuth because of the spell he was under. Besides, he was closer to the younger gods, especially Lugh." Margawt looked away. Still he could find no news of his friend and mentor.

Mearead looked at the youth. He knew how the Morigu had come to his power and he knew that the only creature Margawt cared for was the old wizard. But what was going on inside the Morigu? He was obviously not inclined to talk about the Fomarian's death. What did all that pain really mean?

"Margawt," he said, "we don't know if Dammuth is dead. He was very, very powerful. He could still be alive." Margawt said nothing. Mearead sighed and turned back toward the maker. "Okay, at least we have a partial understanding of who you are, and you say you know who we are. But you still haven't told us how you plan to help us."

"That should be obvious," said the maker. "You want Arianrood." At her name Mearead's eyes went blank and the others, even Margawt, leaned a little closer. "So do we." He stood up and walked to the far wall. From a chest he brought out a map and laid it at the table. It was map of the empire.

"We are here." He traced a circle around a small spot of hills with his finger. "Tolan is there." Again he pointed. "A good eight hours of hard riding away. The capital is completely encircled by an army of about thirty-five thousand. Its leaders include the Ead, the Shadow Lord, a Fomarian of unknown origin, and the Undead Lord, Apkieran."

"The unknown Fomarian," Mearead interrupted, "was Flannlorc ap Laiche, the Ravisher, and," he paused to take a sip of wine, "he's dead."

"Dead?" the maker looked around at the others. "How do you know?" Mearead just pointed to Margawt.

"You felt his death?" Margawt just nodded. "Well," the maker took a deep breath, "that makes things a little easier."

"What things?" Donal asked.

"Well," the monk straightened the map, "let me go on. Inside the city is Lonnlarcan with a host of some three thousand elves and about ten thousand human warriors. The enemy already controls the whole south of the empire up to Comar and the Mountains of Tevulic. Now in Madia," he pointed to a city west of them, "is about another four thousand men, but they are blocked off by a small army, though large enough to defeat them." He paused and took a sip of water.

"Originally," he continued, "we planned to free Madia and, with its troops and what we could gather from the northwest of the empire, free the city from the siege. However, things are bad in Tolan. I don't think the defenders can hold out more than a day or two."

"The main gate is breached," Mearead said, nodding toward Margawt.

"If Tolan falls," added Donal, "the empire will break."

The maker turned from one to another, twisting his lips.

"Exactly," he finally said. "So we must take what troops we have and make a bold bid to free the city. There is no other choice."

"What forces do we have?" asked Mearead.

"Three hundred and fifty of the monks, each of which is worth four warriors. Not far from here we have been able to gather another two thousand. Tomorrow we will be joined by Brasil ap Fin. He has gathered the forces of Dun Scaga and what defenders he could find and made an orderly retreat out of the woods of Ettoro. They are about eighteen hundred strong."

"So," Mearead filled his cup again, "Dun Scaga has fallen." The monk frowned.

"The whole south is theirs now, my lord," he added.

"This, then, is your whole force?" Donal interrupted. The maker nodded.

"With that you plan to break the siege?" Donal's disappointment was obvious.

"Exactly."

"You will die in a futile attack," said Margawt, his voice flat and monotone.

"Obviously we don't plan to just ride up and expect the

enemy to surrender." 'Ah, protect me from unbelievers.'
"Look, think for a moment. What would break the siege?"

"A sizable army," answered Donal, "preferably mobile.
They would need surprise so the enemy could not erect a
defense, and a concerted attack from the city at the same
time would dismantle the besieging troops."

"Precisely." The maker was obviously pleased with
Donal. He put his arm around the Warlord and whispered
conspiratorially, "That is exactly what we intend to do."

"All right, smart guy," Mearead stood up. "You got an
army at your back," he pointed at Madia, "another army
which even with your forces outnumbers us two to one and,
I might add, led by some very powerful beings. No one can
get in or out of that bloody place to let the defenders know
of our plan. Magic cannot get a message through either. For
all your illusions, I doubt it comes near to equal that bitch's
and her band of cutthroats' power."

"I could get through," said Margawt.

"No, you couldn't," answered the maker. "Arianrood has
subverted the earth's power and uses it in corruption. She
would know if you made the attempt. However, the Hunter
can get through. He will be in and over the wall before the
enemy is aware of his presence." He raised his hand and the
others all strove to talk at once. "No more objections, just
listen." They quieted down. "As far as their power is concerned, we do balance it. Inside the city is Lonnlarcan, the
elf lords Cucullin, Ceallac, Teague, and Bairbre. They have
taken casualties. The lord Cainhill has fallen, but Cucullin
has killed the Fire Lord." Donal and Mearead both were
surprised to hear this. It was a victory of sorts in and of
itself. "We have the Stalkers and the masters, and you four
—all warriors. And Mearead and the Avenger are powers in
their own right."

"The plan," said Mearead.

"Is simple," came the quick answer. "The Hunter will
bring our message to the defenders. We do not have the

means to bring a large force against the enemy but we can make them think we do."

"You mean some magic to confuse them, and think we are more than we are?" asked Donal.

"Arianrood will penetrate it and destroy your magicians," Margawt said.

"No, she won't, not in time anyways. The enemy has never come into contact with our magic before. She has no defense against it. We are not strong enough to openly fight magic against magic, but there are things we can do." He looked at Mearead. "She knows of your blood price, lord. She will center on you and the Longsword. Much of their power will be directed that way. They also will know of the Morigu and will attack him, but they don't know us, and they don't know our powers. We, as Trell'dem was fond of saying, are a little surprise."

The discussion continued for some time. Mearead and Donal wished to attack Arianrood before the battle, but the maker convinced them otherwise; they were too valuable. With them in the front ranks, the enemy would be too concerned with them and the Morigu to worry whether all the warriors they saw were really there.

They all had supper with the maker and two human Lords, the leaders of the other force. After the meal, Mearead asked where the other two stalker masters were.

"Hmm, well," said the maker, "you mentioned an army at your back is not a good thing so the hunter and the destroyer with a few other Stalkers and the Hounds of the Hunt have gone off to assassinate the leaders of the enemy army at Madia. They will be back tomorrow." Though he did not show it, Mearead was impressed.

"And the attack?" he asked.

"We leave in the late afternoon tomorrow. That gives us time to gather our armies, reach the battlefield and then attack refreshed the next day." Mearead shook his head, the blood price called to him, yet he knew he must wait one more day to confront his adversary.

Bronwen, Mearead, and this night Donal, too, slept better than they had in a long time. Margawt walked out to the battlements of the monastery. A quiet footstep announced the maker as he joined the Morigu.

"You could not sleep, Avenger?" the monk asked.

"I'm sure you are aware the elven kind do not sleep, at least not as you humans do, and such as I do neither." Margawt stared out at the little valley below.

"The earth calls to you, Avenger?" asked the man.

"It does; even through the stone I can hear and feel the agony the Dark Ones inflicts upon the earth things."

"In the sanctuary, the shrine, Margawt," said the maker kindly, "you could find relief. The Horned One will stop the call for a while."

"No." Margawt's voice was soft and for the first time in a long time he sounded young. "I must feel, so when the time comes I will not forget and fail my duty." The maker shook his head in sympathy.

"You carry a heavy burden," he said. "I fought in the Dark Seign wars, Margawt. I was a mage of a little skill. I befriended one of your kind, a Morigunamachamain. He never even told me his name. He was a great warrior, Margawt, and a noble creature." He sighed and leaned on the battlements.

"He became a Morigu not through the horrors that you faced, but through long dedication and love for the life of the world." He turned to the elf. "But once the pack with the Goddess was made he was driven as you are, never resting, always, always fighting. He had been a gentle elf, a kinder being I have not met. By the end of the war, he would speak rarely—even to me. He was covered with scars inside and out. Two months after the fall of the Dark One, he killed himself." He sighed once more. "The Hunter can be cold, vicious, unpredictable, but never is he cruel. You have a hard mistress, young one." Margawt looked at the man, his eyes black, holding a knowledge the man could never know.

"It is my duty," he said. "What I was died in a nightmare long ago. I am the Morigu, nothing more. It is as I wish it."

"The Morigu." The maker chewed on the words. "Aye, that is what the earth things call you. Not *a* Morigu, but *The*. None think, none remember who you are. Who you are, whether you will it or not. Margawt, a young Shee, a dark elf who does not know you cannot give your soul away, only loan it."

"You do not understand, you cannot understand," said Margawt. The maker turned to Margawt, his blue eyes flashing.

"Don't ever make that mistake, boy, *ever*," his voice rang. "If you learn nothing, learn this. Though another cannot live your experiences, they can understand, always there is a way to understand." He smiled. "After all, that's what I do. I am the maker. I always find a way to understand." With that he left, leaving the dark figure of Margawt standing alone, wondering, for the first time, if any could understand. Though he was one of the most powerful of all creatures, he could not answer that question. He did not even dare ask it.

That night was long in Tolan. The besiegers did not seriously attempt to breach the walls or the barricades at the gate. Their goal was simply to keep the defenders awake during the night, a feat they succeeded at admirably. Niall and Mathwei stood on the wall looking down into the night.

"It's like looking down a great black pit, a pit with thousands of eyes lining its dark sides," Niall said. Mathwei turned to stare at the warrior's hard profile. A fire at the top of one of the towers burned at the level of Niall's eyes, as if that flame came from the warrior.

"It is the nature of what we fight, General." His voice was quiet. "One power, one beast directed at us, and great enough to swallow the world."

Niall said nothing. The strange warrior next to him had unnerved him more than once with his observations. Mathwei had been in the war from the beginning and had seen it all unfold in front of him. The general had met many great warriors in these last days, but there was something elemental about Mathwei.

"You're like that, Mathwei," he said to the night sky in front of him. "You're part of something, laddie, something that connects us all, but you're more than a beast." They were both a little surprised at Niall's words. He had never been one to think things out.

"And what are you, my lord?"

"Hah," Niall dragged his hand through his short cropped hair, "a fool, boy." He turned to his colonel and met those cold grey eyes. "A fool that's unsure for the first time in his life."

They both stood quiet for a moment.

"I was not born into a noble family," Mathwei smiled. "My lord," he added. "I was not brought up a warrior as you were. If there had been no war, I doubt I ever would have made it into the officers' corp." He laughed. "I wasn't born or raised to be a hero." He turned back to the sight beneath them.

"If this wall falls," he patted it, "my family will die, their house will be burned. My sisters and mother, if they are lucky, will die by the sword or, if they are brave, by their own hand." His voice grew hard. "I do not fear for myself. The enemy will not seek me out for corruption or terror. I am still small in the grand scheme of things." He jerked his head. "I fear for those behind us, general. As for myself," he turned to Niall, "they can only kill me, and death is something I no longer fear." With that he bowed and left.

The Shee Dermot moved out of the shadows where she had listened to the conversation. Niall's hand nervously caressed the hilt of his new sword. She watched him quietly for a moment. He stood tall, alone, his thoughts far away. In that moment she saw him as a great elf lord preparing for battle. He turned to her.

"My lady," he said, bowing. The illusion was broken by his mortal voice full of pain and decay.

"Forgive me for listening in," she said. Having a great height like many elves of noble blood, she stood only five inches shorter than Niall. "You humans fascinate me so."

"And why is that, now?"

"Well, that one," she gestured to where Mathwei had walked off, "he has not the training or the strength of your noble families, but he has a will, a spirit that is as great." A dim nimbus of colorless light surrounded her. "I mean that you humans are so bound by your flesh. I have never met any of the elven kind that was so constrained. What we are inside is always expressed in our corporeal form." She said no more.

Niall looked at her. This was one of the famed Shee, the last in Tolan. Her dark eyes were full of strength and knowledge. Her beauty was unreal, untouchable, impossible to hold in his memory. Niall had never had contact with the elven kind before. They were a thing of legend, not reality.

"All my life I have striven against what you call constraint," he said, "to make myself stronger, faster, deadlier. There are few humans who can match my blade," he said with pride. "Mathwei makes light of the fact that he was never expected to be a hero, but I, ah now, isn't it all that I ever wanted?" He could not meet those unhuman eyes. Their beauty did not bring passion to him, just the knowledge of his own ungainliness when compared to her. But his pride reasserted itself. Was it not always so in the legends? and he laughed.

She turned to him. "Why do you laugh?" she asked.

"It is my mother's tales I am remembering. She told me of your kind. In truth, how strange it is to be around you all the time. Aye, but then I remembered I am fighting in a war that wasn't supposed to happen, against a being that is called a goddess by my own clan. Demons, magic, monsters. I am, as the blessed Moriarty said, doomed to live in interesting times."

Dermot struggled to understand her own reaction to the human's words. For some reason she wished to reassure him, but she had not the knowledge. She studied the man's profile again. His chain-mail armor fit tight to his muscular body. She could tell that his body held a strength even an elf would respect. After all, did he not kill a stone troll in single combat? All could see his warriors fairly worshiped him, and the youth, Mathwei, a man of great promise, gave Niall the respect he held from all others.

"By your own words, my lord, you seem the sort of warrior who would wish for such a time if you were not part of it."

"Oh, aye," he turned away, "aye, never did I doubt my ability, my lady. Never did I doubt that I was born in this time, to do something grand, to be," he smiled, "a bright and bonnie hero." He shook his head. "Och, I am counted high among men, but I have learned two new things that were strange to me in the days before the war."

"And they are?"

"Humility, my lady, humility. And most of all, fear. . . ."

CHAPTER

Seventeen

The next day Mearead and the others spent their time checking their weapons and outfitting themselves in armor that the monks provided. Both Mearead's and Donal's armor were in fine shape and the two left Bronwen and Margawt to join the maker in inspecting the troops. They followed a small passage leading through the cliff face to the other side, where another valley was filled with warriors.

Two thirds of the men had already seen combat in the south, the rest were the warriors of Inlit, a small baronial hold to the northeast. Their leader, the Baron Sean of Inlit, was the nominal commander of the armies, as ranking royalty. But the real leader was a Green Branch knight, Conlath ap Lathe.

He walked up to greet the three. He was a powerful man, nearly as tall as the maker, though shorter than the huge Donal. Conlath bowed to the maker and to Mearead, then he turned to Donal.

"It's a great pleasure to meet you, Warlord," he said, wiping a wet lock of brown hair from his eyes. "I've studied your plan at the battle of the Hills of Colmain. It's fine military mind you have."

"Thanks for the praise," said Donal, "but I'm Warlord no more."

"Not if I have any say in it, boyo." Conlath turned to the

maker. "He should be the Warlord, maker. Arianrood was a fool. He's one of the best alive."

"I agree," said the maker. "I suggest the two of you make your plans. Mearead and I along with the other leaders will join you as soon as Lord Brasil joins us." Donal started to protest. "Nay, you are the Warlord. It is decided. This battle will be fought on horse and you've got the most experience and training of all of us in that regard." Donal bowed his head, saying nothing, but none could miss the look in his grey elven eyes. He had no doubts that this was a task he could meet.

"Are you sure that's wise?" said Mearead as he watched the two men walk off. "He has years but little experience."

"Mearead, though Arianrood picked Donal for his loyalty, he is no fool," answered the maker. "He has the best mind for the tactics we need, and in the border wars of Aes Lugh, he stood out and won every battle, with minimal losses." Mearead shook his head.

"Well," he said, "if he's half the man his father was, he'll do." The two turned as a rider approached them. It was the destroyer. He leapt off his horse in a fluid movement.

"The assignment went perfectly," he said with no preliminaries, though the dwarf did not miss the fact that he as well as the maker was addressed. "The leader of the enemy force was a minor demon, one of Apkieran's. He was hard to kill."

"Our losses?" said the maker.

"One dead, five slightly wounded." Mearead recognized his voice from the night before. This was the one that had spoken of the peace of the dark. "We killed five of the enemy's commanders and about forty others, including one minor magician."

"Did you use any magic?" asked the maker.

"It was unnecessary," came the answer.

"Excellent," said the maker. He turned to Mearead. "If it is all right with you, the destroyer will ride at your side. If you can find Arianrood, he will be of great assistance in your quest." The dwarf studied the formidable figure and said nothing. "I will leave you in his hands for now. The preparations for the magic we plan to use are rather lengthy. I must join our mages." He bowed and left. Mearead stared at the silent figure of the destroyer for a moment.

"How good are you?" he asked.

"I can kill her." It was a statement of fact with no room for doubt. "I can kill anything that lives."

"Maybe," said Mearead, "but I'm not sure she is alive anymore."

At midday, the lord Brasil and his men led by the Stalkers, entered the valley. The warriors were a ragged bunch. They had fought steadily since the capture of Dun Scaga some two weeks before. Brasil was a slightly smaller version of his father, Fin. His hair was redder and if possible, a bit more wild. Quickly, the monks started to outfit each warrior with new armor and weapons which they seemed to have an inexhaustible supply of. Mearead's estimation of Trell'dem was once again upgraded.

The companions, along with the rest of the leaders of the small army, sat atop a stony hill overlooking the valley overflowing with warriors. On another hill, two dozen of the monks, now uncowled and in shining chain mail, unloaded a large crate from a wagon. The maker pointed to them.

"As soon as they are done and the horses arrive, we will begin the building of the illusion."

"Horses," said Bronwen.

"Yes, horses," answered Donal, fitting easily into his role as Warlord. "We wish to make the enemy think we have five times the number of warriors we actually do. The monks of the Horned God will make four images of each of the warriors, each image will be slightly different from the original. To make them even more believable, each image will ride a horse."

"A horse?" Brasil's brogue was thick. "How is it these

phantasms of yours are going to be riding, never mind guiding, a horse?"

"They won't," said the maker. "We will. We've collected over the last month and a half over ten thousand horses. These will be directed by fifty Stalkers, directed not by hand, but by magic. And," he added "we will make the illusion of another ten thousand horses."

"So when the attack comes about," said Mearead, "the real horses will be an actual weapon."

"Exactly," said Donal.

"But if the warriors and horses that the illusions are created from fall in battle," Margawt asked, "won't the illusions be destroyed too?"

"In elven, or human, magic," answered the maker, "but not in ours. The images will fight and attack within a limited repertoire, no matter what happens to the original."

"Can the illusions be killed themselves?" asked Brasil.

"No, they are made of light and shadow," said the maker, "but should one believe the arrow shot or the sword thrust is real, then the blows will fall."

"It's a good as if we had the men themselves," said the Baron, Sean.

"Not quite, my lord," Donal added. "They are good until the enemy perceives the illusion."

"Concentration of magic always leaves a trace." Mearead scratched his chin. "Surely the enemy will feel this and attack the spell quickly."

"No," said the maker, "they will not feel such a concentration for it will not be there. The energy will remain here, for it is in this valley we will create it."

"You can create such magic and hold it for so long?" The dwarf did not try to hide his skepticism.

"We can." He stood up and pointed to the other hill. The monks had removed the crate and there stood a glistening object some ten by twenty feet. "The man or horse stands in there," continued the maker. "His reflection is broken into four three-dimensional figures. Imbued by our power, these reflections are dispersed from the prism into five mirrors. The mirrors alone took us twelve years to create. When we reach our destination, the mirrors will be broken and the illusions freed." He looked at the others and smiled. "It is simple, really, and quite unexpected."

Bronwen volunteered to be the first subject of the spell. Since in her armor she would be unknown to the enemy, it was agreed.

Bronwen walked up to the device. It was shaped like a narrow pyramid, its walls opaque and milky. A monk opened the side and she stepped into total darkness. He handed her a bow and spear.

"When the light appears," he instructed, "stand still for a few moments, then draw your sword and wave it around, as if you were fighting. Take the bow and spear and with each do the same. Make sure to shout and talk some. When you are ready to leave, rap on the wall opposite of where you have entered. It will go dark again and we will let you out."

He closed the door behind her and though the light was cut off, for a minute Bronwen watched a dash of light bounce around her. Every time it moved it became dimmer, then it was gone. The whole room filled with a piercing white light.

Bronwen went through the motions the monk had told her of. After a few moments, she realized the reflections were not copying her precisely but adding and changing her moves. They were acting of their own volition!

Quickly she finished her task and banged her hand where she felt there was a wall. She was rewarded with a booming noise and the light was extinguished. She watched in fascination as her thousand selves disappeared one by one. As the last faded, the door opened and she rushed gratefully into the clean sunlight. She looked at the maker who waited for her.

"Don't tell the warriors of what will happen to them," she said. "They will never enter if they know." The maker laughed and linking her arm with his, led her over to where a hundred feet away—actually ninety-nine feet—the others huddled over several monks. They parted ranks to allow Bronwen a look.

There, suspended in midair, seemingly floating on the smoke that came from the braziers below, were four mirrors. At least they looked like mirrors. But they were square and the surface was angular, faceted like a jewel. No reflection came from the surface. The maker pointed to the corner of one where a little flaw made a dark spot. Bronwen leaned close and saw it wasn't a flaw, but a tiny figure. She knew who's figure it was. She stood up and shivered.

"Those things," she pointed at the magic mirrors, "can hold the illusion of the whole army?"

"Oh yes, easily," said the maker. "Indeed, we made them to hold many more. Unfortunately, things did not turn out as we planned and we must make do."

The day passed quickly as one by one, warriors and horses took their turn in the pyramid and prepared for the hard ride they knew would start at midnight.

The four companions sat around a fire on a hill across from the magic pyramid. They stared silently at the fires springing up across the valley.

"I think it will work," Donal said quietly, as he pushed a small branch into the fire.

Bronwen looked up at the Warlord's face and said nothing. The Morigu sat still, the palms of his hands resting on the ground, his face grimacing as if in pain. Mearead rocked back and forth on his heals, chanting to himself, the need of the blood rite pounding in his veins.

"They won't realize we're there until we are within half a mile of them, maybe closer," Donal continued. "Then it's a quick gallop to the city. We'll reach the walls before they can have any sort of chance of breaking the illusion."

"I don't relish the idea of joining the warriors of Tolan in their death trap." Bronwen's voice was strident. Donal turned to her to answer, but just then a grey shadow covered her.

"The maker sent me to tell you that the hunter has left."
The destroyer's armor merged into the shadows, making him
appear larger than he was. "He also requests your presence.
Word has reached him that the defenders of Tolan are in
graver danger than we thought. We will leave in two hours."
Bronwen and Donal looked at one another and jumped to
their feet. Mearead got up slowly and followed them. The
Morigu did not move. He moaned quietly.

"Vengeance," he murmured softly, "vengeance and
death," then he, too, followed the others into the dark, star-
less night.

Two shadow forms looked down upon the valley.

"You have done well, brother," one said. "These followers of yours are strong and dangerous."

"They will be my hand in this battle," the Hunter answered. "And do you to have a sword to aid them?" Death
was quiet for a moment.

"Arianrood is not as the demon princes. She knows me
well in my many forms," he said at last. "She had seen so
many pass." He sighed. "And Apkieran, he, too, is on guard
and I cannot face either in open battle." The Hunter said
nothing, for he heard the anguish in his brother's voice.

"I have touched two fomarians in the space of a week." A
flame burned in his eyes. "I long for more."

"The Morigu has done well," answered the Hunter, "as
have the others."

"The Morigu is corrupted by the Night Hag's magic. We
must watch him carefully."

"What of Fealoth?"

"I have told you, brother, I claim only those that die on
this plane. If Fealoth is truly dead it was not my hand that
touched him."

"Unless he makes himself known, none of us may take
the battlefield openly." The Hunter growled in fury. "Who of
the gods will join us? Which have been corrupted?"

"None will join. We cannot win this war ourselves,"

Death answered. "It is up to the people of the land to save themselves."

"And us," the other added. They both watched the preparations in the valley.

The Hunter said, "Can you do nothing?"

"I can withhold my touch for an extra moment from some, grasp others a bit early." He climbed upon his chariot. "Others turn our way, brother. We must leave. Have no doubts, Death shall play his part." The great steeds reared, and he was gone.

"As must we all," the Hunter whispered, "as must we all."

All that day the enemy had attacked the walls of Tolan. Nearly was the south wall overrun, but Lonnlarcan held the front gate, and none came to challenge him. Fires spread, warriors died, and when the Dark Ones finally broke off the attack many of the defenders simply collapsed in exhaustion. The temples were full of men and women seeking solace: all knew the next assault would be the last for the city.

In the evening, the leaders met in council. Fin and the others humans attempted to persuade the elves to try and break out of the siege and save themselves, but Lonnlarcan refused.

"It is a dark night tonight, but who knows what morning will bring? I didn't ride with the first hosting to return to my people in defeat and disgrace."

"It won't do your people or ours any good for you to die here," answered Fin.

"Perhaps, but I know my fate lies here. We will not leave." With that the council broke up and each of the commanders went to their post to prepare for the last defense.

Lonnlarcan stood upon the high tower next to the emperor's palace. He stared at the dark mass of his enemy spread before him. Like a black worm, the evil army undulated and moved, rank upon rank of destruction. There was no hope, he knew; they could not possibly win. He took a deep breath and sniffed the air. Extending his senses, he could feel the powers swirling around him, the confluence of death, fear, hope, and fate. Though he felt great upheaval ahead, he could not taste his own death and that surprised him. Was he to be the sole survivor?

"My lord?" He turned to face one of his lieutenants. "Important news has reached us. The council is convened. They ask that you join them." Lonnlarcan turned quickly and strode through the archway. 'Help?' he wondered, but dared not hope.

The Hunter stood facing the leaders of Tolan. His leather was torn at the chest and he was covered with blood and gore that was not his. The Ard Riegh stared for a moment and took his seat.

"Now that we are all here," Fin said, "please deliver your message."

"I came from the monastery of the Stalkers."

"Who?" the murmur arose.

"You do not know of us, but your Emperor was our benefactor." Quickly, the hunter told the tale of Trell'dem's suspicion and plans. He then handed them a scroll sealed with the signet ring of the emperor. Fin opened it and read it quietly, handing it to Lonnlarcan.

"Let's say this document is true, and you are who you say you are," Fin said, "what message do you have for us?"

"Hope." He stopped and approached the table. He strode its length back and forth, his head swinging, his nostrils flaring wide. To Fin it was like watching a wolf sniff for his prey. The Hunter stood back.

"No, Dark One here," he grumbled. "You have users of magic here," he said aloud. "Have one of them protect us from unseen eyes and ears."

Bairbre, at Lonnlarcan's signal, stood up and raised her hands in a slow motion about her head. A few feet from the wall of the room a thin silk veil of power appeared.

"We are alone," she said.

"I, the Stalker Master, called the hunter, bring formal greetings from my brethren," he began. "Also, from Lord Mearead, king of the Crystal Falls; Donal Longsword, Warlord of our army; your son, my lord," he indicated Fin with lifted brows, "Brasil ap Fin; Sean, Baron of Inlit; and the Morigunamachamain." At this, he pulled from a sack at his side a fragile-looking crystalized ball.

"The signal," he growled, showing overlarge and pointed canines.

"Signal for what?" asked Fin.

"For the attack. We bring an army to secure the defenders of Tolan." The room erupted in shouts and cries.

As the hunter and the others planned for the battle, in a small room Cainhill opened his eyes once more. There were no attendants to see. He sat up and listened to a voice that only he could hear, and began to dress in his armor. Soundlessly, the elf lord left the room, his once purple eyes now shedding a new light of their own. It was red.

"No we cannot tell any until the moment it is time to assemble," said Ceallac. The others in the council room nodded their heads in agreement.

"Though I grieve to see the people spend one more hour in hopeless fear," said Fin, "the danger of betrayal is too great. We have at least learned that lesson, if none other."

"Then we are agreed," said Lonnlarcan, "we will prepare quietly, without any but those now here and a few of the commanders knowing of the plan." Just then, an urgent knocking filled the room.

"My Lord Lonnlarcan," came a cry from behind the massive door to the council chamber. The elf king signaled to Bairbre and the magic spell was dissipated. Cucullin opened the door and two elves rushed in and bent their knees to the king.

"My King, the Lord Cainhill is gone." With one quick look at Lonnlarcan, Cucullin sped out of the room.

"There is treachery here," cried Ceallac.

"Kianbearac!" Bairbre shouted. With that all the elves ran from the room drawing their weapons.

At that moment, Cainhill stood outside the door of the room where the spear Kianbearac rested. He licked the blood off his sword, the blood of the two elven guards he had slaughtered moments before. He opened the door and entered. It was a small stone room with no furnishings. Lying in the middle of the room, raised up on a marble pedestal, lay the mighty talisman, the spear of the Ard Riegh.

A silver pentagram was etched into the floor, but its magics didn't affect Cainhill. Being of the king's family, the magic was not meant to keep him out. He reached with his hand and he grasped the spear. For a moment it glowed silver, and Cainhill could see the bones in his hands. Both palms began to smoke and the smell of burning flesh filled the room but he took no notice. He turned, and with no sound, no word, left the room.

"The whole city has been searched," said Ceallac, "but he is nowhere and there is no trace of Kianbearac."

The Ard Riegh said nothing. He sat in a thronelike chair in the audience room given to him for his use by Fin. He stared past his cousin, tapping his fingers gently against the arms of the chair. Cucullin entered the room, and shook his head 'no' to the unasked question. Lonnlarcan sighed and stood up.

"There is no choice. Get it," he said to Ceallac, who bowed once and left the room.

"Remember the words of Fiachra. Draw the sword and you unleash doom and salvation," said Cucullin.

"I remember," said the king in a tired voice, "but without Kianbearac the power of the sword may be necessary."

"We may still find Kianbearac," said Cucullin with little hope.

"No, Cu, we have been outwitted. Cainhill has it, therefore the enemy has it. We have a little less than an hour until the signal goes up. We must prepare." Lonnlarcan rose to put on his armor.

Ceallac came back with the sword of Cather-na-nog in its black and silver sheath. Reverently, he handed it to his king.

"My lord," Cucullin said, "if there is any truth in Fiachra's words, I think it best that I wield the sword.

"Nay, my lord," Ceallac answered, "I am the king's cousin, and I am the servant of war. Let me wield it, so that any ill doom shall not touch you." Lonnlarcan smiled on them both.

"Ah, you two," he shook his head and laughed. "I thought you knew me better. A king does not ask of his people what he will not give."

"You do not ask," Ceallac said.

"Nay, lord," Cucullin finished, "we offer."

"It is well done," the Ard Riegh said, "but if there is doom in this sword then it is for me and no other. You forget there is also salvation in the prophecy. Would you keep that from me, too?" Cucullin and Ceallac looked at one another, realizing their efforts were futile. With no further words— for what else was there to say?—the two left.

Lonnlarcan put the sword down and finished buckling on his armor. His mind was a strange place even to him. He haunted the dream paths of all his people. The elf king had no place in his heart for fear, no room to wonder of death. He hooked the sword on his silver girdle.

'This day,' he thought, 'in this war, we all must be greater than we are. We all must face our own private doom.' And as he left for the battlefield he strove unsuccessfully to forget about Cainhill, who had failed his test.

CHAPTER

Eighteen

In the faint predawn light, the Dark army moved about restlessly. Arianrood turned to the skeleton standing next to her.

"Put the Shadow Lord in charge of the army, my lord," she said.

"I thought you would lead?" Apkieran asked.

"Something, something is amiss. Those fools don't realize they are already doomed. They are planning something, I can feel it." She faced the city. Even in the murky light it looked defiant, strong. She turned back to him. "And is our 'ally's,'" she said the word with scorn, "true form here yet?"

"No," he answered, "it should arrive anytime. Do you really think we need him?"

"We hold him in reserve. I don't wish to reveal him until we must." She felt the demon's hate pressing against her, but it did not frighten her. His power could not touch such as she, even if he had turned the elf lord.

"I have another surprise if we need it," she said, playing with her dark locks. She rubbed the inside of her thigh with one hand slowly, and smiled to herself, wondering what could be going through the demon's mind. For all his power there was one pleasure forever denied him. She wondered if he ever felt such a desire. Well, now was not the time to find out.

"Bring the leader of the trolls to me," she said. "I will need them. And, my lord, I wish you to stay here with me and protect the hill with your own legions." He bowed once and strode off.

'It is strange,' he thought, 'for her not to wish to lead the armies to the victory.' He wondered if she was afraid, but no, Dubh might be the most powerful, but there was no doubt that she was the favorite. He turned his mind to the thought of the battle and casually reached out to grab a goblin that was not fast enough to get out of his way. Carelessly, he twisted its head off and drank deep of its blood, never once losing a beat to his stride.

In the city, the astonished warriors were running about, their commanders giving them no time to think about the new orders: attack! In the southeast corner of the city, Lonnlarcan, Bairbre, Dermot, and their new ally, the hunter, searched the skies above. Behind them, two thousand elves supported by five hundred heavy human cavalry waited nervously.

Lonnlarcan's keen elven sight picked out the figures moving around on top of the highest tower of the city. A sparkle of gold danced briefly as one of the figures held aloft the globe the hunter had brought. The sphere rose from the tower moving faster and faster. He ordered the warriors to prepare. They fanned out into three lines, facing the outer wall in front of them. There was a great noise of an explosion and all eyes inside and outside of Tolan looked up to see the globe explode into thousands of tiny shards, glimmering in the predawn darkness.

As soon as all the motes were gone from the sky, Lonnlarcan raised his hand, and as one the warriors' spears flashed and leveled out, pointing straight ahead. The Ard Riegh's hand fell and Bairbre cried a word of power. In front of them, the wall fell outward.

The king led the charge, even as the crash reverberated.

The Dark army had watched the globe burst in the air uncomprehendingly, their leaders completely baffled. They had never seen anything like it, for it was more than a signal: it was a weapon.

The thousands of motes had drifted over the walls of the city deep into the ranks of the besiegers. Some of the goblins in curiosity had reached out to catch the flakes of gold, only to scream in pain when the motes burned through their hands.

The army went mad trying to dodge the gold flakes that now covered the sky. If flake touched wood, it started a blaze. If it touched flesh, it would burn straight through. Metal melted and cloth burned. Fires spread all across the field and the whole army became a confusing montage of fire and pain. Some of the goblins and wolves turned on one another in their agony, striking out randomly. Bolts of power shot out from the Dark Ones destroying the flakes. But even as they stopped falling, and the commanders tried to reorganize their troops, the horns of the elves were heard.

A weary goblin commander turned at the crashing of the wall. As he stared uncomprehendingly, he heard the cry of vengeance from two thousand elven throats. The dust of the fallen wall swirled and out of it came riders. First, one, the dread Witch King himself, then a few more elf lords, one covered with a red aura holding a great ball of fire in her hand, and then more and more, the silver tips of weapons all leveled at him. With a wail of fear, he turned to run, only to be impaled on an elven spear.

The elves hit the enemy like a great thunderbolt. The troops were exclusively goblins in that area, and after only light resistance, they turned and fled. Lonnlarcan's men rode over the ill-manned breastworks, while the air resounded with the thudding of hoofbeats. The goblin leaders knew they were as good as dead. But then from the south they saw a great body of horsemen riding toward them. "Reinforcements!" they cried, and turned to face the elven charge.

The sun broke over the eastern hills, the armor and weapons of the reinforcements glittered. Their numbers blackened the plains. As uneasy whisper flowed through the goblins and then a great cry was taken up.

"The Morigunamachamain leads them, the Morigu comes!" The goblins' ranks broke as all tried to flee the vengeance that was upon them.

A few miles from the city the army of the Stalkers spread out. It was broken into two wings, the strongest led by Donal Longsword. With him rode Brasil ap Fin, Bronwen, Sean of Inlit, the destroyer, all of Brasil's men, two hundred of the Stalkers and three hundred warriors under the Baron.

Mearead rode up to Margawt, who stood by his horse, staring at the city ahead.

"Margawt," the dwarf said. There was no answer. "Margawt, tell me what you see."

"I, I see," his voice was rough, cold, mortal, "I see the Earth Goddess, she holds her hands out to me imploringly. She is naked and her breast runs with blood as do her thighs." The Morigu turned from his vision, taking great gulps of air.

"It's almost time, lad. Mount up."

"I can't. The power flows from the earth through the horse to me. It will kill it."

"Did I hear someone say 'horse'?" The maker's cheerful voice interrupted. "Ta dah," he said, and behind a great bulk pulled itself from the shadows. Margawt's heart leaped. At first he thought it was Anlon, for the horn was clear, but then he realized it was a thing of stone, a magical fabrication that moved.

"This is your mount, Margawt," said the maker.

"Why did you parody Anlon?" Margawt asked bitterly.

"Parody? Parody?" The maker looked shocked. "You misunderstand. You are the only being his lordship has ever allowed to ride him. This construction was built this way in honor of that. The unicorn is ever a strong token for a warrior."

"I thank you, then, and in memory of my friend, I will

ride it." He climbed upon the stone unicorn's back and moved to the front of the ranks.

"'His lordship'?" Mearead raised a white eyebrow.

"Oh, didn't you know?" asked the maker. "Anlon is the son of the Hunter and the Earth Goddess." He smiled at the dwarf lord. "Speaking of horses, are you going to be able to ride that one okay?" Mearead realized how silly he must look, balancing on top, the horse so much larger than himself.

"Just let this thing get me to the battlefield, then I'll be all right. *She's* there. I can smell her." He patted the horse, his eyes deep in shadow. "Just get me there."

Donal looked around at all the riderless horses, and shook his head. He planned as best he could, and if those in the city followed his orders, they could win, but not without the illusion. As the last of the globe's motes settled to the ground the Stalkers broke the mirrors. Donal watched as dark, small shapes flew to each empty saddle, then stretched and molded into human figures. As the elven horns were heard the figures gained color, then movement. The Warlord looked behind him to see. Waving their swords in impatience were, or seemed to be, thousands of warriors, awaiting his orders. He turned to the diminutive Stalker next to him.

"We are ready, my lord," said the man. "We await your orders." Donal turned to his troops, and waving his sword three times above his head, cried aloud, "For vengeance, for victory!" And with a roar the army charged.

In what seemed like a minute—no longer—Donal saw the enemy ahead. The elves were cutting through them like a knife. The goblins were running around in aimless patterns. He picked out a chieftain riding a giant wolf and spurred his horse on. His men had the hardest job, for they had to clear out the whole east wall and get to the north side where they would be joined by defenders of the city.

Donal knew at the corner of the east wall lay a large detachment of undead. There were bound to be several mages among them. He had few magics to fight them with, and only hoped the confusion would keep the enemy from breaking the illusion until they had reached the other side.

His sword swept across the chieftain's throat, geysering its blood into the air. The troops rode over the goblins and continued on.

Margawt urged his mount on, but it would not let him get too far ahead of the others. Behind him rode the rest of the Stalker army. He realized the stone unicorn was cutting off some of the power of the earth somehow, shielding him from the corruption that the enemy had infused into the land here, but still his veins filled with madness and he shook with his need.

The goblins dared not face the Morigu and fled from his charge. A giant troll stepped up to meet him, but was gored by the mount and beheaded by Margawt before it realized what had happened. Margawt plunged into the middle of the enemy ranks, his sword moving so fast that it seemed to be just a flash of color. A line of power splashed against his chest, but did no damage. He just charged the dark mage who had cast the spell and with a casual backhand of his shield, smashed its head to a pulp.

Lonnlarcan turned his men west to fight alongside the troops following the Morigu. Great magics flew from him, wiping out entire ranks of the enemy. He did not draw the elven sword, but his magic, combined with Bairbre's and Dermot's, did more damage than even that talisman could have.

His elves glittered with a silver and gold witch light. The human warriors with them were engulfed in this protective shield also. The elven magic infused the men, giving them an unnatural strength. The enemy could not slow them down, never mind stop the Ard Riegh's advance.

* * *

The Shadow Lord formed his troops at the southeast corner of the city. He threw all the magic he could control at the enemy even as he tried to keep his army from fleeing. His thoughts were cold. Had not his sister and brother fallen before this rabble already? He redoubled his efforts. He had not finally escaped his age-old prison to die.

The demon general that controlled the troops in front of the main gate quickly sent reinforcements to the Shadow Lord, leaving only a handful to hold the line in front of the gate. He looked despairingly behind him, where he knew Apkieran and the witch waited behind the ranks of the Undead Lord's best. He saw lines and wedges of magic fly from the hill, but this time he knew magic wouldn't be enough. He needed those troops.

The maker was nearly knocked off his horse as he strove to blunt Arianrood's magical attack. 'She is so powerful,' he thought, but he knew her magic and she was hopelessly confused by his. He attacked with all his power, linking up with the lesser magics of the other Stalker monks. They had to keep her and the Shadow Lord off balance so they could not shatter the illusion of the warriors.

Lonnlarcan rode to the front of the reinforcement army, his elves taking the vanguard. The enemy fled before them and their whole southern flank was rolled up. The Shadow Lord sent a desperate counterattack led by the elite goblin wolfriders that slowed the assault down for a little while.

Meanwhile, Donal's men smashed into the ranks of the undead. The Stalkers were not sure whether the illusion would fool the undead and the Warlord couldn't tell, but the weight of the horses, massed as they were, was enough to push the enemy back. The slow-moving zombies—horrible as they were—could not fight cavalry effectively. But

through the smoke of the battlefield, Donal could see that
the zombies were just a screen, while a quarter-mile away
the enemy was organizing a defense.

Donal slowed his troops, and after seeing that the zombies were decimated, he reorganized his ranks. He motioned
to the hunter who clapped his hands twice. In response, behind the army a great red streak flashed into the air.

Cucullin saw the flash leap across the sky. He nodded to
an elf mage and again a great rending was heard as the part
of the north wall in front of them collapsed. Cucullin
charged with all the remaining elves behind him. On his
right rode Ceallac, leading the Green Branch knights and
some thousand other warriors, and on his left rode Niall and
Oidean leading another twelve hundred men. All were
horsed and burst out on the unsuspecting enemy. In little
more than fifteen minutes of fighting, they scattered the
goblins, and turned east to meet up with Donal's troops.

Lonnlarcan's army's mad charge was slowed by the
Shadow Lord's defense, but with no reinforcements, the
dark army was forced to withdraw. This, despite the fury of
the elves and men, they were able to do in good order.

Cucullin's men smashed into the rear of the troops fighting
Donal, and caught between the hammer and anvil, the
enemy was destroyed. Quickly the two armies merged and
faced east along the north wall.

The Ard Riegh halted his warriors. It took Mearead's
strength to contain the Morigu. Though the blood price
pounded in the dwarf, he knew the necessities of battle. As
Donal and Cucullin came around the north edge, the barricade at the broken gate was thrown down, and Fin marched
out with the remaining eight thousand defenders. The troops
at the barricades fled and joined what was left of the Dark
army, ringed around the hill where Arianrood blazed in
anger.

The two armies stood silently, glaring across the field at one another. The sun rose higher over the city and right into the eyes of the Dark Ones, and they despaired to see the apparent size of their enemy. For no more than twelve thousand of the invaders were left, ranged around the blasted hill where Arianrood, Queen of Aes Lugh, General of the army, premier wizard of the age, High Priestess of Fealoth, Ead, waited.

Margawt could feel her black hunger, and breaking from Mearead's hold, leaped upon the stone mount and rode to the front of the ranks.

Arianrood hissed when she saw him, spittle flecking her perfect lips. Apkieran strode up.

"I will kill him," she moaned. "I will drink his soul."

"Lady," said the demon prince, pulling back from the look she gave him, "hold your wrath a moment. There is something wrong."

"I know there is something wrong, you dolt, and once I kill that mongrel, we can make things right!" She began to move toward the battlefield.

"No," he said, daring to grab her arm. She turned on him, her hair flying madly about, streaked with the green of her power. "No, lady, those troops, they are not right."

"What do you mean?" she said. Her voice was a deadly threat.

"I don't know, but some of those warriors are not there. They have no souls." He dared to meet her glare.

"You mean they are undead?" she asked.

"No, I mean they are not there."

"Illusion," she laughed. "Of course, where could they have gotten all those warriors? It has to be an illusion." She signaled to the thirteen cowled figures at the bottom of the hill. They approached her.

"The battle is yours, Apkieran. You are in command until I defeat this magic." He bowed once and strode down the hill.

* * *

The Morigu rode out midway between the two armies. He halted his mount and just stood there. Waiting. Behind him, the sun fought the smoke of the many fires, and the army glittered and bristled with armor and weapons. The enemy waited about the hill, restless, like some great storm cloud, fighting to pull itself together, as the wind tries to tug it apart.

"I have come," cried the Morigu. His body gave off great waves of power as if he radiated a fierce heat.

"The earth has called and I have come." He moved closer. "Give me Arianrood and I will let the rest of you live. Now, today, I want only her." No one laughed at the outrageousness of his demand, for in that moment none truly doubted that he could defeat the enemy alone.

"Once more I ask, give her to me, or die." He rode closer. The front ranks of the army were composed of goblins, and they edged away from the Morigu. But behind them lay the rest of the undead, and the goblins' fear of the zombies was enough to force them to keep ranks. Suddenly, at the stone unicorn's foot, Dorrenlassarslany of the pyridin showed up.

"Great unmaker," it said, for once giving a proper bow. "Hurry. Evil. Black traitor, witch, is choosing the path. It leads to the undoing of, great lords people's magic." Margawt looked uncomprehendingly at the little creature for a moment.

"Arianrood," he hissed, "she is finding a way to break the Stalkers' illusion." Dorrenlassarslany bobbed his head once. The Morigu looked back at the warriors behind him. He smiled, showing no teeth. Margawt turned back to the enemy and drew his sword, kicking his stone mount's flanks.

For the first time, the construct made a sound.

"Give 'em hell, Kondo-s," it said. But Margawt did not hear.

The human/elven army was caught by surprise when Margawt turned and alone attacked the enemy. They stared in disbelief as a shower of arrows rained on the Morigu. Those that hit the stone mount bounced off, and none hit the Morigu. Only the elves had sharp enough eyes to see Margawt dodge the arrows, with a speed that no creature of the earth could ever match.

The Morigu smashed into the enemy's dark ranks. Straight through them he plowed. It was as if he splashed through a giant river of blood, for such was the destruction he caused that on either side of him great geysers of red gore sprayed up. With an animal cry of pain, Mearead charged after Margawt, and with a deep, hoarse shout, the army followed him.

Death rode at Margawt's right side, and every stroke of the Morigu's weapons took a life. But Lord Death did not laugh.

He had expended a great deal of power so far and he dared do no more. None had detected him yet. After all, in such a slaughter as this all would expect to feel Lord Death's interest. But the Dark Ones were still holding, and many of their units were reforming to join the fight at the hill. They were not defeated yet.

"Forgive me," he said. But he could not say who he hoped would hear him. He spread his power again to support the charging warriors, and in his heart he said a silent prayer, though there was no god for him to pray to. Still, the thought was agonizing. Would they become aware of him? Would he be responsible for starting the final battle?

And the Morigu stained red by his enemy's blood chanted, "Death! Death! Death!"

CHAPTER

Nineteen

Apkieran watched quietly while the Morigu rode toward him.

"It's not over yet, mad one," he said. He saw a bright gold light shining about the enemy host. 'The same,' he thought, 'as in the battle of Greenway.' But what it meant he did not know.

The demon prince was sure his undead would stop Margawt but the Morigu began to cut through them with the same maniacal fury that had thrown the goblins in such confusion. Behind Apkieran, the hill was covered in a swirl of unnatural light in colors—if they could be called that—that were unfamiliar even to the demon. Arianrood could not help until she pierced the veils of the illusion. It was up to him.

In front of him, staked to the ground, were thirteen figures inside of a hexagram. On the six points rested males: a baby, a child of four, a boy of twelve, a young man of twenty-one, an older man of forty, and an old one of seventy years. Staked in the six small triangles, heads nearly touching the others, were six females of the same ages. In the middle lay a priest of Fealoth; he represented the hope of supernatural intervention.

Apkieran nodded once and his twelve most powerful wraiths descended upon the terrified humans in an orgy of violence and pain. The demon prince strode to the center and

with his bleeding ax began to flail the priest. As the humans'
cries reached a peak, Apkieran soaked in the horror and
transferred it to his troops—undead, goblins, and wolves.
All went into a berserk fury. Screaming in foul voices they
charged to meet the host attacking them.

The attackers were stopped short by the enemy and re-
pulsed completely. As the warriors tried to regroup a horrific
shriek was heard, and Dorrenlassarslany's voice reverberated about the field.

"The unmaker! The unmaker!" Men and elves watched in
horror as the Morigu and his mount were buried under an
avalanche of the undead. The tiny pyridin sped through the
enemy's ranks, nearly matching the Morigu's speed as he
tried desperately to get to Margawt. Dorrenlassarslany did
not fight; he dodged and pranced, ran, crawled—his voice a
long wail that brought shudders to both armies.

"Arianrood!" Mearead's voice boomed out, and the host
cried as one and charged again. The dwarf king leaped off
his mount and pushed through the goblins, his ax a great
scythe of destruction. On came the men and elves, foot by
bloody foot. The enemy contested every step, and imbued
by Apkieran's magic, did not retreat. The Shadow Lord led a
great charge of undead on the left flank, and Cucullin and
Donal were pushed back.

The cries and crashing of weapons were deafening. Niall,
Mathwei at his side, countercharged the Shadow Lord and
forced the undead back. The center and right flank of the
human/elven army merged and pressed on. Under the weight
of numbers they pushed the enemy back.

Then a great light blinded everyone momentarily, and
with a cry, a third of the Stalker mages burst into flames.
The maker, who rode at the front of the army, was thrown to
the ground, his horse dead beneath him. The hunter leaped
to protect him, and using only a pair of clawed cestus, defended the unconscious body of his friend.

The men despaired as the illusion was broken and many
found themselves fighting alongside an empty saddle; or
worse, both horse and man disappeared. The horses, freed

from the Stalker power, went berserk, many fleeing toward the city.

Mearead pounded the earth with his hands, and calling all his power, shattered the ground into great rifts for a hundred yards in front of him. Just then, the Morigu, covered with gore, rose up on his mount.

"To me, to me!" he cried, and as one, every elf spurred his mount and moved toward the center. Lonnlarcan and Bairbre blasted the enemy's magic and the Dark Host's left flank collapsed.

For another hour the battle seesawed back and forth. Arianrood used her strength to hold her army together, freeing Apkieran to take command.

Such was the terror of the demon prince and his twelve dark wraiths, that again the defenders of Tolan were thrown back. Several of the Stalkers were able to retreat with the wounded maker. In order to give them a chance to escape Conlath ap Lathe led a charge at the undead lord. The brave warrior was impaled on a black spear and his men retreated in confusion.

But the hunter continued forward, supported by a handful of his own monks. Right into the ranks of the wraiths they pressed, but their powers were useless against such creatures, and the hunter's broken body was thrown at Apkieran's feet.

The Morigu rode through but was unhorsed by three of the wraiths and his mount was separated from him. Even as he strove to rise, Margawt heard Dorrenlassarslany's piercing cry and the little creature threw itself at Apkieran.

"Aieee!" a wail escaped the demon's mouth as somehow the pyridin managed to hurt him. He grabbed Dorrenlassarslany in his two hands and with a great Word of magic echoing from his skeletal jaw, he ripped the pyridin in half. Such was the power of that Word, that all that heard it were thrown down.

"Apkieran," a great voice shouted, and surrounded by a golden light Cucullin beheaded one of the wraiths. The Dark prince raised his arms above his head and moaned like the wind through the mountains. All the humans who had fallen in Conlath's charge rose, dead but not dead, and at the demon's bidding pulled Cucullin down. A great fog shrouded the area and under cover of the Shadow Lord's magic, Apkieran escaped.

Quickly, he sped to the hill where Arianrood threw enchantments before her. The fighting was barely half a mile away from the foot of the hill and Apkieran could see the humans and elves cutting great holes in his army. Though his dead did not run and fought unyieldingly, Apkieran saw that it was only a matter of time.

"Arianrood," he shouted above the clash of arms, "we have lost. We must retreat."

"Retreat?!" she cried. "Never!" She pointed to the foot of the hill where a hundred trolls stood, each facing a great stake pointed at their breast. "I have not lost yet, not yet!" And she walked down toward the trolls. Apkieran turned to follow even as one of the mages on the hill burst into a black flame and died.

The main strength of the enemy retreated with the Shadow Lord to the north of the hill. There, Donal led most of the men and elves supported by Ceallac, the destroyer, and Lord Brasil. Fin, Sean, Bronwen, and Dermot attacked the remnants of the enemy's right flank, forcing them away from the hill. The other leaders, supported by human horse, a handful of Stalkers, and the rest of the elves, moved toward the hill, one though in all their minds: Arianrood!

Apkieran prepared the defense of the hill with what was left of the undead, a handful of goblins, and the still fresh trolls. But there was no magic to counter the leaders, and following the Morigu, Mearead, and Cucullin, the men and elves began to cut their way through.

At the foot of the hill Arianrood addressed the hundred trolls.

"Do your duty and meet your destiny. Your great lord waits for you in his halls. Let your lord's retribution defeat this scum that dare to defy us." With a deep-throated, "Feth," the trolls as one impaled themselves on the stakes before them.

As the enemy's ranks shattered under the power of their antagonist, a foul smelling wind swept from the foot of the hill. The humans who smelled it fell down in a swoon and many of the elves ran away screaming in fear. The sun darkened and turned blood-red, and there, standing at the hill, was the great god Feth, Lord of the Fifth Plane.

He stood twelve feet high, his body a deep black strewn with grey veins as if he was made of marble. His features were that of a troll but his eyes were large pits of red-black madness promising the tortures of the damned. Such was his mass that he sunk a full foot into the ground. Many who had not run from the deadly wind fell to the ground in terror. The few undead left simply dissolved into the ground while all the others of the Dark army ran shrieking in fear. Only the few hundred trolls remained, ecstatic in the rapture of their worship.

Facing the dread god stood the Morigu, Lonnlarcan, Bairbre, Cucullin, Mearead, Niall, Mathwei, and the old man Oidean. With them also stood thirty of the bravest elves and two human knights.

Niall, covered with blood, lifted himself off the ground from where his terrified horse had thrown him. He dared not look at the troll god before him.

"Trollsbane, trollsbane," he muttered, and staggering like a drunk man, shambled toward the risen god. With almost casual contempt, the god directed his sight toward the man, and a red burst of color flew toward Niall. Bairbre was able to deflect most of it but enough hit Niall to throw him fifteen feet in the air to crash to the ground. He did not move.

But the others did. It was enough to break the spell of the god's rising. As one they charged ahead, meeting with a crash the attack of the trolls. As the others fought the mass of trolls, Lonnlarcan and Bairbre threw their magic at the god. They barely slowed him down as step by step he moved toward them.

All fought but Oidean. The old man just stared up the hill at Arianrood, who stood there laughing. Apkieran retreated up the hill. The nine remaining wraiths waited his bidding. They led a force of fifty vampires, all mounted on skeletal horses. Apkieran pointed to the foot of the hill.

"Down," he growled, "down there. Kill them all." With human-sounding screams the evil ones charged. Apkieran looked at the city and smiled. He, too, had one more card to play.

Oidean felt a hot breath on his neck and turned to see the mount of Margawt staring at him with red eyes. Slowly, the creature's hide changed from stone to a blue blackness of silk hide.

"I know who you are." Anlon showed his thick teeth in a mockery of a smile.

"You!" cried the old man and even as the unicorn's horn pierced his chest, his body melted into a darkness that fled to the sky. A moment later, a great cry of pain was heard, and a black shadow, made more awesome by the lurid glare of the red sun, filled the field. Even Feth looked up.

There swooping down came Oidean, rejoined with his true body. He came down from a great height, the last of the dragons, Cuir re Duriche, the Fire Shade, son of Sessthon.

From wingtip to wingtip he stretched sixty feet, and from his great saurion snout to the wicked tip of his tail was forty. He was covered with thick green scales, his nostrils dripped acid, and from between his four-foot-long fangs poured orange flame.

The dragon's eyes were solid red, slit down the middle by a wicked green stripe. His body was thick and heavily muscled. Only magic could give his batlike wings the strength to lift that great weight. There was an evil power beneath those wings and the air they fanned became dank with fumes.

He was the last dragon, a being of such power that even a

god might take heed. Cuir re Duriche, like all his kind, shared the racial memory of all the dragonkind and was a master of deceit. A great doom lay on him, for if he failed, if he fell, his race would fall with him.

He screamed out his defiance as he floated above the battlefield, his roar shaking the earth, even as his flames scoured her.

'Too soon,' he cried to himself, 'too soon.' He wished to flee, to plan, but first he would have his revenge. The dragon swooped down on the battlefield, his rage taking form in his unholy fires. He breathed it on elves and trolls alike, striking Anlon with the full force of his fury. He hovered above the ground, his great wings beating with a monstrous noise, the wind from them throwing friend and foe about like so many twigs.

The flame covered the unicorn until no sight of him could be seen. With a last shriek, the dragon flew again deep into the air, disappearing within the fumes his own anger had created. The Morigu was the first to recover, just in time to block a great blow by Feth. His shield shattered and the Morigu was driven three feet into the ground.

Both of the human knights died in the dragon's fire along with four of the elves. Mearead shook with outrage. Between him and Arianrood stood a god, a dragon, and the hundred trolls who had withstood the dragon's random flame. And then he saw the wraiths and vampires charging.

"No!" he screamed. He turned to Lonnlarcan. "These are your problem. The horse and I will deal with the dragon." With that he raced to the unicorn.

"I am not a horse," shouted Anlon.

"Shut up," said Mearead as he jumped on the demigod's back.

"No one rides without my permission," shouted Anlon again.

"Shut up and move!" Mearead pointed to a small hill a few hundred yards away. Anlon took off with the dwarf balancing on his back. They rode to the top and the dwarf started shouting insults at the dragon. From Anlon's horn a black streak flew to strike the mammoth beast. It did no apparent harm as Cuir re Duriche hovered for a moment then dived at the two figures and covered them with his magic fire.

Reorganizing themselves, the elves charged the trolls and drove them back as Cucullin and the Morigu traded blows with Feth, but both warriors were thrown down and a score of trolls leaped at them. The god continued his march.

Two score of human knights, mostly Green Branch, with some ten elves came riding toward the fight. Mathwei reared his mount around and met them. Quickly they organized behind him, and Mathwei, white with fear, led them against the wraiths.

Bairbre cried in a great voice as a lance of power struck Lonnlarcan in the chest, and he went to his knees. She stood over her lord and using every last bit of her power, emulated herself in her own magic. She turned into a creature of pure red power, nearly the size of the troll god, and the two locked in mortal combat. With fists, claws, and teeth the two raged at one another. She forced him away from Lonnlarcan, who pulled himself up.

He saw his elves being overwhelmed, heard the fires of the dragon. Soon even Cucullin and the Morigu must fall. As these thoughts cleared his mind of the battle fog, he saw the troll god rip the head off of Bairbre, who in her true form again fell at the king's feet.

Lonnlarcan stared at the headless body for a moment and then looked up at the god. Such was the power in that glance that Feth fell to his knees.

"Doom and salvation, let it be so," the Ard Riegh cried, and in all parts of the field, even to the city the voice was heard. "By my power and strength, I banish you, Dark One, and know that forever will you be the enemy to the elder until the end of time." He drew the great sword which sparked as it slid from its sheath. Lonnlarcan brought it down on the kneeling god's neck. True was that stroke and thousands of sparks flew when the sword made contact. With his elven sight, Lonnlarcan saw the god leave his mortal form which, freed of the power that imbued it, turned to the marble it resembled. A call of horns was heard and warriors, led by Fin, crashed into the trolls, spilling them across the field, others racing to reinforce Mathwei. Donal and Ceallac raced to attack the dragon.

On the top of the hill Apkieran watched all this alone. The hill was burnt and scarred with great rifts where the elven and human magic had contended against Arianrood's enchantments. All her mages were dead, charred heaps, just part of the blackened debris. Arianrood was nowhere to be seen.

The Lord of the Undead lifted his great ax and allowed the constant flow of blood down its blade to cover him. His skeletal frame glowed with a green luminescence.

"Now," he said quietly, and he spoke a Word. His body quivered, then dissipated in a witch wind that came from nowhere. He, too, made his escape from the shambles of the battlefield.

But his command was heard. In a dark room in Tolan, Cainhill stared down at the terrified woman who lay at his feet. The stone flags had been torn from the floor as she lay on the earth. She tried to cover her big belly as if she could protect the child within. For a moment he hesitated, and the spear Kianbearac bucked in his hand. His hands were burnt to the bone. He barely had enough fingers left to hold the spear.

"No," a whimper escaped his lips, but it was too late, and the spear plunged through the woman's belly deep into the ground beneath. In the explosion of power and outrage at the desecration, Cainhill, the woman, and the room were blown to pieces. The tower overhead crashed down as a great earthquake shook the land as far as Ruegal and Cather-na-nog.

Only Anlon remained on his feet and Mearead stood upon his back, but they were both distracted by the cries of the elven host for their loss. Not so the dragon. He swooped down, his claws ripping through Mearead's mail. It grasped him and turned to fly away.

Donal, supported by a tree, had risen first of all the host, and seeing the dragon dive, ran toward Mearead and the unicorn. As the dragon turned to fly away with his prize, Donal's sword swept at the claw, and the stroke, backed by all his incredible strength, dug deep, the runes of the Horned God blazing a sharp blue. The dragon dropped the dwarf king and flew high into the sky, screeching in pain and agony. Its black blood splattered and burned Donal, and he fell to lie next to the Lord of the Crystal Falls, his friend.

All elves everywhere felt the desecration of Kianbearac but none in such a manner as Lonnlarcan, the Ard Riegh. A great ache swept through him. Falling to his knees, he felt the crack of bones within him as he, first of the elves, felt age. And time drove deep in him, and the dark breath of mortality filled his lungs.

He opened his eyes to see a strange land of grassless plains and leafless trees. There was a bright directionless light that came from the land itself and hurt the elven king's eyes. Before him stood a grey shadow. Lonnlarcan felt the power, but this being he did not know.

"No, you don't know me. I am not for your kind," said Lord Death. He was silent for a moment, then cocked his head to one side. "I will not take you. Long have I desired one such as you in my halls, Lonnlarcan. But I will not take you."

"You must," came a sibilant voice, and Lonnlarcan shivered at the evil in it.

"No!" Death shouted to the empty sky. "I am master here." He turned to look down at the Ard Riegh. "Go back, Witch King, there is still much you must go. Go back." Lonnlarcan blinked his eyes once, and still feeling the burden of time, fell in a swoon.

* * *

Somehow Mathwei pulled himself to his feet. Around him lay the dead. A few forms moved in pain, and he could see some of the knights were recovering. But all the elves lay still.

"At least," his voice was small on the field of death, "the undead are gone." He felt buoyed by that thought. Mathwei knew he could never again do anything as brave as attack the wraiths and vampires as he had. He still shuddered as he remembered their glowing eyes thirsting for his soul.

He moved to remove his lance from the breast of a dead vampire.

"I don't even remember killing that thing," he said aloud.

"Yes," answered a voice, "it's like that sometimes. I forget who I've killed quite often." The voice came from behind Mathwei. It moved closer. Silky, soft, and murderous, the voice continued. "But you know, Mathwei ap Niall, I never forget those I miss."

Mathwei's body froze in fear. Some part of his mind registered the fact that his bladder had just evacuated itself.

"You're dead. The arrow killed you." His voice was hoarse and tears streamed down the young warrior's face. He did not turn around.

"Shame on you, Mathwei. You know that it takes more than a toothpick to kill such as I. You do remember me, though. That's good, very good. Makes our acquaintance that much more sweet, don't you think?" Mathwei still did not turn. He knew this was the monster he had crossed swords with and nearly died fighting at the battle of Greenway. The vampire had marked him for death and would never accept anything else.

"Now, now, my brave young knight, no need to fear me so. Soon you will realize I'm not such a terrible monster after all." It laughed, a bark like a hyena. "After all, you'll have all eternity to get to know me." A hand, cold, dead, flashed out and wiped blood from Mathwei's wounds. Behind him he heard it lick the fluid from its hand.

Mathwei knew if he turned and looked at the vampire it would control him. Worse, he realized the beast would bring no easy death. It didn't wish to kill him. It wished to make him a vampire, enslaved to its will. That thought was enough to cut through his fear. His body tensed and he gripped his sword tighter.

"Now, now, Mathwei, your sword cannot harm me. Why don't you just turn around so we can talk this out man to man, as it were?"

The compulsion was strong and the warrior found that he was turning slowly around. He strove against himself. His body jerked like a demented puppet. In despair, he tried to shout his defiance but nothing came out. The vampire's words rang in his head. "Your sword cannot harm me." 'I have no weapons,' he cried inside himself, 'no way to fight.'

The vampire reexerted its will, its dark hunger taking over its game of cruelty. Mathwei let his knees buckle, but his body continued to try and twist around. 'Sword cannot harm. No weapons. All eternity. Death. Death.' The word caught hold and then Mathwei knew a way out, a way to win. His hand ripped the vial of poison from his neck, and his teeth crunched down on the splintering glass, cutting his mouth, causing him to cry in agony.

"Enough, mortal, you are mine. Your blood is mine." The voice controlled him and he turned, but instead of facing the vampire, Mathwei saw a grey shadow between him and the monster. The shadow was manlike in form. It spoke to the vampire.

"This one belongs to me, leech. Leave him be." The poison began to work and Mathwei felt his limbs grow thick and heavy.

The vampire, a pale shadow to Mathwei's eyes, hissed at the grey shadow. "Away, Grey Man. You have no power over me. My master is greater than you. This one is mine." The pale shadow leaped at Mathwei, and one taloned hand tore his throat wide open. It dug its face into the spraying blood. The grey shadow watched as the monster filled itself with Mathwei's blood, and laughed.

The vampire tore away from the dead warrior and faced the shadow. "You are defeated by me, by my master." The vampire shrieked. Then it grabbed its throat and gasped, drawing air into its withered lungs. But it didn't help and the vampire fell to it knees, drowning in the poisoned blood coursing through its veins.

"Poison?" it questioned the shadow. "Poison cannot kill me." Its voice was a whimper.

"Death claims His own. That noble warrior is mine and you go back to your master." The shadow looked down on the gasping creature. 'None escaped death; your master has forgotten the law. Return to him and tell him this. He over-reaches himself. I am aware. I am watching. I am waiting. I will come. Return to him and give my message." The grey shadow's hand reached out and extended, touching the vampire on the chest. It shrieked one last time, and from its chest a twisting, turning shape, brown and black, flew into the air.

"I am sorry." The shadow turned to Mathwei's body. "Third time, and I must take my payment." Mathwei's soul spun from its body and dashed straight into the heart of the shadow. "My halls wait for you." Death's voice was soft. "Your place is ready. You have done well." A wind came across the field and the grey shadow drifted apart as if made of dust. It was Fin who found Mathwei ap Niall's body spread eagle amongst the corpses of war. Though he mourned the dead warrior, he was puzzled that despite the gaping throat, the features of the body were peaceful, and the young hero's face held a beatific smile.

The field was covered with dead. Broken weapons and ghastly shapes blackened the plain. The sun turned yellow again, but its light was cruel as it showed the agonized countenance of dead and dying warriors. At the foot of the hill the elves slowly gathered around their fallen lord. Though he lived, they stared in fear at the wrinkles that lined head and hands. Others moved to the Morigu where he lay prone upon the ground, blood dripping from his mouth.

Margawt breathed shallowly. The Dark Ones' latest desecration of the earth had nearly overcome him. Cucullin pulled Bairbre's head from Dermot's grasp. Dermot sat there sightlessly, her silver elven tears staining the blooded ground.

Slowly, the survivors came from the city and the wails of anguish filled the air. The battle of Tolan had been won, but many wondered if it was worth the cost.

CHAPTER

Twenty

The victorious army quickly reorganized itself. The dead were buried and the wounded were treated. There was no victory banquet. Even if there was time, none wished for one. For no man or elf had not lost a friend or relative in the desperate defense of Tolan.

Two great mounds were made in sight of the gates of the city. Here, the dead, elf and man, were buried together. A smaller mound was made that lay between the two. Here, Bairbre, sorceress of the elves, was buried, and alongside her lay the young warrior Mathwei. Many were surprised at this, but it was on Lonnlarcan's insistence that it was done.

"He deserves this," was all the Ard Riegh would say. Niall Trollsbane laid his sword by Mathwei's side. "I'll remember," he swore quietly as the tomb was closed.

Upon the hill where the Dark Ones had made their last stand, all the enemy's bodies were heaped. It was by Mearead's magic they were burned and a dark cloud overhung that place for three days and nights. Forever after nothing grew there and no animal would come near it.

Two days later a relief force was sent to Madia where they quickly routed the enemy forces there. A garrison of two thousand was left and the rest marched to Tolan, bringing all the noncombatants from that city.

The army was heavily reinforced by troops from the

northern cities of Tinnafar and Althman and the many strongholds of the north and west.

Anlon rode off with fifteen hundred men and five hundred elves, to reinforce Ruegal. Now that Oidean had been revealed to be the dragon, all felt sure he would return to the halls where Niall had found him. Anlon had fought in the Dark Seign wars; his father had trained him well in the defense against dragons. The unicorn had to leave before Margawt regained consciousness and for that he was sorry, but he knew what part he must play in this war.

The next day, a thousand elves came from Cather-na-nog to replenish the badly wounded first hosting. Of the original four thousand elves that had ridden to Tolan's defense, less than half had survived. The reinforcements came with stories of a new danger. The raids from Maegul, the haunted lands, had increased. Lonnlarcan must return.

Mearead, through his magic, contacted his people but there would be no help from that corner. The Crystal Falls was surrounded by the armies of Aes Lugh, led by Bronwen's sorcerous father, Remon. The allies had no troops to spare to help the dwarves. They were on their own, and Mearead could not return. The blood price must be paid.

The charred splinters of Kianbearac had been recovered but the body of Cainhill and the woman he murdered were utterly destroyed. The city rang with hammers as the people of the city worked to repair the damage done in the battle. The blacksmiths' fires smoked day and night as arms were repaired and new weapons made. And all men and elves wrestled inside themselves with the knowledge that this war was far from over.

Fin retained the title of Warlord of the East, but by popular agreement Donal Longsword was made the Warlord of all Tolath. The irony of using Arianrood's ex-Warlord as the leader of the Alliance's forces appealed to all.

So it was that Donal called the council meeting one week after the battle, and it was he who stood to the right of the emperor's empty seat. The surviving thirteen heroes of

the Allied army seated themselves around the room. All save
Cucullin and the destroyer had been wounded in the battle,
but thanks to the elven healers only the maker and Lonnlarcan were still recovering.

The Ard Riegh took his seat slowly, each breath painful
for him as he tasted the decay of the mortal air. His face was
deeply lined with wrinkles and his once silver hair was now
a pure white. His great shoulders slumped over, bowed by
age, the only elf ever to feel its burden.

The maker looked in little better shape. He had taken the
brunt of Arianrood's magic when she had destroyed the illusion. Even now his breath came in painful gasps. Also
seated at the table was the Duke of Tinnafar, the Earl of
Althman, the Baron of Mathia, and Cormac, the son of
Cainhill, who had led the elven reinforcements to Tolan. The
others tended to eye him nervously since he was the image
of his father. The elf lord ground his teeth together, his
whole attitude showing his private battle of rage and despair
at his father's fall.

"I have called this council, for it is time for us to take the
initiative in this war. But, first, it is also my sad duty to
inform you that less than an hour ago the Baron Sean of Inlit
finally succumbed to his wounds and died." There was silence at this announcement. All had been touched by the
man's struggle with his wounds. He had been no great warrior but had acquitted himself well in the battle, attacking the
Shadow Lord himself. If was that fomarian's magic that had
frozen the lungs of the Baron and the man had died a linger-
ing and painful death.

"It is one more black deed the enemy must pay for."
Donal's voice rung with his anger.

He went to the middle of the room where the large map of
the known lands lay. Such was the size of the Warlord that
only the elf lords and Niall were near his height, and none,
not even Cucullin, had his breadth of muscles. Donal
pointed to the map, his hand still bandaged from the burn of
the dragon's blood.

"As you can see, we have mopped up the forces of the enemy as best we could. The lord Mearead assures me that his people will keep the armies of Aes Lugh from our borders. We now know that the kingdom of Cather-na-nog is facing an invasion from Maegul, but I don't think this is our main concern. The enemy's plan, I'm sure, is to first deal with the other allies, saving the elves for last, since they are the strongest of us. That makes sense. So what does that leave us with?"

"A mess," mumbled Mearead, and the others laughed.

"A fine mess," continued Donal. "The whole south of the empire is in enemy hands. I think it is safe to say we have hardly dented their power, while we have taken losses we could barely afford. Our first step is obvious. We must continue to gather what forces we may. We have sent the emperor's couriers throughout the land to gather all the warriors we can. We've sent some to the borderlands in the south and even to Ibhire, though I doubt there is any help for us in that quarter."

"Even if there are any of them left, they could never reach us," Brasil ap Fin's bass voice rumbled.

"Probably true. Still, if the couriers can find them, there is a chance that they could bring other men safely through, albeit a small one."

"And what has happened in Maihan, I'm wondering?" asked Niall.

"The free states of Maihan." Donal pointed them out on the southern end of the continent. "Your father has sent emissaries to all nine. So far none have returned. We sent out another squadron of ships. I'm hopeful. Those cities were all prosperous before the war. I'm sure the enemy must have attacked them but some may have survived. Whether they can help or not is another story."

"Anywhere else we can look to?" asked Kevin, the Duke of Tinnafar. Donal sighed. "Well, we have sent couriers to the northeast, each paired with an elven rider. Maybe there is someone or something out there in the devastation that can help."

"So," said Mearead, "that leaves Cardoc-nae-corond."

"Yes," said Donal. "I know that you have tried to contact them before, Mearead."

"With no success."

"In the council meeting at Fealoth's celebration," said Fin, "the question of the dwarves of Cardoc-nae-corond came up. It seemed to me that the emperor put a great stress on the need for their magic."

"It wasn't so much their magic," Mearead took a sip of wine, "but their ability to create magical weapons."

For the first time Lonnlarcan spoke. His voice no longer had the power of old, but was a thin whisper that the humans had to strain to hear. "The spear, Kianbearac," he said, his silver eyes heavy and sad, "was made with the help of the dwarves of Cardoc-nae-corond long years ago."

"Aye, I remember now," said Fin. "The emperor hoped they could make more weapons of magical quality, or at least have some that could be used."

"Yes," said Donal, "the one nation that still retained its former power in creating magical items. They have something we are so desperately in need of: magic."

"Of course," said Ceallac, "Trell'dem, Dammuth," the Morigu looked up at that, "all those early assassinations, Arianrood's betrayal—this whole war the enemy has been a step ahead of us. If I had been them I would have attacked the dwarves first, too."

"Which," said Mearead softly, "is probably exactly what they did."

"Dammuth dead!" Margawt shouted out.

"We don't know, lad," said Mearead, "but it's a safe bet." Margawt stared at him for a moment, then leaned back in his seat. Those nearest noticed his hand gripping his sword hilt with white knuckles.

"But how could they do it without anyone knowing?" said the maker.

"I don't know," answered Donal, "but I think we had better find out."

No one said anything. "I have already sent messengers to Cardoc-nae-corond," he continued.

"Is that enough?" Ceallac asked.

"I don't know." Donal stared at the map.

"Don't know, don't know," Mearead mumbled. "There's too much we don't know."

"Sure, and that's not a problem the enemy has had." Niall's voice shook.

"Arianrood," Margawt said. The others sat quietly. Mearead's hand tightened on his ax handle.

Cucullin cleared his throat and looked pointedly at the Warlord.

"Yes," Donal looked down at the map, "yes, every step, every move we've made, the enemy has countered. They know we will try to gather allies."

"And the master, Lord Anlon," said the maker, "surely Arianrood at least realized he was fighting with us. The dragon was the perfect way to draw him from us, his power and his council."

"Why?" asked Kevin, scratching his greying hair.

"Only Lord Anlon was able to pierce the illusion the dragon cast."

"An illusion I fell for easy enough," Niall said bitterly.

"We all did," said Cucullin.

"It isn't a magic to pierce," said Mearead. "A dragon of that one's power can leave his body, shape an image by the force of his will, even use his powers to a limited extent."

"It was him who animated the dragon skulls," Dermot's voice was gruff.

"It was he who killed Teague," Lonnlarcan added.

"Yes, the dragon's body stays animated, but his mind is far away. He called his body to him before the battle, in case his disguise was unveiled."

"As Anlon did," the maker said.

"As Arianrood expected," Mearead mumbled.

"We get off the track." Lonnlarcan looked to Donal. "You have an idea?"

"Offense," Donal's voice rang out. The others looked startled.

"Offense," Niall shook his head. "Oh, that's grand, and what, by the Martyr, are we going to use to start this great offense, that, I might add, you said they'd be expecting?"

"Imagination," the maker said. Niall snorted.

"Exactly," Donal continued, "exactly. We must strike, quick and hard."

"Aye, lad, that's the right of it," Cucullin's form shimmered golden in his excitement. "Over and over they have hurt us where we could least afford it. Now we must do the same."

"Killing Arianrood would do that," Mearead spat out.

"Arianrood is not your enemy, my lord." For the first time, Bronwen spoke up. "You forget I have fought Arianrood for five long years. She is powerful, but full of whims. Many times she could have destroyed me and my people but for some purpose of her own, pulled back."

"She lost interest!" Donal shouted. "That's it, she lost interest!" The others just stared at him. "Listen, I served her for many years. Many times she would give me some needless task, stop the armies, give us conflicting orders. We have all been thinking of the witch as our enemy, as the leader, but she's not. She can't be."

"Apkieran," Cucullin's eyes were bright.

"No, the other demon who was leading the armies at first," said Fin.

"No, you're all wrong," said Mearead. "I should have known, I should have seen. . . ." He put his hands onto his head. "Ah, Fealoth," he said, "what happened to you, my friend?"

"Fealoth?" several cried. Mearead just shook his head.

"All that power," Lonnlarcan smacked his hand on the table, enough strength in him still to shake it, "all that power! The armies from nowhere, the turning of the Ead, the despoiling of the earth powers, the rising of the fomarians and the troll god . . ."

". . . demons striding the earth once more," Cucullin continued, "dragons revived, the Hunter, Death himself taking sides."

Margawt stood up. "Only one has the power, only one could do it. . . ." He stared at the others, his hands gripping the table, his fingers burying into the stone. "My lords, we fight the Dark One himself!"

After that pronouncement, the council was quick to break up. One by one the leaders left to confer with their advisors and themselves. Soon, only Donal, Lonnlarcan, the Morigu were left.

"You wished to speak to me?" Margawt said to Donal.

"How did you know?" Donal asked. The Morigu just shrugged. The Warlord looked over at Lonnlarcan, who nodded slightly. Donal sat directly across from Margawt, his eyes holding the Morigu's.

"The Ard Riegh and I have been planning these last few days," Donal started, "trying to devise a way to strike back, to take the initiative."

"You knew all along," Margawt smiled slightly, "you knew it was the Beast we fight."

"Donal supplied me with the missing pieces," Lonnlarcan's voice rasped. "It was a matter of putting them together in the proper order."

"You wish something of me," Margawt stated. Donal studied him for a moment. The black eyes seemed feverishly bright. The Morigu unnerved him. He watched Margawt's chest rise as he breathed, but the elf made no sound. The silence spell Margawt shrouded himself with made him even more uncanny, more unreal.

"Margawt," Donal said, "you are the Morigu, perhaps the most powerful that has ever existed. You have abilities no other creature possesses." Donal licked his lips. "You can see, feel wrongness in things, living or dead, right?"

Margawt nodded once.

"Can you see the soul of everything?" Again, Margawt nodded.

"Even a god?" Donal's voice was hushed. Margawt stared at them for a moment.

"If the god has contact with the world, if enough of his essence is here, I can know his heart." The other two leaned back, a smile of satisfaction touching Donal's lips. Lonnlarcan lifted his hand in an arcane gesture. Outside the council chamber chanting was heard. Margawt felt a great barrier of power surround the room and those inside. He said nothing, waiting for Donal to continue.

"Margawt, we are brethren here," Donal said quietly. "I am half-elven but enough of the elven blood runs through my veins that I, like you two, can shield my heart and thoughts from any being, including a god."

"You wish to trick a being from the outer planes." For the first time Margawt's voice showed interest.

"Not so much trick," said Lonnlarcan, "as reveal." Margawt looked confused.

"You know that three days ago," Donal continued, "the people of this city attacked and desecrated Fealoth's temple." Margawt nodded. "The humans have turned to Lugh of the Long Arm, or to the Horned One for solace and guidance. Fealoth has been no help in the war, his priests are completely ineffective."

"In the last weeks," Lonnlarcan said, "at least three fomarians have been freed of their eons-old binding. Arianrood called up the spirit of Feth, a lesser god, to be sure, but a god nonetheless."

"I have spoken with the Hunter," Donal said. "Lonnlarcan has seen Death himself, and you are the Earth Goddess' own messenger."

"The barriers have been weakened between this world and the domain of the gods," Lonnlarcan added.

"The enemy does this for a purpose," said Margawt. Both

elves nodded. Donal licked his lips and took a sip of wine. He turned back to Margawt.

"We think the enemy is not just led by the Dark One." He took a deep breath. "We think they hope to free him and bring him to the earth once more." Margawt said nothing as he took in this pronouncement. He played with the goblin teeth that adorned his chest.

"You don't need me to tell you of the wrongness of the Beast."

"No," said Donal, "not the Dark One." He stared straight at the Morigu. "If the enemy seeks to bring a god to this world, cannot we do the same?"

"But the gods dare not directly intervene." Margawt paced back and forth. "That would bring the intervention of other deities, leading to a confrontation that would destroy the world."

"It was just to avoid that," said Lonnlarcan, "that Fealoth was raised to Godhood, so that he could intervene before accepting his place in the Bright World."

"Something we can't hope to do again," Donal added.

"Fealoth." Margawt nodded, "you wish to raise Fealoth."

"Yes," Donal became animated, "yes, he is the missing piece, the key to all this."

"So," Margawt smiled, "this is your offense."

"The first part," Donal added.

"But won't that weaken the barriers more?" the Morigu asked.

Lonnlarcan nodded. "Yes, probably, but we know that Arianrood for some time contacted him regularly. One more time can't be enough to tip the balance."

"And the enemy?" asked Margawt.

"Will probably expect us at some time or another to try it," Donal said.

"Which is probably why Arianrood let us know that she could speak with Fealoth, to plant the idea in our heads." Lonnlarcan looked hard.

"So, again we fall into their trap."

"Not exactly," Donal stood up, "because, you see, the enemy had no idea you existed. We're sure of that. He could not have prepared for you. It usually takes years upon years for a Morigunamachamain to come to his power." Margawt looked away as once more his mind tortured him with the events that led him to become what he was. The other two waited quietly for Margawt to speak.

"They would expect you to call Fealoth." He looked at the two, a smile of defiance forming on his face. "But they would not expect you to test the god you created."

"Can you hide yourself completely from Fealoth's power?"

"It will be hard, take a lot of concentration, but I can do it." He began to chuckle, a soft, deep-throated sound, the promise in that near-laugh plain to the others. "When do you plan to try this?"

"Tomorrow," said Donal. "You must leave before then and return unknown to anyone."

"None must guess what we do in case they inadvertently give us away." Lonnlarcan's eyes burned silver. "You must leave on some mission, to be gone for a day or two, then hide in a chamber in the temple." Margawt nodded.

"I think tonight and tomorrow I will have to confer with the Goddess." The other two smiled.

"We must know," Lonnlarcan's voice was urgent, "is Fealoth alive or dead, and if alive, is he with us or against us?"

CHAPTER

Twenty-One

That night Donal resumed the council meeting. When all were seated he took his place by the map.

"Now," he said, "we must decide what our first move is."

"We need more information." Mearead's voice slurred.

"Indeed we do." Donal gave them a look of smug satisfaction.

"I assume, my lord," said Ceallac, "you have a plan?"

Lonnlarcan answered. "Yes, we do." He stared at the others for a moment, sweeping them all with his silver gaze. "We must call Fealoth." Immediately the room exploded in bedlam.

"He is dead," someone shouted.

"He has betrayed us," this from Kevin.

"What help are human gods?" Ceallac's voice rose above the din.

"Can we do it?" Mearead's voice quieted the others.

"We know that Arianrood did, before the war," Lonnlarcan answered, his once melodious voice harsh and rough, "and since that time we have seen the barriers between the Bright World and ours grow steadily weaker as the enemy has used other powers to help their cause."

"I have spoken with the High Priest here in Tolan," Donal said. "He is anxious to try, since," he added wryly, "adherents to the faith have become few and far between." The humans looked nervously at each other. None could now claim to be a stout believer in the faith of the Bright God.

"The people of Tinnafar," said Kevin, "have always been followers of Lugh. Should we not try to call him instead? He has never wavered in his alliance to men."

"No," said Mearead, "it makes sense. Fealoth was supposed to have defeated the Dark One forever. He lies in the middle of this."

"Yes, yes," added the maker, "how is it that Fealoth allowed Arianrood to go so far, to betray what he supposedly stood for?"

"My old *friend*," Mearead stessed the word, "has a lot to answer for. We will call him and he will come." His statement left no room for refusal.

It was decided that the next day they would attempt to call Fealoth and then, armed with whatever knowledge gained from the event, they would plan for a military offensive. As the council meeting adjourned, the dwarf king rose to his feet.

"It will behoove us all, my lords," he said, "to remember one thing." He paused for a moment. "There is no doubt, Trell'dem was right. The enemy was just rebuilding their strength. This is the same war we fought so long ago. The Dark Seign wars are not ended yet." The others said nothing and left one by one to wait to see what the next day would portend.

Much was made of the Morigu's departure that night and Donal made sure all the human lords, plus Ceallac, were there to see the elf ride into the night. As soon as the lone figure was lost in the grey shadows, Donal went about preparing the temple of Fealoth for its divine visit.

This had to be done quietly, though. Not a few people, priest and mob, had died in the riots earlier, and the populace was ill-disposed toward the temple. In darkest secrecy, special troops—all consisting of members of the royalty and the Green Branch knights—went about cleaning the place and preparing it for the great ritual.

The temple was a monstrous edifice of stone and marble. The inside vast enough to hold three thousand worshipers at once. Once entered, the faithful would pass beneath the tiered seats for the royalty. These were at the very back, forming three sides of a rectangle that surrounded the tomb of Ellawyn and Lir, the mother and father of the god Fealoth.

Twelve columns marched across the floor, six to each side, each the thickness of a large wagon wheel. Between each pillar was an alcove where a painting presented part of the story of the rise of the god. At the opposite end of the temple stood a stone altar, overshadowed from behind by a twenty-foot sculpture of Fealoth.

To the left and right were two silver doors leading to the inner sanctum, where a series of three circles merged to open to the inner chamber where the bones and armor of the god were interred in a crystal case. For when he ascended to godhood, Fealoth had no more need of his physical body and left his bones and armor on earth. Only the shield and sword did he take with him, their mystical element essential in his rise.

The mob had not been able to reach the inner sanctum since the narrow circular corridors were easily defended by the priests. All the priests of Fealoth were able fighters, since Fealoth was above all a warrior god.

The High Priest set a limit to how many could be present. Seven, being a number of power and good luck, was chosen. So it was that early the next morning, Donal, Mearead, Kevin, Lonnlarcan, Cucullin, Ceallac, and Niall entered the hushed interior of the temple.

The temple was clean, but all the marks of the attack could not be erased in a night, so all stared as they walked in at the defaced paintings and chipped marble. Surprisingly, the statue and tomb in the main hall were barely touched as if the mob, so recently converted, could not quite bring itself to attack these monuments.

"Where are the benches?" Ceallac murmured as the temple rang with the ching of armor and weapons that all wore.

"Fealoth is not a god you kneel to," answered Mearead, "even if you prayed to him."

The High Priest waited for them at the altar. He was a tall man, his long white hair in a thick braid reaching his waist, emulating the hair of his god. His piercing green eyes took in the party as he bowed deeply. If he felt it a little unorthodox that the group was armed, he said nothing.

"All is in readiness," he said, his high-pitched voice disturbing the image of the patriarch he obviously cultivated.

The others followed him as he led them into the inner sanctum. None could fail to notice the hard-scrubbed walls and floors marking the spot where blood had been shed where the priests had taken their stand.

The inner chamber was completely bare except for the enshrined bones placed at the very center. They were raised on a short platform made of a chunk of solid jade encased in a crystal coffin. The top had been opened and the crown of Tolath was placed upon the skull. Also in its thin grasp rested the sceptre of the emperor.

"They have been placed there," explained the High Priest, "to give the god earthly objects to focus on." Along the curved walls of the room stood twelve priests in bright blue robes, heads completely covered by long hoods as they chanted in a sonorous monotone. Each swung a thiruble of incense that clouded the room with a thick, cloying smell that attached itself to clothes and hair. But around all the elves an unseen force pushed the multicolored smoke away from them, forming a clear aura an inch off their skin.

The High Priest positioned each of the leaders around the casket, then he bowed once to the skeleton. He retreated to the foot of the casket. He joined the chant, speaking in an archaic tongue that only Lonnlarcan of all there was familiar with.

For an hour the priests chanted, making gestures, crying in loud voices. Each of the leaders tried to help by concentrating, but the elves could not follow the paths of the humans' desire with their own magic. Mearead became more exasperated as he became sure that no real power was being exerted by the priests. Just wishful thinking.

After another half hour, the High Priest raised himself slowly.

"Nothing, my lord," he addressed Donal. "I am sorry but there is no response. The god does not wish to be disturbed." The Warlord and Ard Riegh looked at one another. This was not a turn of events they expected.

Mearead sighed, then moved toward the skeleton. He reached down to touch the hand feebly clutching the sceptre. All the priests cried aloud and the patriarch grabbed Mearead's shoulder to pull him away. But he might as well have tried to pull down the pillars of the temple as budge the dwarf.

"My lord," Donal cried, "you go too far." He pushed the priest away. "Do you forget who the Lord Mearead is?" The man just stared back, his green eyes bright.

But Mearead paid no attention. He was remembering days long gone by. He was not thinking of the god, but of his friend, the young, cocky emperor of Tolath, more comfortable with drunken jest than godlike utterances. And he remembered—a dark field, two great hosts facing one another and he walked across the length of the field, alone, to face the giant shadow, to face the Dark One himself; to issue the challenge of Fealoth.

He remembered and his old heart ached, ached with the blood and pain of the old wars, ached for the deaths of his people in the last months, the constant fight inside himself over the fear of betrayal by his friend. He reached out with mind and heart and for a moment he felt a touch, light, then pull away. He groaned and shouted to the ceiling.

"Fealoth!" he cried in a great voice. "You owe me! You

owe me, Fealoth!" He lifted his ax and shook it toward the empty ceiling.

"Damn you, Fealoth! You owe me! Fealoth! Fealoth!" he cried and some force, some power carried his words so in all of Tolan, in every house, in every shop, the cry was heard, not loud, but there. None could avoid it, not even the god.

He came as he knew he must. The others he could ignore, but not Mearead, never him.

In the room the clouds of incense whirled around and around. The incense was burned down in seconds and the thick vapor drove into the casket. There it wrapped around the bones, obscuring them, filling out the forms of muscles and sinew, fat and flesh.

Inadvertently, all save Mearead and Lonnlarcan took a step back. Slowly, the vapors quit whirling about the bones and formed into a semi-opaque body. In agonizing slowness, the body pulled itself up and off the platform. The others crowded at one end to face the rising of the god.

But it wasn't the proud figure of the statue that faced them. This being stood at an angle seeming to barely hold itself up. Great rents in the flesh covered the body as if an ax had chopped it randomly. The bright blue eyes were missing; in their place were empty holes, dark and blind. The smoke-flesh had turned the silver so closely associated with Fealoth, but it was a dirty and tarnished color and made the apparition only that more ghastly.

"I have come," the mouth barely moved and the voice was hollow, sounding as if he spoke from a great distance. Not soft, but from far, far away. The priests fell to their knees in a mixture of joy and horror. Mearead took a step closer, but even he dared not reach out and touch the God.

"Fealoth, what has been done to you?" he asked, his voice husky.

"The war never ended, my friend." Fealoth shook his head sadly. "I have fought and fought, but my strength has not been enough. I have been cast down, and barely manage to survive." He sighed, like a great breeze through the evening trees. "The Bright World, is not all bright . . . I had no time to adjust to my new power, my Godhood." He backed against the walls as if for support. "I could not warn you. I could not help you. He was too powerful. *He,*" Fealoth stressed the word, "always blocked me."

"The Dark One," Mearead's voice was sad and old.

"Aye," Fealoth looked down at the dwarf, "our ancient enemy. I chained Him. Even at my height I could not kill Him. But always, always, there were those eager to do His bidding, always there were those who strove to free Him." He fell silent, his breathing great rasps that echoed about the chamber.

"Can you offer us no help?" said Donal.

The god looked up. "Help? Help, Warlord? There is no help for you . . . you are all doomed. He will rise and none can stand in His way. He will rise and stretch forth His great black hand and this world will be His." Unnoticed by the others, the thirubles lit and again the clouds filled the air. But whereas before they had been multicolored, they were now grey. They drifted to enshroud each of the figures. It seemed to each person there—man, elf, and dwarf—that it was as if the others dwindled to shadow and only he was there, alone, facing the Bright God's despair.

The smoke grew thick, and unknowingly all there drank deep of its fumes. Even the elves became encased in a cloud that began to wrap tighter and tighter around them, pressing on them, forcing them to relive the scenes of the war, all the deaths. And for what? A brief respite, a moment in the sun? Fealoth himself, a God, was helpless. What could they do for all their vaunted power?

This was the message that Fealoth brought them, the message that weighed down their hearts and souls. The message that was one by one destroying them. Already two of the priests had fallen to the ground; their hearts burst as their wills shattered.

And it would have worked. He would have destroyed them all in that moment. But He did not know, He did not know that one other listened, one other was in that room, one who could see Him for what He truly was.

Margawt's form flowed out of the wall. For a moment he stood, concentrating, using all his power to blind the God to his presence. The vision he saw was not the same as the others'. For he saw Fealoth unhurt, strong, a ruthless grin twisting his handsome features. And the Morigu saw more, he saw the Darkness within, the evil and corruption a thick sludge that was the true body of the God. Margawt restrained himself. The agony of Fealoth's evil scraped his nerves like a razor, but though tears of blood streaked his face he moved one slow step at a time, closer, closer.

Fealoth felt something, the threat, the hate, something. He concentrated, putting more of his essence into the earthly form. More, he poured it in. And as more of his power infused the skeleton, the God began to register something, something narrowing in, He would have it in a second. . . .

Then He did see something, but it wasn't the Morigu. It was a thick, pale shadow, a shadow not of evil, but of doom, and it reached for Him.

"This is my world," Death hissed. For the first time since his ascension, Fealoth felt fear. He pulled away from the earthly coils He had created, rising away fast before Death's cold hand could touch Him.

And the Morigu struck. With a great cry he brought his sword down, crashing the skull to slivers, the force of the blow shattering every bone, cleaving the crown in two. Though Fealoth escaped, the Morigu howled with delight, for he knew he had hurt Him, he knew he had hurt the blackest traitor of them all. And as the others strove for consciousness, the Morigunamachamain's howls rang through the temple as he did a mad dance amongst the God's bones.

It was a few hours before the others recovered. The events of the night were explained to the other leaders. After everyone had time to think about it, Fealoth's betrayal was not such a shock as it could have been, and it was offset by the knowledge that for once they had trapped the enemy and ruined at least one of their intricate plans.

If Mearead was quieter than ever, no one took notice, nor did anyone blame him that he alone of the seven did not congratulate the Morigu.

Margawt said nothing, for he realized he, too, must seek to find the answer of a friend's part in this war. Was Dammuth dead? Or did he follow the path of Arianrood and Fealoth?

There was one more casualty of the traitor Fealoth that night, as the High Priest, feeling the betrayal perhaps more than anyone, slit his thin old wrist. When Mearead was given the news he just nodded and continued to sharpen his ax, as he had been doing since he awoke from Fealoth's power.

Two shadows watched it all. Silent, they stood above the city as the inhabitants hurried about trying to find the strength to continue the war.

"You have shown yourself," the Hunter said. Death just shrugged.

"It was worth it, to attack that traitor."

"What now?"

"Red war. The people of the land must rearm, hold the evil hordes back."

"They will try to release our Dark Brother."

"He is no brother of mine!" Death's form expanded and he looked down at the Hunter. "The people must hold."

"What good if they bring back the Beast?"

"Evil," Death hissed, "evil, brother, works against itself. Give them time and the leaders will fight amongst each other, each trying to rule." He laughed. "Even the Black Soul would have a hard time controlling Arianrood, and the Demon Prince Dubh has trebled his own strength."

"What of us?"

"You must seek the answer to the riddle of when and how they will bring the Beast back."

"And you?"

"I am going to find a way to kill the unkillable." His form expanded into nothingness. "I am going to kill the Lord of the Undead."

Epilogue

In a room that was not a room, a place that was not a place, in darkness that was more than darkness, a thick, black chain rattled and for the first time in one hundred and fifty years a shadow stood. The chain was still too thick, but it was weaker, weaker.

The shadow in shadows smiled, if that is what it could be called, for the gesture would have crushed any mortal soul that saw it.

'The maggots fought back, and their latest victory was greater than they realized.' The thoughts whirled in the not-place, giving shape to gibbering creatures of talon and claw. 'But it was to be expected.'

"Not long now," the darkness gave voice to its thoughts, and the newborn creatures whined in pain and horror. "I can wait. I know patience. I can wait." And in the world, the sun got darker and many of power great and weak felt a touch of despair, but there were few who could know the meaning of it, and of those few, they kept their own counsel.

The shadow lost form and slid back into the darkest of darkness that surrounded it, one thought vibrating the evil that it was.

"Not long now."